The Cindra Corrina Chronicles
BOOK 4

THE BLACK EAGLE

MARK RUDE

All persons, gods and monsters appearing in this work are fictitious. Any resemblance to real individuals, living, dead or immortal is purely coincidental.

Conversely, if any of the gods or monsters described herein turn out to be real after all, the author takes no responsibility.

ISBN 978-0-9848275-4-1

Printed in the United States of America.

To Family and friends who have supported and encouraged me, and to my fellow authors and artists who have inspired, helped, and enriched me with their creative energies.

Really, I'm like a creative energy vampire.

Slurp, slurp, slurp

Acknowledgements

A big 'thank you' goes out to Elora K. for sharing her humongous art reference files with me, including lots of tutorials for Photoshop. It was a big help with my new cover art.

Also much thanks to the Facebook community for offering "Likes" and feedback on my rebranding efforts.

Finally, to all those nice people I met during my first major convention, who took a chance on me and dropped some cash for my humble little books.

Contents

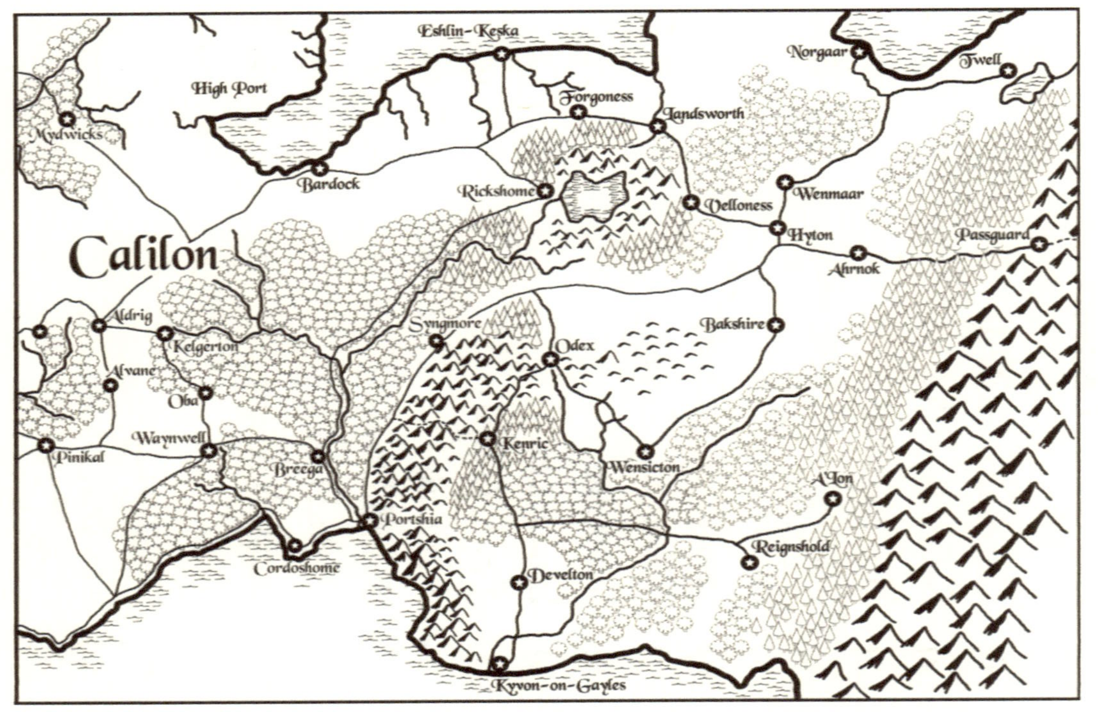
Calilon
Eshlin-Keska
Norgaar
Twell
High Port
Forgoness
Landsworth
Mydwicks
Bardock
Rickshome
Velloness
Wenmaar
Hyton
Passguard
Ahrnok
Bakshire
Aldrig
Syngmore
Odex
Kelgerton
Alvane
Oba
Kenric
Wensicton
Waynwell
Ayon
Pinikal
Breega
Reignshold
Portshia
Develton
Cordoshome
Kyvon-on-Gayles

Chapter One

Unexpected Arrivals

The crash of distant waves and the cry of sea gulls created a lulling chorus as the procession made its way along the Red Coast Road. Ten horsemen escorted a cart bearing a simple pine coffin, along with the personal belongings of its occupant. The solemn riders wore the red and black tabards of their fighting school and carried whatever personal weapons they thought to bring. They also bore spears taken from the school's armory, to which were fastened black banners that fluttered and snapped in the salt air. They were bound for Cordoshome, the sleepy fishing town that was the home to their schoolmaster, as well as his deceased student.

Schoolmaster Cord Freekirk felt the loss deeply, for he knew the boy's family; they were vassals of his father, and had trusted him to return their son as a well-trained warrior, not a corpse. So he undertook the expense of seeing him home, even to the point of having a wizard cast a spell of preservation upon the casket. It was a six-day journey in the summer heat, and Cord would have the body fit to lie before the lad's parents before its final rest. The cost had been ruinous, but the need was deemed fit and necessary, and the only smells that assailed the nostrils of the company were their own sweat-laden clothes and the occasional elimination of their mounts.

"We should be there by evening," Sir Jaron said, riding at Cord's side at the head of the column. Sir Cord knew the road better than anyone, but Jaron just needed to speak aloud. "The lads will be happy for a roof over their heads tonight."

They had spent the last week sleeping under the stars, for lodging expenses were not factored into the trip. The procession was made up of those students who felt the need to attend and would not mind a little hardship on Halvoy's behalf.

Sir Cord nodded absently, his eyes locked on the horizon. His sandy hair looked golden in the sunlight, his face as impassive as stone.

Jaron sighed. Cord had been in a gloom all week. The young knight had never known the big man to dwell upon things he could not change; that was Jaron's domain. Now the roles were reversed and Jaron was at a loss for words. He ran a hand through his sweat-laden brown hair, brushing his forelocks back before replacing his knight's beret. He glanced back at Dillan, his squire, looking for support.

Dillan DePort, known to a trusted few as Cindra Corrina, simply shrugged at him; she had no idea how to draw the man out of his thoughts. Her own mind had been spinning in odd directions since leaving the distractions of the city for the tranquility of the road. All the omens pointed to something dreadful coming. Some even whispered of a second Time of Chaos, a thought that caused her to shiver in the warm afternoon sun. It didn't help that she and her beloved

Jaron no longer had the privacy of their quarters to share and comfort each other's fears.

She glanced back along the line of riders. She and her teammates, Adric and Inis, represented the Dread Wolves. Farther back were most of the Fire Steeds: Bradric, Filbert and Mat, all teammates of Halvoy. Terrus and Gaius represented the Thorn Bears and Ice Drakes respectively. Those pretentious names, once a source of school pride and competition, now rang hollow with false bravado. She didn't feel like a dread wolf. Not at all.

Evening approached and the sun sank low over the distant hills where Cord's ancestral home stood, overlooking the town built into the sloping sea cliffs. The rose light of sunset carried an odd haze usually seen only in the winter months when all the town's hearths were lit. Cord squinted at it, his face drawn in concern. He raised his hand and brought the procession to a stop.

"What is it?" Adric asked. He had only just gotten the feel for his horse and reined it in at Cindra's side, a bit too close.

"Not sure," she answered. Her voice was pitched a bit too high for a boy of sixteen; she had spoken so rarely on this trip that she had forgotten to deepen it. "Sir Jaron?" she called to her knight. "What is it?"

But it was Sir Cord who answered. "Smoke. It's too warm an evening for that many hearth fires, unless…" He turned in his saddle, "Carter! Make for the manor house. The rest of you, follow me as best you can!" He spurred his horse to a gallop, racing towards the town.

The students did their best to keep up, though riding at speed with spear in hand was not something they had practiced yet. Cindra alone was able to keep pace with Jaron and Cord, her bay pony, T'ózha, was eager to prove himself. Jaron had a twinge of doubt as he saw her riding beside him. He wanted to order her to stay with the wagon, but Cindra would certainly argue all the way to town and make him regret it later.

The sight that greeted them as they rode over the crest of the hill was something from a nightmare; Cordoshome was being attacked from the sea. Through the thickening smoke and glowing flames, the red sails of a Minozhian longship glowed in the hellish light, its ramming horns pinning the remains of a hapless fishing boat against the docks. Upon the open deck stood ranks of archers unleashing flaming crossbow bolts into the buildings high up the cliff face, setting fires between the docks and its defenders on the hill. The massive shapes of bull men could be seen carrying torches and weapons as the terrified townsfolk fled before them, braving the growing flames as they headed for higher ground.

Cord spurred on his mount to the gates, leading his students past the terrified townsfolk who were fleeing their burning homes. He halted before the lone guard and shouted, "What happened? Where is the militia?" The guard recognized his lord's son, and stammered, "T-they came with the fog, milord! There was no sign... The militia had no time to rally!"

Cord raised his voice to a thunderous boom, "Citizens, get to the keep! Take only what you can carry!" Then to the guard, "Let our wagon get through, then close the gates! Then make sure we have a bucket brigade to put out those fires!"

The guard saluted, happy to have some direction amid the chaos. "Gods above and below," Cord said under his breath, his eyes watering with rage and the stinging smoke. He looked over his shoulder to survey his students, as if seeing them for the first time since leaving Portshia. They were young and inexperienced to the man, save Mat Belvine who was a mercenary soldier. Then there was the count's daughter. Damn her, but she was the only one of his students who could claim to have fought Minozhians. She even had that black Gali bow and a quiver of arrows. Damn her, he needed her with them.

"Dismount!" he bellowed, "Spears at the ready and

follow me!" The carter drove his wagon through the portal and the gates were closed and barred. "Dillan!" Cord called, giving Cindra a glowering look he felt she deserved, "Stay behind us and put that fancy bow to good use!"

Cindra nodded, having no desire to be in front with nothing between her and the advancing Minozhians but a length of wood. She strung her bow and adjusted her quiver. Her heart had been pounding with fear and rage when she saw the red sails in the harbor; since that fateful morning her ship was attacked and her friend Mineth was killed, most of Cindra's nightmares featured the shaggy, bull-headed men emerging from the mist.

She looked to her schoolmates, seeing the fear in their eyes that reflected her own. No one had expected combat on this somber journey, least of all with monsters from the Horned Isles. She thought, *My father's ships have been hunting all along the Red Coast for Minozhian raiders; how had they gotten past them? They are just days from Portshia!*

Cindra pulled her school tabard up to cover her nose and mouth in the choking smoke as Cord and Jaron led them through the crowded streets. People were trying to save whatever they could and flee, while Cord ordered them to head for the manor house. Militiamen in their red tabards and helmets were attempting to organize, but Cindra could see the shock in their faces. This was beyond their meager training.

Mat called over the din, "Minozhians are just like men! They have the same weak spots, and wear naught but boiled leather armor."

No one spoke or offered any more advice. Everyone knew the enemy was bigger, stronger, and more fearsome than any man, light armor or no. Besides, the students wore none.

When they reached the fourth turn of the street above the dock, they found a line of fighting men who were holding strong against the attackers, though their situation was dire. There were twenty in total, but some had been wounded and dragged to the back of the line. They bore swords and shields and fought in a defensive phalanx, but the Minozhians wielded long, double-headed axes, and swords as tall as a man, making the defenders' weapons of little use. All that kept them at bay was a desperate salvo of diminishing arrows shot by a lone archer behind the ranks.

The archer spared a glance over his shoulder, noting the arrival of Cord and his students. He smiled at the sight of spears and shouted, "Re-enforcements!" He loosed another arrow as a bull man's shaggy, horned head presented itself.

Cord bellowed, "Spears! Work them back!" He rushed to the line and reaching high, thrust his spear at an advancing Minozhian. The enemies were bulky and tall, standing at least a foot or two over the defenders. The narrow street was an ideal choke point, but if the Minozhians pushed the line back another ten feet, the defenders would be tripped up on the stairs behind them where the archer stood. The students rushed forward and did their best to thrust past the fighting men, but few were as tall as Cord.

Cindra joined the archer on the steps, noticing his young face and tanned skin under his hood. He was perhaps Jaron's age with a golden, trimmed, and styled beard. His eyes were intense in the firelight and his jaw was set with determination. He nodded to her and said, "Keep them from rounding the corner; we cannot repel more than three at a time." He loosed another arrow, catching a beast man in his thick, muscled shoulder. The creature snarled in pain, but otherwise paid it no mind.

Cindra set her spear in the doorway and notched an arrow. She had not used the bow in over a year and realized a new danger; if she shot too low, she might hit her allies. Adric and the larger Bradric were just a foot below her aim. She raised the bow uncertainly, waiting for a shot. A bull warrior with shield held high came around the corner and swung low with his great ax, drawing a bloodcurdling scream of pain from a swordsman. She saw a helmeted head drop from the front line, and the ranks closed further as one of the man's fellows dragged him back with the wounded. He was missing a leg below the knee, and gore gushed from the severed stump. The metallic, rusty tang of fresh blood assaulted her senses.

Cindra's breathing came quickly as she tried to shut out the horror of the sight. She heard the Minozhian roar in pain and saw him back away as someone scored a lucky thrust past his shield. She drew her bow, hoping to finish the beast, but something in the corner of her vision distracted her. Glancing at the adjacent building, she saw a horned, muscled figure rising over the tiled rooftop. It raised a crossbow directly at her position.

"Our flank!" she cried, and grabbed her fellow archer by the collar, pulling him aside just as a whistling bolt sunk into the door where he had been standing. The archer made a startled gasp, but took in the situation immediately and struggled to regain his weapon. Cindra drew her arrow and took her time to aim, knowing the enemy's weapon would be slower to reload. But to her dismay, the bull warrior braced the crossbow against his hip and pulled back the heavy cord with one hand, loading another bolt far too quickly.

She felt a moment's thrill of panic as she sucked in a breath, held it, and released the arrow. She saw the moment as if it were painted in her mind, her focus was so intense. The Minozhian was a dark form, lit from behind with crimson and amber flames that colored the black, billowing smoke. Embers flew upward in a slow dance as she saw her arrow flex, fishtailing for a moment before flying true, sinking into the creature's chest. She let out her breath, and everything resumed its frantic pace.

The beast man stumbled back, grunting at the impact, but raised his crossbow and tried to take aim.

The archer, having regained his footing, buried an arrow into the Minozhian's neck, making him tumble off the roof as the bolt flew high and wide.

But there was no time to exchange thanks or praise; a cry from the lines brought their attention back to the phalanx. A shaggy warrior had come around the corner swinging a long ax and lowering his head to gore a hapless soldier, flinging him over his back to land in a heap with dead and wounded bull men. More came around the corner with shields and axes at the ready, anticipating the death of the defending archer. They crashed into the men and shoved them back upon each other, creating bedlam in the defenders' ranks. Most of the spearmen were able to move back in time, but Bradric and Mat were knocked down by the flailing bodies of swordsmen. Bradric was pinned beneath a man almost his own size.

"Fall back!" called an older man, his voice deep and commanding. He and nine other defenders pulled their comrades to their feet and retreated behind the remaining spears. The captain shouted, "Swords, to flanks; spears, to center!"

Those few left behind were not so lucky, and the beast-men hacked at them as they waded forward. One sunk an ax into the shoulder of the swordsman who had fallen on Bradric, and the blow sprayed the big lad's face with the man's blood.

Adric cried out as he saw his friend under the ax stroke, but was backed into a doorway and had his spear cleaved in half. He struck at his attacker frantically, but only succeeded in scratching the monster's thick hide.

Mat lost his spear in the crush of bodies, so he drew his sword and hamstrung one of the creatures, bringing it to its knees. He drove his blade into the creature's neck and then yanked his weapon free to face another attacker.

Terrus found himself facing the shaggy bull man who had broken the line. The young man attacked with perfect form, but the Minozhian countered with sheer strength, thrusting the pointed head of his ax at his opponent's chest. Terrus gave a shout of pain, and crimson bloomed from his tunic.

Cindra shot an arrow into the beast man's eye before he could finish Terrus; she could hardly miss, they were so close. She wanted to rush down and pull the boy to safety, but the only safety in this narrow street was behind her bow. The remaining Minozhians advanced with savage efficiency, only their eyes and horns visible over their round shields, which were a yard in diameter. She knew she would have to retreat soon.

Inis DeGhat dropped his spear and pulled Terrus back a few precious paces. The shaggy bull man raised his long ax to strike him, but the captain took up the boy's spear and fended off the attack. His men had regrouped, their steel blades adding to the meager thicket of spears, which darted in and out like striking serpents. Inis covered his classmate with a discarded shield, and searched for a weapon. Filbert, Mat and Adric rallied around their teachers, though there was precious little room to move.

Gaius Corrina fought shoulder-to-shoulder with his schoolmasters, thrusting low when they struck high; a fierce fire was in his eyes, his teeth bared like an animal's.

Sir Jaron and Sir Cord, working as one, harried the invaders' every step, threatening to pierce feet, knees, thighs, or heads. Nevertheless, they came on.

Cindra and the archer were forced to retreat to separate sides of the street as their position became compromised. Cindra remembered to grab her spear, and she rushed to a doorstep, wishing she could find a higher vantage. She thought she might enter a house and find a high window, but she didn't want to leave her friends.

Adric held half a spear in each hand, a fearsome look of determination on his youthful face. He called, "Don't let them any closer! Protect our wounded!" Although his spear's reach had been halved, he stood his ground, holding a length of wood like a shield and the other ready to strike.

Such valor, Cindra thought. She wondered at her own courage, that fierce spark she had felt in the past. Her heart was hammering, her breathing was quick, but that warm, angry courage she remembered was buried somewhere. Sweat stung her eyes, and the smell of blood and burning timbers filled her nose, along with that odor she had come to associate with Minozhians, a bearskin left out in the rain, or a wet dog that had been playing in the surf. There was also a sour smell that came with them; it was the smell of her own terror. She could smell it now, and it grew as she shot her bow; she felt her quiver emptying fast.

A crash could be heard across the street where the other archer was standing; it came from inside the house, as though a wall had collapsed. The man lowered his bow and moved out of the door frame, his eyes searching the windows above for signs of smoke. The crashing grew louder, accented by the sounds of breaking crockery. It was as if something was plowing its way through the house.

The archer stepped back further, raising his bow towards the door as it suddenly flew off its hinges, throwing planks of jagged wood into the street. A Minozhian warrior emerged, striking the archer in mid-charge, flinging him to the ground. The beast man turned to Cindra, lowered his horns, and rushed at her.

Cindra had screamed and dropped her bow as the door exploded, shielding her face instead. Now unarmed, she stumbled back into the non-existent cover of her door-frame, flailing about for anything to put between her and the nightmare that filled her vision. Her hand found her spear and she lowered the tip to meet the charging creature, even as her feet slipped out from under her.

Hearing the commotion, the captain of the swordsmen withdrew from the line shouting, "To the black!"

Jaron heard the man say 'black.' Surely he meant 'back?' He dared a glance to the rear and witnessed the beast charging into Cindra. "No!" he cried, and disengaged from the line.

"Jaron!" Cord barked, unable to spare a hand to yank him back in place.

Cindra hit the ground and gripped the spear with white knuckles just as the Minozhian impaled himself upon it. It did not stop his momentum however, and his horns pierced the door on either side of Cindra's head. She found herself face-to-face with the creature, its hot breath like a summer wind over the stockyards, saliva and blood spattering her. She gave a wordless scream of terror and defiance, unable to move as she felt the warm rush gushing over her hands.

But the beast man was far from dead. His hands were free, and using one to support his weight, he brought the other up to his enemy's neck.

Cindra fought to stay the creature's hand, but to no avail. Desperately, she reached back for her Minozhian *Kos* knife in its belt sheath. It was a war trophy of her first kill, given to her by a Galindri woman whose life she had saved with a well-placed arrow. Cindra had hated the large, wicked blade, since one like it had killed her handmaiden. She only wore it because it was intimidating and impressive to her fellow students. Now, it would earn its keep.

She drew the blade and thrust it into the creature's armpit. It was harder to do effectively than she imagined; the point was broad and single-edged, not ideal for piercing thrusts. Her shoulder ached with strain as she shoved upward with her weak arm; her sword arm now feebly protecting her neck from the massive, gripping fingers. She felt them close on her face, pushing into her eyes, enclosing her head.

Once, as a child, she had become so angry that she had squeezed an orange until her fingers sank through the skin. Now she was that orange, fighting for her life against the monstrous hand. Hot blood ran down her knife arm. The rank odor of urine stung her nose, whether hers or the creature's, she could not tell. Footfalls approached; were they her friends, or her opponent's?

Finally, the Minozhian let out a long, rasping breath. The pressure ceased. She kept working the knife deeper until a hand grasped her.

"*Cindra*," Jaron hissed under his breath, "Cindra, are you hurt?"

Her voice was weak and choked. "I-I'm fine," she stammered. Jaron pulled her from under the sagging body as the Minozhian slumped in death.

A horn sounded above the din; two repeating notes that echoed along the walls of the cliff harbor. The Minozhians roared in defiance and beat a hasty retreat, leaving their dead and slaying any wounded that could not make it back to the longboat on their own. Before the men knew what was happening, the fight was over.

Cord took a moment to catch his breath, and then yelled, "Dunlorden!"

Jaron flinched, gave Cindra a weak smile, and returned to the older knight. "Dillan is unharmed," he reported, as if Cord had asked.

Sir Cord was not unrelieved at the news, but he was no less angry. "You left the line, boy." Jaron flinched again; Cord only called him 'boy' when he was furious. "You weakened our defense and endangered everyone."

Jaron knew Cord was right and there was no use arguing. He had learned *that* much since his own training days. "I am sorry, Sir Cord. I should have trusted the swords to deal with it when they left as well."

Cord's eyes narrowed. He too had heard the captain call for his men, had witnessed more than a few of them fall out of line to rush to the aid of their archer friend. What surprised him was the ease with which Sir Jaron had shifted the blame. *He's gaining survival skills, the kind you need when you live with a woman.*

"Since you like running about so much," Cord continued, "You can follow them back to the docks and report on their retreat. Find out what in the name of Rath's golden member is going on."

Jaron saluted, gave Cindra one last look, and made his way down towards the docks.

The swordsmen were seeing to their wounded, performing a grim triage. The students aided as best they could, though only Mat Belvine had experience with battlefield wounds.

Sir Cord spoke to Inis, who was examining Terrus, removing his tunic before the fabric stuck to the wound. "DeGhat, I need a runner," he said.

DeGhat's steel-blue eyes met the schoolmaster's with his typical dry humor, "Had I known, I might have left sooner, master."

Cord smirked despite himself. "Run up the hill and check on that fire brigade. Tell them the streets are clear until I say otherwise. Then inform the manor house that the Minozhians have withdrawn for now and we need healers, as well as extra help putting out the fires. Confirm that their ship has moved off, and report back to me. I'll see to Drakthorne."

Inis gave Terrus a last worried look and ran up the street, and Cord used his own tabard to staunch the blood. The lad might live from a wound like this, depending on how deep it was. He looked up at the sound of running feet, and saw his family's Lelonethan priests in their orange robes rushing towards him. They had been near at hand, readying their Divine Alchemy just out of sight of the battle. *Gods bless them,* Cord thought.

The archer approached Cindra after conferring with the captain. He clapped her on the shoulder and said, "I thought you were finished for certain, lad. You are luckier than an alley cat. What is your name?"

Cindra was shaken, but still managed to reply. "Dillan, Dillan DePort."

"Well, Dillan!" the archer exclaimed, "How does it

feel to be a Minozhian slayer?"

Cindra could not answer. She could still feel the hot breath of the creature on her face; or was it the waves of heat from the burning buildings? She only smiled weakly.

"Bradric!" cried Adric, helping the big lad out from under the body of a swordsman. "I thought you were killed, you big ox!"

Bradric's face and chest were crimson with the dead man's blood, and he looked like one of those macabre temple paintings of the war god Balkon, minus the bushy beard. "I thought I was too, so I figured I'd stay that way until the Minozhians had passed by." He rubbed at his cheek, finding a gash where the bull man's ax had cut him. "Vina's tits, but that's a close shave!"

Adric laughed and hugged him, gore and all.

Chapter Two

Secrets Revealed

All told, the swordsmen had lost half their number. The Lelonethan priests used their alchemy to speed the healing of the injured, and ease the passing of the mortally wounded. The bodies were arranged in a row with swords held to their breasts in the manner of knights in effigy, while Minozhian bodies were dragged to the docks and piled in a heap. Frantic townsfolk passed buckets of water to quench the flames, and all around were the cries and wailing of the distraught.

In the midst of the chaos, the ten men-at-arms met with the students and their school masters. The archer spoke for the men, something which Cord thought odd; he had assumed the older captain was in charge.

"Your arrival is timely, sir knight! Never have I been so glad to see so few." The archer clapped Cord on the shoulder and smiled.

Sir Cord answered grimly, "It was ill cause that brought us from Portshia, but it seems fate had need of us. You are not with the town's defenses." It was not a question. He spent little time in his home town, but he knew that the man's chain mail shirt was too well-made, the clasp of his cloak was too expensive, and the gear of his company was top quality.

"No, we were to be staying the night before moving on. We had barely stowed our luggage when the Minozhians attacked," said the young archer with a confident air, "What is your name sir knight, and whom do you serve? I see the arms of Houses Freekirk and Corrina about you, and the badge of a hound."

"I am Sir Cord Freekirk, knight commander of House Corrina, and the count's faithful hound." he answered. "The tabards we wear are of my family's Daerbrik School; we are here on school business. May I ask your name, friend?"

The archer only smiled, "The young bowman in your company, what is his name?"

Cord blinked, mindful of his question being ignored. He answered carefully, "Dillan DePort, a student of mine."

The archer said, "You have trained him well! The lad saved my life back there, not once, but twice."

Oh, damn her thrice, Cord thought, *She just can't keep from being noticed.* "He is one of my better students, although we do not train with the bow. He brought that skill with him."

Cindra and Jaron were unaware of the scrutiny of the men-at-arms. Cindra had wandered from the other students and Jaron had followed, noticing her stumble once or twice. She began to shake, and bent over, hands on knees.

Jaron patted her back saying, "Breathe in through the nose, out through the mouth. It will pass." Never mind that the scene stank of smoke, fish, and gore, it was good advice.

She said between breaths, "It will pass? I don't even know what 'it' is." She began to shake.

"It's the battle frenzy wearing off," he explained, "You may feel sick for a while. It's normal."

"Ugh..." she took several more deep breaths, and then

had to sit on a nearby crate as her legs became too weak to support her. "I killed them, Jaron. I killed those... monsters."

He nodded, though her eyes were cast down at her feet. "That you did," he said, "You nearly made my heart stop back there, but you did well."

"Then why do I feel so guilty for it?" she sobbed, suddenly choked with tears, "They deserved it; they all deserve it for what they did!"

Jaron knelt beside her, doing his best to shield her from the others. "To Mineth, you mean?"

Cindra nodded, "She was family, did you know? We were distant cousins on my mother's side, but I never thought of her as family. Was that wrong of me?"

Jaron didn't know what to say. He just rubbed her back and said, "Keep breathing."

She stammered, "S-so why do I feel guilty for killing those... those gods-damned butchers?" She began to sob, wiping tears and blood from her face.

Jaron said, "Taking a life has a price, even if you think they deserve it; even if they are unnatural abominations. Minozhians walk like men, they think and speak like men, their ancestors used to be men once, if the tales are true."

Cindra didn't answer. Her deep breathing increased.

Jaron said softly, "My first battle was at Lintheid, about five years ago. I was younger than you are now, and squire to a loud-mouthed, uncouth knight by the name of Sir Cord Freekirk." He looked back at the man to make sure he was out of earshot. "After the fighting was over, I shook for hours. I gave up my breakfast too."

Cindra huffed, "Don't talk about throwing up, damn you."

"Sorry," he said, grinning. Then he sobered and leaned in close, lest anyone hear. "Your first encounter was soon after Mineth was killed, wasn't it?"

She nodded. "Days after."

"You've had time to cope with it," he said, "The pain

was fresh, and your desire for revenge was strong."

"You think that I feel differently about them now?" she asked, looking accusingly into his eyes, "You think that I've stopped hating them for what they did two years ago?"

"No," he replied, "I think you're a warrior now, like it or not. You know what it's like to fight alongside your brothers-in-arms; watching them stand or fall. The stakes are higher, and it takes its toll."

"Does it ever get easier?" she asked weakly.

Jaron's face grew troubled, "Do you want it to?"

She recalled that she had felt guilt even two years ago, when she had earned her war token. The feelings were not as acute as now, or she didn't remember them to be. Maybe it was because she and Teya had escaped uninjured that day, whereas today, soldiers had died horribly before her eyes.

Jaron rose as he heard men approaching, and helped Cindra to her feet.

The archer came over with his company and Sir Cord in tow, gave them a salute, and clapped Cindra on the shoulder. "Your first battle, I take it?" he asked, noting her state.

Cindra only nodded.

"Well fought, master DePort! Well fought indeed. You saved my skin a time or two." He turned to the other students, who were gathering out of curiosity. "All of you! You have done your master credit! Well fought indeed!"

Turning back to Cindra, the archer noticed the large Minozhian knife at her waist. "What is this?" he asked, fingering the still-bloody, horned handle, and noting its custom-made sheath. "This is one of their blades, is it not?"

"Yes it is," Cindra answered, her pride giving her a little strength, "from my last run-in with Minozhians. It's a token of my first kill."

The archer laughed and mussed Cindra's hair roughly in the way that men like to do to boys. "Hah! The gods have sent a Minozhian killer in our hour of need! Splendid!" He turned to Jaron saying, "Sir Cord tells me Dillan is your squire. I presume you are Sir Jaron Dunlorden, son of Sir Fedrick, the Farmer Knight?"

"I am," Jaron nodded, unused to this nickname for his father, accurate though it was. The bold archer was clearly the youngest of his company, perhaps matching Jaron's twenty-two years. His dark golden hair, now free of his hood and mail coif, hung about his shoulders, thick with sweat and grime. The man's speech was odd, like someone from the far west; his vowels were clipped in that particular way.

"An honor, to be sure. Your father's good service to his count is well known." He glanced down and said, "Is that an Honor Sword at your hip?" He motioned to *Valdiroth* at Jaron's side, its distinctive hilt and pedigree giving it away. "It might have been good to see it unsheathed today."

Jaron flushed, "Our spears were better suited for the day's work, I think."

The archer smiled and gave a nod, moving on as he conferred with his captain.

Cord, Jaron, and the students all gathered together as they watched the men-at-arms heading for a plundered warehouse. Cord had his arms folded, as he often did when trying to figure something through.

"Who in blazes are they?" Jaron asked.

"Not sure," Cord answered, "They wear no badge or heraldry. Fine gear though; maybe they're a band of mercenaries?"

Mat Belvine who was a mercenary himself, said, "That'd explain how they fought. Loads of experience between them, or I'm a milkmaid."

Gaius Corrina remarked, "I've heard that manner of speech before. It's from the far western lands; I'm sure of it. My father would receive ember swallows using that kind of speech."

Cindra's father had as well, though she couldn't say so. However, there was something more to this man, something personal. She had the feeling she had seen his face before.

"Well," Cord said, "Let's stop acting like a flock of gossiping hens. There's work to be done!" He began directing his students to aid the villagers, who were surveying the wreckage of their lives in a haze of smoke and shock.

As the others departed, Cindra received a shock of her own. She grabbed Jaron's arm, yanking him close. "Jaron, I *do* know that man! I've *seen* him before!" she said in a hushed voice.

"Who, the jolly, opinionated bowman?" he asked, "Perhaps he's some fellow who traded with you and your Galindri friends?"

"I think..." she lowered her voice to a whisper, "I think he's the king."

"The king?" Jaron hissed, turning serious, "What makes you say that?" He eyed the young man with disbelief.

Cindra took him aside saying, "I saw the prince two years ago in Highseat, before Galen II died. And yes, I was with my Galindri family, in disguise. He rode right by me!"

Jaron stole a look at the young man who was now stepping into the looted warehouse. "So this was the prince known as the Black Eagle, now Galen III? What is he doing here?" His question died on his lips as the answer became obvious; the king was moving east towards the enemy, preparing to either attack or defend in the inevitable civil war. Jaron whispered, "But if the king is here, where is his army?"

Cindra shook her head at the question, not wanting to ponder the answer.

The archer emerged from the warehouse moments later, holding aloft a lantern. "This is the only building they plundered," he said. "I want to know what was kept here and what is missing." One of the swordsmen nodded, hurrying off. The golden-haired archer turned to Sir Cord and asked, "What did you say your business was here, schoolmaster?"

Cord felt himself compelled to answer just by the look on the younger man's face. He said, "We were traveling from Portshia to return one of my students for burial. He was killed by a vemlok in the city."

"Indeed?" gasped the archer, "A vemlok, you say? The scourges of elder days are returning it would seem; beast-men, dire creatures of the wild, and now the undead... None can argue that dark times are upon us again." He shook his head, his expression grim.

"I never got your name, stranger," Cord said, folding his arms.

The archer smiled and took Cord by the shoulder, "Blunt as the mace on your standard, sir knight. All will be told, but first I would like to ask the hospitality of your house, after our dead are tended to, of course. We will all need a safe place to sleep."

Cord scowled at being put off yet again, but sensed the weary resolve in the young man's voice. Clearly he was hiding something, but he felt no treachery in the archer's manner. He agreed to the man's request, keeping his reservations to himself.

The archer walked up the street to kneel by his fallen comrades, his cloaked form partially obscured by the falling ash and wandering citizens returning to their homes. It was only then that Cindra and Jaron approached Sir Cord, and Jaron whispered in his ear.

Cord's jaw dropped as he uttered, "Rath's Blood!"

Baron Saul Freekirk of Cordo did not receive many visitors these days. His mental state had deteriorated over the last decade or so, and his wife Mytha tried her best to shield him from too much excitement. This had been impossible today, for upon seeing his town in flames, Saul had doused himself with a pitcher of water.

It fell to Lady Cordo to see to the defense of the town, the security of the townsfolk in the manor house, and the chaos in the aftermath. She did not notice that her husband was soaking wet and hiding in his bedchamber, until Cord and the healers arrived bearing a wounded young man.

The lord and lady now stood in the main hall of their manor house, as dignified and formal as possible. Saul had been hastily dried off and dressed to receive guests, and the townsfolk had returned to their homes, leaving behind an unwholesome atmosphere of fear and anxiety. Sir Cord stood beside his parents, having quietly informed his mother once, and his father thrice, about the identity of their new guest.

Jaron and Cindra were present also, along with their fellow students. The air was thick with anticipation, and if the rumors were true, they would be representing the Freekirk School before the king himself. No one wished to slouch or show pain as they stood at attention. Only Terrus Drakthorne had suffered a grievous blow and was absent. He lay bandaged in Cord's own bed; his chest wound being tended by the healer priests.

The surviving swordsmen stood tall, bandages and all, as their captain stepped forward and filled the room with his resonant voice, "I give you His Royal Highness Galen III!" He bowed before the young archer and the swordsmen sank to their knees as one, followed by everyone else in the room. Only Lord Saul was surprised.

"Your highness!" proclaimed the old baron, sinking precariously to his knee as Cord and Mytha supported him. Then to his wife, he half-whispered, "I thought the king was much older."

"Rise friends," said the king, "I had intended to impose upon you tomorrow morning, but our inn has suffered the fire, and we need shelter for the night."

"It is no imposition at all," Lady Mytha said in her most gracious tone. "Your Highness may not recall, but our poor house once received your person, in the company of your royal father and his queen, in better days." Her northern accent was melodic and soothing, and well-practiced at speaking to royalty. Cordobal Province was the ancestral home of the royal family, and Cordoshome was a frequent stop on the king's annual sojourn to the Winter Palace in Portshia, though the old king had not made the trip in years.

Galen III nodded, saying, "I do recall, though I was only a small lad at the time. I thought your sons to all be giants!" There was polite laughter, and the king gestured to the older man at his side, "May I present Field Marshal Valthór, leader of my southern army."

Cord was puzzled, "Southern army? I was not aware that an army was being raised, highness."

The king smiled, "That, sir knight, is the purpose of my mission. We are raising a force in our wake; it is currently marching down the Red Coast Road from Pinikal and Woodcourt, Abandi and Ghat, and shall soon pass through your lands. We require that you send all available men-at-arms to Portshia as soon as possible. They are needed for both the city garrison and a march against the Dissenter Houses."

Lady Mytha replied, "Of course, highness. We shall send out the call tonight. I regret that we do not maintain much of a standing force, and it might be a few weeks before our troops can be mustered."

"As my good wife says, highness," Lord Saul said cheerfully.

"Majesty," said Cord, "We have heard little news here in the south. Has the situation changed with the Dissenter Houses?"

The king answered, his young eyes hardening, "My father was poisoned, his attempts to gain allies thwarted by vile conspiracy," Cindra realized he was referring to her 'death' at sea and the failure of her wedding plans, "I shall not wait for an attack to come at their leisure. I will take the fight to them and settle all scores."

No one spoke, for the king's voice had a keen edge to it. It was not a rebuke, but it hung in the air like a headman's ax, ready to fall upon any who questioned his resolve.

Cindra stepped forward and knelt before she could think the better of it, "Highness?" she asked.

The king's face softened, "Yes, young Dillan of Waynwell, Minozhian slayer. You may speak."

Lady Mytha's eyes went wide as she recognized the girl she had trained to act as a boy, having blended in so well with the other students that she had quite mistaken her. She had assumed Jaron and Cord had sent her back to her family by now. *What were they thinking?*

"There are other tidings from the south that may not have reached your ears, highness." Cindra said. "Portshia has been beset by strange storms and stranger happenings. There are rumors of Llomaakitte priests plotting against the crown, and a mad wizard heralding evil times has been seen in the city. Sir Jaron and I encountered this man by chance, and he wields unknown powers."

The king held Dillan in his gaze saying, "House DePort must have either a noble lineage, or excellent teachers, as well-spoken as you are. I have heard rumors of that ancient cult's involvement in my father's death, but I did not know of this mad wizard or the pall over Portshia. Is it known if this cult is present in the city?"

Cindra said, "It may be so, highness." The memory of her near-assassination over a year ago sprung freshly to her mind. *Julen Gordon is dead, but his wife Lemorea was never found.* She thought, *How do I tell him what he needs to know without revealing how I know it?*

"Oh," cried Lord Saul, "She's the spy!" He chuckled to himself as Lady Mytha's heart leaped to her throat, and Cord and Jaron stood agape.

"Forgive my lord husband, your highness," Lady Mytha interjected quickly, "he grows confused in this late hour. The excitement of the evening..." She summoned the household servants to assist the baron to bed.

"Indeed," said the king as he gave the baron leave, and then turned his attention towards Dillan.

Cindra kept her head down, hiding her furious blush. *Of all the things the old man could remember!* During the months she and Jaron had stayed in the manor house, they had told the baron she was a spy disguised as a boy, looking for the king's enemies in the fighting school, but they hadn't revealed her true identity. That was just as well; what he did recall was bad enough.

The king returned his gaze to Jaron, "Your squire is most knowledgeable, sir knight. Could it be that the baron speaks true about his profession... if not his gender?" His playful smile told them he took none of it seriously.

Jaron was at a loss, being unable to spin a lie in front of the king, "He uh, he is kept in my confidence, highness. I would recommend consulting the Arch Mage Ildric Finnael in Portshia for more information. He is the source of much of our knowledge."

"I shall do so," said the king, "and I thank you, young Dillan DePort, for bringing such news to my attention." Cindra bowed again and backed away, taking her place behind Jaron. The king then turned to Sir Cord, "Have you any knights in your fighting school that may be summoned?"

"Only myself and Sir Jaron, highness," he answered. "The students are esquires, freemen, and sell-swords, mostly. We had only just begun basic mounted training when... I lost a lad to the vemlok."

The king nodded, "It is the way of things in this age; fewer trained knights, and more skilled infantry. So be it. My northern army should be in Rickshome-on-the-Joshian by now, and the southern forces will assemble at Portshia into the winter. We will require every fighting man available upon the spring thaw."

Cord answered, "I shall see to it, highness."

Cindra shivered. Early spring would bring war, and the melting snow would mingle with the blood of Calilon as the Loyalists and Dissenters clashed over control of the vast country. Waiting in the shadows would be the evil priests of Llomaak, the Countless Lord, their dark designs unknown and ominous.

There were details of her encounter with the wicked priests in Pinikal two years ago that she could not recall, for they didn't seem as important as the threats she understood; now she felt that every element of that night was vital and she struggled to remember. The man she later recognized as Julen Gordon had found her eavesdropping on their secret meeting and captured her; it was only the timely arrival of her Galindri friends that saved her from a vile fate.

"Highness," Jaron said quickly, "One of the students in Portshia is the son of Baron DeKenric himself. It might be best to send him away before news of this reaches the school."

Cindra flinched, as she could quickly think of many more uses for Grigor DeKenric that the king might consider. Jaron may have signed the lad's death warrant, or condemned him to prison or ransom for the duration of the war.

"Interesting," said the king. "I shall have to consider that on the way. In the meantime, I will require a supplement to my escort for the journey to Portshia. I give you two days to conclude your business here, Sir Cord. I hope it is sufficient."

"More than sufficient, highness." Cord bowed.

Galen III turned to the students and said, "You have all fought bravely in the service of king and country. I shall reward you each as I see fit. Good evening." They all bowed as he strode from the room, followed by his royal guard.

Bradric sputtered in his coarse voice, "Vina's tits! The king! We helped save the king!" He sat down heavily on the floor. "Reward us, he says. Gods!"

Adric patted Cindra on the back, "He called you 'Minozhian slayer.' How many did you kill this time, eh Dillan?"

Inis DeGhat said, "One that I saw. He set a spear

against his charge and impaled him!”

“That would be two,” said Filbert, who had seen the one on the roof. “He picked off a crossbowman who’d climbed the rooftops. He and the king finished him before the final push.”

Cindra blushed, “I did no more than the rest of you. I wasn’t even face to face with them; I was safely in the back.” She didn’t need to mention it was actually three.

“Safe,” Jaron shook his head. “Safe, my eye.”

Gaius Corrina approached Cindra and clapped her shoulder, “Well done, DePort. You’ll make a fine knight someday, I warrant.” It was the nicest thing her unknowing cousin had said to her all year. Cindra blushed even more.

“I wonder if he’ll knight us all?” murmured Filbert, “Honor though it’d be, I can’t afford it.” He smiled as the others silently took account of their situation and prospects.

“Hire us, more likely,” said Mat. “It is skilled troops his highness will need, if I caught his tone proper.” He looked at Sir Cord for confirmation.

Cord nodded grimly, “The king will need to fill his ranks, and the best offers will go to those with the best training. This winter will be a busy time for us, make no mistake. If it’s to be war come springtime, then I’ll have you make a good showing of it.”

“Will we have time to visit our families before... spring?” asked Inis. The others looked expectantly to the school master.

Cord folded his arms, troubled. “For some, perhaps. I won’t lie to you; some of you may have already said your last goodbyes. Take my advice. Save your money for decent equipment and provisions, not for a last trip home.”

Morning brought fresh tears as the townsfolk surveyed the damage in the light of day. The fire had burned nearly a third of the buildings from midway up the cliffs to the manor house, which was protected by a wall of stone and outcropping of rock. Dozens of families were displaced but only a few people had perished in the attack, either by Minozhian hands or the flames set by them.

An accounting had found that indeed the bull warriors had only looted a single warehouse, leaving most of the town unspoiled. Since Cord and the other students were returning Halvoy Quenlorden's body to his family, it fell to Jaron to investigate. He had spent many years in Cordoshome and knew it well. Cindra accompanied him, eager to learn what the Minozhians were after this time.

The owner of the warehouse, a merchant named Narvek, was being questioned as he surveyed the damage. "I can't account for it," he was saying, "Of all the goods they could pillage; they took off with my wine."

Jaron examined the ax marks and the crates thrown aside to get at the corner where the wine was stored. The straw-packed remnants of pottery and spice jars lay about the floor as Narvek gathered what he could, muttering to himself.

"Are you sure the wine was the only thing taken?" Jaron asked again.

"It was... I-I can't account for it," he repeated.

"What kind of wine was it?" Cindra asked.

"Oh, ah um, an Aurilonian port," he said absently. "Quite a nice vintage."

"Is there anything else you can tell us about it?" Jaron pushed. "They burned half the town to get it, and I would know why."

Cindra had an insight. "I take it you sampled some?"

Narvek stammered, "I-I'd sampled some, yes... I wasn't skimming from the stock if that's what you're implying. I was offered a cask as partial payment to keep it here until fall. After that it would be picked up, I was told, by a foreign customer." He chuckled without mirth, "Foreign customer indeed!"

Cindra considered this, "Do you still have the cask?"

"I do," Narvek nodded, "I've not drunk the whole thing yet, though I may start heartily soon." He led them from the warehouse to his office upstairs. The little room held a desk full of parchments, scrolls and ledgers, as well as tokens from previous dealings. Among them was a cask of port that had been tapped, a symbol painted in stencil upon the side. Cindra squinted at the markings.

"Jaron, this trademark..." she said, pointing. Jaron peered at the label.

"It belongs to Maron Theenix," Narvek explained. "He's a top man in the Portshia Trade Guild; I'd hate to tell him his shipment was taken."

Cindra turned to Jaron, who was puzzling it out. "Master Theenix was at the Lady Cindra's engagement feast, same as the treacherous Gordons," she said, reminding him of the dinner where she and Jaron had first laid eyes upon each other. "The count wanted to know the guild's position on new purveyance contracts if there was a civil war."

Jaron spoke softly, "Do you recall what their position was?"

She replied in a low voice, "I was a bit distracted by a certain knight who kept staring at me."

Narvek was occupied with his ledgers and his muttering, and so heard nothing.

Jaron examined the barrel, rocking it to and fro absently, as if the answer would spill out. He pulled the stopper and let the liquid slosh about within, issuing a heady aroma. Something felt odd however, as if the port was not the only thing weighing down the cask. He hefted it, testing its balance, and then picked it up and strode out to the top of the stairs above the warehouse. After checking below, he threw the cask hard upon the dock, breaking it asunder. Narvek screeched in dismay as the last of his precious port seeped between the cracks in the boardwalk.

The bottom of the barrel held a waxen mass that seemed to glitter in the morning sun even as the port drained from its surface, leaving a ruby stain. Jaron leaped down to the broken cask with Cindra close behind, kicking aside the splintered wood to reveal the secret within. What they found was a mass of beeswax poured over hundreds of gold coins, cunningly concealed from anyone unwilling to smash open the merchandise.

"A payment!" Cindra exclaimed. "They knew exactly where it was... someone must have told them about it, setting it up to look like a raid."

"Payment for what?" Jaron asked as Narvek arrived, his eyes going wide at the incriminating coins.

"Either something they've done or something they're going to do," she said unhelpfully. "They must have carried off thousands of coins if this amount was in each barrel."

Jaron turned to Narvek, folding his arms. "I'd like to see all of your records that pertain to this shipment."

The frazzled man nodded absently.

The documents were strewn on the table in the hall of the Freekirk Villa as Field Marshal Valthór read aloud from the lading forms, "The casks came from the port of LuQuivost, via an Aurilonian tradesman. They were shipped to Portshia, received by the Theenix warehouse and moved to Cordoshome by wagon."

Galen III glowered at the lump of wax containing what was certainly treasonous blood money. He idly chipped at the golden-yellow mass with a dagger, seeing his father's face stamped on the coins beneath the surface. "Maron Theenix," he said. "Why? What has he to gain by employing Minozhian pirates?"

Valthór said, "The obvious motive is profit. But without knowing what they were paid for, we cannot say for certain."

Cindra stood beside Jaron and Lady Mytha, trying not to give herself away by joining in the conversation. She knew that her father had been dealing with the Trade Guild to avoid war profiteering, securing agreements in advance. She sorely wished she had paid more attention when her mother had explained this several years ago; she had been preoccupied with being gloomy.

"But why deal with Minozhians? Why not supply the Dissenter Houses directly?" the king asked.

Valthór considered, "Any number of reasons. It all depends on what their goals are. We need to speak with Master Theenix." The tone of his voice made Cindra realize he meant more than simple conversation. Dungeons and sharp instruments would be involved.

"Agreed," said the king, "Have our dead been given the proper rites?"

"Yes highness," answered Valthór grimly.

Galen III turned to Lady Mytha, who had been silent until now. "Baroness, I expect the forces of Cordobal to march to Portshia within the week."

"Yes, your highness," she said. The forces of Cordobal Province included her sons and their older children who held lands to the north. She did not let the worry show in her eyes.

He said to Jaron, "Sir Jaron, I intend to make your squire a knight for services rendered to the crown. I hope this does not inconvenience you overmuch."

Jaron and Lady Mytha both gasped; the knight's face turned red as the lady's turned white. Cindra was in shock, her stomach went all quivery as her world tilted for a brief second. *Knighthood?* Her mind reeled. It was what she had always imagined for herself in her silly fantasies, but the reality of it hit her like a fall from a horse. Knighthood meant riding to war in the name of a lord. Even a poor knight such as Sir Jaron, who had to borrow his jousting armor, who was buying his plate mail a piece at a time, was expected to ride to war when called. And war was upon them.

"Well," Galen III said to Cindra, "What say you to that, young Dillan?"

Cindra tried to form words but failed.

Lady Mytha spoke, "Highness, you do the boy too

much honor. He should complete his training first, surely?"

"Nonsense! I am in need of brave knights of quality, and if he can meet the Minozhian beasts face to face, surely he can cope with my traitorous barons." He clapped Dillan on the shoulder saying, "Kneel, and lets have it done." He drew his sword as Cindra sank to her knees, too shocked to speak.

Now? He's doing it now?

Jaron and the baroness stood by helplessly as a stern look from the field marshal told them interference was not advised. They were here to raise an army after all.

Galen touched his sword to her shoulders, right and left, then the top of her head saying, "In the name of the Most High King Arathus, and his son Kraal the Great, I make thee a knight. Arise, Sir Dillan."

Cindra found that she could not. She just knelt there on the stone floor, trembling. Galen took her hesitance as confusion. "Worry not about the formalities, young knight. Ceremony is for times of peace. If you wish for a more formal procedure, there's plenty of time for that." He helped her to her feet.

Lady Mytha wrung her hands as Jaron stood with his mouth open. Cindra felt a welling of pride and achievement, but her better sense squashed that almost immediately. This was a greater matter than fooling boys at a fighting school. She had to tell the truth now, for this was her king.

"Highness," Cindra began, "I... There are things we must speak of now, vital things that... that you must know."

Galen looked to his field marshal, who shifted uneasily. "Oh?" he said. "What vital matters must we discuss, sir knight?"

Cindra chose her words carefully, keeping her eyes lowered. She had often imagined how she would tell her close friends at the school, but she never thought she would meet the king and have to explain her deception. She took a deep breath, "For the last few years I have been in hiding. Assassins sought my life and I did what I had to in order to elude them. I used my influence to bend others to my way of thinking. Any fault your highness finds is mine and mine alone."

Galen frowned, his eyes searching the lad's face. "I think you'd best explain, Sir Dillan."

Cindra could not think of any other way to say it. She began to break into a cold sweat, and felt her nerve slipping away. What consequences would befall her? What about Jaron? Cord? Lady Mytha? All were complicit in her deception.

Before her courage failed completely, she stepped back and curtsied, bowing her head. "Royal cousin," she said in her natural feminine voice, "I am Lady Cindra Corrina, daughter of Lord Amon and Lady Zara, Count and Countess Casselvane. I beg your highness's forgiveness and... understanding."

The king was quite taken aback; confusion, amusement and incredulity played across his face. He looked to his field marshal, who only had a look of horror. "Is this a joke?" Galen asked, not knowing whether to laugh or be enraged. "Lady Cindra died at sea, a victim of Minozhian pirates..."

Cindra straightened and continued, feeling relieved to unburden herself so completely. "My ship was attacked at sea, but my life was saved by a magic trinket given by Arch Mage Finnael. I was found by a Galindri family and lived among them for over a year; I was present, though in disguise, in the city of Highseat when your highness arrived and your royal father died. I saw the purple smoke over the castle."

Galen's mouth dropped as he recalled the day he became king by tragic circumstance. He motioned for Valthór to bring him a chair and he sat heavily in it.

Cindra said, "By happy chance I met Sir Jaron in Pinikal." Her mind flew to the day she and her adopted sisters had been bathing, and Teya caught the knight spying on them. She did not share this detail. "He escorted me to Cordoshome, where Lady Mytha kept us over the winter, awaiting the time of Jaron's banishment to end. I asked her to teach me to pass as a boy so that I could hide in plain sight at the fighting school and learn to defend the honor of my house. Sir Jaron and Sir Cord were acting under my command, and for the purpose of keeping me safe from our enemies." She stood silently with hands folded, waiting for the king's reaction.

But Field Marshal Valthór spoke, "What perversion is this? 'Defend the honor of your house,' you say? House Corrina will never live down the shame of it! You have made a mockery of the fighting school, the knighthood, and your own virtue! Living amongst the squires, serving a knight in all manner of..." He glared at Jaron, "What have you to say, sir knight? Did the lady sleep in your chambers, as a squire should? What would you have us believe now?"

Jaron bore the assault silently, his face reddening in shame. The moment he had been dreading had finally arrived and he made no answer.

But Cindra was having none of it; she had endured too much to be ashamed. "I have been a fugitive for the last four years, living in disguise, afraid to show myself even to my family. In that time, I have faced more dangers than many who would now be called to war. Should I sit idle? Have I so little to lose?

"My gender has been a curse on my family, robbing my father of another heir. My marriage was prevented by treachery, so is my usefulness at an end? Am I to go back and wait in my father's castle while our enemies close in around us? Was I not just knighted because I proved myself worthy?"

At this, Valthór snorted in disgust and turned away. Galen only watched her impassively, his face unreadable.

"Highness," she entreated, "I seek nothing beyond my station but the freedom to defend my home and the crown. Had I been married I would be a duchess, unable to lift a finger to aid my country-"

"Had you been married," Valthór interrupted, "we would have allies in Rokvynnar at our backs instead of the Minozhians!"

She replied curtly, "They poisoned the duke I was to marry, they tried to have me killed, and they murdered the king himself! Do you really think all would be well if I had simply announced my survival and wed as planned?" She raised her eyebrows in the manner her mother used when scolding someone. "Besides, no one would know these events were related had I not heard it from the conspirators' own mouths!"

"Enough," said the king quietly, raising his hand. "Lady Cindra," his eyes flicked up and down to reconcile with her appearance, "No one doubts the perils you have faced or the value of the intelligence you have gathered. I thank you for it. What is in question is your deception. A woman is not permitted to dress as a man or engage in manly activities; such is the law of the land and the way of our people. This cannot continue."

Cindra shook, "Does his highness mean to debase me now? To revoke my knighthood?"

The king sighed, "It should never have been, lady."

She nodded sullenly, "Does his highness revoke my training and experience? Does he command the fire in my heart be extinguished and my courage to be forgotten?"

Valthór chided, "He commands your obedience, lady."

She kept her eyes on the floor as tears clouded her vision. "What is to become of me then? I am no longer marriageable, surely. My virtue is intact but there is no more proof. No one will have me."

This surprised Valthór as he looked accusingly at Sir Jaron. "What do you mean, 'no more proof'?"

She explained, "I have not been intact since I learned to ride a horse Galindri-style during my time in the wilderness. Such matters are not important among their women."

"What the Galindri do with their women is not our concern," Valthór said. "You are not one of them."

She answered softly. "Among them I am a warrior; the headband and knife I wear are symbols of that. I did not lie when I said I have dealt with Minozhians before, highness." She sniffed back her tears as she touched the handle of the deadly weapon. "This is from one of the pirates who attacked my ship; I felled him with a single arrow to save the life of a friend. She too is a warrior."

The king looked impressed, though it only showed in a slight widening of his eyes. Valthór scoffed and folded his arms.

"I admit," said the king, "that you would be a most worthy young man, were it for deeds alone," he sighed and rubbed his temples, "but regardless of your deeds, you are a woman and you have broken the law in pretending otherwise."

"Then let me continue as a woman!" she offered. "I will pretend no longer."

"That is out of the question," said the king. "You seek rights above your station. If a commoner pretended to be a noble, would it do to reward his crime by making him one for true?"

"Highness," she said carefully, "I am already of a noble house. I could remain a squire-"

"In the name of the gods," spouted the field marshal, "By what manner have you been raised? Did your father and mother not teach you your place? Are you so very confused that you think this is a matter of choice or... or... *petition*?"

Cindra answered a bit more forcefully than she intended, "I was raised to believe that I was not as *important* as a son! I was a disappointment to my father, especially after my little brother died. Even though I was everything he might hope for in an heir, I was not his heir. I was *raised*, field marshal, for life in a cage. And by the gods, I will *not* be caged!" Without thinking, her hand gripped the *Kos* knife, her knuckles white upon the horned handle.

"That remains to be seen," said Valthór, resting his own hand on his sword hilt.

The king spoke, "You have a fire in you Lady Cindra, I will say that for you. It makes me sad that you are not the young man I thought you to be. As for your fate, that will be decided later in the presence of your father. In the meantime, I order you to dress no longer in the manner of a man." He turned to Lady Mytha. "Baroness?"

The woman stepped forward, afraid to look up.

"Find her something suitable, will you? She will be presented to her parents properly as their daughter." He rose from his chair and strode from the hall, his field marshal at his heels.

Cindra could only stare after the king. Everything had been taken from her with a few words, leaving her a helpless, useless girl once again. Her chest heaved, her heart pounded with mute fury; she wanted to scream, to cry, and to tear at her clothes.

Boy's clothes. Clothing she would never wear again.

As the boots of the Black Eagle vanished to distant echoes in the hall, the only sounds she could hear were the distant preparations of the kitchen, the soft footsteps of the baroness, and her own pulse pounding in her ears.

Chapter Three

First Meetings

It was late the next evening when Sir Cord and the students returned from the country home of the Quenlordens, having paid their respects and buried their comrade. They tried to enter the main hall quietly, but the noise of booted feet and weary voices carried up to the room where Lady Cindra now sat.

Sir Jaron occupied the other chair at the dressing table, watching as Lady Mytha and her handmaid tried to make something more feminine of Cindra's short auburn locks. Her hair drooped just above shoulder length with barely enough for a modest braid, and her forelocks stubbornly hung free in a boyish style. For a squire seeking knighthood, the hair was kept longer in the back to accept the traditional *tipok* knot. Cindra had worn it longer to keep up appearances, or so she told herself. The foolishness of her original dreams was painfully apparent now.

Lady Mytha's handmaid had a selection of her own

daughter's clothing to choose from, and Cindra picked out a blue cotton dress, yellow ribbons for her sleeves and waist, and yellow shoes. They were her family's colors, and they gave her a small amount of comfort. After all, she would be reunited with her parents in a week's time, and that was worth celebrating in spite of all that had happened.

Cord's heavy feet could be heard climbing the stairs as he responded to his mother's summons. He knocked once, entered the room and stopped dead in his tracks upon seeing Lady Cindra in her new clothes.

"Oh, gods save us," he muttered before shutting the door behind him.

"Welcome back, son." said Lady Mytha with a sigh.

Cord was turning white, "What in the name of Balkon's balls...?"

"Language!" Mytha scolded. "There is more than one lady here, and one is your *mother*." Then she sighed, "The ruse is at an end. His highness knows."

"H-how?" Cord was turning red now, making his sandy hair appear as a pale wreath about a blustery furnace.

His mother explained, "The king decided to bestow a knighthood upon young Dillan yesterday morning, before anyone could say anything." She shook her head, "Once it was done, Lady Cindra correctly saw fit to inform him of matters that could no longer remain hidden."

Cord searched about for a chair, and finding none, pitched Jaron out of his. "What does this mean for the school?" he asked as he sank into the upholstery. "What did the king say?"

"He will leave the matter to rest until you reach Portshia," said the baroness. "In the meantime, Lady Cindra is to be a boy no longer."

Cord groaned, "Ugh, I knew this would happen someday, but I thought it would only be the count finding out. Now it's the king..." he buried his face in his hands. "We could lose our license for this. Our house could be disgraced like the Greenfellows..."

Cindra lifted her eyes at the mention of that house; Jaron's family had a long-standing rivalry with the Greenfellows that had ended in blood, if ended it had. She did not wish for House Freekirk to be disgraced because of her. She retreated into her thoughts as her eyes sank to the floor once again.

Jaron was trying to maintain his dignity after being hoisted from his chair. He straightened his tunic and said, "If the Freekirk School could turn a noble girl into a fierce Minozhian slayer, I'd call that an endorsement."

Cord glared at him, "What in the Abyss are you doing here anyway? Should you be lurking in a lady's private quarters?"

Jaron folded his arms and said, "I am hiding; what do you think? There is no place for me to go without having the eyes of the king's men leering at me. Suppose one of them decides to insult Cindra or myself? I'd have to take up the challenge."

"And I don't want Jaron being so stupid," Cindra said to the floor.

"I think," said the baroness, "that Lady Cindra should be introduced to her former classmates. It will make tomorrow's journey less awkward."

Cord shook his head, "Less awkward! That's a laugh! How am I to explain this?"

Cindra rose to her feet and straightened her simple dress saying, "I shall speak for myself, Master Cord; I require no one to explain for me. You might, however, have them stand at attention when I enter; it could make for a more proper introduction."

It took a moment for Cord to realize who was addressing him; he had gotten used to her being Jaron's troublesome squire, not the count's daughter. "I suppose you're right about that, milady," he said as he rose. "I'll have them ready." He strode from the room, muttering under his breath.

Lady Mytha motioned for her handmaid to join her

and said, "We take our leave now, Lady Cindra. Do not keep them waiting overlong."

Cindra walked up to Jaron and offered a weak smile. "No turning back now," she said.

Jaron said, "Turning back isn't in your nature," and he leaned in to kiss her.

She returned the pressure of his lips with a sudden urgency, not knowing if she would ever feel them again. Something told her their time together might be at an end, and it made her heart skip with dread. Her arms surrounded his neck as a whimper escaped her tightening throat, threatening to lead to tears. If this was to be their last moment alone, she would not have it be in tears of despair.

Jaron's hands caressed her back and pulled her close, their breath mingling as he lifted her to her toes. His fingers found their way to the nape of her neck, intending to hold her closer, but nearly undid the meager braid that tamed her auburn locks. He withdrew his fingers, not wanting to spoil her appearance.

She was still strong and firm beneath the cotton dress. She was the same young warrior who had earned the scar on her chin, giving as good as she got in the training ring. The wrapping that hid her breasts had finally been removed for good and her true shape was now apparent for the first time in years. She was glorious, graceful and powerful, like a Kyraine: winged battle maidens of Balkon that carried the fallen to their final judgment.

But Jaron couldn't escape the feeling that she had become frailer somehow; that all of the strength she had gained was now at the mercy of laces, ribbons, and bows; that she was now bound more tightly in the loose, flowing dress than she had ever been in the concealing garb of a man.

"Are you going to be alright?" he asked, seeing his reflection swimming in her eyes.

"I-I think I will be," she breathed. "I'm afraid of what

will happen when we reach Portshia, though." Her fingers brushed the hair from his brow. "I don't want you or Master Cord to suffer for my decisions."

Jaron held her face in his hands, "And I don't want you to suffer either. They must be made to understand. They *must!*"

"We've made mistakes, Jaron love; both of us, with full knowledge of what we did." She took a deep, shaking breath.

He nodded, "I know," he said. "But I'd not live the past few years any differently."

"Neither would I," she said. "Neither would I."

He stroked her hair. "What should we tell them if they ask about our... intimacies?"

Cindra rested her head against his chest, listening to his beating heart. It was so strong, whether from passion or worry, she could not tell. "I think... I think it would be best if we keep our answers within the bounds of Perfect Love."

"Sorry?" Jaron said, truly puzzled.

"Perfect Love," she repeated. "Selvina's guide for loving those beyond our reach."

His voice carried more than a hint of irony, "You mean like between a knight and the lady he serves, for example?"

"Yes," she said, realizing how silly it sounded now.

"I think we are a few years too late for that," he chided. "No one will believe that we have been as chaste and pure as Selvina's poets envisioned.

"Then hold your silence about my honor, as a gentleman should," she said. "Let our questioners come to me, if they wish to pry out the secrets of our bedchamber."

Jaron frowned with concern, "Are you sure?"

She nodded, "I am well-versed in Selvina's teachings, and I can demand that a priestess be present when answering such questions; perhaps even Reverend Sister Lyneth herself. I can tread as thin a path as they can lay out for me, if it comes to that."

"Let us hope the king has greater things on his mind than the misdeeds of two people in love," Jaron said, and he kissed her again.

No answer was spoken aloud, but was expressed in the pressure of their lips and the beating of their hearts.

Cindra approached the top of the stairs, looked down on the assembled lads and sighed. When they had last parted ways, they were her friends and peers. But in the next few moments... who could tell? Would any of them ever speak to her again? They all looked tired from their journey, eager to roll out their blankets and sleep where they may in the warmth of the main hall. They were uncertain and unsuspecting; she could see weary confusion in the fire-lit faces. More than half were expecting bad news, maybe about Terrus Drakthorne. They had indeed lost another companion, but not in the way they feared.

Master Cord was waiting at the bottom of the stairs. He saw her in the shadows above, nodding as she and Jaron descended. He turned to his students and said in a voice soft and respectful, "Lads, I present to you... Lady Cindra Corrina."

The students just stared in confusion as their eyes focused in the dim light. As Cindra's face entered the light, the mutterings broke out, half in disbelief, half in amusement.

They think it's a test or a joke, she thought, keeping her face as calm as she could. Her lips tightened in a nervous grimace that might have been a smile.

Gaius Corrina was not smiling or muttering, but other eyes were on him; other voices asking questions he could not know.

"That really her, Gaius?"

"Isn't she supposed to be dead?"

Cindra felt badly for him, the cousin she had never met properly. His eyes were intently seeking hers, though she could only hold his gaze for a moment.

Adric could not help himself and he stepped forward, ready to be let in on the joke. "Dillan?" he asked in a wry whisper, "Is that you under that?" His eyes ran down the dress, lingering where they shouldn't. "Dillan?"

Some came closer, trying to reconcile the face they knew with the body and clothing they didn't. Others stood where they were, folding their arms or watching Master Cord for some sign that it was all foolishness.

Cord's face was a stone, and Jaron's eyes were cast downward.

Cindra smiled as best she could while keeping a proper distance. "I know this may be difficult to accept," she said, speaking in her normal, higher voice. "But it is true, and it is a secret that can no longer be kept."

The students looked at one another, a mix of aversion and incredulity prevalent on most faces.

She took a deep breath and began, "I survived the pirate attack that was meant to stop my marriage to a Rokvynnar duke. I was found and sheltered by a Galindri family, who disguised me as one of them. During that time in disguise, I learned that the men behind many important deaths were living in Portshia, among other places. I could not come home as myself, and I think they knew of my Galindri disguise.

"It was decided- *I* decided- that I would be safest where no one would think to look; where I could be close to Sir Jaron and Master Cord, my father's most trusted knights. Dillan DePort was a mask I wore for almost two years, but I can wear it no longer. I am sorry..." She almost choked on the word. Her throat closed up and she could say no more. The looks on the faces of her friends was too much to bear; they were masks of shock and mistrust, lit by orange flame and hidden by deep shadow as they turned from her.

Master Cord spoke up, his usual booming voice tamed and regretful. "Both I and Sir Jaron have been a party to this, obviously, but neither Gavadaire nor any other student knew about it." He cleared his throat, which was unusually tight. "As you may recall, Gavadaire LuVestra found an intruder with a crossbow in his room above our training hall last year. Gavadaire believed the assassin was there for him, but I can reveal now that the man intended that bolt for Lady Cindra."

This revelation caused a few sympathetic eyes to drift back to her.

Jaron spoke up, "He was the same man who was behind the lady's attack at sea, and the death of Galen II. There is a cult of wicked priests at work in our lands, and they want to bring about a war!"

Cindra stepped forward, regaining her voice. "None of this really matters!" she said, waving her hands as if to push it all away. "Not the why or the how. What matters is that I deceived you. I broke the law, I dressed as a man, and I trained by your sides. I am sorry if you feel betrayed; I never meant to bring any shame or dishonor to anyone. But never before have I had so many friends worth fighting for, and it has been the single greatest honor of my life to be counted as a friend and fellow student. I hope you can find it in your hearts to forgive me."

She sniffed and wiped her eyes, trying to remember how to do it in a ladylike fashion. The tears were flowing freely now, though she tried to blink them away. The faces of her friends were unreadable blurs of light and shadow, and their shifting feet conveyed the awkward emotions that went unspoken. When she could take no more of the silence, she gave a slight curtsy and withdrew up the stairs, holding the handrail lest her weakened knees betray her.

Master Cord cleared his throat again and said, "It's time to retire for all of us. We share a roof with the king tonight, so I'd thank you all to keep your voices down until morning. We leave at first light, so get some rest." He and Sir Jaron retreated to the corner of the hall and unrolled their blankets. The students followed suit, lying on tables, benches, and wherever the warmth of the fire would reach.

Once they were all settled in for the night, Bradric broke the silence. "So... Dillan's been a girl the whole time?"

Adric sighed, "Ever since she was born, I'd imagine..."

"Gods!" the big horse trainer's son remarked, "All the things I said in front of a noble lady..."

"She told you not to blaspheme so much," Adric chided.

Mat Belvine chuckled and said, "Well, this has been a capital day. We've seen one comrade put in the ground, and another put in a dress. Makes you wonder what tomorrow will bring."

Inis muttered, "I expect we'll get to see that Gali pony with a sidesaddle, that's what."

Filbert spoke up. "What are they going to do to Lady Cindra, do you think? I mean, if a woman was found practicing wizardry, she'd be called a witch and hanged for it." The Gaddisen family had a long tradition of sending their sons to the Mystic College, though Filbert was an odd exception.

Bradric said, "A girl learning to fight with men is crazy, sure enough. But look at what she did! She beat that Ratham kid in a fair fight, and she's a Minozhian killer, make no mistake. That's got to be worth something."

"Worth what?" Filbert asked. "It's proof that she wasn't just hiding there, but learning what she oughtn't. It'd be better if she pretended to be old Elmore's granddaughter or something; then she could've had reason to be at the school."

Mat laughed, "What, and have the likes of us slapping her rump as she poured our ale? Aye, that'd be better by far."

"My point is," Filbert said, "she wouldn't have been taking privileges beyond her station and sex."

"Like being stomped upon by bigger lads is some kind of privilege!" Adric laughed as he leaned on an elbow, "If they punish her for it, they might as well punish me too. I'm naught but a commoner's son, though we've got a little money. I chose to be a sell-sword instead of a cobbler, and who knows, someday I might even become a knight!" He lay back, staring at the chandelier high above. "This Lady Cindra, she picked a hard way, not an easier or better one."

Bradric scratched himself and nodded, "My dad's common, same as you, mate. He put up the money so I could earn a good wage as a bodyguard or sell-sword, seeing as I got too many older brothers to get a piece of the family business, as it were. I figures, hard work is hard work, ya know? I never thought of it like taking more than I ought."

"And you aren't!" Filbert said, getting flustered. "We are all commoners here, except for Inis and poor Drakthorne, but that's not the point! We are *men*, and war is the province of men."

"What about the Kyraine of Balkon?" Inis asked. "Are they not warriors?"

"Kyrai-" Filbert stammered, "They aren't *proper* women, are they? They've got wings, for starters, and talons instead hands and feet!"

"So to clarify," Inis said, "if Lady Cindra had bird feet and wings, she'd not be a proper woman, and *then* she could be a warrior?" The others could hear his smile in the darkness; mental games like this were his hobby.

"Kyraine are servants of the gods," Filbert said, exasperated. "They were *made* to be warriors, they didn't *choose* to be."

"Whose side are you on, Fil?" Adric asked.

"No one's side!" Filbert said with exasperation, "I'm not passing judgment on... on the lady; I'm trying to explain the position of authority!"

"Well," said Adric, "We haven't heard from you, Gaius. What do you think about all this?"

The room went silent as they waited for Gaius to speak for the first time since the revelation. He said nothing.

"If I understood things aright," Adric said, "you're the

only family she's been around in years. You even stood up to Ratham for mocking her, when you thought she was dead."

Still, the young man said nothing.

"Figured you'd be happier to see her is all..." Adric finished. Only the popping of the wood in the fire gave answer for the rest of the night.

King Galen III, who had been listening in the shadows, withdrew quietly to do some thinking.

The morning came sooner than desired, and the students were rousted from an uneasy sleep. Once the main hall was made tidy again, they were served a small breakfast, given provisions for the next few days, and thanked their hostess. Lady Mytha was gracious as always, telling them that their comrade, Terrus Drakthorne, would be given their best wishes as soon as he awakened. No one spoke of Cindra.

Lady Cindra awoke before dawn, dressed with the help of a servant girl a few years her junior, and took a private breakfast in her chambers. She donned a travel cloak over her dress, checked the lacing on her boots, and headed downstairs. Her baggage had already been seen to, and was now set upon T'ózha as if he were a pack mule. Her old clothes had been donated to the needy in town. Her weapons were wrapped up and packed out of reach; apparently she would not need them on the journey home.

When she said her goodbyes to Lady Mytha and Lord Saul, the other men were already in the yard waiting for her. It gave her a brief moment of privacy with her hosts.

"I want to thank you for everything, baroness," Cindra said, holding the woman's big, soft hands; her own were delicate, but strong and rough. "You have done more for me than you know, and I can never repay you."

Lady Mytha touched the girl's cheek, "Was it so much? I only passed on the bad habits of my men-folk to aid in your deception."

"You made it possible for me to find a home for a time, and to experience things I may never know again." Cindra replied.

The lady of Cordoshome drew her into a hug, kissing the top of her head as Cindra's mother used to. She then gave a traditional northern farewell, "Theil yegn vastr frahn." *Treasure by calm waters.*

Cindra answered, "Haldif iven dobis mayn." *Peace under blue skies.*

"Fare you well," said the baron, uncertain of who was departing. Cindra gave him a kind smile just the same.

Upon entering the courtyard, she was informed of her travel arrangements. Since her own horse was never trained for sidesaddle, Cindra found she would be riding on the cart that had borne Halvoy Quenlorden's body from Portshia. The king himself was standing at hand to help her onto the bench, and she was thankful that at least she wouldn't be in back among the provisions.

Galen III offered his hand saying, "It is an honor to meet you at last, Lady Cindra. I hope your journey will be a pleasant one."

Cindra made her way onto the bench with as little support from him as possible, and replied, "It would be more pleasant upon my own horse, riding with my friends."

He said, "Think of this as a chance to make new friends, milady. For a certainty, few among us truly know you as yet."

She flinched at that.

"You shall ride safely and comfortably in the wagon, with my men in front and Master Cord's men behind. We have need of haste however, so the best time to talk will be at nightly camp."

Cindra could read between those lines. Camp, whether along the road or at an inn, would be for eating and sleeping, neither of which she would be expected to do in the company of men. She would have her own tent or room, and be expected to stay inside it.

The road home was a cheerless one, almost more so than when they were bearing the body of their schoolmate. Halvoy's death had been tragic and unexpected, but Cindra's revelation was bizarre and unsettling in a way that death could not be. When she managed to turn and catch the eyes of her schoolmates, they averted their eyes or pretended to be looking at something else.

Only Jaron met her gaze, and it was heartbreaking to see his expressions. He would try to smile, try to reassure her, but the distance between them grew with every mile. He was never so far as a few dozen paces behind, but they did not speak, could not speak, lest it draw the attention of the king or his men.

It had not been spoken of, but by the way the king's men looked at Sir Jaron, especially the field marshal, it was obvious that there would be disapproval of further contact between the knight and his erstwhile squire.

During their nightly stops, it was Adric or Inis who volunteered to bring her evening meal. Cindra was grateful for the contact; for it meant that they did not hate her at least.

"I think it's brave, what you did," Adric said, bowing clumsily. "It was a mad idea, mad as a mongoose, but brave; joining the school, I mean."

Cindra grinned as she accepted the strange praise, "I suppose it *was* rather mad. So you aren't angry with me?"

"Nah," Adric said. "You worked just as hard as the rest of us, harder even. I expect some of the lads won't believe you didn't have help or special treatment, but we're teammates. I know better."

When Inis DeGhat spoke with her, he was far less awkward. He said, "I often wondered why you were so shy on laundry day and bathed alone. I suppose I should have suspected sooner; I have three sisters, after all."

"What was to suspect?" Cindra asked. "You couldn't

have guessed I was a girl, surely?"

"Oh, we knew something was going on, Morrin and I," he smirked.

"Morrin LiKeska?" Cindra gave a sly smile, "What does *he* know about girls?"

"Who said anything about girls?" Inis replied with a sly smile of his own.

"What are you...?" she broke off, suddenly comprehending. "Oh, not Jaron!" she laughed. "I teased him *once*, just once about liking boys-" she broke off into a giggle.

"We never shared our suspicions with anyone, mind you," Inis reassured her. "It's a fighting school, not the pleasure gardens of Vinius the Wicked." He rubbed a hand over his cropped, sandy hair. "But you can't blame us for thinking it. Sir Jaron always seemed jealous of Gavadaire's attentions for you..."

"A sordid little love triangle, is that what you thought? A tangle of spears?" Cindra feigned outrage, "You squires are worse than a pack of chambermaids on laundry day!"

"Morrin was about ready to cast it into verse, he was so certain!" Inis laughed.

Cindra wiped her eyes, "If Morrin wants to play the Bawdy Bard of the Bedchamber, then he had better do it away from armed men."

"True," Inis said, his own eyes moist from laughter. "But he was so inspired!"

"Well, I'm sorry to disappoint," Cindra said, arranging her food before her. "Perhaps you should tell him to look to his own reputation, when you see him next?"

"I shall, milady." Inis smiled and departed.

The last part of the journey was mostly spent in the company of the king himself, who rode alongside the wagon, much to the chagrin of his bodyguards at the head of the line. The Black Eagle was a cautious one, Cindra came to realize. Despite his reputation for being imposing and aloof, he was a friendly man once he got to know someone.

It was *how* he got to know someone that made him misunderstood. He watched and listened, allowing others to interact in his stead. He learned how a person acted when among inferiors, superiors, or equals. He spoke as a king, but never assumed he was speaking to loyal subjects. He did not trust readily, and those who had earned it were surely men of high standing indeed.

"So you never felt threatened or ill-at-ease among the Galindri wanderers?" he asked, as they discussed her years in exile.

"Never," she said, "I was suspicious at first, not sure how they would treat me if they learned who I was." She recalled the evening her identity was revealed; she had saved Teya, the huntress, from a Minozhian knife, the same knife that now sat useless in her saddlebag. "But they owed me a debt, and they know what it is to be hunted and live in fear."

Galen considered this with narrowed eyes. Finally he asked, "Do they live in fear, then? Fear of whom? They are free by ancient edict to wander the lands as they will."

Cindra shook her head, "They are free to wander, but they are not trusted or respected. Villagers hide their children from them, and sometimes... sometimes they are preyed upon by Outlanders." She recalled the story of how Teya Two-Knives came by that name. It still made her shiver.

"Outlanders." He sounded bemused.

"It is what they call us," she explained.

"This is a problem that plagues many, not just the Galindri," he said. "Brigands travel the wilderlands, preying on whoever crosses their path."

"But majesty," Cindra said, "Who can the Galindri turn to if they are wronged? The local lords will not seek justice on their behalf. The only justice is what they make for themselves."

At this, the king turned to meet her eyes, "Justice

must come from the law, not the hands of the wronged. The law must encompass everyone, or there will be chaos."

"Fine words for the temple of Arathus," she said, "but so easily forgotten when put into practice."

"You question your king?" he asked.

"I question every lord, great and small, whoever ruled over so much as a patch of land," she said. "Can you say that they all upheld the highest ideals of the law?"

"Would that include your father?" he asked with slight smile.

"I do not know how my father rules every corner of his lands. It was never meant to be my concern," she replied.

Galen noted the tone of rebuke in her voice saying, "What would you have us do, milady? How would a king seek to undo every injustice in his lands?"

Cindra thought for a moment and replied, "One could start by remembering the past. I am not saying that all Galindri are good and blameless, or that every lord turns a blind eye when it suits him. I just think that we must remember why Kraal the Great gave them his blessing to continue their old ways."

The king said, "In thanks for their protection in his youth, and for their military aid in his time of need."

Cindra nodded saying, "Yes! Then you know the story of how they disguised him as one of their own and raised him to manhood?"

"The story is known to me, yes." He said, "A prince learns many things growing up, including different versions of history from different sources."

"Well," Cindra said, "I learned it for the first time when the Galindri gathered *b'ámava* berries to color my skin. The edict of Kraal the Great was to repay a debt of honor. *That* is what we all must remember. There would be no Calilon without them."

Galen nodded, "Well spoken, milady. I find it interesting that Kraal's story parallels your own. Perhaps it is your way of reminding me of the future, as well as the past?"

She shook her head, "I cannot speak for the tribes, or offer an army of horsemen in your time of need, majesty. I owe a debt of honor to them; they owe me nothing."

The king appraised her as she sat on the wagon bench, while the driver tried to mind his own business. "You are indeed a remarkable young woman, Lady Cindra."

She held his gaze and said, "Your majesty knows better than most."

He paused, gave her a curt nod, and rode on ahead.

The day of their arrival at Portshia was a growing dread that crept across Cindra's skin. As they crossed the bridge over the canal to the Copper Gate, she could not help but feel unprotected, even amid the armed escort. The armor of her disguise had been stripped away and she felt naked to the enemies that were surely still looking for her. The towering walls and buildings, once comforting, now enclosed about her like thorny thickets, ready to snag her dress and cut her flesh.

It occurred to Cindra that the king was still dressed as a bowman, and no banners were flying to identify his men as anything other than sell-swords. The only recognizable colors were the red and black of the Freekirk School, which followed behind her wagon. If anyone was on the lookout for strange visitors heading to the castle, *she* would be the most obvious one, not the king. They would look like her bodyguard as she sat there in blue and gold, the colors of House Corrina.

Gods above and below, she thought with a stab of fear, *I am a diversion! I am bait!*

Did her friends even realize? She looked back at Jaron, who was watching the windows and rooftops. He realized it by now; he also looked none too happy.

The people they passed had fear in their eyes, though she did not think the riders were the cause. Something else had happened in their absence, something that hung like a pall over the heads of every man, woman and child they passed. Faces were pale and drawn, lips were tight, and eyes were downcast.

It was then that she noticed the rats. There were rats everywhere, rats in the gutters, rats in the doorways, rats on the windowsills and rooftops. The streets were littered with droppings and debris, resisting any attempts to keep them clean. Rats fought over bits of food or anything that could line a nest.

The furry bodies caused portions of the street to move before them like a brown tide. The creatures scampered out of the path of the horses and wagon, only to flow back in their wake. There was a smell that overpowered the common odors of the canals and gutters; it was the smell of decomposition and rot. Little bodies littered the ground everywhere, too many rats among too many people. Those that were not dragged away and eaten by cats or their own kin were left for the flies and the summer sun. Men and boys wearing the mark of the rat catcher's guild could be seen on every street, though they welcomed any non-guild help they could get. Rats were a common sight in any city, but this... this was a plague of rats.

Cindra's mind went back to the night of the freak dust storm, when she and Jaron had encountered the strange old man at the inn. Ever since he came to town, bizarre things had happened, culminating in the vemlok attack. The pale woman in her burial gown, her fiery red hair aglow in the flashes of lightning; the memory made Cindra flinch, like the touch of a cold hand upon her spine. Could this be just another effect of the old man's presence in the city? Was it an omen from the silent gods, or something worse?

They finally crossed the drawbridge at the High Gate and rode past the noble villas lining the avenue in the walled Highcourt. The rats had not spared the wealthiest district of the city, but the lawns and pathways were broad and open, making their numbers seem thinner. Cindra paid the rats little heed as her eyes darted to the gates of Casselvane Keep, now closer than she had seen it in nearly four years. Her heart leapt at the thought of reuniting with her parents, regardless of her circumstances. As she imagined the scene playing out in her mind, it alarmed her that she could not recall little details, such as the color of her father's hair, or the shape of her mother's ears. *Has it really been so long,* she wondered, *or am I just a poor excuse for a daughter?*

As they reached the main gates, there was a brief halt and conversation as the men-at-arms explained their business to the guards; then the company rode into the bailey, drawing questioning looks from all eyes within. A runner was sent to inform the lord and lady of their guests, and a welcome would be prepared in the main hall.

The fresh ocean breeze was tainted by the closeness of the kennels and stables just inside the gate, and Cindra wondered if Nixyalderthor was near at hand. The last she heard he was doing well, though in his innocent foolishness he had given away her secret. He unwittingly sent an Ember Swallow messenger that found her in the fighting school, leaving a trail of smoke and flame in its wake. The evil priest she knew as 'Julen Gordon' had apparently seen it, for he had checked into the adjoining inn that night, and was caught the next day in the act of attempted assassination. The man's wife, Lemorea, was never found.

Nixy DuQuayne was also not to be found, at least not in the stables or kennels. She gave a disappointed sigh as the cart passed through the last gatehouse to the inner courtyard. She had hoped to see Nixy's happy face among the grooms and stable boys.

The courtyard was even lovelier than she remembered it. The white circular walls towered above her; its creeping ivy, glazed windows, arched doorways and ornate balconies softening its original defensive design. The castle had long ago become a grand home, rather than a mighty fortress.

Upon the newel posts at the foot of the stairs were carved cats of stone, painted gold and seated upright; they held aloft crystal orbs which would be lit by wizard spells at night. The broad stairs led to a pair of large, iron-shod doors, beyond which were the halls of her childhood home. She would see them again within moments, she knew.

A feeling of comfort washed over her and she leaped from the cart unassisted, beaming a smile for all to see. Once these walls had felt like a prison, but now they encompassed her happiest memories of home and well-being. She felt truly safe for the first time in many years. She could not even feel angry at the king for placing her in harm's way to vouch-safe his arrival.

The horsemen filled the courtyard, dismounting as grooms, stablemen, and even the lumpish stable-master himself rushed in to see to their mounts. It was chaos for a brief time, and Jaron took advantage of it to speak with Cindra.

"You know the king was using you for cover back there?" He asked under his breath.

"I know love," she said. "Say nothing of it, and don't let your feelings show. We are all in danger now."

Jaron gave her a look of deep concern, but backed away as the king himself approached.

"Lady Cindra," said the king, "Will you give me the honor of escorting you home?"

She smiled and curtsied, taking his offered arm.

The party was shown into the main hall to the left of the grand stairs. The king and Cindra led the way, followed by the king's men, and lastly Master Cord and his students. Cindra heard the mutterings of her friends behind her, awestruck by the beauty of her home. It gave her a touch of pride, but she recognized that as a dangerous thing now. Her pride had led her to say some sharp things to the king, and his mood had altered since their last conversation. He was marching against his defiant barons, and it would be foolish for his supporters to give him reason to doubt their loyalty.

Still, all sense of danger was wiped away as she gazed across the hall to the gathering of people there. Her parents were in the main hall, with Constable Fingelm and numerous advisers behind them. Cindra held her breath as their eyes focused upon her, hardly seeing anyone else.

Zara Corrina gasped and cried, "Cindra!" She crossed the floor with long strides, arms outstretched.

Cindra rushed forward, embracing the countess with all her might. "Mother!" she cried, tears streaming down her cheeks, and the woman's arms enfolded her as if they would never let go. Her world was reduced to the texture of crushed velvet, the scent of rosewater and lavender, and the beating of the first heart she ever knew.

When the pressure relented, she saw her father's face as well, glowing with joy. She was soon caught in a fierce embrace that took her breath away. They covered her in kisses, laughing, crying, and speaking her name as if it were a spell, binding her to them so she could never depart again.

The sight of the reunion was enough to lift every heart in the room. Servants wept, officials choked back tears of joy, and the students smiled broadly at each other, not realizing until this moment what their former comrade had endured. Sir Jaron and Sir Cord were not immune either, though they tried their best to hold back tears. The king and his men waited patiently with gentle smiles, for even though their purpose was grim, there was room for sentiment to make light of their burdens, at least for a while.

Cindra's eyes were blurred with happy tears as she beheld her parents once again. Her graceful mother and stern father were older and more careworn to her eyes, for their grief and longing had cost them in years. Her father's hair was whiter than it had been, and the golden luster of her mother's locks had dimmed somewhat, though her emerald eyes had lost none of their sparkle.

She wondered how she must look to them; taller perhaps, more tanned and filled out, leaner and not as soft. Her training had beaten her into a firm and fit specimen to compete with men twice her size, but she worried now that she might not look the part of her parents' daughter. Her mother kept trying to brush back her forelocks, which hung stubbornly in their boyish style.

A commotion from her companions drew their attention as two people descended the grand stairs behind them. Cindra turned to see a strange woman, ethereal and beautiful, with skin like honey and cream, eyes like violet gems, and hair of sunshine and gold. She wore a simple yet elegant silken gown of green and blue, and her hands were painted with symbols of earthen brown. Her ears were up-swept in faerie points, accenting her delicately angled face, and she had a radiance about her that stole one's breath away.

The men parted mutely as she approached, and Cindra saw that beside her walked a young, well-dressed lad with a round face. His blue eyes were wide with surprise, and his blond hair, though meticulously trimmed, managed to stick up in a cowlick.

"C-Cindra?" the boy gasped, "Is that you?"

"Nixy!" she cried, opening her arms as the boy ran towards her. When last she had seen him, he was as tall as her chin; now he was up to her nose. Thankfully, he was far better groomed than before. His face had lost much of its baby fat, but he still looked like a young scamp, despite his fourteen years. *Fourteen years,* she thought. *I was his age when we met.*

"Nixy, how I've missed you!" she said, hugging the little ex-pickpocket. "I have so many stories to tell." Her fingers ran over the fine, rich fabric of his tunic, and she felt very under-dressed all of a sudden.

"Me too, me too," he laughed, embracing the girl who had saved his life. "There's stuff you wouldn't believe! I don't even believe it mostly." His voice had deepened noticeably, but still had a boyish squeak.

When the commotion died down a bit, Field Marshal Valthór stepped forward to address the room, "Lord and Lady Casselvane, may I present His Royal Highness Galen SuCordobal, the third of his name; King of Calilon, Duke of Maylione, Count of Regala, Count of Cordobal, Defender of the Realm, and Keeper of the Law."

Galen stepped forward, his face a mask of regal benevolence and dignity. Never before in their brief acquaintance had Cindra seen him looking so kingly; his manner and bearing had altered as his titles were recited, as though a final layer of disguise had been shed.

"Rise," said the king, "I am happy to facilitate this joyful meeting, but I'm afraid my business here is pressing. Count Casselvane, it is well to finally meet you. My father spoke often of his stalwart in the south." He turned to the countess, "Lady, it is a supreme pleasure."

The countess replied, "The pleasure is ours, Sire! But... we heard nothing of your visit."

"As it should be," he said. "We are traveling in secret, gathering forces in our wake. We have much to discuss... but first-" he turned to the golden woman, "Who is this enchanting vision before me? You are an elf, or I am much mistaken."

The count presented his guest, "This is Wenyssaya, emissary of the elven lands of the eastern wood. She is here on behalf of the Lord of the Shadowood Forest, who offers his goodwill to our house."

"Indeed?" said the king, awestruck. "These are fair tidings! We remember well the tales of the Ilves who fought with Kraal against the tyrant Orthicus. Might they be willing to aid us once again?"

Wenyssaya replied, "I speak neither for the Ilvayiin nor the Shadow Lord, great king. I am only here to protect and guide his heir, and perhaps bring him to meet his father in the dark woods. The Shadow Lord has not shared his mind on any other matter, but offers his gratitude for those who have sheltered his heir from harm."

"His heir?" asked the king, searching the room for another impressive-looking elf.

Wenyssaya gestured to the ordinary, blond boy beside her, "May I present Prince Nixyalderthor, heir of the Lord of the Shadowood Forest."

Nixy bowed awkwardly to the king and then gave Cindra a sheepish look.

She muttered the first thing that popped into her mind.

"Balkon's balls!"

Chapter Four

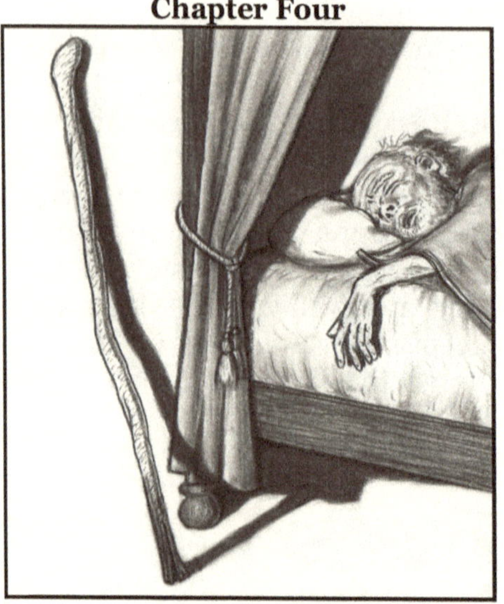

Planning for Departure

"Intolerable," Maveezh said under her breath. DuChat was keeping her waiting yet again. She had been his 'guest' for over a year, hiding within the halls of DuShonmaer while the count's men scoured Portshia for 'Lemorea Gordon,' wife of the dead traitor 'Julen.' DuChat had kept her occupied, granting her resources only he could summon, but she still felt she deserved more access to her host.

Her poor husband Ghethas had acted impulsively, risking everything to kill the girl who had eluded him twice. Unfortunately he had chosen the wrong room in which to do the deed; the occupant returned, catching him in the act. Maveezh had not been allowed to take revenge on his killer, or even give her husband a proper burial.

DuChat was alone in his office, she knew. Yet still he made her wait. "Intolerable," she repeated.

"Perhaps he is attempting to teach patience yet again." She heard the voice of her dead husband in her mind, as clear as a remembered song. *"Sacrificing our*

brothers from the north like that was wasteful."

Maveezh tensed, *It came to us, did it not? They found him in a jail cell, and he might be there still, had I not sent them to retrieve it.*

Ghethas reminded her, "*You ordered them to 'test' the Mad One, to take it from him. Now they are dead, all but poor Omiras Bevek.*"

He should be honored, she thought, *to be the chosen servant of the Prophet of Mash.*

Ghethas scoffed, "*I wonder if either of us would feel so honored.*"

Her lips tightened at the thought. She could picture his expressions, his smirk, the tilt of his head and raised eyebrows. Her husband's arguments had become more frustrating now that he only lived in her memory.

That bland-faced servant, the one she was never able to intimidate, entered the foyer and gestured to her.

Finally! She thought. *Lead the way, you dreary scarecrow.*

The servant led her without comment into the study of Kobus DuChat, wealthy merchant and man of many secrets. DuChat's curly black hair and beard were neatly trimmed as usual, and his clothing was fine and immaculate, for he had returned from a business engagement an hour ago. He looked up from a sheaf of parchments.

"Sit," DuChat said, offering a chair across from his polished desk. "I trust you have news?"

"Yes," Maveezh said, "It seems my latest scheming has borne fruit. Many months ago, I passed information to Maron Theenix about a good investment opportunity; I told him that a shipyard in Aurilon was raising capital for a new merchant fleet." She smiled, "In short, I got Theenix to send a large sum of money to one of your Circle of Gold men across the sea."

DuChat raised an eyebrow at that. He had given Maveezh the names of many contacts in the Circle of Gold, his vast criminal empire. He had to admit, he was interested to learn what she had done with her time.

She continued, "The gold was smuggled back in casks of port, and delivered to the Theenix warehouse. They were received, stamped with his mark, and delivered to Cordoshome by land. I then sent word to our Minozhian friends that the gold was theirs for the taking." She sat back in satisfaction. "I just heard that Theenix has been arrested for treason."

DuChat cocked his head, "What was the point of this mischief?"

She folded her arms, "Theenix was the count's greatest advocate among the merchant class. His 'betrayal' will shatter the confidence of investors, destabilize the wartime trade agreements, and lead the government in circles as they try to figure out what his ultimate plans are."

DuChat nodded, "Mayhem for mayhem's sake? I can appreciate that. Pity about poor Theenix though, such a nice fellow." He took a pinch of snuff from a silver box on his desk.

Maveezh settled back in her chair, waiting for him to inhale his snuff and make those silly facial twitches that always followed. *Absurd habit,* she thought. "There is another matter I'd like to discuss, if it's not too much of a burden."

DuChat only smiled at her impatience, "I assume you are referring to the Mad One and the Dark Heart?"

"Of course I am!" she snapped. "He is here; *it* is here, in this very house! We have been under the same roof for nearly a month, and I haven't been allowed to see it!"

DuChat explained, "The Dark Heart is within the Mad One's chest; it cannot be seen unless you cut him open, as one of Bevek's companions did."

"Then when is the Mad One going to give it up?" she asked.

He smiled, enjoying her frustration. *She has suffered enough,* he though. *It is time to reward her faith.* He rubbed the scar on his eyelid as he spoke, "The identity of the scion was revealed to me two days ago. He is indeed in the city, but is not yet in place to receive the Dark Heart. It seems the Mad One arrived here too soon..."

Maveezh blinked, sensing the rebuke. She heard her husband's voice again, *"So he was meant to rot in that jail cell a bit longer? Pity about those men you wasted..."*

She pushed the guilt from her mind and said, "Might I ask the identity of the scion?"

DuChat said, "I... don't know if that would be helpful."

She furrowed her brow, unsure of his meaning. "It isn't... *you,* is it?"

"Hah! No," he said. "The blood of Llomaak will not work much of a change on me. Let us say that its intended recipient is someone who will be completely unprepared to cope with its influences."

Maveezh said, "The first victim was an ancient Sorcerer King; the second was Orthicus, chosen of Arathus, but otherwise ordinary; it seems to be a downward path towards mediocrity."

"Only at first glance," he said. "Many things are not what they seem."

"So who will deliver the Dark Heart to the intended?" she asked. "Will it be that skull-faced man from your Circle of Gold?"

"Dexer? No, no..." he sighed, "I'm afraid Dexer is missing. I sent him on an errand three months ago and he vanished without a trace."

"What a pity," she said without emotion. Maveezh didn't like the gaunt man; he was a killer without subtlety, a naked blade dripping with poison. "Did he accomplish his task at least?"

"No," DuChat said. "But it was for the best. Game pieces are best used once their full value is known."

She sniffed, "More mysteries?"

He grinned that infuriating, mocking grin. "His target was a boy, a member of my Circle. I had sent him into the count's house as a spy, but he turned out to be far more important."

"How so?" she asked, pleased that he was being so forthcoming.

"I find it hard to believe myself, but the lad is the heir of an elf lord; a very *old* elf lord, if the rumors are correct." DuChat chuckled and shook his head. "An elven emissary arrived last year to serve as his guardian and instructor."

"I heard there was an elf in the castle," she said. "A woman of surpassing beauty, I am told." The thought struck her: *Is it him, this boy? Is he the one?*

"If Constable Fingelm's descriptions are even half-true, she is marvelous to behold," he said. "The flame-haired fool has dried up as a source of good information, but he can't help but burble his opinions over a bottle of wine."

"You still meet with him?" she asked.

"To keep up appearances," he said. "He offers his hospitality and shares his little stories; in return, I neglect to press him about his outstanding debt."

"So what was Dexer sent to do, kill the boy?" she asked, thinking to herself, *Wouldn't **that** have been a blunder if he is the scion!*

"It was believed that the boy represented a possible alliance between House Corrina and the lord of the Shadowood," he said. "Such an alliance would not serve our purposes."

Maveezh gaped, "The count's daughter and the boy, of course! Oh, if only my Ghethas had succeeded..." Her anger rose once again, "Have we any further plans to thwart this alliance?"

"Our priorities have changed," DuChat said. "The arrival of the Black Eagle at the head of an army has altered things."

"How so?" she asked. "Does it not make a resolution more critical?"

DuChat leaned forward saying, "One would think. However, it seems that the Lady Cindra has done our work for us."

Maveezh frowned, not understanding.

"We know that Ghethas found her hiding in the fighting school with her disgraced knight, Dunlorden. What we did not know until today was *how* she was hiding; the girl has been disguised as a man, training as Dunlorden's squire no less! She has doomed herself, and the king is bound by law to see to her punishment."

For the first time in over a year, Maveezh laughed.

DuChat, in a rare moment, shared her amusement. "Indeed! She is hardly fit to be a fishwife now, much less the bride of an elven prince. If the king is to maintain the respect of his barons, knights and common conscripts, he must deal with her harshly. She has made a mockery of their profession. I understand she even attended services at the temple of Balkon!"

"If Ghethas could be here now..." she smiled, imagining his laugh and his wicked, wolfish grin. "He would love to see her death delivered by the king himself."

"So for now, we wait for the comedy to play out," DuChat said, growing serious again. "Omiras Bevek has told me of the Mad One's prophecies, such as he can interpret them. The Dark Heart will remain here until the king's armies are ready to march in spring. The scion shall receive it before he leaves the city, and he shall carry it into the heart of the conflict."

Maveezh waited for more, but there was none. "That is it? More waiting?"

"Not for you, Maveezh. I have said our priorities have changed; I should have said *your* priorities. I have a task for you."

"I cannot risk moving about the city," she said. "Even if I am masked or disguised, the lord's diviners will find me if I leave DuShonmaer."

He said, "No, they will not. At some expense, I was able to retrieve the warding amulet lost with your husband. You may use it to leave the city and travel north."

"North?" she said in alarm. "What is to the north that

is so important?"

DuChat ran his fingertips through his beard as he studied her. *Is she up to it?* Then he thought of Omiras Bevek and the acolytes that died retrieving the Mad One; men she had sent to their deaths for her impatience.

He said, "I have a special mission for you. Bevek spoke of a Guadim his party encountered at the Woodcliff Bridge near the northern border."

A Guadim! Maveezh could not help but shudder.

He continued, "The creature claimed that it had been driven from Portshia by a vemlok, a 'rare, tamed one' as it said."

"What does that mean?" she asked. "There was a vemlok attack in the Commons last month, but it was slain."

"That was a woman, recently buried. According to the Guadim, the vemlok called Portshia 'his' city," DuChat explained. "I have been told that a rare few vemloks are able to tame the thirsting spirit, becoming far more powerful. If such a one has claimed this city for his own, I would know who he is."

"So," she said coldly, "You wish me to seek out one immortal monster to help find another immortal monster. Whatever have I done to deserve this honor?"

"As if you couldn't guess?" she heard her husband say. *Be quiet*, she replied, as a muscle twitched under her eye.

DuChat fixed her with his gaze, "The Final Days are near at hand. If we are to succeed, then all the children of Llomaak must join in common cause. Travel north until you find the Guadim. Take whatever Divine Alchemy you require. Convince it to join our efforts, or at least offer it our assistance. If it knows the identity of the vemlok, then perhaps we can sway him to our cause. If the elves are returning to the world in force, the Guadim will stop at nothing to prevent it."

Maveezh took a deep breath before nodding her acceptance. Guadim were an ancient evil from a time shortly after the awakening of humanity; beings spawned from the seed of the Countless Lord, spilled upon fertile, but fetid earth. They did not breed, so each one still living in the world was as old as the Age of Man.

"It will be done," she said gravely.

DuChat rang for his servant and the blank-faced man entered, carrying a small amulet which he presented to Maveezh. She took it gingerly, examining it before placing it around her neck. It was the same amulet her husband had worn since returning to Portshia from his mission abroad. It had kept him safe from detection by the likes of Arch Mage Ildric Finnael himself, and so would do for her. Yet wizards would be the least of her worries if her mission was a success. She rose and intoned, *"Mash bah havaath."* Then she solemnly left the High Priest's office, probably for the last time.

The servant saw her to the door, closed it, and chuckled to himself. His formality melted away as he strode across the room with casual ease. He sank into the chair across from his master, undid the neck of his jacket, and put a foot up on the desk.

DuChat gave him only a glance before rubbing his eyes. "What?" he demanded.

The servant cricked his neck loudly and ruffled his thinning hair, somehow causing it to lengthen and become fuller. His face pulled and twisted on its own, bones stretching and contracting stiffly, making popping, grinding sounds as muscle spasms twitched across his brow and cheeks. His brown eyes changed color, one turning green and the other going blue; above them his eyebrows thinned and arched, one higher than the other, the lower one tweaked and up-swept on the end. His nose became long and bent, and he cracked a yellow-toothed half-smile. He began to fidget in his chair, tapping his fingers on the wooden arm and wiggling his foot on the desk. The twisted man was a bundle of pent-up energy, his eyes darting about the room as his tongue roved over his teeth behind his lips.

"Lovely lackey you have there," Twist said in a lilting voice. "Tell me, did you take advantage of her sad and lonely state?"

"I'm sure you would know if I did," DuChat answered. "You can't seem to keep your nose in your own business."

"Ha!" he barked a laugh. "Your business *is* my business, at least all of your important business. Has the old goat said anything else today?"

"You mean the prophet of Mash, the Chosen of Llomaak?" DuChat asked, chiding him. "No, he has not. The Mad One is resting, though obviously the Dark Heart is not."

Twist looked about the room, searching for signs of the creeping chaos that was slowly engulfing the city. "You seem reasonably free of rats, plague, and aberrations of nature in here."

DuChat looked up and raised his eyebrows. "Oh? Look again." DuShonmaer was protected by many powerful warding spells, defending the mansion against intrusion, divination, and even unwanted pests. Still, there were two aberrations of nature in this very room.

"You and I don't count, boy." He rapped his knuckles on the desk, "So have you decided when you will strike your great blow for the cause?"

"After the army departs in the spring," DuChat answered. "They will be most vulnerable when their troops have marched and the king is otherwise occupied with his little war."

"I assume," Twist said with a sidelong glance, "that you plan to survive the party?"

"You presume correctly," DuChat said. "I shall see the ending of creation with my own eyes, Llomaak willing."

The crooked man looked about the room at nothing in particular. "I think I will miss existence, or at least the idea of it. I hope the ending is something spectacular; otherwise it will all seem a waste."

"The Mad One has assured me that the cataclysm will be beyond our imaginings," DuChat said, allowing a touch of anticipation to creep into his voice.

"So much the better," said Twist. "I'd hate for creation to go out with a whimper."

Omiras Bevek had not found rest in the halls of DuShonmaer, not like he had hoped. Delivering the Mad One to High Priest DuChat had earned him a bath, a warm bed, and good food, but it did nothing for his dreams. He could still see the deaths of his companions; still hear the sounds, still smell the blood and offal.

The old man had looked up at Bevek that day and told him, 'You're the one who lived.' Then his companions started dying. Young Felithor, who had been examining the Mad One's staff, had run head-first into a wall. Colm had been next, using that crooked staff to stoke their fire, but the fire consumed him like a starving beast. Helvert had been chased into the dark woods by clawing ravens and never seen again, swallowed by the unnatural forest. Marvek... poor Marvek. He had known the senior acolyte for years and considered him a friend, so he had no choice but to take his head and end his suffering.

Through it all, the Mad One had known. He had spoken of their deaths before they happened, though it sounded like gibberish at the time. Bevek had learned to hang on the old man's every word, sifting through the droppings of the addled mind for those nuggets of pure prophecy. The effort had cost him more than he could have imagined.

The Mad One was sitting by the hearth in their room, basking in the warmth of the fire. Bevek sat farther away, unable to stand the additional heat. The old man never seemed to be warm enough, even at midday in late summer. Still, the fire kept him happy, and when he was happy, he was quiet. His bent, white ash staff leaned against his chair, ever near-at-hand.

Bevek had once examined that staff for a brief moment, his morbid curiosity getting the better of him. What he saw had caused his already fractured mind to recoil in terror. He saw words resolve themselves from the intricate carvings that wove around the staff; he saw names, places, and events that he recognized; he saw his own past, present, and future flowing into a coherent narrative. The carvings had become a skein of threads, twisting and weaving into the very fabric of existence. He had to tear his gaze aside lest the words propel him to his death, or showing it, taunt him with all of his futile attempts to avoid it.

But one detail always stuck in his mind, drawing his eyes to the staff from a safe distance. The base of the staff was cracked, as if it had been struck hard against a stone. It ruined the carvings and disrupted the strange magic that had terrified him so. The narrative lost its structure, as if the people and events depicted in the carvings were unbound to its power. *That,* he thought, *or nothing anyone does will matter so near the end.*

As if sensing his thoughts, the Mad One turned in Bevek's direction, looking somewhere beyond him. He said in a voice that was hoarse and unbelieving, "No... you are not meant to be here... Why are you here?"

Bevek wondered if the old man was speaking to him, or someone else beyond the present. He answered, "I was the one who lived. I am bound to you, Prophet of Llomaak."

The Mad One's eyes fell upon Bevek and pierced him fiercely, "I am no one's prophet, least of all Llomaak's! I am myself! I am... me..."

"I found you," Bevek said carefully. "I took you south to Portshia, where you sought the 'face under a face,' the one to whom you will give the Dark Heart."

The old man's gaze grew unfocused as the brief anger in his voice died out. He turned to stare into the fire, muttering softly, "You? You are here. You helped me... in my time of need. You found me, took pity on me and rescued me. You do not deserve this fate, young one. You do not deserve to be here with me."

Bevek could not help but agree. But he asked, "It is Kobus DuChat, is it not? The face under a face?"

"He is not Kobus DuChat," answered the Mad One.

This gave Bevek pause. "He... is not? You mean the man you seek is not DuChat? Or do you mean our *host* is not DuChat?"

The old man rocked himself gently, "Long since turned to dust and bone, that one. Dust and bone, under a stone."

"A dead man?" Bevek grasped at the riddle, "Are you saying Kobus DuChat... is dead?"

The old man looked from the fire, his eyes retaining some of the brightness from it. "Most of us are dead... at one time or another."

"But the face under a face, it is our host, is it not?" Bevek did not like the doubts this was raising.

The old eyes widened as he nodded.

"So our host... is not the real Kobus DuChat? That man is long dead?" This made some amount of sense, Bevek realized. No one knew how DuChat had become the high priest and crime lord, coming from an ordinary merchant household. But then, it was rumored that none of his close friends from his younger days still lived. "Who is he then, this man claiming to be DuChat?"

"He's half a man, only half," said the Mad One. "The better half, if better he's got."

Bevek saw the old man nodding, heard his voice fade. Before he could drift off again, he asked him, "But is he committed to the cause? Will he help us?"

"He will do his part," the Mad One said softly. "It will all be over very soon, very soon... a dreamless sleep awaits, with no waking on this side of the veil or the other..."

Bevek watched as the miserable, ancient fellow drifted off into a troubled slumber.

Chapter Five

A Time for Tales

Cindra spent almost every waking hour of the next three days with her parents. She had told them all she could remember of her adventures with the Galindri, her encounters with Minozhians, and the brush with the evil priests. When the subject of her time hiding in the city arose, she mentioned only being kept busy while in the care of decent folk.

"They must have kept you very busy indeed," Zara had said, feeling her daughter's muscled arms. "You have become quite robust." Cindra just shrugged and redirected the conversation.

Meanwhile, the security of Casselvane Keep had been increased to an alarming level, with guild wizards and Corrina knights everywhere. The house staff was subjected to rigorous questioning by the king's field marshal, and all provisions brought from the city were examined by poison sensing spells. Even the guild's ward master, Syvin Wyngaard, was brought in to add extra protections to the king's rooms.

Then there was the celebratory feast. The return of Cindra and the king called for the grandest celebration since her fourteenth birthday, and the cooks did not disappoint. The kitchens had been preparing since their arrival days before, and as the cooking began in earnest, the dining hall hosted the aromas of roast pheasant, venison, beef, pork, fish, and dozens of vegetables, sauces, and baked delicacies.

The revelry lasted for many hours, culminating in a reenactment of the king and his allies defending Cordoshome from Minozhian hordes. Cindra noticed that there was only one mummer pretending to shoot arrows, and he wore a crown. Also conspicuously absent in the reenactment was Sir Jaron, although the reinforcements were led by one blond, blue-capped Corrina knight, no doubt meant to be Sir Cord.

The two knights had been required to decline their invitations to the banquet, she later learned, for reasons of their involvement in her deception. The king had not wanted them present, and so his field marshal had made their excuses to Cindra's parents. The king's alterations had left a very bad taste in her mouth, despite the succulent dishes served.

Cindra and Nixy left the feast together and met in Cindra's old private chambers, which had gone unused and mostly unchanged since her departure four years ago. There were scant few personal belongings, since most had been packed aboard her ill-fated ship. One that remained was a tapestry she had received from Maron Theenix on her fourteenth birthday; its cheerful, frolicking ponies danced in the low light of the fireplace, adding vibrant color to an otherwise barren patch of wall.

There were guards posted at the door, and servants silently cleaning the dayroom by candlelight. It was all the privacy they could hope for; after all, he was an heir to a great lord, and she was a criminal awaiting her fate.

How the tables have turned, she thought.

"So, you're actually a prince?" she shook her head in disbelief. "A half-elven prince?"

Nixy just nodded, "I still can't believe it myself. Nothing in my life makes sense anymore. Not that I'm complaining much." He smiled sheepishly, tugging at his nice silk jacket.

Cindra smiled, wondering what it would be like to grow up poor and miserable, run away from home and steal for a living, only to learn that you should have been brought up like... well, like she had been. She knew nothing of elves, but imagined they must have better homes than Nixy had known, especially an ancient elf lord. She searched the boy's face for the ethereal beauty she had seen in the emissary and saw only the same happy-go-lucky child with the unruly blond hair. It was so hard to believe.

"So now we know why Black Will was after you," she said, "your father rules the whole of the Shadowood. He wanted to use Blood Magic to hurt him through you."

Nixy nodded silently, remembering the horrors of the night they met. He had snatched Cindra's purse and she had run him down, only to save him from the monster man.

"Black Will is dead," he said without thinking.

"Is he?" she asked, "You know that for sure?"

"Yeah," he said, cursing himself for mentioning it. He wondered, *How much can I tell her? Does it even matter now that Clavemont is gone?* He decided to confide in her, for he would surely burst if he didn't tell someone, and a little voice in his head told him this was too big a secret to keep to himself.

"Um, you know after you left, you wanted me to stay in the castle?" he asked. She nodded. "Well, I- I didn't stay for too long. It was too miserable and I couldn't stand it anymore, so I left. I went back to the Circle of Gold."

"Oh Nixy..." Cindra sighed. She had risked so much to keep him from harm and he had run right back into danger. *Foolish child. This must be how poor Mineth felt watching over me*, she mused.

"Anyway... Dexer, that was my boss, he told me I could have a second chance if I passed another test." He added in a hushed voice, "A *breaker test.*"

"What's a breaker test?" she asked.

"Housebreaking," he squeaked. "You break in and steal something personal." He avoided her disapproving gaze, "Anyway, I was told to break Clavemont Manor..."

"Clavemont Manor!" Cindra gasped. "Lord Clavemont has all kinds of magical alarms and traps in that house. He likes to boast about it."

"That's not the half of it," he said. "He had magic traps, but I... I managed to get past 'em. I'm not even sure how. I think it's 'cause I'm... special."

With noble elf blood in his veins, he *should* be special. "Did you steal something?" she asked.

"Yeah," he muttered. "But I was caught by Black Will. He dragged me out a window and climbed up to the cathedral roof with me. A troll was up there too."

She blinked in disbelief, "Wait, a troll? A *real* troll?" He nodded, and she could see the fear in his eyes. "If they took you all the way up to the roof, how did you ever escape?"

Nixy saw the servants were leaving, and waited for the door to close behind them. He hoped it would be alright to tell his best friend. "Lord Clavemont... came to get me."

She peered at him suspiciously "He came to get you... on top of the cathedral."

"Yeah, it sounds crazy..." he agreed. "Long way up, but he was there. See... he's a... he's a vemlok." There, he said it. Lightning hadn't struck, but he did feel a creeping dread along his spine.

"A vemlok? Arton Clavemont?" she laughed, "He's just an albino, not a vemlok. He was at my engagement party, for Selvina's sake!"

"He's a vemlok," Nixy whispered. "He's a really old

one. He knocked Black Will's head right off, and told the troll to leave the city. Then I fell off the roof, and he caught me in mid-air."

"He caught-?" she *had* to stop repeating his words. It was getting ridiculous.

Cindra tried to maintain a smile, but it slowly faded as she saw how deathly serious and terrified Nixy was. He kept looking about the room as if something bad was going to happen any second. Cindra took his hands and said, "Are you sure Nixy? Because I've seen a real vemlok and she was nothing like Clavemont."

Nixy nodded, "I know, I heard about the attack. That's why I went to his house to ask him about it that same night."

"You what?" she gasped. *Had he no sense of self-preservation?*

Nixy cringed at her expression and explained, "He told me he had the thirsting spirit under control and he wouldn't drink me again! I figured it would be safe enough..." It was a lie; he had been dreadfully afraid that night, but he had needed answers.

"Again! Drink you *again*?" she exclaimed. *Stop repeating him*, she thought. *You sound like an ember swallow.*

"Anyway," he continued with shoulders hunched, "when I got to Clavemont Manor, it was deserted. The furniture is all draped with cloth and no one's home."

Cindra considered this. "It sounds like he left on a long trip. He isn't the only one; many nobles are heading for their country estates because of all the rats and sickness."

"I think he's leaving because of all the weirdness, but it's not because he's afraid of rats or getting sick," Nixy said. "The trolls, *Guadim* he called them, wanted to start a war to mess up the world. Last time it happened was the Time of Chaos, and that's when Clavemont, um, died." He squirmed at his own words. "Maybe things are going bad like that again. Maybe there are more vemloks coming, or maybe he's not himself anymore."

Cindra could not help but agree. Things were going bad again, that much was obvious, but she wasn't yet ready to believe that another Time of Chaos was coming.

Nixy sat by the fire, letting it warm away the chill in his heart. They both listened to it crack and pop for several minutes before he asked, "So, what have you been doing all these years?"

"That is a long story," Cindra said. She got up and called for refreshments. As the servants entered with wine and cakes, they were followed by a familiar calico cat. "Rufi!" Cindra exclaimed. The cat sniffed her fingers and leaped onto her lap, purring in welcome, but that was the extent of the animal's enthusiasm for her safe return.

Cindra told of the voyage, the attack at dawn by Minozhian pirates, the murder of her poor handmaiden Mineth. She told of the magic bracelet that saved her life, and the Galindri wanderers that took her in. The fascinating things she had learned and places she had visited constantly sidetracked her story, but Nixy didn't seem to mind.

It had been the adventure of a lifetime on the road, free of responsibility and duty, caring only for the needs of the day. She talked until her jaw ached, and her audience of one sat enraptured; the cat left once the petting stopped.

Hours later, she came to the turning point in her tale. "We were at a gathering in Pinikal, when I discovered evil priests that were plotting against my father and the crown. I learned that the old king had been poisoned, as had the duke I was meant to marry. I wish I could remember more of the details, but I didn't think I'd make it out alive."

She sat deeper in her chair and hugged herself, remembering. "It was horrible, they all had these beast masks over their mouths and they said such vile things. But I saw one of them unmasked, and he looked familiar."

"You knew him?" Nixy asked.

"I'm getting to that," she said. "Anyway, Jaron's wanderings led him to the same town. We had been camping within a half-mile of each other for two whole months! Can you believe it? We eventually made the journey back to Cordoshome for the winter, and it was there that I convinced Jaron to train me as his squire at the Freekirk School."

He asked in amazement, "You've been learning to fight for real?"

"Yes," she grinned, "When you sent Gavagul to deliver your message, he flew right into the mess hall during dinner. Nearly gave me away right then and there."

"Sorry about that," Nixy's head drooped. "It was stupid."

"It was sweet," she said. "Stupid, but sweet. Anyway, remember I said that one of those evil priests looked familiar? Well, it turns out that he was a local merchant named Julen Gordon. After the ember swallow came to the school, he made an attempt on my life."

Nixy looked sick at the news.

"It's alright," she said, comforting him. "He died in the attempt, thanks to Gavadaire LuVestra. In a way, you helped flush him out of hiding."

He considered this, not quite wanting to forgive himself so easily. Eventually he changed the subject. "I thought girls couldn't do stuff like that?" he said. "Learn to fight at those schools, I mean."

"No, we can't. It's illegal," she sighed. "I was disguised as a boy named Dillan DePort. No one had any idea I was a girl except Jaron and Master Cord. Now everyone will know."

"How did they find out?" he asked, worried that this might somehow be his fault too.

She replied, "I was too brave for my own good. I fought to defend Cordoshome against Minozhians; I killed three with my bow and... managed to save the life of the king. He was so impressed that he knighted me the next morning."

"You're a knight?" he said. "That's amazing!" Cindra had always been his hero and he was happy that she had finally been rewarded.

"I don't think I am," she said sadly, "I had to tell the king who I am. Now I've been commanded to give up all I've worked for and be a lady. They might even put me on trial for my crimes and... there could be harsh punishment." It sounded melodramatic, but for all she knew it would bear out as the truth.

"They can't!" Nixy jumped from his chair. "I won't let them do nothing to you! You saved me, the king, and a bunch of people! You don't deserve punishment for that!"

She smiled weakly, "We may not have a choice, Nixy."

"That's *Prince Nixyalderthor!*" he said boldly. "My father's the Shadow Lord, and if the king wants the elves to help him, he's not gonna hurt my best friend!"

He was fuming now; his face was red in the firelight, contrasting his blond hair. More disturbing than his sudden temper was the way the shadows in the room seemed to grow deeper and encroach upon their cozy space, and the air grew thick and muffled. Only the fire seemed untouched by the odd change.

Cindra sat in awe of the little boy she had pulled off the streets. He had grown only a little in size, but there was a new confidence and power about him now. It wasn't the arrogance or superiority that nobles were raised with, but something he had earned. He had been special all his life and never realized it, but now he was becoming aware of his importance and would not forget that. He had been through too much in his short life to let even the king take anything away, least of all his hero.

A plot began to form in Cindra's mind, a way to cheat her fate. She was too useful, too vital to throw away or censure. She had connections to the Galindri and an elf lord; even if those ties were weak and didn't amount to much in reality, she could make the most of it if she was clever. All she had to do was make her position officially acknowledged, and it might just save her a great deal of trouble, maybe even her life.

"Nixy- I mean, *Prince Nixyalderthor*," she said with a smile, "we need to talk to the elven emissary about this. You might be in a position to make some special requests."

"That sounds good I guess," he said, calming down a little.

The shadows receded and it made Cindra's skin tingle with goosebumps. She hadn't imagined it; the boy's anger really had an effect on the gloom. She pushed the thought aside and said, "The elf woman said that she might take you to the Shadowood to see your lord father. She could request that I accompany you, since I was the one who saved you in the first place. I could represent my house, as well as the king, assuming I am still his knight."

Nixy was getting excited now, glad he could finally help. "Maybe she can do more than that. She knows how to bring back memories; she might help you remember more about the priests who caught you!"

"She can do that?" Cindra asked, impressed. If she could recall all the little details of her brush with the Llomaakittes, she might be able to save more lives. "Get her at once! We have a long night ahead of us, my little prince!"

Wenyssaya had enjoyed the feast immensely, for not only had she been the center of much attention, but she had the chance to observe the highest peerage of the dwivayiin at their best. It was a revealing engagement, and she longed to discuss it at length with her tutors back home.

The feast was to celebrate the return of a long-lost child as well as the arrival of the new king, yet the joy was tempered with worry and fear, especially from those who should be happiest. Her hosts, the count and countess, were afraid of losing their daughter to the king's justice. The king was worried about losing the support of his most vital lord because of what he must do to placate his other lords. Lady Cindra was happy to be home again, but missed the life and love she had been forced to give up. The priestess of Selvina was torn between her happiness for Cindra in finding love, and her need to contain such enthusiasm before those who would disapprove. The other nobles in attendance, when not trying to gain the king's favor, were concerned that he had finally brought war to their doorstep. Prince Nixyalderthor seemed to be the only one who was truly happy without reservation, though she knew that was due to his abundant innocence about such matters.

The celebration had ended an hour after sundown, and Wenyssaya was content to be entertained by many competing gentlemen as Lady Cindra and the little prince retired to talk in private. Her worry peaked however, when she felt a tug of spirit energy, of *Hanna*, from upstairs. Something had upset her little prince, and she felt his anger ripple in her mind. It subsided, but she was not surprised when a summons came for her shortly thereafter. She excused herself from her adoring admirers and went upstairs.

The guards let her pass and she entered the young lady's chambers, where Cindra and Nixyalderthor were sitting by the fire waiting for her. There was a conspiratorial air in the room, and the servants had been sent away.

"My prince," she said with a little bow. "You summoned me?"

"Yeah," he said. "We um, we need to make a perposal to the king."

"Proposal," Cindra corrected.

"Yeah, one of those," he said. "I'd like Cindra to come with us if I go to see my- er, the Shadow Lord."

"I understand," Wenyssaya said. "You wish to preserve your friend and her honor, to make sure that she is not unduly punished for her... crime." She said the word with distaste.

"Right!" Nixy said.

"Consider it done, my prince," she said.

"Also, there's another thing," he said, glancing at Cindra. "Could you help her remember something, like you did with me?"

The woman's violet eyes turned to the girl, and Cindra flinched under the gaze, feeling again like that awkward girl who used to live in this room.

"How may I help you, Lady Cindra?" asked the elf woman.

"I, uh, I need to remember the details of something that happened two years ago," Cindra said. "I was briefly captured by a band of evil priests, and they were talking about the murder of the old king and a plot against my father's house."

"Oh my!" the elf maiden exclaimed. Her eyes widened, gathering more of the dim light, and Cindra could swear that they sparkled like polished jewels. "I shall do what I can. I take it this is not a pleasant memory?"

"Not really," Cindra said.

"Very well," Wenyssaya said. "It is an experience we must share, so I will steel myself. I will place you in a light sleep, but you must guide me to the memory." She offered her hand to the girl.

Cindra's eyes wandered over the light brown markings drawn on the woman's hands, appreciating their beauty and complexity. She took the offered hand and was led over to her old bed, which had recently been prepared with a new mattress. She lay back as the woman sat beside her. Rufi jumped up and curled near Cindra's feet.

"Try to relax," said Wenyssaya. "If the memories disturb you, do not be afraid to embrace the fear; it will make the recollection stronger."

She turned to Nixy and said, "My prince? Please inform the guards outside that there might be loud voices, and they are not to disturb us.”

Nixy nodded and did as she asked, casting Cindra a worried glance.

Wenyssaya began a whispering chant, passing her delicate hand over Cindra's face in a graceful dance of painted fingers. Her voice was melodious and soothing, lulling the girl into a fast and peaceful sleep. “Vothii, navíthive... navíthive di thesnasúve...”

Cindra heard the words, strange and foreign, but knew their meaning deep in her heart. *Sleep, dream... dream and remember.* She could not tell if she was dreaming yet or not. Perhaps she only dreamed that she understood the words? Her grasp on reality had already slipped, yet she could still feel the woman holding her hand. Its soft warmth was like an anchor, keeping her from drifting away over a black sea of time and remembrance.

Wenyssaya closed her eyes, allowing the girl to pull her into the Sleep of Memory. She drifted into the twilight realm of partial consciousness, bobbing like a cork above the fathomless night, waiting for the young lady to find what she sought.

Two years ago in the lands to the west, Wenyssaya's mind prompted gently. *You were among the dark-skinned wanderers, the-*

The memories came like a great weight, threatening to pull her under the dark waters. She felt Cindra grip her hand tightly as the visions swam into view, emerging from the inky blackness like a terrible predatory fish.

She saw horned warriors emerging from fog, saw them bursting through the hatch of a sailing ship. *“Get away Cindra!”* called the young woman, just before a wicked knife pierced her heart. *Mineth!* The cry was shrill in her mind as the dark sea rushed up to meet her, engulfing her in cold terror as the waters pulled at her nightclothes.

Suddenly she was holding a spear, staring into unfamiliar trees as a hunter prowled the shadows around her. There was a flash of horrible jaws and teeth, and the feel of warm blood flowing over her hands.

An arrow flew from her bow, striking a massive, bull-headed warrior in the ribs, just before his knife could fall on a defenseless neck. The beast-man's companions searched for her with wild, unseeing eyes. They were so close; she could smell musty leather and sea salt, firewood and smoke, beech trees and earth...

Wenyssaya almost broke the connection, but Cindra's grip stayed her; the young girl, alone in the dark, keenly felt the threat of abandonment. Her breathing and her pulse quickened, and a pitiful whimper escaped her lips.

The elf maid, feeling ashamed for her sudden panic, squeezed the girl's hand reassuringly. *I am here,* she told Cindra. *I will not leave you. We must find what you have lost. You were taken captive by a band of evil priests...*

"Yes," came the weak reply. "I remember."

The images turned to a pleasant scene of a Galindri gathering; cook-fires burned amid painted caravans, laughter and music could be heard under the trees, and leaf-green eyes peered out from dark faces. A lovely young woman walked beside Cindra, her colorful, layered skirts flowing with the swinging of her hips. Her dark, honey-colored hair was woven in long, thin braids that draped over her shoulders. Bangles jangled at her wrists and ankles.

"*Haani,*" Cindra thought, as nostalgic longing flowed through her. "*Saya.*"

A man with curly blond hair and a beard walked by, nearly bumping into them. Wenyssaya felt the fear in Cindra's heart as the man glanced at her. "*Julen Gordon!*" The name coursed through Cindra's mind, though it had not been a part of the memory.

"I've seen that man before, Haani." Cindra had said. "I don't know where exactly, but I swear I recognize him!"

She watched him go into his room at the inn, saw his companions waiting inside with bestial masks snarling in the dim flickering light. Cindra dropped the logs she had been carrying, making Haani jump aside.

"What is it?" asked Haani.

Cindra hissed urgently, "Haani, g-go get Teya, tell her the masked priests are here at the inn!"

"Me-ni-ka!" Haani chided as Cindra hurried off to follow the man.

Wenyssaya noticed that Cindra's skin was only a shade lighter than her companion's. *A disguise,* she thought. *Like the old story of Kraal.*

"I am in disguise," Cindra echoed. *"They cannot recognize me. I am in disguise."* It was repeated in her mind like a litany. It was not part of the original memory, but a conscious effort to endure what was coming next.

A man was saying, "Now that His Majesty is no more, the barons will begin to move. I've also learned from the High Priest that the scion is in Portshia, and soon the Dark Heart will be turned over to us."

The Dark Heart! Wenyssaya gasped. *The scion!*

A different man's voice asked, "What about Casselvane? We hear there is talk of a new alliance?"

"We will use this new alliance to place blame for the death of his daughter. He will see plots where there are none, and miss the one right under his nose."

Then it happened; Wenyssaya felt Cindra tense as the arm shot through the window, grabbing her by the hair. More hands took her and pulled her inside the room, and suddenly she was surrounded by men, their beast masks snarling at her with fangs bared and tongues lolling.

"Well, it looks like we have some entertainment," said the blond man. "Looking for something to steal, perhaps? Or maybe you came to sell your beauty? We aren't the paying kind."

Someone said, "Ha-ha, but Ghethas, you're married!" The others laughed.

"My wife is the understanding kind," the blond man said. He was now wearing a mask like the muzzle of a wolf, and had taken her *Kos* knife from her hip.

"Look at this," he sneered, "she's got a Minozhian knife. Isn't that charming?"

Cindra struggled and cried, "*Ne, ne! Doha erenáya!*" A big hand covered her mouth.

Wenyssaya found it hard to breathe. Her own heart was hammering in her chest.

"We can take her into the woods and show her how to use it..."

"Too many other brownies around, best stay in the room until we finish with her."

"Leave a surprise for the innkeeper."

The door burst open and many angry Galindri men stood outside, knives drawn. A wave of relief flooded through both Cindra and Wenyssaya. *It is almost over,* the elf maid thought. *I hope.*

Cindra wrenched her arm free; her bangles rattling as a few fell away. *This is where I lost Ildric's bracelet,* she thought. *That is how they learned I am alive.* She turned and ran past her Galindri saviors, shouting back at the masked men, "*Neko-fáche-beh!*" Her legs were shaking as she walked back to safety, her adopted family enclosing around her protectively.

The dream ended. Wenyssaya opened her eyes and found that she had been crying. Ever since she was a child, she had dreamed disturbing dreams. They had been strange enough to attract the attention of the elders, but those dreams had never frightened her like these. In Wenyssaya's dreams, she was strong, brave and capable; the memory of those dreams had been terrifying, but her dream-self could bear them even if her childish, waking self could not.

Cindra's dream memories were not the memories of a heroic girl like the one Nixyalderthor described when he spoke of her. They were the memories of a girl with less than two decades of life, who had been forced to face great dangers and overcome them or die. A trembling went through the elf maid's limbs, and it was then that she realized how very sheltered her two and a half centuries of existence had been.

"Are you alright?" asked Nixy, looking concerned.

Cindra started to answer until she saw Wenyssaya's face; the woman looked deeply shaken.

"I shall be," said the elf woman. She wiped her eyes and stood, her hand still holding Cindra's.

"What were you saying, Cindra?" he asked.

"I spoke out loud?" she asked, looking embarrassed. "I had to keep up my disguise when they captured me."

"Your last words to them did not sound very kind," Wenyssaya said.

"They weren't," Cindra agreed, sitting up with the woman's help. "Thank you, Wenyssaya. I take it we learned something very important?"

"We did," said the elf maid, "We did indeed."

Chapter Six

Enemies of the State

Sir Jaron and Sir Cord had returned to the Freekirk fighting school shortly after Lady Cindra was reunited with her parents. They had been ordered to make themselves scarce, but to remain within the city to await the king's judgment. It was a sign of trust in their personal honor that the king had not had them clapped in irons for their part in the lady's deception.

Later that evening, after the mandatory rat-killing, Master Cord had all the students gather in the mess hall for an important announcement. Jaron and his fellow instructing assistant Gavadaire LuVestra were present, as were the old caretakers Elmore and Celia. Adric Hywahl sat with Padison Pemwreth, who had been out of commission for a few weeks due to a broken rib. The short, tow-headed boy was hard to keep down and he would have accompanied the party to Cordoshome if he had been permitted.

"Where's Dillan?" Padison asked.

Adric just gave him a peculiar smile.

Cord began, "I have gathered you here tonight because I have news that concerns all of us." His big voice filled the hall with somber tones, "Upon my return to Cordoshome two winters ago, I learned that a member of a noble house was being sheltered at Freekirk Manor with Sir Jaron Dunlorden. This person had been the target of assassins and was still in grave danger. The only way they would survive a return to Portshia would be in disguise. An idea was put to me to hide that person in the school. I was against it at first, but later felt that it might be the safest place, considering." He paused before confirming, "The student known to you all as Dillan DePort was the noble in question."

The others began muttering among themselves and Padison whispered to Adric in shock, "DePort was a nobleman?"

"Not exactly," Adric said.

Cord cleared his throat, not really wanting to go on, "During our trip to deliver Halvoy Quenlorden to his final rest, we encountered the king himself, traveling to Portshia." This news was met with stunned murmuring as everyone considered the ramifications. "The king became aware of Dillan DePort's true identity, and has ordered... DePort to put aside the disguise and return to any previous... ah, duties."

The students who had returned from Cordoshome only looked at each other in embarrassed silence, feeling sorry for their schoolmaster's predicament. It had been awkward enough the first time.

Cord glanced at Jaron, who only shrugged. Cord stumbled on, blushing, "The, ah, identity of the noble in question... ehem," More throat-clearing ensued, "That noble person was- er, *is*..." he sighed in resignation, "the Lady Cindra Corrina, daughter of our lord Count Casselvane."

Laughter burst through the room. Most of them were sure the schoolmaster was having a joke, odd though it was. Everyone knew Lady Cindra was supposed to be dead and Sir Jaron was romantically linked to her, which somehow made the joke all the more funny. It was the worst kind of humor; the kind people hated themselves for enjoying. The idea that not only had she survived, but had been living and training alongside them... it was obscenely hilarious.

A few did not find it overly funny. Maadi Gaavi, the dark-skinned Gozhiman, was apparently no stranger to female warriors if his stories were to be believed. Minas Koorla, the copper-skinned mercenary of Maanok descent, was never one to join in anyone's fun. Celia, who had tended one of Cindra's injuries, tugged at her husband Elmore's sleeve as if to say 'I told you so.'

But the loudest laughter started with Rejick Ratham and his friends Lukas and Demel. The little cabal had spent the last few years tormenting Dillan for being the squire of the man who killed Ratham's cousin, Sir Earnold Greenfellow. Their smiles and mirth died down a little as they saw that Master Cord, Sir Jaron and the students who had gone to Cordoshome were not joining them.

"I am being damned serious!" Cord boomed. "This was undertaken at great risk to the integrity of the school. Now the king knows about our deception and he might very well revoke my license." He rumbled into the sudden silence, "As some of you may have heard, we arrived at Cordoshome to find it under siege by Minozhian pirates. It so happened that the king had just arrived there, and several of his own men died protecting the town. Terrus Drakthorne was injured as well, but the healers say he will recover.

"Now the king is in Portshia for the winter and troops from all along the Red Coast will come following behind. War is coming in the spring, and he personally asked me if there were any good fighting men at my school that could be called upon. I told him you were all good fighting men."

"Unless more of us are women," Ratham said as the

weight of the news sank in. A rage was growing in the young man's chest. A *girl* had beaten him in a sparring match. A girl! His face was turning red even as he sat there, his shame amplified beyond the ability to swallow it. He rubbed his left hand, the one she had broken in their match. It still hurt.

"At ease, Ratham," Cord said. He had expected some backtalk and outrage, but had no patience for the boy's mouth. The other students did not utter a sound.

"How do we know we've been trained as men?" blurted Ratham, "Was it all made easy enough for your secret pupil? My uncle Waliss will die of laughter when he learns what this school has done! His own school is forced to gather students to a backwoods, one-temple town, but at least they don't train girls!"

"Oh, you question your training, do you?" Cord said, hands on hips, "The fact is that Lady Cindra was able to rise to meet the challenge, much to my surprise. Had you had taken the training as seriously as she did, you might have fared better against a smaller, weaker opponent. That's the *Maurbrik* way, after all."

This struck Ratham silent, but the redness spread to his ears and neck until he looked like a glowing iron drawn from a furnace. He wanted to rise, to storm about, but he could only sit and shake under the headmaster's gaze.

Padison spoke, breaking the tension a little. "So what's going happen to Lady Cindra? Is she going to be in trouble too?"

"Possibly," Jaron said. "The king said that her fate would be decided after reaching Portshia, and in the next few days there might even be a trial. No one knows for certain." The thought of it sickened him; after all they had been through together, for all she had sacrificed and suffered, to be marked as a criminal... it was unthinkable.

It was Gavadaire's voice that drew Jaron out of his thoughts. "I knew there was something special about DePort, but I had no idea it went so deep." He smiled wryly, "Still, I must say I am honored to have had such a student. Sir Jaron, you must be proud of her, yes?"

"Yes," he said, "she was a marvel and never ceased to surprise me." He realized he was speaking of her in past tense, as if she was already gone, and he cursed himself for it.

"I'll bet she did," Ratham said, just loud enough to be heard. The students tensed. Jaron glowered at him, his hand twitching for his sword.

Padison spoke up loudly, "People who get bested by little girls can't talk here."

Ratham stood, infuriated. Adric stepped between him and his injured friend.

"Still on the mend or no," Ratham snarled, "I'll make you eat my fist, Pemwreth!"

Padison was undaunted as usual, "I'll bet it tastes better than shame pie. How's *that* going down, Ratham?"

"Enough!" Cord bellowed. "There will be no infighting here! And the next man who disrespects a teacher will get sent home with a silver mark and a boot to the ass!" The students calmed down but Ratham still stood there, glaring at the wounded boy. "Ratham, sit down!" Cord commanded, but Ratham was not cowed.

"I don't think so, *Master Cord*." He sneered, "I am returning to Breega to train in my uncle's school. I'll let him know his money here was wasted."

"Oh, I'll see he gets a full refund, Ratham," Cord growled. "I'm sure House Greenfellow needs it more than I do." Several students groaned at the well-placed strike, seeing Ratham stiffen. The young man glared and stalked from the hall, heading for the dormitory to gather his things.

Going up the stairs, he shouted, "A curse on all Freekirks, Dunlordens and Corrinas!"

Under his breath, Jaron said "Ambassador of good will, as usual, Master Cord."

Cord folded his arms. The schoolmaster was looking at Lukas Korbison and Demel Victhor, waiting to see if they were such loyal friends to Rejick Ratham that they would throw away their time here and follow him out. Neither boy moved.

"Now I want to get one thing clear," Cord said. "You have been trained as hard as any students that have passed through that gate. Harder even, since Gavadaire started his Su'Kraal lessons. War is coming and I'll see you all ready. If the king doesn't close us down, I'll keep the school open through the winter. When the call comes up, you'll have the credentials to earn a good wage if it's pay you're after. For those without the finances to support a knighthood, I'd recommend that route. Don't sell yourselves cheap.

"As for the lady, who lived and fought among us, imagine what I can make of you if I could make that of her? Just train with the same fervor the Lady Cindra did, and mark me..." His words trailed off as the sound of horses thundered into the courtyard and booted feet marched up to the inner door.

A voice called, "Open in the name of the king!"

Old Elmore rushed to the door, opening it at Cord's nod. Five armed men stood there, led by one of the king's bodyguards. They strode in, hands on weapons, followed by half a dozen rats.

"What is this about," Cord demanded. He had a sickening feeling that he and Jaron would be arrested right in front of the class.

The leader unrolled a proclamation and read it aloud. "Grigor Evenast DeKenric, esquire, son of the Baron Kenric, stand forward!" All eyes went to the boy in question, and he stood uncertainly, shaking a little. "Take him," said the leader, and the men closed in to clap the lad in irons. Several of the students got to their feet, causing the swordsmen to draw weapons.

"Hold!" Cord waved off his students. He turned to the king's man and barked, "What is the meaning of this?"

The man faced him, fully aware of his own authority. "You know that you are training a member of a Dissenter House, an enemy of the crown? He is possibly a spy."

"Nonsense!" Cord said, "There's nothing to spy on here, unless it's my training yard."

"Master Cord," said the king's man, "The count may have been lax with your practices, if he was even aware of them," he looked at Jaron pointedly. "But His Highness takes the safety of the kingdom much more seriously."

The men led the DeKenric boy out of the room as the students turned to Master Cord for direction. Cord could only stand by as Grigor gave him a pleading look.

Jaron's heart sank; this was his fault. He had mentioned the boy to the king himself, hoping to alert him to a potential problem. Yet the DeKenric lad had done nothing suspicious; he was a model student but for the fact that many didn't trust him and he had few friends.

"What is to be done with him?" Jaron demanded, though he knew it was a bit late to be indignant.

The leader answered, "He is to be questioned, of course. Then it is for the king to decide."

"Questioned like Maron Theenix?" Jaron asked pointedly. "I understand you could hear his answers through the walls."

The king's man replied, "Maron Theenix was accused of treason. I believe you were responsible for turning him in as well."

The rebuke hit Jaron like a slap, and he fell silent with shame.

Cord asked, "What if someone comes looking for DeKenric here?"

"Then I am sure you will inform us immediately," said the man. "Anyone wishing to contact him will be suspect as well." He turned on his heel, following the men and their prisoner into the courtyard. An extra horse had been brought for the prisoner and his hands were bound to the saddle horn as he was led away. The students poured out into the yard to watch them depart. Dark little shapes moved around their feet as a light rain flecked their faces and struck the dusty training yard with tiny, sodden craters.

"What's going on, master?" asked Padison.

Cord frowned, "The king is shaking the tree, seeing what falls out. Grigor is no spy, but his arrest might make others nervous. When word of this reaches Baron Kenric..."

"Do you think he wants to hold him for ransom?" Jaron asked.

"If I were to guess," Cord replied, "I'd say he will use him to keep the baron out of the fight. That means keeping him safe and sound."

"Maybe he'll use him to avoid a war?" offered Morrin LiKeska hopefully.

Inis DeGhat said, "Even if it neutralizes Kenric, there's still the other Dissenter Houses to contend with. No, there'll be a war come spring."

"My, what a wet rag you are, Inis," Morrin said. Inis shrugged.

Adric launched a rat that climbed on his boot. He said, "The war hasn't even started and we're down five of our number. Not a good omen."

Just then, Rejick Ratham came out of the hall with his baggage over one shoulder. He stalked past his former classmates, eyes burning a hole in the night as he made for the school's gate. No words were spoken, and the only sounds were his stomping feet and the occasional squeak of a rat that was too slow to get out of his way.

"I'm gonna miss him," Padison said finally. "He had the warmest smile and the funniest stories."

Stansig, the big stoic Norsican, burst into a rare laugh. Chuckles followed as the tension eased, and Cord was grateful for it.

"This term will go down in the history of the school, that's for certain," Cord said. "Too many unique events..."

Gaius spoke up, "Have you ever trained two Corrinas in the same term?"

Those who had been to Cordoshome looked at him curiously; it was the first time he had acknowledged his cousin since her revelation.

Cord answered, "Not since I have been master. I think in my grandfather's time there were three at once, but I'd have to check the records." He placed a hand on the boy's shoulder. "Frankly lad, I thought you'd be happier to learn she was still alive."

Gaius flinched at that, but collected his thoughts and replied, "I was taken aback, like we all were. But you understand that our family has been grieving for her for years? I thought... I thought that if anyone could be trusted with a secret like that, it would be family."

Cord nodded, "It was regrettable, true. But the fewer people who knew, the safer she was."

Gaius folded his arms defensively saying, "When I first came to the city to train, I visited my uncle and aunt. I offered my condolences, and they accepted. Did they know she lived? They knew I would be training here... did they not trust me with the secret?"

Jaron spoke up, "The lord and lady knew she was alive and in hiding, but they did not know the particulars. If it is any comfort, Cindra wanted to tell you on several occasions."

"Then why-?" he began.

"If you knew," Adric broke in, "would you have stuck her in the armpit with your training sword like you did? You'd have gone easy on her and made everyone suspicious."

Gaius blushed at the thought. Everyone got and gave injuries in training, but knowing he had inflicted such a blow on a lady made him deeply ashamed. Adric was right: he would never have been so aggressive if he had known.

The raindrops became larger, pelting the roof tiles and filling the courtyard with a growing patter. The students retreated to the covered porch before the main hall, cleaning the mud from their boots.

Finnas, the more agreeable of the two Avenoth

brothers, asked no one in particular, "So how did the king find out about DePort anyway?"

Adric answered, "She saved his life in the battle, and he made DePort a knight."

No one outside of the Cordoshome party had heard this detail before and a general clamor arose.

"A knight!"

"*She's* a knight now?"

"Of all the damned luck."

"Wish I could have seen the look on the king's face..."

"That's hardly fair..."

"Balkon's balls!"

Gavadaire only laughed.

"That's enough, all of you!" Cord barked. "It was the worst thing that could have happened. She was duty-bound to reveal her identity after that, and now she'll pay the price." *We all will,* he thought. "Before the lot of you starts bleating about how unfair it is, consider what the consequences might be!"

There were still mutterings, but they were mostly drowned out by the falling rain.

Padison asked, "What are they going to do to her?"

Cord said, "No one is certain, but the penalty might be harsh. The laws are clear; women are not permitted to dress as men to obtain rights and privileges above their station. There are also the laws of the church to consider."

Demel Victhor said, "Gods, she was in Balkon's temple with us every Massday! That's a burning offense!"

"Burning??" Padison was aghast.

"No one's burned a heretic for over a century," Inis said. "We live in a more enlightened age now."

"So what do they do to heretics in this 'enlightened age' of ours?" asked Bradric.

Inis was reluctant to elaborate. He cast a glance at Jaron, who was listening intently. "Eh, well... there are ways to um..."

"It's not pretty," Morrin said. "Public shaming,

flogging, branding, even a quick death if they are feeling particularly aggrieved."

Jaron began to look ill. He left their company and went upstairs.

"Idiot," Inis chided. "You didn't have to go that far."

"Farther than your stammering, you mean?" Morrin smirked. "He deserves to know the truth. She is in grave danger, and so is he."

"Sir Jaron's in danger too?" Padison asked.

"You can't think it will be ignored that they were living in the same room for two years," Morrin said. "Everyone knows they were lovers before-"

"That's enough Morrin," Cord interrupted.

Morrin shrugged, keeping silent.

"Is there anything we can do, master?" Adric asked.

"Pray," Cord said. "Pray that the king is just and wise, and pray that Balkon is in a forgiving mood."

Chapter Seven

Tokens and Favors

Tavenji heaved a sigh of relief. The walls of his little tent realm had stopped trembling ages ago, but the trickster god was going to be cautious. The last two pranks on his elder brother had left the war god in an epic rage, and Tavenji was sure that Balkon would be brooding and planning his revenge. It was all great fun, but it came with risks.

On their last visit to Balkon's realm in the Fields of Strife, Tavenji and his sister Lelonetha had been set upon by Balkon's Dishonored, reanimated corpses of soldiers who were meant to tear the little trickster limb from limb. Lelonetha persuaded Balkon to let them go by bribing him with the Peaches of Bliss. It had been a brilliant move, bringing her along; it had saved him from an enormous amount of torment and trouble, and father's message would never have been delivered otherwise.

Tavenji didn't like being threatened with pain and

dismemberment, so before they departed, he made the entire Dishonored army put on a performance worthy of legend: spears were spun like batons, shields clashed like cymbals, and rotting armor flashed with each high-kick and twirl. The ranks of doomed souls pranced upon the blood-soaked soil of Strife with happy feet and they would not stop, not until Balkon smashed them into dust. Worse, Balkon had to suffer Tavenji's presence soon afterward during an audience with their father the King, forcing him to swallow his anger.

But when the audience was over, Balkon had pursued Tavenji and Lelonetha through the Void until the trickster had given him the slip, escaping into his little tent-realm of throw pillows and collected treasures. They had stayed there for quite a while now, and Lelonetha was getting anxious to return to her place in Haven.

The little god's face poked out of the nothingness of the Void, looking this way and that as he sniffed the ethereal winds. "I think he's finally gone," he said, ducking behind the velvet curtains of his blanket fort. "I thought he'd never give up! He's persistent, I'll give him that."

The Mother of Mercy reclined on a pile of pillows as she yawned and stretched. She had never spent so much time with the little god before, and she had to admit it was taxing. He was always such a bundle of energy; a bouncing, darting figure in his yellow and black motley, green silk jacket and red sash. His slight, athletic form was topped with a mane of platinum hair and up-swept, pointed ears. His boyish face broke into a wide grin as he turned to Lelonetha, bouncing on the pillows opposite her. He was always moving, never at rest. It was difficult to relax around him, even in a cozy setting such as this.

"I think we can leave now if you're ready. But I wouldn't take an Ether Dragon this time; they're too easy to track." His eyes darted about the makeshift shelves hanging between the ancient dragon ribs that supported the walls and star-spangled ceiling. "Where did I put that thing?" he muttered as he began looking under pillows.

The Mother of Mercy arranged her yellow robe, gathering the fabric about her waist and shoulders. The action was unnecessary of course, for it would look as she desired when she desired, but it was something to do. She bound up her golden hair in its golden ring, feeling the soothing softness of her locks. Her pale skin glowed with a soft radiance in the dim light of the tent, lending it an ambiance of gentle serenity.

She said, "I do not think our brother will track my movements, little one." Her eyes showed concern as she reminded him, "It is you he wants, after all."

"You can never be too careful," Tavenji said. "He didn't seem very reasonable when last we met." His words offered caution, but his face said he was enjoying himself. "I think it would be best if- Ah-HA!" he exclaimed, pulling an object up from under a pillow.

It looked like a brass pole with a small window near the top, but he kept pulling it upward and upwards from the floor, raising it towards the roof of the tent. Then came what appeared to be an eyepiece, then a pair of handlebars and a steersman's wheel below that, and the whole assembly locked into place as the pole poked through the top of the tent. Tavenji looked through the eyepiece above the handlebars, and he turned the assembly this way and that.

"What in the Nine Realms is that supposed to be?" Lelonetha asked.

"It's a looking-tube!" Tavenji proclaimed. "It uses mirrors to let me see outside without leaving my realm!" He giggled with delight as he spun about, his arms resting on the handlebars.

"And the wheel?" she inquired, a little smile warming her face.

"It's so I can steer a course, of course!" he said, and he spun the wheel about, adjusting it until he was satisfied. "Forward to Haven!" he cried, and Lelonetha felt the tent shift under her.

"Are we moving through the Void?" she asked, amused and impressed.

"Yes!" he said, grinning. "Well, *under* it, really. You don't expect me to keep my realm in one place, do you?" He sank back into a pile of pillows and said, "It's not as fast as an ether dragon, mind you, but it's safer. We shall be at the fiery gates of Haven in a little while, not to worry."

Haven had barriers of pain that one must pass to reach it, and hence, to appreciate what Haven offered. This especially applied to gods, and that was why the Mother of Mercy received so few divine visitors. Tavenji had always tried to sneak through, but the barriers had only gotten trickier for him.

"So sister, are you sure you don't want to come with me?" he asked, a bit of sadness creeping into his voice. "It could be fun..."

Lelonetha shook her head and smiled, not wanting to disappoint her favorite brother, but not wanting to commit to another adventure with him either. "My place is in Haven, brother dear. I will offer what help I can, but I cannot travel to the other realms with you. I have duties of my own that have been too long neglected."

Tavenji nodded and pouted, accepting her refusal. "I suppose I understand," he moped. "I've always done better on my own, just me. A loner, that's what I am. Self-sufficient, independent, I'll be fine." He heaved a sigh for effect.

"I know you will be," she said as she patted his knee. "And I think you are being very brave to try. I would not be so brave."

"Well, it *is* my fault after all," he said gloomily. "If it wasn't for me, the whole of creation would be safe and father wouldn't be so angry."

"It is not your doing, dear one." She sighed, "It is our poor lost brother. You were only showing him compassion, and I could never fault you for that."

"Father might," Tavenji said.

When Arathus told the gathered gods that the Dark Heart had been removed from its hiding place and taken back to the mortal world, Tavenji knew he had been an unwitting accomplice. *He* had found his brother calling from beyond the Void; *he* had pulled him through and taken him to his former realm. It was there that his poor, lost, elder brother had found what was hidden and took it unto himself, fooling the Lord of Fools into delivering him back to the mortal world. Tavenji had made it possible for the End to begin. He had only shared this knowledge with his dear sister, who had always been more like a mother to him.

"The judgment of King Arathus will be harsh," she agreed. "But it is better to try and make it right. After all, if you fail..."

"Then nothing will matter," he said. "Everything ever created will be undone, all but Father, Uncle, and the Great Mother. I wonder if they'll start things over again, or just give up on the whole idea."

"You are assuming this has never happened before," she smiled slyly.

He blinked at that, searching her face. "H-has it happened before, a creation before this one?" *Surely someone would have mentioned that.* The thought chilled him.

"Who can say?" she replied. "Perhaps they were hoping this one would turn out differently. Perhaps the same mistakes are made again and again?"

Tavenji stared at her for a long while before shaking his head to clear it, "Is *this* what you think about all day long? You sound like one of those human philosophers who spend their lives contemplating their navels. Why would the elder gods keep making the same mistakes? They aren't like the mortals who build empires only to see them fail for the same reasons. They're too wise to... to keep... creating someone like me..." He hugged his knees to his chest and looked crestfallen.

"Tavenji dear," she said, "You are not a mistake.

Arathus made you for a reason, a good reason. If this *has* happened before, perhaps you were made to correct it. If there has never been another creation, then what of it? You will make things right, I know it." She crossed the little tent to put her arms around him. "You have never truly felt like one of us. The others call you 'half-brother' because they cannot see the good in you, because they do not know the mind of our father. But it is not for them to question.

"You are the only one of us who would dare defy father to help our brother. Not even I would risk such an act, though my heart yearns to aid him in his exile." She lifted his chin to look in his eyes, "I have always felt that father made you for a reason, perhaps a reason too deep for us to comprehend. You are a child of Order but you carry Chaos within you, therefore you know the ways of the enemy better than any of us. Perhaps that is what father was thinking."

Tavenji sniffed, "So you think father made me to disobey him? You think I was made the way I am to... to be his champion against Uncle?"

Lelonetha shrugged, giving him a warm smile. It was all the encouragement he needed.

"Then that's what I shall be!" Tavenji said, straightening as his mood brightened immediately. "I will defy father, just like he wants me to, whether he admits it or not! I will save our brother and save creation, and save everyone, and then the others will see when the king rewards me for it. They'll see, even that big, dumb, bloody lump of a war god. I'll show them all!"

He jumped up and peered through the looking-tube, adjusting their course a little to the left. The tent continued on its way as its captain whistled and did a little jig behind the wheel, content with his newfound purpose.

It was a while before they arrived at their destination, and Lelonetha spent the time contemplating what she had done. Tavenji needed no inspiration to get into trouble, but she had given him a big push regardless. Was it the right thing to do? Time would tell. But one thing was certain: she would not leave her elder brother to wander the mortal world alone and in pain. Her father's wishes be damned.

"Here we are!" Tavenji exclaimed, peering through the tube one last time, "Right on your doorstep!"

She arose and removed the golden ring that bound her hair, giving it to her little brother and holding his hands in hers. "Take this on your journey, dear one. You may have need of it, as might our brother."

He smiled and hugged her, then stepped back to open the side of the tent. The curtain parted and before them shone a bright sun hanging in the ether, a lone star in the endless Void. The sphere of fire was the first layer of Haven's gate, and might either be the last, or the first of many, depending on the life one led. Those who suffered in life would pass with little effort, and those who led a life of comfort were condemned to many layers of suffering before reaching their reward. Such was the wisdom of Lelonetha. It also kept certain people from stealing her peaches.

"Farewell, dear brother," she said. "I shall be watching you." She touched his cheek, and then stepped from the tent into the ether, gliding across space to enter the tumultuous flames and disappear in a flash of light that broke into little bits, drifting on the ethereal winds like leaves.

"Farewell sister," he said, and he closed the tent flap. "Onward to glory," he muttered as he stepped behind the looking-tube and spun the wheel. "With just a few quick stops first..."

The market went on forever, with row upon row of stalls, tables, tents, and blankets spread on the ground with all manner of goods for sale. Items never before seen in the mortal world could be found here, alongside the more 'average' treasures and wares found in every age of recorded history.

There were colored rockets from the Storm Isles of Onkanshu; Gozhian ivory and jewelry; bottled charisma from the deepest wishing wells; masks of gold, and precious cut stones from Rakaal; jars of rare, pickled dragon organs; exotic fruits from the Haeylic and Lazbrish Islands; scrolls and artwork from ancient Bythia; armored suits and crystal weapons of elven craft; skulls of lesser dragon-kin, long turned to stone; sculptures from the Celvestrian Empire's height; enchanted toys from the courts of the Sorcerer Kings, and graven idols from the labyrinthine tombs of Rasha, to name but a few of the wares found within a minute's walk.

Aromatic scents wove around the little trickster god, promoting spices from a thousand lands, as culinary delights of every variety were being prepared for eager customers. Merchants called out to the endless crowd of patrons, who appraised everything with wary eyes, and paid with purses bulging with minted desire.

Tavenji skipped through the crowd with unnatural agility, pausing to gaze at the more exotic and ancient wares he passed, and smiling to the wary shopkeepers who fixed him with sharp, mistrustful eyes. *These souls have long memories,* he thought. *That just makes it more fun.* He bit into a juicy bread-berry he had just pinched from a display, as the spirits of deceased mortals mulled about him, seeking to quench their desire for material goods, or make the fortunes they were denied in life.

Tavenji quenched his desire for a fried laughing beetle; swiping the delicacy from a vendor's table and eating the little bug with relish, letting the creature's venom work its trick. He began to giggle helplessly as he walked, drawing a few glances from the wandering spirits around him. The laughing beetle was one of his favorite ideas, and was once used by his priesthood in their Divine Alchemy. Alas, his priesthood was no more, and the poor laughing beetles were almost all gone. Some things were simply too good to last.

Towering above the hordes of buyers and sellers was the Great Treasury, the palace of Obamir. It rose over the textile landscape of silken pavilions to dominate the center of the market, always in sight but never in reach, no matter how one navigated the twisting paths that surrounded it.

The edifice was rather squat, broad and rounded much like its owner; its sides bulged outward as if it could scarcely contain the riches within, and its bulbous, onion-shaped dome topped it like the cap of a mushroom. About its sides were three smaller towers, each devoted to one of the three virtues the god cherished: luck, prosperity, and benevolence. It had a stubby, phallic shape that Tavenji found hilarious, but the little god was too wise to joke with its owner about it. A person only stood before Obamir when something was desired, and the purse strings of the Lord of Luxury could close tighter than a duck's ass if he felt slighted.

Gaining an audience with his brother would not be a problem; Obamir knew of Tavenji's arrival the moment he entered the market. All he had to do was await his escort.

"My Lord Messenger," said a stern, feminine voice from behind him. Turning, he beheld three Kyraine, resplendent in their silver armor and short, white raiment. They held golden spears in their taloned hands, and their wings folded behind them like majestic feathered cloaks.

"Oh, hello!" Tavenji said, "I was wondering when you'd show up." He looked the women up and down as if they were part of the market's offerings. "My brother is so kind to send such lovely female Kyraine to escort me." He grinned, "Very lovely indeed."

"There are no male Kyraine, my Lord Messenger," the leader intoned. "As I am sure you know." Her porcelain-perfect complexion showed no sign of emotion. Kyraine had a severe beauty that was accentuated by their tightly bound hair and silver, reflective eyes.

"Is that why you're all so tense and irritable?" he asked. "How awful; what was father thinking when he made you so?"

"I do not presume to know the mind of our creator," she said coolly. "But clearly, he did not think they were needed." She motioned with a taloned hand, "Please accompany us, and we shall take you to our master."

Tavenji nodded and gestured with a flourish, "Lead the way, my lovelies..." Two Kyraine flanked him as the dark-haired leader walked before them. "...and put a little wiggle in those wings!" Tavenji called, and the woman stiffened ever so slightly. He couldn't help it. People with no sense of humor brought out the worst in him.

The Kyraine led him on a hidden path through the tents and merchant stalls, turning this way and that, until the way opened before them and the path became a road. Such a road was only imagined in the mortal world, though some had tried to emulate its grandeur.

The Golden Path was paved with bricks of gold and cemented with blood, sweat and tears. It followed a course like a winding river bordered on either side with living statues of toil and hardship, their faces etched with endless suffering, muscles taut with eternal strain. They were the Insatiable, the cursed souls who had taken and taken, never giving back any of the fortune they had acquired in their lives. No kindness, no charity, no altruism or generosity had existed in them in life, and none were given to them now. Their presence here reminded any guest of the Lord of Avarice that the path to riches was a treacherous one. All wealth flowed from his blessings, and to deny others even the smallest share was to scorn the gifts that the god had given. It was a harsh fate, but that didn't stop the path from growing, or new statues from populating it.

The Golden Path ended at the platinum gates of the Great Treasury, which parted to admit the Lord of

Thieves and his escort. Tavenji's gaze took in the awe-inspiring beauty that Obamir surrounded himself with. The vast hall had a great vaulted ceiling, gilded and encrusted with gemstones, and painted with frescoes that moved with a slow, graceful life of their own. Dancing statues of alternating gold and silver spun in place on their pedestals, weaving their limbs in time to an unearthly music of harp, lute, and flute, that wafted in from hidden galleries. Pillars of polished rhodonite supported the vaulted ceiling, giving the space rosy warmth; tiny diamonds sparkled on the black marble floor, mirroring the twinkling splendor above. Incense burned in decorative censers shaped like birds that glided lazily about the chamber as they dispersed their fragrant smoke. Similar ornate hallways broke off to either side, curving around the vast circumference of the palace. A grand stairway led to the upper levels, past enough riches to purchase a continent. It was all Tavenji could do to keep from bumping into his escorts, so distracted was he by the spectacle.

Finally they reached the inner sanctum, where Obamir entertained his honored guests. It was an intimate, cozy setting compared to the vastness of the palace. The chamber was circular and entirely upholstered with sumptuous cloth. Swaths of silken fabric draped from a central point above, curving down towards the walls and gathering at the floor. It gave the chamber a tent-like appearance, though to Tavenji's eyes it looked more like the view from the inside of a privy seat; he half expected the ceiling to break wind.

"Dear Tavenji! Welcome to my home!" The voice was high, rich and refined, oozing charm; it came from an ample figure reclining in a large cushioned couch, adorned in a plum silken robe lined with fine white fur. Obamir's bejeweled fingers held the stem of a water-pipe, and the red curls about his head and face were currently being stroked by the taloned fingers of a Kyraine servant behind him. His ruddy complexion made it hard to tell where his hair ended and his round face began.

"Greetings to you, brother Obamir," Tavenji said, bowing low. "It was kind of you to send such an attractive and friendly escort." The women bowed and turned to leave, and Tavenji was tempted to slap the leader on her shapely behind, but sadly, her wings were in the way.

Obamir gestured to a nearby couch saying, "I would not have wished for you to wander aimlessly in my market, as I am sure you have pressing matters."

That was diplomatic of him, the little god thought. He plopped onto the couch with a hop and made himself comfortable, taking a pipe stem from the holder and drawing the aromatic smoke through the hose. "Mmmmm," he hummed as he puffed smoke out of his ears. "Lovely. Yes, I do have a rather pressing matter to discuss with you, brother." He propped himself up on an elbow and motioned to the Kyraine servants with his pipe stem, "Might we have some privacy first?"

Obamir smiled and waved his hand, sending the winged women away, their taloned feet plucking softly at the carpet. Once they had closed the doors behind them, Tavenji spoke. "I was wondering, that is, I was hoping that I might trouble you for... for a coin."

Obamir raised his bushy eyebrows, coughing slightly on his smoke. "A coin? One of *my* coins? One of my three?" He would have sat up in surprise, but Tavenji imagined it was too much effort.

The little god nodded, "Yes, one of those three. I am going to try and correct a mistake, and I could use all the help I can get."

The opulent god observed his guest for a long moment before replying, "You are aware that I always weigh the profit and risk of every venture. Might I know what this mistake might be, and how you intend to correct it?"

"Er, best not," Tavenji said, blushing. "It is a rather *big* mistake, and the less you know, the better, I think."

He sat up, the pipe forgotten. "You see, if father finds out, he will be a bit cross and that won't help anyone." Obamir frowned and Tavenji fidgeted, "I wouldn't ask for such a favor unless it was *very* important. Lelonetha has already given aid, and she thinks I'm doing the right thing."

"So," Obamir said, "she knows what you are planning to do? Is her help worth so much more than mine that you should confide in her and not me?"

Tavenji said, "No, it's not like that. You know we are very close, and I had to discuss this with someone. Besides, we were stuck together for a time and we got to talking..."

"Ah, so that was what all the bluster was about," Obamir sat back with his fingers crossed over his belly. "You maligned Balkon again and he sought you out."

The little god grinned sheepishly and shrugged, "He had it coming. I was delivering a message, official business mind you, and he tried to have his little minions attack me! It was a serious breach of protocol. I could have gone to father and complained, but that's... not really my style." He hopped up and paced the carpet, "It's not that I don't want to tell you, it's just that I... I don't want this to get back to father."

Obamir gave him a measuring stare, "Would it help if I arranged for a writ of confidence?" A sheaf of paper appeared in the opulent god's hand and dark writing bled to the surface, spelling out the agreement. He handed it to Tavenji, who took it and gave it a read.

"I suppose this will do," the trickster said, signing his name with his finger under his brother's signature. He heaved a sigh, "I know what happened to the Dark Heart and I want to fix it."

Obamir's eyes widened and he hoisted himself upright on the couch, "What? You were behind the theft after all? I did not think even *you* would be so brazen and foolish!" He tossed his pipe stem aside and huffed.

"No!" Tavenji cried, "No, I didn't take it. All I did was

pull brother through one of the old gates and-and take him to his realm and-and..." He spun about and sat on the floor, his legs and arms crossed, "I didn't mean any harm. He was calling to us, he was suffering and I wanted to help. He only wanted his cloak and staff! I brought him to the Sands of the Ages and he got his things, but he took something else, something I didn't know was there! I can't help it if no one tells me these things! If I knew it was hidden there, I would never..."

"None of us were told where it was hidden," Obamir said, "That is the point of hiding something." He leaned forward, "But how, *how* did you manage to pull our lost brother through a gate? The portals were all shut, surely!"

"I know, I know," he said. "I didn't think it could be done either, but he was so weak, so very weak. I couldn't pass through, but I could pull him into the Void. It wasn't easy for him; I don't know how he survived it, but he did. He shed what little power he had; I could feel it sloughing away. It was... it was horrible."

Obamir was listening with rapt attention, now sitting on the edge of the couch, his hands resting on his knees. "How... how is he?"

Tavenji glanced up, grimaced and said, "Close your robe; I can see your jewels." Obamir mumbled an apology and arranged his clothing.

Tavenji lay back with his hands behind his head. "He is not all there, our brother. The mortal world has done something to him. Or maybe it was the banishment. Or maybe it's because he saw it all in advance. Who knows? But I do know that he is not himself. He's almost- well, I don't want to say 'mad' but I suppose it applies."

The portly god huffed in distress and stroked his beard thoughtfully. "I had always wondered what had caused such anger in him. When he cracked his staff, it sent vibrations across the Ether that could be felt in every realm. Had he seen his obsolescence I wonder?

Had he seen his banishment, the End of All Things, and his part in it?"

Tavenji wondered just then if he had also seen a certain trickster god helping him through the gate, knowing his little brother could be blinded by compassion to aid him in his mad scheme. The thought made him feel sick.

"If he carries out his plan," Tavenji said, "it will spell the doom of us all. No more realms, no more gods, no more Creation; just the Mother, Father Order, and Uncle Chaos. Just like in the Beginning."

Obamir stood and began to pace the room as Tavenji got to his feet glumly, watching the decisions cross his brother's face. Finally, the god came to a halt and said, "A total loss. That is what hangs in the balance. In the face of such odds, it would be foolish not to render aid. Even the wrath of Arathus would be preferable to oblivion." He turned to the little god and said, "I shall grant your request. Which of my coins do you require?"

Tavenji brightened and bounced on his toes as he answered, "Luck! I shall need a great deal of luck." He had considered this on his journey here; he could make his own luck with his skill and cunning, but his own resources were not going to be enough to save everything in existence.

Obamir nodded and reached into his sash, drawing a gold coin from its folds. He tumbled it across his thick, ringed fingers before holding it out for the little god to take. "Try not to lose it," he said, "I have plenty of others of course, but I do not grant them lightly."

Tavenji took the coin, spinning it on a fingertip. "I won't lose it, and you have my eternal thanks, brother Obamir."

"Then make certain that eternity lasts, brother Tavenji," Obamir said solemnly.

There was only one more realm he needed to visit, only one more sibling whose assistance he would beg. Not Selvina, the goddess of love and beauty; she would be of little help. Besides, she didn't much like the trickster god for some reason. Valdak... well frankly, Valdak frightened him. The god of judgment and divine retribution was not the most caring and compassionate of his brothers and sisters; he might judge Tavenji harshly for even *considering* breaking the law of Arathus, plus he always had that hooked, bladed staff with him. And those blind eyes, they could see *everything* a person had done. Maybe even everything a god had done. Then there was Balkon... No, he'd not ask for aid from Balkon, not even with creation in the balance. The war god would be furious with him for ages to come, that is, if there *were* any ages to come.

That left Eyorona. She was not warm with him like Lelonetha, nor was she harsh with him like Selvina; Eyorona was always cool and even-tempered, tolerating his jokes and antics, but never driven to the point of anger or distraction. She was infuriatingly stolid, relentlessly stoic. He was essentially powerless against her, and that was a terrible annoyance for a god.

One thing Eyorona had in abundance was wisdom. Wisdom was her province; she was teacher, guide and adviser, the source of all crafts and the font of the arts. She always knew the wise course, which was one reason Tavenji rarely spoke to her. Wise was never *fun*.

Eyorona had long ago chosen Alhanna for her realm, though it was not of her making and she could claim no dominion there; she only wished to be close to her precious Ilvayiin. When the Ilvayiin gave up their flesh, their spirits would return to Alhanna to dwell with Eyorona for all time. She was the most beloved deity of the Ilvayiin, for though she did not create them, she was their teacher and patron.

After making the five elements, Mother Jayda created Alhanna. It was a spirit world populated with all manner of spirit creatures; beautiful, perfect and dreadfully dull. That was likely the reason why Jayda decided to make a world of elements instead, full of life, death, and rebirth. It was called *Alsuvath* by the elves and 'Jayde' by mortals. Alhanna served as the spirit of that world, and was the source of what mortals called magic. As such, it was the closest realm to Jayde and the most permeable; if there was a way to enter the mortal world from Outside, it must be through Alhanna, or so Tavenji hoped.

Finding the spirit realm was easy; it was in the middle of the Void. Tavenji steered his little tent-realm towards the faint glow, following the streams of Ether as they flowed from their source. He was still on the lookout for Balkon, certain the war god would not have abandoned his search completely. As Tavenji arrived at Alhanna's borders, he scanned the Void one last time with the looking-tube. The blackness was still and calm and the Ether flowed gently outward with no ripples or visible signs of trouble. If Balkon was out there with his geese-drawn chariot, fuming in his wrath, there would be signs. Finally satisfied, Tavenji lowered the tube until it disappeared into the floor, and then opened the tent flaps.

"Hellooooo...?" he said to the blackness. No one answered, so he pushed himself out of his now-invisible tent and drifted toward the world below. It radiated a calming light, as if peace and happiness had become colors in the spectrum, visible to the eye. It was vast and grand, quickly filling his vision as he fell towards the surface, and a spirit-wind ruffled his hair, tugging at his jacket and sash as he broke Alhanna's borders.

His body now flared and flashed like a meteor, streaking towards the valley which in the material world was called Du-Dwithian, the Place of Beginning where the First Ones chose to dwell. Closer and closer he flew, until he could see a vast forest near a lake, and the upturned eyes of hundreds of tall and noble spirits watching his approach. A slight adjustment of thought and he was right over them, glowing like a miniature sun, trailing fire and sound. With a *whoosh* he pulled out of his dive and looped just over their heads, making more than a few of them duck. Finally he landed before them with a satisfying, echoing *boom*, hands on hips, legs apart and head held high.

"Greetings, Ilvayiin!" Tavenji proclaimed, brushing nonexistent dust from his shoulders, "I hope I'm not disturbing anything?"

The gathered elven spirits sank to one knee in welcome, an act which put the tallest of them at eye-level with the little god. "Welcome to you, Lord Tavenji, brother of Lady Eyorona the Beloved," said the one nearest him. "Welcome," the rest intoned as they rose to their feet. They were genuinely pleased to see him.

A god could get used to all this kissing up, Tavenji thought. He surveyed the lands of the vast valley, recognizing the place where, in the world of Alsuvath, stood the Crystal City and the High House upon the shore of the distant lake. Here in Alhanna, there was nothing constructed, nothing built for comfort or shelter. There were no homes to live in, no beds to sleep in, no crops to tend or chores to do. There was no need.

Boring, Tavenji thought.

"If you seek Eyorona," said a male elf spirit, "she is in the Dark Glade with the First Ones. No doubt she has sensed your arrival." He said this last part with a smile, and Tavenji wondered if they missed such surprises here in Perfect Land.

"My thanks," he said, and he skipped off through the forest path. Spirit rabbits and spirit deer capered aimlessly around him, ignoring the spirit grass and spirit predators; nothing ever got hungry here, not even the predators. He wondered, *Are they 'predators' if they don't prey on anything?*

The Dark Glade was the counterpart to a site in the 'real' world called the Spirit Glade, a place where the veil between worlds was thinner. Such places existed all over, but the Spirit Glade of Du-Dwithian was sacred to the Ilvayiin. The Dark Glade was not truly dark, but its radiance was noticeably dimmer than its surroundings.

As the Spirit Glade made the elves feel closer to Alhanna, the Dark Glade made them feel closer to Alsuvath. *The grass is always greener on the other side of reality,* Tavenji mused.

He found Eyorona and a group of powerful elven spirits conversing in the glade, their radiance only accentuating the relative gloom of their surroundings. The elves were the First Ones, created here before manifesting bodies of flesh in Alsuvath. But they had left that world long ago, returning to their place of creation. They were tall, beautiful, graceful and elegant, wearing garments that seemed almost lighter than air, drifting with the slightest movement.

Eyorona appeared as one of them, sharing their fine features, pointed ears, almond eyes and pale, golden skin. Yet, she was taller and even more beautiful somehow, perfecting perfection in a way that only a goddess could manage. Her hair was a flowing cascade of copper curls, her eyes shone like the brightest sapphires, her skin sparkled subtly as if dusted with gold, and her garments were of the richest coral hue.

She turned as he approached, spreading her arms in greeting as her long sleeves flowed like liquid gossamer. "Welcome, half-brother. This is a rare visit." The First Ones bowed in deference to him, parting to the edges of the glade as the gods exchanged salutations.

Calling me 'half-brother' in front of her minions, Tavenji thought. *That is as close as she will come to a reprimand for my entrance.* Still, his dramatic descent had been worth it.

"Greetings, sister-and-a-half," he said as he craned his neck to look up at her. "It has been too long since last you scolded me." He made a little bow and she made a slight curtsy.

"Not so long, as I remember," she said, guiding him into the woods with a hand on his shoulder. "It was only a short time ago that father told us of the theft of the Dark Heart. I assume that is why you are here?"

He ducked out from under her hand, affronted. "Sister! Do you accuse me of stealing something so vile? Well, I never!" He folded his arms and pouted as they walked.

"Accuse?" she smiled, "No, Lord of Thieves, I do not accuse. Yet I sense that you are involved in some way. Is this not so?"

Tavenji gave up his facade and sighed, "It is so. But I was not the one who took it; I'm blameless there."

She nodded, "So you say, Lord of Lies. What small part did you play in this disaster, if I may ask?"

He looked about to make sure they were alone before replying, "All I did was answer a call for help, a call none of my siblings chose to hear." It wasn't often that he could be self-righteous, so he made the most of it. "I did a good and noble deed, a compassionate deed, and it led to disaster. I wasn't looking for trouble! I didn't even realize what had happened until father told us it was missing!" He was hopping around as he spoke, energized by his own rare innocence.

"Yet, it is gone and you had a part in it," she said evenly. "I ask again, what part did you play?"

He shrugged and leaned against a tree. "I heard brother calling for help. I heard him calling from the other side, Eyorona."

Her up-swept eyebrows raised in mild surprise as she exclaimed, "Brother Thesram? You... *interacted* with him?"

Tavenji's ears reddened at the tips. "Of course I *interacted* with him. He was calling for help! And he hasn't gone by 'Thesram' since the First Ones came home. He is known as Epoch."

Eyorona pinned him to the tree with her gaze, "He is known as 'banished,' half-brother. Arathus stripped him of his power and duties and cast him into Alsuvath. We are not to interact with the world of elements, and we are not to interact with him! This was no 'noble deed' as you claim, but an extreme act of malfeasance!" She put her hands on his shoulders, gently yet firmly.

"You must go before Arathus and tell him what you have done."

Tavenji shrugged her off, "Is *that* the wise thing to do? Is that all you have to offer?" he scoffed, "I came to you for help, sister. I want to fix this, and I can't fix it if father banishes me too."

"What did you hope for, coming here?" she asked. "You have committed a terrible act, no matter your intentions. If you wish for counsel, I cannot counsel you to be a fool."

"I'm not really looking for counsel," he said pleadingly, "I'm looking for help. I need to get into Alsuvath, and I figured you might know a way, maybe through that Dark Glade. If not, maybe you can give me a favor, a token? Anything would be appreciated..."

The expression on her face was not promising. "You want me to help you break father's edict, his last great command? Tavenji, you risk more than you can imagine with this folly."

His frustration boiled over, "Imagine this, sister!" he squeaked, "Everything will end! Me, you, Alhanna, Alsuvath, all of it! Brother Epoch wants to destroy creation for some reason, and I am trying to stop him! Now, are you going to aid me, or would you like to start saying goodbye to all your little spirit people?"

Her face became a mask of uncertainty as she considered his words. She turned and paced a few steps with her head bowed, copper curls swaying gently as she shook her head. Finally, she straightened, gathered herself, and said in a soft voice, "It seems I have little choice. Unless it is the will of Arathus to end all of creation, I cannot stand idly by."

"It's not his will, I'm pretty sure," Tavenji said. "He wouldn't have gone through all the trouble if it was."

She turned to him, and for the first time Tavenji saw tears in the eyes of another god. They sparkled like diamonds as they rolled down her cheeks, and where they fell upon the ground, there sprung small clusters of new flowers.

"There is no way to pass into the world of elements, not even from Alhanna," she said dismally. "The portals will not allow a being as powerful as a god to pass. Not even the First Ones could return if they wished, though their power is so much less than ours. The world repels us now, denying our influence. As it is with us, so it is with the Lord of Chaos. That was father's plan."

Yet Tavenji would not be thwarted. "But there are powers that pass the barriers! Selvina's butterflies did it not long ago, and there are denizens of the Abyss that still influence the world. I've heard rumors from the recently deceased; things are happening again, another Thinning."

Eyorona nodded, "Yes, the power of the Dark Heart causes a thinning between the worlds, and the lesser powers seep through. But this cannot allow you to pass; a god cannot shed so much power, it can only be taken by our father." She placed a hand on his shoulder again, this time in support. "If you truly wish to enter the world of elements, you must go before father and face banishment. Only he can take from you your godhood and let you slip through the portals, but once done, there is no coming back."

Tavenji sighed and hung his head. He was committed to this course, and if it meant going before father and being banished, then it's what he must do. It wasn't going to be fun, and it wasn't going to be pretty.

"I suppose it's no less than I deserve," he said glumly. "If father made me for a reason, maybe it was this."

Eyorona gazed down upon her little brother, the youngest of the gods. He had always been such an irritant, such a confusing little enigma that flew in the face of all the Divine Court stood for. Their father was Order and Law. Tavenji was more like Chaos, like an offspring of Llomaak. It had never made sense that Arathus should claim him as his own creation, but now perhaps there was a method to the apparent madness. It gave Eyorona little comfort, however.

"I can grant you a favor, little brother," she said, "for

I do believe you will need the gift of wisdom before this is over." She held out her hand to him, and resting in her palm was an acorn.

He took it gingerly, saying, "Thank you, sister. I will remember this always... and I will try to make sure that 'always' lasts a long time."

She smiled at this. It was the first time he could recall her smiling at one of his jokes. *It is a day of firsts,* he thought. *Perhaps it will be a day of lasts as well.*

"Sister, may I ask you a question?"

She smiled, "Of course."

He said, "The other gods made realms to serve the spirits of dead mortals. Valdak judges them and they go where they must. But you and I are the only ones who don't serve mortals in their afterlife." He asked, "I know my reasons, but what are yours? Surely mortal souls would have a need for your lessons and gifts on their final journey?"

She considered for a moment and replied, "The spirits of the Ilvayiin are immortal, and were always a part of this realm, it is true. Why then do I not have a place for mortal souls to come, and learn or create to their hearts' content before they move on? It is simple, really." She explained, "The dead have little need for wisdom, and I give mortals a chance at immortality in life. Who could be immortalized in story or song were it not for the scholar or singer? Whose image would live outside of memory, were it not for the sculptor or painter? A people long dead can be known by that which they built, by that which they crafted or learned. My gifts give a measure of immortality to any who would use them. They need only put forth the effort."

He might have said something funny, something sarcastic and cutting. He might have once, but not now. He was too somber to make jokes, his burden too heavy to shatter this unlikely moment of kinship and congeniality.

"I see," he said. "Thank you, sister."

It was time to head back to his little realm and travel to the Plains of Dromoth at the top of creation, where the city of Dormos stood, perfect in its symmetry and efficiency, the very seat of Order. He knew King Arathus would be furious, and he wondered if being stripped of power and banished would hurt. *Perhaps he will make it hurt,* he thought uncomfortably.

Another thought occurred to him and he took out the three favors he had been given, the ring, the coin, and the acorn. He had to make sure they passed into the world of Jayde with him. If he lost even one it might spell disaster, to say nothing of losing all three. Epoch had hidden the Dark Heart inside himself somehow, so Tavenji figured the safest thing would be to do the same. Shrugging, he popped all three items into his mouth and swallowed. *That will have to do,* he decided. *It's either one end or the other.* Leaping into the sky, he left the world of Alhanna behind and headed for the open Void.

As soon as he cleared the boundaries of Alhanna, he felt a tremor in the ether, like the beating of a moth's wings. Panic rising in his chest, he made for the spot where he had left his realm; its entrance lay just beyond, waiting like a hole in space. He could almost feel the fabric of the tent under his fingers as he stretched forth, willing the portal to appear and part for him. But before he could push it aside and enter, a force came hurtling down from somewhere above, grabbing him about the waist and pulling him away from safety.

What in the Nine Realms? His mind whirled as he tried to right himself. *How did that sneak up on me?* Another tremor, then another streak of movement came from below (or was it above?) and grabbed his legs. He struggled with his attackers, still unable to see much more than flashes of metal and wings.

Then two more figures came rushing at him from the darkness, winged women with taloned hands and feet, the ethereal glow flashing off of their silver armor and the swords on their hips. None had drawn their weapons, but instead wielded thin chains that they spun about, making a hissing whirl in the darkness before casting them at his flailing limbs. The chains snaked around his wrists and ankles, binding him. He was certain he could escape given a few moments, but the Kyraine did not allow him the opportunity.

"Was it something I said?" he asked.

A Kyraine flew before him and drew her sword, pressing it to his throat and effectively ceasing his struggles.

He gulped, "T-this isn't because of those jokes I made, is it? I have the deepest respect for the Kyraine, really I do. Beauty and brawn are a sexy combination. And brains too! I've always admired your um… tactical skills. Sneaking up on me is no small feat…"

She did not seem moved, nor did she move the tip of her blade.

He squeaked, "Does your master Obamir know you're doing this?"

The Kyraine before him glared and said, "Lord Obamir is not our master." She then withdrew a war horn from her belt and sounded it, producing a deep, rising tone that made him tremble.

It was then that Tavenji recognized the woman. *Ziowyn. Her name is Ziowyn, and she belongs to Balkon.* Panic took him for true and he struggled to break free, tossing the Kyraine left and right and wriggling against the chains, yet they did not loosen. *Have these been forged just for me?* They were getting tighter the more he shifted and pulled at them, restraining his power in a way that nothing had done before. *I am the Trickster, the Lord of Thieves and Master of Escapes! I can get into and out of anything!* Yet the chains held fast and the Kyraine rushed to hold him again, digging their talons into his body.

As he felt himself tire and grow weaker, he heard a dreadful noise; the responding call of another horn sounding in the Void, deeper and more ominous. The honking of geese arose, and Tavenji saw the trail of fire left by the spinning wheels of Balkon's chariot. The war god was in his shining armor, covered with red gore and draped with a crimson cape that flew out behind him as the chariot came on. The three bronze geese that drew the chariot flapped their mighty wings and echoed the god's war horn. Tavenji could make out the wild, thick hair of his beard, dark but matted with blood. His cavernous mouth was agape, laughing and roaring with crazed blood-lust beneath his helm's open visor. In his hand was a long spear with a silver shaft and a golden head, broad and sharp. He had it raised to his shoulder as if ready to cast it. His eyes were bright and fixed on the little god with murderous intent.

Steering the geese to the side, Balkon leaped off his chariot and let it fly away as he drifted towards Tavenji, a look of imminent victory on his brutish face. He placed the tip of the spear on the hollow of the little god's throat as he leaned in close, the smell of blood and death reeking about him. "So now I finally have you, little bastard spawn of Llomaak." The tip of the spear pricked Tavenji's flesh, making a red glow spread about his neck.

"Y-you might hurt me with that little pig-sticker," Tavenji said, his voice shaking, "but you can't make me bleed. Only one blade was ever forged that could bleed a god, and that's not it."

Balkon's voice was low and soft now, so different from his usual booming bluster; Tavenji found it more terrifying by far. "Oh, we all remember your little gift to the world, your god blade. That arrogant fool of an elf certainly made use of it, didn't she? Are you happy now, Chaos-Son? First you made the Dark Heart possible, and now you've sent it back to the world."

"I didn't!" Tavenji blurted, "It was Epoch! He-" The spear point pushed hard to silence him and he winced in pain. The tip broke the skin and red fire burned around the wound until Balkon withdrew it; not a mark remained to show Tavenji had been hurt. The Kyraine held him fast, watching dispassionately.

"You dare blame your misdeeds on our brother in exile?" Balkon roared. "What do you take me for?"

Tavenji grinned despite the pain, "Oh, where to begin..." he said, but the war god stuck him in the throat again, making him cry out in agony.

"I was furious indeed for your little stunt, cursing my Dishonored to do that stupid dance," Balkon snarled, "but when I heard father say the blood of Llomaak was missing and loose in the world again," he lowered the spear point to the little god's chest, "I knew you had done far worse than any prank done unto me."

"Worse than your hair loss?" Tavenji asked, seeing his reflection in the war god's armor; he was surprised to see himself smiling despite his predicament.

Balkon's scowl worsened and his face flushed almost as red as the blood on his hair and armor. But as infuriated as he was, he stayed his hand. "Oh, I am going to enjoy this. I have waited long and prepared for this day, when I might get my hands on you for true."

"I hope you aren't expecting father to reward you," Tavenji said, sounding bolder than he felt. "He likes to reserve the right to punish his children himself." He actually rather hoped the king god would appear and settle this; it might be worth getting banished if he could see Balkon get berated. Yet no such intervention came.

The war god drifted back a few paces, hefting his spear in both hands. The Kyraine held their prisoner firmly in place at arm's length. Tavenji realized he had only seconds before his brother claimed vengeance for eons of taunts, pranks and mischief at his expense. His mind racing, he groped for anything that might save him. The favors of his siblings were within him and he felt for their power, grasping for anything that might aid in his escape. *Luck, luck, luck, lots of luck needed right now...*

But his luck had run out. Balkon struck him full in the chest with a mighty thrust, the spear blazing with godly fury as it punctured his spirit, ripping him from all sense and feeling. He could not cry out, could not even think, as the blackness of the Void became a blinding light to swallow him whole.

Chapter Eight

Inquisition

It was only two days after the celebratory feast when the king ordered a meeting in the main hall of Casselvane Keep. The preparations were for a hearing or a trial, and two men had recently been brought to the castle dungeons. The count had been dismayed to find that one of them was Maron Theenix, chairman of the city's Trade Guild. The other was the son of a Dissenter House who had apparently been training at the Freekirk School.

Amon Corrina spoke to his countess over a light breakfast in the lady's dayroom. "The king is wasting no time in flushing out his enemies, though I wonder if more prudence is needed."

"I wonder if he intends to carry out these deeds in our home, or if he will be moving on to the Winter Palace soon." Zara was not so much dismayed by the imposition of the king as by the cold, ominous wrath he brought with him. She did not wish to see their castle turned into the center of an inquisition. Casselvane Keep had not heard cries in its dungeons in many generations.

"I think he is only waiting for the Winter Palace to be readied; there was no advance news of his coming, after all." said the count.

"It can hardly be so inadequate for his needs," she remarked frostily. "Prisoners and soldiers don't mind a bit of dust."

"They do enjoy food and drink however," the count reminded her. "The larders have not been stocked in years, not since his father fell ill."

"Not since he was poisoned, you mean." Zara said.

"Yes..." Amon agreed.

"What is poor Master Theenix supposed to have done? How can he deserve such treatment?" she asked. The man had been a guest at their table more than once.

"The king found evidence that he may have paid off Minozhian pirates that recently sacked Cordoshome," he said.

"Nonsense!" she said. "Do you believe it?"

"I don't understand what he would have to gain," he replied. "The king believes Theenix either intends to spread our navy thin chasing Minozhians, or is working for either the Dissenters or the Aurilonian king. None of it makes sense. Maron Theenix is Portshia born and bred; he has dedicated his life to this city and its interests."

"Perhaps he has other interests," she said. "If Julen and Lemorea Gordon were actually evil priests of Chaos, then Maron might be as well." The countess never liked Maron's wife Madred. The woman wore a permanent expression of distaste and disapproval, as though she had been raised on lemon juice.

"I cannot believe that," he said. "I never knew the Gordons, but Maron..."

Zara cocked her head, "How did the Gordons get an invitation to Cindra's engagement feast in the first place?"

Amon frowned, trying to remember. "I believe they were... I think... You know, I'm not sure. You did not invite them?"

"No," she said. "I arranged most of the invitations, but there were several endorsements from advisers."

"Yes... Now that you mention it, I think they were requested by Fingelm," said the count. "They were friends of friends, or some such thing." He fell silent and looked very uneasy.

"You don't think... Fingelm is involved?" Zara shuddered.

"No!" the count said firmly. "No, I don't think he knew about them."

"Should we not confront him about it?" she asked.

The count shook his head, "If there is any question of Fingelm's loyalty, I will see to it when the king has left our halls. I will handle my own justice; none of our household will come under the Black Eagle's talons if I can help it."

All bowed as the count and countess entered the main hall. It was indeed arranged for a trial, with rows of chairs opposite each other for spectators, and a head table for those who would sit in judgment. Five chairs were set behind the head table, and Amon Corrina suspected one was for him. As the chief justice in the province, he would normally take the center chair and preside over a trial, but he was no longer the highest law in the land.

A tear-shaped piece of polished Shadowood served as the official court gavel. Resting in a concave base, its wide grains of black and gray swirled across the shiny surface, awaiting the hand of the king. In the middle of the room was a raised dock surrounded by a wooden railing. The count wondered what state Maron Theenix would be in when required to stand there. He had little concern for the condition of the DeKenric boy, since a noble hostage was always treated well. But Theenix...

he had been told of the cries coming from the prison halls, and it had chilled his blood. He wondered if the king had bothered to call upon any guild wizards to aid in the questioning, or if he had gone straight to the thumbscrews.

There were many nobles in the hall, having been summoned last night by the king's messengers. Many looked confused and worried, and rightly so; their attendance had been required, but few explanations were given. High officials of the faiths were present, but for the conspicuous absence of priests of Valdak, the Blind Judge. There were representatives from the Order of Astrellaris, the council of wizards based in the Tower of the Silver Moon. Arch Mage Ildric Finnael was among them, and he offered the count a slight smile.

It was half an hour later before the king entered, accompanied by his field marshal and personal guard. Valthór announced the sovereign's entrance in a loud, clear voice. "His Royal Highness Galen III SuCordobal, King of Calilon, Duke of Maylione, Count of Regala, Count of Cordobal, Defender of the Realm, and Keeper of the Law!"

Everyone bowed low as he entered, though he paid little mind, striding purposefully to the center chair behind the table. He sat, prompting the rest of the room to sit as well.

"Count Casselvane," said the king, "Join me, will you?" He motioned to the chair beside him.

The countess squeezed his hand before letting it go. The count strode to the table and took the offered seat at the king's right hand.

The king looked about the room as the field marshal handed him a list of names. "Baron Midcassel of House Drakthorne," he said. A dark haired man in deep green finery stepped forward. He was in his mid-thirties and fit, though he walked with a limp. He took a seat next to the count.

"Lord Clavemont," the king read, looking about.

There was a muttering in the hall. The pale man was not present. "Lord Clavemont?" he repeated.

Constable Fingelm stepped forward. "Highness, it seems that Lord Clavemont has taken leave of the city. I am afraid no one knows his present whereabouts."

King Galen's eyes narrowed. "Very well," he said, looking down the list, "I call upon Arch Mage Ildric Finnael."

Finnael stepped forward, "Highness, I fear I must recuse myself. I am too close to the matter in question."

The king raised an eyebrow, "Arch Mage, I have not announced what the matter is."

"Begging your highness's pardon, I would not be much of an arch mage if I did not already know." He smiled wryly, leaning on his staff. The other members of his order looked at him with disapproval; apparently Finnael had not shared his insight with them.

"I see..." King Galen stared at him a moment, then looked at the list. "Arch Mage Ravilus Tage, are *you* able to serve, or must you recuse yourself as well?"

The gray-bearded man next to Ildric stiffened. "Snooping on royal persons is not my area of expertise, so I am at your disposal, Your Highness." He haughtily strode to the judges' table, his purple robes flowing behind him as the crowd made nervous laughter.

The king announced his final choice, "High Commander Reynard Fenwald of the Temple of Balkon." The high priest, a tall man in black and red robes strode to the table. His dark hair and beard were dyed red, as was customary for all Balkonittes not blessed with natural red hair.

"Bring in the accused," said the king in a loud voice as he rapped the gavel. One of his men left in haste towards the grand stair, his footsteps echoing between the walls.

When he returned with the prisoner, the crowd let out a gasp followed by a loud buzz of conversation that resonated confusion and outrage. Lady Cindra Corrina strode between two guards, wearing a simple servant's dress of blue linen. Her hair was braided in the back and she wore a striped band of burgundy cloth across her brow. Disturbingly, her wrists were bound by shackles that clinked as she walked. Following behind at a distance were the young half-elven prince and the lovely elven emissary.

"What is the meaning of this?" the count demanded. His eyes sought his wife, who was staring in shock at their daughter. "Of what is my daughter accused?"

The king motioned the count to be still as he asked to have the charges read. Cindra took her place in the dock, looking calm and confident, though the hesitation in her footsteps betrayed her fears. Nixy DuQuayne and Wenyssaya took up a place several paces back.

Valthór strode forward and proclaimed, "Lady Cindra Corrina, hereafter known as the accused, has been charged with the following crimes: that she willfully took the disguise of a man to attend the Freekirk Fighting School; that in that disguise, she trained and cohabited with the unknowing students there; that she played as squire to Sir Jaron Dunlorden, who was fully complicit in this scheme; that she attended regular services in the Temple of Balkon in this disguise," at this, the high priest stiffened, "and under false pretenses, acquired a title of knighthood from His Highness, King Galen III."

The room was shocked into silence. The countess gripped a chair to steady herself, her green eyes wide and filling with tears. The count stood from his chair, searching his daughter's face for a denial. "What madness is this?" he demanded, "Cindra...?"

"How do you plead?" asked Valthór.

"Innocent," she said calmly. The charges were true of course, but the mitigating circumstances could not be ignored. If this was going to work, she had to remain sure of her actions and their necessity.

Valthór smirked, "Very well. Let the plea be entered into the record. Who will speak in your defense?"

"I shall speak on my own behalf, field marshal," Cindra said.

This brought more murmuring from the crowd. Everyone knew the lady had the right to ask for a priest of Valdak to represent her.

"Majesty," said the count, his face ashen, "Must I sit in judgment over my own daughter, whom I have just had returned to me? I do not understand-"

"My good Casselvane," said the king, "would you not be the one to decide her fate otherwise? She is your responsibility now as ever. Would you truly be recused and give the decision to others?"

The count looked stricken as he held his daughter's gaze. He slowly sat back down as Cindra gave him the slightest nod.

Valthór looked to the elven woman standing behind Cindra and said, "Will the elven emissary attempt to sway this panel with her charms? What is her purpose here?"

Wenyssaya replied, "I would not presume to sway you with my 'charms' as you say. I am unfamiliar with your laws, but Prince Nixyalderthor made a diplomatic request yesterday, and we have not yet received an answer."

"My lady emissary," said the king, "I think this is not the proper time to inquire."

"Forgive me, great king," she said, "but among my people, such debts of honor and gratitude are considered first before minor infractions."

"These infractions are not *minor!*" barked Valthór.

"I shall convey that to the Shadow Lord, if ever I see him," she said.

"Enough," said the king. "My lady emissary, the answer to your inquiry will be decided by this trial. There is far more at stake here than you realize, and I would invite you to sit and observe with the young prince."

They took his meaning and took their seats. Wenyssaya placed a hand on Nixy's to reassure him.

Nixy had been sure the proposal would work, but the king hadn't called off the trial. His one chance to save Cindra from trouble had gone nowhere.

Valthór said, "You recall, Lady Cindra, that you informed His Highness of your deception yourself. Your plea of innocence carries no meaning."

Cindra summoned all her training and dignity to respond, using the voices her mother taught her when addressing an audience, "I was aware that I was violating the laws and traditions of the kingdom and the fighting school, but my first duty was survival. My second was to bring news of treason to my father and the crown. If I had entered the city as Lady Cindra, I might not have reached the keep alive."

Valthór said, "And yet upon entering the city in disguise, you did not go to the keep. You enrolled in the fighting school as the squire of Sir Jaron Dunlorden!"

"Yes," she said, "I learned that King Galen II had been poisoned in his own castle. How safe could it have been for me, not knowing whom to trust?"

The king shifted in his seat at the reference to his father. The culprits had still not been found and it rankled him greatly.

"And on your admission to the school," Valthór continued, "you saw fit to perpetuate the lie, training with the men and acting as one of them?"

Cindra said, "I could not hope to avoid suspicion by staying in my quarters for years." There were nervous chuckles about the room, but most faces were scandalized.

"So I suppose that attending regular services at the Balkonitte Temple was also part of your disguise?" Valthór said. "Entering a sacred house under false pretenses, partaking of the ceremonies and sacraments, receiving the blessings meant for men who would fight and die in battle; this was all part of your elaborate deception?"

Cindra shook her head, "I was raised to honor the gods. My mother taught me the Songs of Selvina from an early age, but I found that I was meant to follow another path." She touched her headband; "This cloth marks me as a warrior of the *Gatéth-sho'a* people. I earned it by saving the life of another warrior from Minozhians." This caused a small uproar of unbelief, and the king had to strike the gavel for silence. "The warrior I saved was a woman named Teya Haana-Majii; she witnessed the Minozhians receiving payment for my death from a masked priest of the Countless Lord. Later, she saved me from that same priest and his fellows as they talked of the poisoning of the king. I feel that Balkon's hand is guiding me for a purpose."

This brought a frown to the face of High Commander Fenwald as he spoke. "I understand you have invoked the name of Balkon in the past to cover for your antics. There was an incident, I believe, in which you cajoled several peasant children into firing a cannon from the wall of your father's keep? You said that Balkon had ordered it, did you not?"

Cindra stiffened, horrified that her foolish childhood prank had come back to haunt her. It wasn't fair. She really meant it *this* time.

"That is not fair!" It was the voice of the countess raised in anguish. "That was a youthful indiscretion, not an adult's heresy! Would any of us wish to be judged by our younger days?" Cindra had never seen her mother so angry. She recalled now that the countess had shared the story with their guests at the banquet for their amusement, never suspecting it would be used against her in a trial.

Cindra leaned on the railing, her voice strong and certain, "I make no claim to hearing the voice of the gods or knowing their will. I only think that they have a hand in my life, else why would I have survived through so much?" She turned to the king saying, "Majesty, I have learned even more about the plans of these evil priests! Wenyssaya used a spell to help me remember details that are vitally important."

This brought a hush over the assembled witnesses

and the wizard Ravilus Tage darted his gaze between the elf woman and Cindra. Everyone knew women could not use magic by law.

Ildric spoke in the silence, "The Ilvayiin are not bound by the laws of the Mystic College, nor the kingdom, or the laws of humanity itself. Magic is their birthright and it matters not if they are man or woman. They train those who show promise." This brought mutterings of understanding if not acceptance.

Yet Tage was suspicious, and asked the elf woman in a professional, albeit condescending tone, "What manner of spell was used, madam emissary?"

Wenyssaya said, "It was a guided dream, nothing more."

Tage pressed, "Was it an augmentation, a divining, or a charm? What was the methodical basis for the spell you used?"

She shook her golden head saying, "These human concepts hold no meaning for me, arch mage. You might well ask a fish the name of the river in which it swims." Mild laughter spread about the crowd. Tage tugged at his long gray beard in dismay.

The king raised his hand for silence. "Lady Cindra, if you have gained new information, you will share it with the court immediately."

"Of course, Highness," she said. "As you might know by now, the man who delivered payment for my death and who I later overheard in Pinikal was a local merchant named Julen Gordon. He was killed last year attempting to fire a crossbow into the fighting school. I believe I was his target."

Gasps spread through the room. Even the count and countess were not immune to the revelation; they had heard that Gavadaire LuVestra was the intended target.

She continued, "He was also known by the name of Ghethas. His wife Lemorea Gordon is still unaccounted for." She turned to address both sides of the room, "He also said that he 'learned from the high priest that the scion is in Portshia,' and they will soon have the Dark

Heart. I do not pretend to know what this means, but Wenyssaya seemed to think it very important."

The elf maid placed a painted hand on Nixy's shoulder; her lovely face held a grave expression that broke the heart to behold.

The news caused an uproar among the wizards and priests in the hall. Everyone else just sat dumbly by, hoping someone would share whatever was so important.

Ildric Finnael exclaimed, "The Dark Heart! Is this true?"

Wenyssaya nodded grimly, "It is what Lady Cindra heard. I think it may well answer for all that has befallen the city of late. I fear the Dark Heart is already here."

"The Dark Heart was destroyed by Kraal the Great!" argued High Commander Fenwald, "It is written in the scriptures!"

"Then why," countered Ildric, "is there also a prophecy of Kraal's return? Perhaps it is to complete a task unfinished?"

The priest blustered, his face turning red. Outcries came from the high commander's fellow priests of the war god.

Ravilus Tage called to Ildric, "Finnael, you have been warned about spreading such unfounded theories!"

"Heresies!" cried Fenwald. "Kraal's Return is not recognized as canonical!"

Ildric said, "Since when does the Order of Astrellaris care which scriptures are accepted as canon? We are scholars and students of history, and Kraal's Return was reported by official sources-"

The king rapped his knuckles on the table. "Order! Let us return to the matter at hand. If that ancient unholy relic is indeed in this city, then the argument becomes academic. For now, we must hear the Lady Cindra's crimes."

"Your Highness," said Amon Corrina, "Surely my daughter has demonstrated the value of her folly, whether the gods favor her or not. I would not have approved of her conduct had I known, but-"

The king interrupted, "It is her conduct that is on trial, not the unintended benefits of her behavior."

The count made as if to argue, but could not form words. He closed his eyes and took a deep breath to calm himself.

Marus Drakthorne, the Baron Midcassel, spoke, "I wish to know more of how my son was injured in Cordoshome. I understand that... Lady Cindra was present in the battle." He shook his head as he tried to imagine the scene. "I want to know what led to his injuries. What part did you play in the fighting, Lady Cindra?"

He thinks my presence must be to blame, she realized. *Why did the king chose him as a judge anyway?*

She said, "Several of my schoolmates had offered to speak for me if there was to be a trial. By chance, were they summoned?"

"They have not been," said the king, "since their own judgment is in question."

Cindra blinked, wondering what he meant by that. *Does he think they would lie for me?* Now she began to worry, for it felt like things were indeed going too fast and in one direction. "Highness, you were there. I fought by your side. Was I to blame for anyone being injured?"

"I am not on trial for my actions, lady," the king said. "Speak on your own behalf, or do you require the emissary's spells to help you remember?"

She frowned and looked about the room. The faces were expectant and concerned, especially those of her parents and their retainers. She realized that the king was testing her father's loyalty by roasting her over the coals.

She addressed the judges carefully, "When we arrived at the battle in the street, I was ordered by Sir Cord to stay at the back and use my bow while the others held the line with spears. I took a position next to an archer, whom I later learned was His Royal Highness. I recall pulling His Highness aside as a bolt struck where he had been standing. We shot the bull man with the crossbow, but the others pressed the attack. Many, including Terrus, fell before the onslaught. I remember killing one with an arrow before it could finish Terrus where he lay injured. After that, we fell back to a better shooting position."

Drakthorne nodded slowly, coming to grips with his doubts. Most in the crowd were trying to picture this girl shooting arrows at monsters and saving the king and her fellow students. It was an absurd notion, but no one saw the king disputing her testimony.

"Lady Cindra," asked Galen, "what were your intentions in training for knighthood, an honor which I bestowed upon you unknowingly? What did you hope to gain by attaining such a rank?"

Cindra thought for a moment, finally deciding to give the answer that was deep in her heart, the one she rarely admitted to. "I wished to be the son my father needed, not the daughter he did not."

She heard her mother suck in a breath and begin to weep, but Cindra could not bring herself to look. The count bowed his head, staring at his hands, which trembled upon the table.

The king said, "Even though it might bring shame and misfortune upon those who helped you in this deception? The Freekirk family, Sir Jaron Dunlorden-"

"Myself," Ildric Finnael interjected. "Yes, Your Highness. I learned of her whereabouts in the fighting school but did not divulge them. I advised Jaron Dunlorden when needed, and I hid her from magical prying eyes. That is why I could not sit in judgment at this... trial."

The day was full of surprises, it seemed. Cindra allowed herself a tiny smile at the old wizard's boldness, liking him even more. She said, "If there is to be punishment, then I wish to bear it myself. There is no need to drag anyone else down. I am a lady of high birth and I used my influence to convince others to help me. There is no need for further trials or consequences. Let me carry them myself."

The eyes of the gallery beheld her in awe. Never had the assembly heard such bizarre testimony or such selfless culpability. Many in the audience were moved by her decision, and others wondered if she really knew what she was asking.

"As you wish," said the king. "We shall take this into account as we decide your case. This court is now adjourned until noon today." He struck the gavel and rose saying, "Casselvane, we shall need a private room to come to a decision."

The count nodded absently and followed the king and other judges out of the hall, his eyes locked upon his daughter. They were bright with welling tears.

The countess gave them pleading looks as she watched them go, not wanting to believe this was really happening. She wrung her hands helplessly, wanting to hold Cindra close and protect her from this farce of justice. She caught her daughter's eyes and saw the resignation there, but also something else. It was a spark of caution, a warning. Zara Corrina could only stand by as her remaining child was taken away in chains.

Cindra was escorted to her chambers by the king's men, followed by Nixy, Wenyssaya and Ildric Finnael. The guards were reluctant to argue with a wizard, an elf, and a prince, so they admitted them without comment. Besides, they had no orders to keep the lady in isolation.

Once behind closed doors, Nixy burst into anger. "It didn't help at all! You said the king would be stuck if I asked to have Cindra take me to the Shadow Lord!"

"I sensed doubt in him when I asked his decision," Wenyssaya said gently. "I think he will consider it."

Ildric said, "One must tread carefully when trying to manipulate a king. It was a risky tactic, and might easily have blown up in your faces."

Cindra turned to the wizard, "Master Ildric, you knew about the trial in advance. Do you happen to know what will the verdict be?"

He held her gaze for a moment and sighed, "I cannot deny that I looked into the river of possibilities. There is much turning about this moment, Lady Cindra; as there was before your ocean voyage. I fear that things will become more difficult soon."

"But my father is a judge; surely he can sway the king..."

"The king only needs three of the five judges to agree on a conviction," said the wizard. "However... you are guilty as charged I'm afraid."

"What?" Nixy gasped. "I thought you were on her side?"

"Peace, little prince," said the wizard. "It is clear that she did all the things of which she was accused. The king made it clear that it is not the unintended benefits of her behavior that were on trial, but her conduct." He folded his arms saying, "What worries me was the expediency of the trial. There were no Valdakian priests present, neither as witnesses nor counsel."

Wenyssaya said, "Valdak is Justice, and his priests show no favor to highborn or low. Would they not side against her?"

"They would be obligated to make sure that she had representation or at least fair treatment under the law," Ildric said. "This king is playing a dangerous game by omitting them."

The elf maid considered. "Would not the trial be invalid without their involvement?"

"No," he said, "just very hasty and controversial." His eyes were troubled and he sighed deeply.

Cindra studied his face. "You saw," she concluded, "You saw what happens."

Ildric scratched his beard with his good hand. The Eye of Omithys bound in the palm of his silver hand was a powerful relic of divination and made him perhaps the greatest diviner in the world. It came with a heavy price however.

"I have," he admitted as he drew some items from his robe. "I have seen what will most likely happen. Therefore you must listen to me very carefully..."

The judges had deliberated for many hours, with a fair share of impassioned arguments for and against. Finally a decision had been made and they were allowed to adjourn until noon. The count and countess took the time to visit Cindra in her chambers, for her father had grave news for them both.

"The judgment is in," he said, his voice shaking. "I am afraid... we all-" His words faltered.

"What?' Zara was aghast. "Surely not?"

"You all found me guilty as charged," Cindra said.

"No!" Zara cried. "Amon, you didn't!"

Amon could not raise his head, could not look at either of them. His hands shook in his lap, and his shoulders heaved with sobs. "Forgive me Cindra."

"It's alright, mother," Cindra replied, holding back tears of her own. "I forgive you, father."

"How can you?" asked Zara, her voice throaty and raw. "And how could you condemn your own daughter?" She squeezed Cindra's hand fiercely.

"He had no choice," Cindra said. "The king demanded it of him, and there was no doubt of my guilt; only my intentions were in question."

Zara chided him, "But you said that *none* of our household would fall under the Black Eagle's talons!"

"Mother," Cindra said as calmly as she could manage, "It is a test."

"What?" her mother blinked away tears.

"He is testing us, testing our loyalty. Think about it; we have had traitors in our own house. Sir Greenfellow betrayed us over a family feud with Jaron-" she cringed at the way she said his name, so familiar, so protective, "with Sir Jaron Dunlorden. We even had would-be assassins at our own dinner table. How much more careful must the king be? He needs to know we will do our duty, that we will be loyal to the end. That is why I took full responsibility for all the actions of my friends; the Freekirks, Jaron," there it was again, she knew, the unmistakable love in her voice, "they have risked so much for me already."

Amon rubbed his temples, "Do not speak of Jaron Dunlorden, Cindra. I am not so old that I have forgotten what is was like to be young."

She said nothing. There were rumors, no doubt; many were likely true. She was not going to deny that they were very close, that they were lovers. She needn't go into the specifics with her parents if they did not ask. She was just thankful that it didn't come up at the trial.

"But such a test!" Zara exclaimed. "Must we all sacrifice our children to prove our allegiance?"

"He will ask much more of us in the coming months," Cindra said. "Noble and commoner alike will be thrown into war come springtime. Many will sacrifice their sons..."

"But not their daughters!" Zara said. "This is barbaric! Are we to be like the Maanok, slaughtering virgins on the eve of battle?"

Cindra blushed a little, wondering if that title still applied to her.

Zara regained some of her composure and asked, "Why, Cindra? Why did you not ask for counsel from one of the blind priests? It is your right."

The count muttered, "There was no doubt that she did what she was accused of. The issue is whether or not she can be pardoned in light of what has happened. The king may have wanted the freedom do decide without involving them."

"Did he say as much?" asked Zara hopefully.

"The question was brought up in deliberation," said Amon. "These matters were 'too delicate to leave to their dogmatic interpretations,' or so he said."

"But he has offered no pardon," Zara said.

Amon shrugged, feeling miserable, "He may yet... but he fears it will anger his lords and knights. It is no small thing making a girl into a knight, and many will not swallow it. All I know is that he is deciding her sentence now. We will know his mind in half an hour."

"Then you must do nothing to shake his faith in you, father." Cindra said. "Whatever the punishment, if there is to be one, you must abide by it. He must not see weakness in you. He is testing the table before he stands upon it."

The count smiled meekly, looking her in the eyes for the first time since revealing his decision, "I see not all my lessons were ignored."

She smiled in turn before replying, "You and mother must be strong. I might be facing something terrible, but you are both in danger as well."

Cindra was brought before the court at the appointed time, but King Galen was busy dealing with some rather irate members of the clergy. Three men in black robes, the eldest of them ritually blinded by his own hand, confronted the king as Cindra took her place on the dock.

"You cannot try a member of the nobility without proper council!" cried the bent old priest, his wiry beard jutting out from under his hood. "It is the sacred charge of the Valdakian order to oversee all proceedings of justice, especially those with such... such ramifications!"

"I am well aware of your duties, High Arbiter," Galen said frostily, "But the accused confessed her crimes to me personally, and I have the right to decide her fate without your participation."

"But having her own father sit in judgment! A priest could have taken his place and avoided the conflict." The old priest's companions reached to steady him, ready to pull him back if he lurched with too much enthusiasm.

The king was unmoved as he took his place behind

the head table, indicating the priest's assistants should move the old man away. "It is decided. You may tell me afterward if you think I am being unjust."

The priests moved to the edge of the gathered crowd of witnesses, the elder sputtering under his breath. The count and the other judges were excused from duty, leaving the king alone to pronounce the girl's fate.

"Lady Cindra Corrina," said the king in a voice that rang through the hall, "In light of your actions and the aid you have given the crown, I am unable to find a suitable punishment for your crimes. However I cannot grant a pardon, for there are great principles at stake. Also, you have offered to bear the punishment for your accomplices. So be it." He paused, looking about at the waiting faces. "According to the elder traditions of our land, I shall leave it to the gods to decide. You shall face a trial before the elements. If you survive, you shall be considered worthy to bear that which you have sought under false guise. If you are judged unworthy... you shall die."

There was silence as the crowd digested this news, followed by a rapidly growing cacophony of confusion. A trial of elements was an ancient practice that had fallen out of use centuries ago. The gods of the Divine Court were the only ones who ever took interest in the affairs of men, and they no longer interceded; the gods of nature were a part of the world, yet rarely stirred but in wrath. A trial of elements was therefore in the hands of gods who cared nothing for the fate of an individual.

"Highness!" cried the old Valdakian priest from his dusty dark robes, "This is most improper! If the will of the gods is to be known, there must be a Reading! Everyone knows they only speak through omens, not intervention, as they did in the ancient days."

The king turned to the priest saying, "My dear High Arbiter, Portshia is under a shroud of ill omens, in case you haven't noticed. Would it be fair to interpret her fate in the running of rats in the street, or perhaps the buzzing of flies as they circle diseased bodies? No, I will not leave her fate to the readings of these dark times." He turned to the count and countess, who were now standing at their daughter's side, their faces drawn in grief and anguish. "I am told there is an ancient pillar atop the mountain bluff overlooking the sea. I decree that Lady Cindra be taken and bound to the stone for a period of four days."

A collective gasp rippled through the audience. Four days on the mountaintop was just short of a death sentence. No food, no water, and no shelter against the trade winds and summer sun... and the weather had become so unpredictable of late, with choking dust and hailstorms preceding the plague and infestation.

She was no witch! She was a noble lady of a great house and surely deserved better. Still, her crimes were an affront to decency and her family honor, but this... The gathered nobility collectively shuddered at the thought. What could happen to one could happen to all.

Only Cindra did not react to the sentence. The wizard had told her what to expect if the worst befell her. Drowning, branding or exposure were the options he had foreseen as most likely. Ildric had the magic bracelet that had saved her from drowning at sea, but no magic trinkets would be allowed in her punishment. All he could offer was that she would not be alone.

Her parents moved hurriedly to her side, wanting to embrace her, to shield her from unfriendly hands that would pull her away. She had warned them to be strong and resolute before the king lest he doubt their loyalty. To her relief, they did not protest or break down in despair. They each laid a hand upon her shoulder, giving her strength to bear the coming ordeal.

The king leaned on the table saying, "In the first morning light, Lady Cindra will be brought to Tirgrim's Bluff and bound to the stone, to be brought down after sunset on the last day. Until that time, I grant her the comfort of her quarters for the night." He gestured to the guards to escort her from the hall. As they led her away, the king said, "We are prepared to see to our next prisoner. Bring in Maron Theenix."

As she reached the stairs, Cindra caught a glimpse of a disheveled, balding man being dragged between two guards; Master Theenix had not fared well. She stifled a shudder as she saw his bruised and burned skin, his sunken eyes, and raw fingers.

Gods keep you; she thought bleakly, *traitor or no.*

Chapter Nine

Letting Go

Sir Fedrick was looking thin and haggard in his meager quarters in Casselvane Keep. He had listened to the morning's proceedings from the hallway outside his room, stifling his cough in the crook of his elbow. The effort had tired him out, but he heard much of what was spoken. His heart had gone out to the count and countess, and he questioned the wisdom of this young king, so guarded and unreadable, so unlike his tempestuous father.

He also sympathized with his son, though the news that Lady Cindra had been living and training as his squire was news indeed to the old knight. He didn't want to think about what might have gone on between them. *Stupid, reckless boy,* he thought. Or maybe he said it aloud. He couldn't always tell anymore.

Jaron was beside himself with misery and helpless anger as he sat with his father in the cushioned chairs by the fireplace. The evening had brought news to the school of Cindra's sentence, and Jaron had entertained all manner of rash deeds, judging each one as either highly improbable or downright suicidal. He was not in the habit of throwing his life away, but he needed to act.

"What am I to do?" Jaron asked with his face in his hands.

"Do nothing!" Fedrick rasped, grabbing a half-eaten bun from the table and throwing it at his son. "You've done far too much already. It's a wonder the count hasn't seen you hanged. It was bad enough you went and got banished, but you come back..." He was racked by a fit of coughing, "...you come back and put that girl up at the school, sharing a room with her, no less!" He glared at his son, daring him to deny the implications. "She's taken your punishment upon herself, boy. Don't louse it up by doing something stupid."

Jaron picked up the thrown bun and replaced it on the small table near the fire. "She's going to be chained to a rock under the summer sun for four days," he said, his voice quivering. "She could die up there!"

"So what do you expect to do?" Fedrick asked, "Fight your way up the trail to the rock, break her chains and escape over the mountains with her on your shoulder?"

Jaron stammered, "I-I can... I can give her water and food, maybe shade... the guards are only stationed at the base of the trail, so if I can find another way up... I have to do something! The gods certainly aren't going to help. They've all gone."

Fedrick shook his balding head and squinted at his son through the smoke as he lit his pipe again. "You've been a city boy too long if you think that. There are gods who never left, who were always a part of the world and can't be shut out of it. They're the gods of the common folk, the ones who depend on the rain and winds and rivers, the gods of farmers like me."

"The Mother and her Children," Jaron said, nodding, "The Jaydecean Wheel."

"Aye, the Wheel," Fedrick said. "Those are the gods

you might want to pray to tonight."

The Wheel was a symbol of the seven gods of nature. There was Arahn the sun, Lieutrella the moon, Obesh the oceans, Rolona the rivers, Hwessa the winds, Pokaht the rainstorms, and Jayda the World Mother. All were enclosed in a circle like spokes in a wheel, with the Mother at the hub, being both the center and outer circle all at once, all encompassing. Jaron remembered when his own mother told him about the gods of the Wheel when he was a small child. It was one of his earliest memories of the woman who bore him.

"Mother taught me long ago," he said, smiling. "She somehow made me understand how they were all part of a whole."

Fedrick ruminated on his own memories, fuller, farther-reaching, and bittersweet. "When your mother died, we lost the only person who could make you understand anything. She was a woman wise beyond her years, gods keep her."

"She didn't pass it to me, it seems." Jaron said ruefully. "I know I can't interfere with the trial, but I can't just sit back while Cindra dies up there."

Fedrick puffed on his pipe, gazing at the fire. Finally, he spoke into the silence. "When your mother caught the sickness... it was all I could do to keep her alive. She couldn't hold anything down, not even water; I had to wet a rag in the rain and drip it into her mouth, a bit at a time." Jaron looked into his father's eyes, which were still focused on the flame and on a time long past but as fresh as yesterday. He had never heard him speak of his mother's last days, and Jaron had always been too respectful or fearful to ask.

The old man continued, "I sent you to stay at the Grenward farm, to play with their hound's new pups so you wouldn't have to see her like that. It was three days since she took to bed, and she wasted away before my eyes." He drew a ragged breath, "I prayed to all the gods to help her. I prayed to Mother Jayda, the sun and the moon, any who would listen. I prayed to Lelonetha for her mercy and healing, and to Eyorona for the wisdom to know what to do. I even asked Valdak to take me instead, if this was some kind of retribution for my misdeeds... nothing helped, nothing.

"All I could do was hold her hand as she... slowly died. The village priest was with me at the end; he gave her the rites, I'm thankful for that." He looked up at his son with moist eyes full of pain. His lower lip quivered and his throat was tight, and Jaron thought in that moment that his father looked very, very old. "Sometimes all you can do is watch and hope. Pray for her if you want, pray to Arahn to go easy on her skin and Hwessa to keep the winds gentle. Pray for rain so she has something to drink. But you have to prepare yourself, son. People die, no matter how much we love them or how much we want to prevent it. It's simply out of our hands."

Jaron could not accept it, not after all they had been through. On his way back to the fighting school, he revisited all of the wild plans to intervene, to come to her rescue. It was the only way he could calm the anger and pain that threatened to burst his skull.

He could not fight his way up the mountain, which was for certain. He had no doubt that his skill with a sword was superior to any of the men who might stand in his way, but one crossbow would be the death of him. No, he needed cunning to carry out this mission, and cunning was something he was not known for.

The evening meal had ended when he arrived at the school, and the lads were helping to clear the training floor, using wooden swords and brooms to herd rats out of the building so they might be disposed of in the yard. Thankfully no one in the school had come down with the camp fever that was spreading through the city's districts; the plague had claimed almost a hundred lives since the arrival of the rats, though everyone knew it could become much, much worse. Whole armies had been decimated by camp fever, winning in the field but losing on the long march home.

At Jaron's request, Cord and Gavadaire met him in the Master's Hall once the students had finished their evening duties and retired. The fire was lit, the drinks were poured, and they had each settled into a chair before Jaron came to the point of the meeting.

"I intend to do something about Cindra's trial of elements," he began.

"By the gods, you will not!" Cord replied.

"The king, *your* king, has decreed this," Gavadaire said. "Would you commit treason against the crown?"

"For Lady Cindra, yes!" Jaron said with conviction.

"Listen to me, lad," Cord leaned forward for emphasis. "Nothing you can do will help her. Not unless you can fly or become invisible."

"I have a plan," Jaron said. "If I leave tonight, I can climb up to the bluff and camp in the woods, out of sight. I will wait until nightfall to tend to Cindra, giving her food and water."

"Suppose they intend to post a guard on the bluff to watch for such a thing?" Cord said. "And what makes you think you can survive in hiding on a mountainside for four days? No fire, no shelter, and only what food and water you can carry for the both of you?"

"What if you are caught?" Gavadaire said. "What if they look for you here at the school?"

"I don't care if I am caught!" Jaron replied angrily. "Damn it all, she was your prize student, Gavadaire! Don't you want to help her as well?"

"Of course I do," he said. "But she is taking the punishment for Master Cord, his family, *you*, and anyone else who was an accomplice. Is it not best to trust in the gods-?"

Jaron scoffed, "The gods! The only gods who can help her now are the ones who don't care about fate. Wind and rain, sun and moon, if the weather of the last few weeks is any omen of their moods, she doesn't stand a chance."

Gavadaire said, "If there was a way to help her, it is

past. This trial was brief and without witnesses of character. I would have been first to speak on her behalf, but no one asked for my opinion. It is the will of the king."

"He is not your king," Jaron said. "You owe him no allegiance."

"But Lady Cindra of House Corrina does," he replied. "And she has accepted her fate. Let her face it bravely, like the warrior she has become, no?"

"I was going to ask the two of you for your help, your support," Jaron said through gritted teeth. "Now I see you're both too concerned for your own skins-"

Cord stood from his padded chair so fast that it skidded a foot backwards. He loomed over Jaron, his hands balling into fists. "Now you listen to me, Dunlorden. I've tolerated your childish moods and idiotic notions for years. When your little romance with that Deliah woman got you into a duel, did I thrown you out of my school? NO! When you and Lady Cindra got struck by that love spell, who was it that saved your neck? Who took a risk inviting a disgraced knight to be an instructor? Who let you keep the count's daughter in your tender care for two years?" Cord's voice grew louder and his face turned a deeper shade of red with each question.

"I have cut you as much slack as you are going to get. There are bigger things at stake here; *she* knows that far better than you do. If you go charging off to save her, you'll destroy everything she suffers for."

Jaron had been ready to be hit, yanked from his chair, or kicked over. He was thankful that none of those things happened, though he realized too late that he had deserved it.

Instead, Cord stomped to the door saying, "You have two choices. You can stay here and train these men for war, or you can leave tonight and never return. The same goes for you, LuVestra." He slammed the door behind him and was gone.

The two instructors sat in silence for a time, looking

into the fire. Gavadaire finally spoke, "You two are brothers in arms, are you not?"

Jaron blinked, coming back from his thoughts. "Yes, we... fought at Lintheid, in Quivost province in 1111, then in Vale and Vaness later that year."

"A bloody campaign by all accounts," Gavadaire said. "The old king was a ruthless one."

"He was," Jaron agreed, not really wanting to get into a political discussion. "But Cord and I made it through intact. I owe him my life several times over."

Gavadaire said, "My teachers at the Su'Kraal monastery used to tell me that the king god Arathus gave us a great gift in withdrawing from the world. It was the gift of choosing our own destinies. But in doing so, we must rely upon ourselves, our brothers," he paused, "and our sisters."

Jaron leaned forward and stared at him curiously. "Are you saying that I should try to save her?"

Gavadaire returned his look and smiled, "I am saying that she has chosen to save you, and you must rely upon her, if you think you can."

Jaron sat back with a huff. "Have you ever been in love, Gavadaire?"

LuVestra's handsome smile became bittersweet as his bright eyes were cast to the ceiling beams. "Oh yes," he said. "Many times. My first love though, ah I will never forget her."

Her? Jaron thought. *So the Aurilon peacock likes girls...* He knew Cindra would chide him for thinking that way, but old habits die hard.

"I lived at the monastery from the age of six," he began, running his fingers through his thick, blond hair. "I never saw a woman in all that time, until I turned sixteen. The monks brought me a girl from the village; beautiful girl, soft and fair, with hair of fire and skin of cream. I thought she was Selvina herself."

Jaron's mouth was agape, "The monks brought you a girl?" He thought it more likely that they *bought* him a girl, but he didn't say as much.

"Yes," Gavadaire said. "We had such a night as I will never forget in all my days. I was young and eager, but she left me utterly spent. She was my first love, and she is the one I will remember when I am old and gray."

"What became of her?" Jaron asked.

Gavadaire looked into the fire, its light shining harshly in his blue eyes. "After that night, I never saw her again."

Chapter Ten

Tirgrim's Bluff

The morning came too early for Cindra; she awoke in the late watches and was unable to go back to bed. Her nerves were frayed, but at least she had good dreams during her brief sleep. She dreamed of soaring like a gull over the coast, seeing the entire world beneath her as the wind bore her up on white wings. It was a wonderful dream, but waking made her heart sink.

She decided to use the time to prepare for the trial with the items Ildric Finnael had brought her before her sentencing. The first was a salve made of calamine and olive oil, and she rubbed it on her bare skin before donning a simple white linen dress. It was supposed to lessen the burning effects of the sun, or so Ildric said. The salve made her skin look pasty, but she imagined looking pale was to be expected of her this morning.

The wizard had advised against undergarments, saying that she would likely have to relieve herself standing up. That made her balk, but he was just being practical. When she asked if she might wear a dark-colored dress to hide the stains, he said that the white linen would keep her far cooler in the sun. *Besides*, she thought grimly, *in all the old legends, the sacrificial victim always wore white.*

Next, she drank an herbal water mixture from a wineskin that the wizard had prepared, and ate several handfuls of little brown seeds that looked uncomfortably like the rat droppings that covered the city. Ildric explained that these would help her to retain her body's moisture, giving her a better chance to last out the ordeal. She trusted him, but wished he had used magic instead.

She had asked, "Isn't there some spell or potion that can protect me? Something like the bracelet that saved me at sea?"

Ildric and Wenyssaya had exchanged a glance, and the wizard said, "A potion might be possible, but there is no time to make one. As for a spell, what protection either of us could give you would not last nearly long enough. We will not be with you on the mountain, and they will not allow us to cast a spell upon you in the morning. The king is making sure that no one interferes with his *justice*." He said the last word with distaste.

Wenyssaya had placed her painted hands upon the girl's shoulders and fixed her with those beautiful violet eyes. "You *shall* survive this," she said. "You are strong of will and sound of body, and your friends will not abandon you."

She had even made Cindra believe it. *Perhaps it was an elf thing*, she thought.

The light of dawn turned the sky a deep shade of blue that bent to a fiery gold on the horizon. The sun would not rise over the nearby mountains for a few hours, but she would be climbing to meet it. It would be a beautiful day and an awe-inspiring sight, and she meant to enjoy it while she could. She took several deep breaths to calm herself, a technique she had learned from her adopted Galindri father Majii. She slipped on her shoes, tied her hair back into a pony's tail, and sat on the edge of the bed. She was going to survive this. She was ready.

Yet, when the knock came at the door, it made her jump.

There were tearful farewells and somber faces as the castle's population turned out to watch the lady being led away. By then, the news had reached everyone within the castle walls that the daughter once thought lost had returned, and had now been judged by the king himself for crimes against the social order. The king was present, as were her parents, and Nixy and Wenyssaya. Priests of Valdak were there as well, the eldest observing the proceedings with his remaining four senses. The disdain seen on his face was echoed in the eyes of many in the crowd. They either did not know the full chain of events that had led to this, or their loyalty was first to their grieving lord, and second to the king who was bringing an army to their peaceful city.

The journey was thankfully made in secret and under light guard. Had it been a 'regular' punishment, there would have been an announcement, a large procession, and the townspeople would turn out to throw rotten fruit. However since it was widely believed that Cindra was already dead, she suspected King Galen was trying to avoid a public outcry. *He knows my people would rise up and save me*, she thought, then immediately giggled at the absurdity of it. *Desperate wishes*, she mused. Her guard gave her a curious look.

Cindra was in an open carriage with one of the king's men sitting across from her and four more on horseback behind, their purple and gold livery worn publicly now. Their presence was just enough to discourage a foolish attempt to rescue her, but no more.

Jaron, my dearest Jaron, let me do this for you. She

knew he was twisting himself in knots over whether or not to act; his gallantry at odds with what little sense he possessed. She hoped Sir Cord was keeping him in line as he always did. Yet, she desperately wanted to see his face before ascending the mountain. *One last time, love.*

No, she thought. *I shall survive this.*

It was as if the goddess Selvina was playing a cruel joke, letting them fall in love. She imagined the goddess picking two roses from opposite ends of her garden and placing them in a vase, watching them bloom together before returning them to their respective bushes. It would have been kinder if she had let them wilt and die, let them lose their fragrance and fade. *But then,* she thought, *I would have one less thing to keep me strong.*

The small procession made its way across the bridges as the city came alive with early morning striders, shopkeepers and workers. The rats were out in force this morning, taking advantage of the sleeping city before making a partial retreat to the shadows as the humans awoke.

The stench of the canal was stronger than she remembered it, and to her horror, there were bodies in the street. She saw a total of seven along the route, slumped over in doorways, lying in the dark corners of buildings, or laid out on the curb with minor dignity to be buried by priests. They might have been only sleeping, but for the rats. No sleeping man would abide the gnawing of rats. She shuddered and chose to look at the mountaintop instead. *If I survive this, will I ever see that mountain as beautiful again?*

The carriage turned onto the North River Walk and made for the Sea Gate, which separated the city proper from the ancient fishing village that stood since the city's founding. The worn and curving marina was abuzz with activity as the fishermen prepared their boats for the day's labors, and many turned to watch the strange sight as Cindra and her guards rode past on the Lighthouse Trail.

The lighthouse had long ago been rebuilt to accommodate wizard lamps, which were lit nightly by a resident guild wizard. The glow was shielded from the city, but out on the open sea, it was a beacon of hope and comfort. Cindra would not see that light from her vantage, and she needed hope and comfort.

They rode up the trail to the base of the tower, where the path turned and headed back along the opposite side of the rocky spine that shielded the harbor. Before her was a little-used path carved along the wave-beaten rocks, too narrow to accommodate the carriage. The guard across from Cindra stepped off the carriage and helped her down with an offered hand, a grim look on his face. The men on horseback stayed behind as the driver returned to the city, leaving the prisoner and her escort to proceed on foot.

The sea spray misted her skin and moistened her dress, making it cling to her legs as she ascended the steep trail. Her shoes were inadequate to the task however, for the trail had uneven footing and was littered with sharp little rocks. She found herself wishing for the soft, sturdy-soled boots she wore with her Galindri family, but they had been sold when she began dressing as a boy.

They approached a ramshackle guardhouse manned by three of the king's men assigned to watch the passage up the mountain. The men greeted each other with wordless nods, watching the condemned girl with unreadable expressions. While two stayed behind, the third accompanied Cindra and her guard up the mountain path. Tirgrim's Trail it was called, named for the first lord of Casselvane who planned out the first fortifications where Cindra's home now stood, back in the days before Portshia was Portshia, and Tharvus IV of House Wolvert was king, and the land was called Calilaar. In later years, Tirgrim's Bluff became known as a place of endings rather than beginnings.

The climb took the better part of an hour. By the time

they reached the top, they were all out of breath and Cindra was sure she had blisters. Her leg muscles were burning and they had needed to stop a few times, but the exertion had helped to clear her mind.

When they reached the top however, she got her first glimpse of the stone monolith that dominated the bluff and she froze in her tracks. The guards took her gently by the arms to urge her forward, and for a brief moment she wanted to scream and run, but there was no place to go. The path below was the only way up or down, and to the north and east were the taller peaks of the Cassel Range that stretched as far as the eye could see. The sun had risen above the far mountains and bathed the world in a glorious golden light, but her eyes were fixed on the short carved pillar and the shackles hanging near the top. She began to tremble.

"Come, milady," said one of her guards. "Let's be done with it."

They guided her firmly towards the stone, weathered and bleached by the centuries. Her legs almost refused to step upon the plinth, but before she knew it, her back was to the cold stone and her hands were being bound above her head. The shackles closed with a 'clink' and it made her stomach churn, threatening to give up her precious water and little brown seeds. Looking up, she saw they were new and recently installed, fitted for her small, feminine wrists.

"Comfy?" said the other guard. "You let us know when the crows come to pick at your eyes. Just give a yell, and we'll come running." He smirked at her, making her fear turn to anger.

"Leave off," said the first guard. "She saved His Highness in Cordoshome, don't forget that."

"Huh, my own lady wife can pull a bow," said the other man. "Doesn't make her a knight, does it?"

These men are knights, Cindra remembered. All the king's escorts had been knights, though they wore no heavy armor. Their plate mail and great chargers would likely be brought up with the southern army's baggage.

These are men I fought beside in Cordoshome, men I have offended by existing. She didn't feel bad about it, and why should she? Did they feel like lesser men because of her deeds?

When she made no answer to the boorish man, he pressed her, leaning close to her face. "So what say you, milady? *Are* you a knight?"

She leaned close to his face, "Let me down, give me a sword, and we'll see." It was probably not the best thing to say. The knight made to backhand her, but his companion stopped him.

"What are you doing?" He barked, "She's the count's daughter!"

"That doesn't mean I have to take her impudence. You wouldn't last but a minute against me, girl." He spat at her feet but at least he backed away.

The other knight reminded him, "We swore to deliver her unharmed to her fate and that's what we'll do. Survive or no, you think no one will notice if she's been mistreated?"

"Depends on whether or not the beasts get at her." The surly knight snorted a laugh, saying as he departed, "After a few days, you'll wish I'd taken you up on that offer, girl. You'd have died quick. Now, the sun is going to burn your skin and bake your brains, and the crows will have the rest."

I shall survive this, she thought. *I am strong of will and sound of body, and my friends will not abandon me.* She said nothing, but stared at him until he disappeared from view, the sunlight giving fire to her eyes.

The other knight stood before her. "If you survive, do you intend to retain the knighthood our king unknowingly bestowed?"

"I do," she said. "If I survive, it will be because I am worthy in the eyes of the gods." *With a little help from my friends,* she added silently.

"Do not," the man implored. "It will cause dissent in the ranks, and that's something the king cannot afford."

"Is their loyalty and honor worth so little?" she asked, feeling angry and bold. "Would they abandon their king in his time of need?"

"They would abandon their king if they thought him a fool, or if he made a mockery of their traditions," he said.

"My father has not abandoned his king, even though His Royal Highness has set me out to die," she said coldly. "How fragile is the disposition of lesser men."

The knight flinched at this, but gave her an appraising look. As he turned to leave he said, "Gods keep you, lady. We will return at the end of the fourth day, be you alive or no. Farewell." He walked into the morning sun and was gone.

"Perfect day to be out-of-doors," she muttered to herself, defiantly.

The view *was* incredible, now that she took the time to appreciate it. She could see the entire city from here. The castle, the wizard towers, the cathedral, they were all so small. The towers of the Winter Palace, which stood by the mountainside, were not quite as high as she was. Cindra saw all the ships in the harbor, all the people in the market square, and even the little houses and structures of the Outwalls, though she had to strain against the chains and lean far around the pillar. Looking from this height, one could not imagine that the city was plagued with rats, disease, and the occasional undead vemlok. *Perhaps that is why the gods ignore us? Everything looks fine from up there.*

The hours passed slowly as she tried to find a comfortable position in which to stand. Her shoulders ached, the top of her head was too warm, and her wrists chaffed against the irons. She tried to pass the time by turning in place to examine the carvings on the stone, but the words were almost too archaic to comprehend. She could barely recognize one word in ten. *I might not like what it has to say,* she considered.

It was noon when she decided she had to pee. She tried holding it for over an hour, but it became more and more urgent. *I will have to do it sometime, and I'll be here a while*, she thought glumly. She tried a few maneuvers to hoist up the dress a bit, but to no avail. Resigning herself to the futility of her situation, she widened her stance and relieved herself, cringing as the warm liquid ran down her legs. The shame of it was foolish, she knew; she was all alone up here and no one would see her, but she felt shame nonetheless. She was a lady, after all. Worse, the stone plinth did not absorb the puddle or let it run off easily, so she was forced to stand in it. She grimaced and allowed that this was just the first of many indignities to come.

The wind picked up later in the day, cooling her off as it blew away the lingering stench from her puddle. She was sweating now, but not terribly so. The day was hot, baking the stone and irons and making them uncomfortably warm. "I am a lady of the south," she said aloud. "Warm summers are nothing to me." It was only discomfort, not pain. She wiped the sweat from her face with her sleeve, smelling the scent of calamine-laced olive oil on the fabric. "I have some protection," she said to the sun. "You won't hurt me so badly." It made her feel better. She could survive this.

The evening crept up slowly as the sun set over the forest, and the wandering stars could be seen near the horizon. Cindra was exhausted from standing all day; her wrists and arms hurt almost as bad as they had during her sword training and her knees were weak and pained. She had managed to rest by leaning against the rock with her knees locked for support, but now she was paying for it. *I shall have to sleep like this*, she realized.

The night grew steadily cooler, which was a blessed relief. The ocean breeze smelled wonderful as it carried up the mountainside, fluttering the fabric of her dress. She was far above the smells of the city and for a brief moment, she recalled living out in the wild with the

Gatéth-sho'a, sleeping under the stars and living off the land. She thought of Teya bringing home food from the hunt, helping Luka and Haani prepare a meal while Navo played his flute and Majii tended the fire. *That was a happy time*, she thought, and smiled to herself.

The thought of food made her stomach rumble. She had only had those seeds to eat early this morning, and the ache was becoming noticeable. "Three more days," she said to herself. "One day down, three to go." *I shall survive this*, she thought. *I am strong of will and sound of body, and my friends will not abandon me.* But where were her friends now? They were sitting down to a decent meal, probably. Her stomach rumbled again, making her throat squeak and gurgle. Her mouth was dry and she felt tired, so tired.

"Is anyone there?" she called to the night. Maybe the guards were within earshot? Maybe someone had a bit of food or water? "Hello?" No answer, only the sound of the wind and the sea crashing on the rocks below.

Suddenly, an inspiration took her and she felt up for the iron hoop upon which the shackles were secured. She began to pull and push against it with all her might, hoping to work it free. The thought of putting her arms down and maybe curling up on the ground drove her to try all the harder, but to her dismay, the iron would not budge. When she finally gave up, she was weak and all the more sore for it. She slumped, defeated, against the stone, letting her hands drop from the hoop to hang above her head.

Finally, she began to cry. Long, drawn-out sobs soon wracked her body, making her ribs ache, making her throat close up. She felt utterly helpless, totally hopeless and alone. She was stuck here, possibly for the rest of her life, unable to sit, to eat or drink, unable to even lie down to die, and for what? For putting on boy's clothes and learning to use a sword, that's what. It wasn't fair, she had saved lives, saved the *king's own life*, and this was her reward. Her sorrow turned to anger, and her sobs became frustrated wails.

Cindra was shedding precious tears, she knew, using precious energy. *I have to save my water; I have to save my strength...* She gulped the night air, taking deep breaths and letting them out slowly. She tried to relax her aching muscles, tried to stretch and flex in the way that Sir Cord taught at the fighting school. It was difficult with her hands bound, but it helped. She recalled the jeers of the man who left her here, telling her she'd never make it. She would prove him wrong. She would stare him in the eye as he opened her shackles, and she would snap her fingers in his face. She dried her eyes and looked at the heavens as they filled with stars. *I shall survive this*, she thought. *I am strong of will and sound of body, and my friends will not abandon me.* She made herself believe it.

In the city below, lights were being kindled in the streets as the guild wizards made their rounds, lighting the wizard lamps with their magic. The night looked so much darker up here, the way it looked in the wild. She could see more stars now than she had seen in almost two years. Then her eyes were drawn to her father's castle by a flickering she did not recognize. A flame was leaping high from the battlements of the main keep, and for a panicked moment, she thought the ember swallow's aviary had caught fire. Gavagul would not be hurt of course, but if his flames somehow ignited the roof of his enclosure... No, it was a tended fire, she realized. Someone had stoked a large brazier on the roof of the keep, but why?

Hope came with the realization, and she laughed even as she cried anew. *It's for me. They are keeping a vigil. They want me to see the fire and know I am not alone.*

But she was alone. The night grew late and cold as the day's heat leeched out of the rocks and out of her body. She had been resting her eyes, using each leg in shifts to give the other a rest, when the chill ran through her. *Gods, it's cold*, she thought. *I am only wearing a thin dress, and the breeze...* Just then, the wind picked up and blew steadily, penetrating the fabric. She shivered and blinked as dust was kicked up and flecked her face. *The trade winds are weakest in summer*, she thought, *this will pass and it won't get much worse.*

But the wind continued, picking up larger debris and stinging her exposed skin with tiny little missiles. Her dress began to blow upwards, exposing more flesh to the onslaught. She tried to press herself against the stone to trap the fabric, keeping it about her thighs, but her legs were at the mercy of the wind and blowing dirt. Her face was hidden in her arms, yet dust got up her nose and in her mouth. She again recalled the freak dust storm a month ago, on the night she and Jaron encountered that crazy old wizard. If a storm like that came again, she could well suffocate out in the open. The fear that she might not even last the night shot through her, and she saw the brazier on the castle roof flicker and dance in the wind.

Just as quickly as it came, the gust died down to a gentle breeze and did not come again. Cindra felt her dress settle around her ankles and she coughed and snorted to clear her nose and throat. There was little enough moisture in her mouth to turn the dust into mud, but her runny nose was making up for it. Miserable, she went back to shivering against the stone pillar.

The sound of wings caught her attention and she started, wondering if she would have to fend off an owl, or if indeed the crows had come to peck at her eyes. The sound rapidly grew louder until she felt the buffeting of wings above her head and heard the rake of claws on the top of the pillar. *Merciful Mother, what now?*

"Hello, milady Cindwa!" came a light, high voice from just above her head.

"Drahn!" she squealed, "Oh Drahn, I am *so* happy to see you!" She began to cry despite herself.

"I am happy to see you too!" said the dweedragon, as

the corners of his reptilian mouth curved up as much as they could. "I have brought you some water and a bun. It's not much, but..."

"Anything! I'll take anything!" she exclaimed. It was then she noticed the little dragon-kin was clutching a fresh-baked bun in his forepaws and had a small wineskin fastened around his long neck. "Oh, I'm starving and so thirsty!" Her voice sounded rough and cracked, but maybe it was the dust.

Drahn eyed her situation and tried to figure out the best way to feed her. She could reach the bun if he handed it to her, but her hands could not reach her mouth. "Um," he said, "maybe I could climb down... Do you mind if I hold the bun in my mouth for a moment?"

"Not at all," she said, shaking her head. "What's a little dragon spit?"

He began to climb down head-first onto the chains and swung his cat-sized body down to perch on her suspended arms, being careful not to scratch her with his talons or whack her face with his tail. "I am showwy I couldn't be hewe shooner," he mumbled around the bun, "but de shtwong wind made it hawd to fly." He sat on her shoulder and took the bun out of his mouth, offering it to her pinched in his claws. "Caweful you don't bite me please," he said.

It smelled wonderful. Gingerly, she took a bite of the soft bun. *Bliss.* Lelonetha's peaches couldn't be this good. There was just one problem. "Water," she said around her mouthful.

Drahn blinked, looked things up and down to work out the mechanics of the deceptively simple request, and took the bun in his mouth again, stretching his neck to pass it to her suspended hands. He then held the wineskin and worked it free of his neck, pulling the stopper out with his teeth. "Dwink slowly," he said, holding it up to her lips.

The water flooded her mouth, soaking the bread and turning it to sweet mush. She chewed the wet mass a little before swallowing and took another gulp. A little dribbled down her throat, but she didn't care. Drahn helped her until the bun and water were both gone, and he replaced the stopper and climbed back up to the top of the pillar.

"Thank you so much, Drahn. I needed that."

"You are welcome," he said, sounding pleased. "Master Ildwic and Wenyssaya send their wegards, and hope you are not suffewing too badly."

"I think I have not begun to suffer," she said wearily. "I still have to figure out how to sleep like this." She clanked the shackles for emphasis.

"Hmm, that is a pwoblem," he agreed. "Is there something I can do to help?"

"I don't suppose you could open these shackles for me and let me sleep on the ground?" she asked, daring to hope.

"I'm afwaid not," he said glumly. "I never learned the spell to open most locks, just the ones in my master's tower."

"Can't you ... I don't know... levitate me or something?" she asked.

"Oh my, no!" said the little dweedragon. "I don't think such a spell could be done without a spiwit well; certainly not by me anyway." He fiddled with his tail contritely. "Sowwy," he said.

"It was a wild hope anyway," Cindra sighed, "Seems I'm stuck here. Will you be able to return tomorrow, I hope?"

Drahn nodded, "Yes, after nightfall when I can't be seen easily. Master says there are watchers during the day that use spyglasses to make sure you are alone and bound. At night they are all but blind, especially with a horned moon in the sky."

Cindra glanced up at the moon rising high overhead, its crescent shape reminding her now of the horns of a Minozhian bull-man. "Horned moon? I've never heard that before. We call it a waning vanity."

"Why is that?" Drahn asked, interested.

"As the story goes, Tavenji the Trickster found it

difficult to sneak about at night with Lieutrella's radiant face shining so bright," she explained. "So he marked her with a spot, and every year he places a tiny new blemish on her once-perfect face. It's said that she checks now once a month, and the shadow is the mirror passing before her face. Once it's fully covered, it's called a vain moon."

"Waxing and waning vanities," Drahn smiled. "I like that. I shall have to study more about weligions. I have only looked into interpreting omens from the gods."

"Really?" she asked. "How did that go?"

"Not vewy well," he replied. "There doesn't seem to be any weliable way to tell one omen fwom another. Experts disagree on many aspects of the pwactice, and there are many contwadictions."

Cindra snorted a weak laugh, "That figures. The king seemed to think the Valdakian priests would give me a poor Reading with all the miserable things going on in the city. I wonder if that's true." She couldn't imagine she should *thank* the man for sticking her up here.

Drahn considered, "It may be. His Highness is in an awkward position with his twoops marching to Portshia. He has to pwease his nobles and knights by doing something harsh, but at the same time not make an enemy of the count."

Cindra's anger flashed, "Drahn, if you came to plead the king's case to me, you can fly away now."

"Oh no, I don't like it at all!" said the dweedragon, hastily. "It just seems to me... er, I mean, to my master and Wenyssaya... that the king wanted to give you a fighting chance, wather than have your fate decided by a pwiest's omen or pwessure from his nobles." He fanned his wings a bit, making a purple shadow over her face. "My master says that a pwoper twial would take many days to pwepare, and the new southern army will be here by then. Many a knight would hear of what has happened and demand something... extweme."

"Drowning," she said quietly.

Drahn replied casually, "Oh, dwowning is just the twaditional punishment. Death of any kind is an option, and for a noble lady they might have decided to be quick and chop off your head."

Cindra had nothing to say to that. She just stood there, wondering what it would feel like to have her head lopped off. *They say the head lives for a brief time afterward...* She pushed the thought away.

Drahn nervously cleared his throat in the silence. "Um... I guess that wasn't important. Sowwy."

Cindra took a deep breath, but it made her ribs hurt. "It's alright," she said quietly. "How long can you stay?"

Drahn answered, "Until just before dawn. The watchers must not see me leaving."

She leaned wearily against the rock, her mouth already feeling a bit dry. "Thank you again Drahn. I appreciate the company."

Cindra jerked awake in a wash of pain. They had talked of little matters long into the night, and eventually she must have dozed off, her eyelids growing heavier and her body twitching from little spasms, like she used to get after a hard day's training at the fighting school. Now her wrists and shoulders were afire and her ribs hurt so much she was afraid she could no longer breathe. At least her full weight had not been on her arms; her legs were propping her up against the pillar, but her upper body had been dangling like a forgotten puppet.

The sun was almost breaking over the far peaks of the Cassel Range, painting the eastern landscape in shades of purple, and the sky in fabulous gold and gray-blue. The clouds were like an ocean of fire as they fanned out across the distant lands beyond the range, and for a moment she thought of the war to come. *Which will burn, the east, the west, or both?*

Straightening her body and whimpering with the effort, she looked to the top of the pillar. Drahn had left, probably less than an hour ago, leaving no evidence of his visit. So that was their plan, to send the dweedragon with a bit of food, water and conversation. It was as good a plan as any she supposed, and it didn't involve fighting guards or a dishonorable escape that would make her a fugitive. *I shall survive this after all,* she thought. *I am strong of will and sound of body, and my friends have not abandoned me.*

Sound of body. That could change, she thought. *My body might break before this is over.* Her shoulders ached and her wrists felt detached as she moved them in the shackles. Rotating her wrists, she found that her hands were numb and purplish; she tried to raise her arms slightly, letting the feeling creep back into them. That only succeeded in making her shoulders ache more and sent little needles of sensation to pierce her fingers. Her hair was slipping its binding and she could not reach it to pull it back. It would fall loose soon, making her look properly bedraggled. *Little indignities,* she thought.

The sun grew hot, hotter than the day before, and the breezes were barely enough to stir the hem of her dress. She began to sweat in earnest, as the preparations of the previous morning had likely run their course. As the day wore on, she smelled less and less of the olive oil concoction that was supposed to protect her skin, and more and more of her own unwashed, befouled body. The white dress was not so white anymore, and the tops of her feet were growing pink from the heat. The stone plinth became a small torment to stand on; it was so very warm. The shackles grew even warmer still, making her already tortured wrists burn as the skin became raw.

The fire on the roof of the keep was still burning; a pillar of white smoke marked it amid the sun's glare. As she haggardly surveyed the cityscape below her, she saw what seemed to be a haze of dust in the far west along the coast. *Perhaps it was the king's southern army, arriving at last? What will they say when they learn of my trial?* she wondered. *Will the barons and knights from the western lands refuse to march if one little girl is granted a knighthood?* It seemed so ridiculous she almost laughed, but the pain in her ribs made that unwise. *How had I slept like this anyway?*

For once, she began to wonder why she had carried things this far. She had always believed herself to be in the right, and it was her society that was wrong. She knew the history of her father's people; the Norsicans from across the Emerald Sea had fierce women among them, and some were even queens in their own right. How had everything changed so much?

She began to suspect it was the gods' fault. Norsicans and *Gatéth-sho'a* alike worshiped the Jaydecean nature gods, taking totem animals for themselves as they hunted the lands and fished the seas. Then the old Celvestrian Empire brought the Divine Court to its conquered lands, ruled by the King God Arathus, Lord of Order. There were five male gods and only three females in the Divine Court, hardly a fair balance to her mind. The goddesses governed the softer aspects of culture, such as mercy, wisdom and love; and the male gods dealt with the more practical matters of law, war, wealth, and justice. Then there was Tavenji the Trickster. *Why was there a trickster god among them anyway?*

It seemed to Cindra that inequities came with the gods of society and order, the gods her people had been made to accept in ancient times. It was just as well that they were silent and absent, since they probably would have killed her off by now.

"Merciful Mother," she said weakly, "If you have any care in this world, grant me some relief."

She waited... and waited.

"Arahn, be merciful," she said towards the sky. "They say the gods of the Wheel never left, but rarely listen. Hear me now, please?"

But the sun shone warmly as ever.

Briefly, she wished that Jaron would come up the trail to rescue her, but she pushed that thought from her mind. *No, my love, I am here in part to save you from punishment. Besides, I am not a damsel in need of a knight. I am a knight in need of a drink and a good meal, and perhaps a little shade.*

The day wore on and she suffered in silence. She thought she had known thirst yesterday, but she had been wrong. She thought she had known hunger yesterday, but even in the depths of winter, while living with the *Gatéth-sho'a*, she had had a little to eat each day. Smoked venison jerky sounded *so* good it would have made her mouth water if she had the moisture to spare. She thought she had known pain yesterday, but again, she had been wrong. She had born injuries at the school, even hurts that had made her bedridden for a time, but at least there had been a bed. Now she felt like a broken old woman, aching in her joints and wishing for death just a little more each hour. *I shall survive this*, she thought. *I am... strong.*

A passing shadow caught her attention, and she felt the cool gust of wind as flapping wings buffeted her, and the sound of claws scratched the rock above.

"Drahn!" she exclaimed, invigorated but worried, "I thought you could only come after dark, but I'm glad..." she looked up, not into the purple-scaled face of the dweedragon, but the dark eyes of a black crow. It cawed noisily as it inspected her. "Oh..." she said. "Come for my eyes, have you?"

The crow took a few tentative steps along the edge of the pillar, inching towards her bound hands. She rattled the chains but the bird only hopped back a few paces, cursing at her in its hoarse, throaty voice.

"Shoo!" she said, but the crow only ruffled its feathers. "Damned bird," she muttered, leaning her head against the stone. "Try for my eyes and I'll bite your beak off."

But the crow was more interested in her hands. Once she had stopped watching it, the black bird leaned down and pecked at the tender flesh between her fingers.

"Ow!" she cried, and shot her hands up to grab the creature, clutching its body as it beat its wings and scratched to get away. Finally she released it and it flew off, only to perch on a nearby rocky outcropping. Cindra examined her bloodied hands and cursed, "Balkon's balls, that's all I need." Blasphemy was not her way, but she was angry and pretty sure the war god wasn't listening.

Evening was approaching too slowly and the breeze had picked up, warm though it was. The merciless sun cast long shadows on the red clay-tiled buildings, giving shade to the people in the busy, sun-bleached streets below. A heat shimmer danced in the distance, making the castle and the tops of many buildings look like insubstantial phantoms; spirit constructs that could not quite coalesce in the world of elements. Cindra's eyes were stinging from sweat, but the inside of her eyelids felt grainy and rough, so she kept them open. Arahn was dying his daily death, and she would watch him fall.

The clouds had all burned away, leaving the sky clear for the sun's last rays. The wandering stars were out again and shining brighter than their more reliable cousins, taking no part in constellations and engaging in their own special dance. *That's me,* she thought, *a wandering star. I follow my own path...* She watched the sun shrink to a half-sun, like the one on her family crest, and watched it diminish even further until it was nothing more than a dim crescent of its former glory, red and feeble, like an ember that flies from the fire and cools on the hearth stones. Then it was gone, leaving a mournful sky of pale yellow and deepening cobalt.

Drahn will come soon, bearing food and water, she thought with a slight smile, feeling her lips crack. *Two down, two to go.*

She examined her hands in the failing light. The scratches were deep but had mostly clotted and baked in the sun. *The wounds should be cleaned, and Drahn is only bringing a little water*, she thought grimly. *Maybe he could make two trips?* She had no idea how much effort it took for the little creature to fly up here carrying water and bread, but it couldn't hurt to ask.

No sooner had she thought of this than a howl broke the silence of the bluff. Somewhere off in the low mountain heights, another wolf answered the call, then another. Soon a chorus of wolves greeted the night, sending a cold shock of terror down Cindra's spine. *They are far away. They are not close. They do not smell my blood.* She repeated this in her head until the howling stopped. She had not anticipated wolves. There were no wolves for miles around the city, or so she had thought.

The mountains east of the city were a different matter, apparently. The Cassel Range was estimated to be some thirty to fifty miles wide between Portshia and Kenric, the nearest eastern province. That left a lot of room for wolves all along the length of it; wolves that had to hunt their prey, seldom as lucky as to have it chained to a rock, unable to defend itself. Memories of her encounter with the dread-wolf two years back made her begin to tremble and she had the urge to soil herself. *I will do so because I have to, not because I'm scared*, she decided. *Maybe the smell will scare them away.*

She had learned to lean as far along the pillar as she could, so she wouldn't have to stand in her own filth, but it did nothing for the smell. She wondered if her reek would drive away Sir Jaron if he came up to rescue her, or if Drahn would stay no longer than he had to. The thought of being brought back down the mountain like this made her ashamed again, but what else could she do? There was no lady-like way to be chained to a rock to die.

The wolf howled again, and this time it seemed much closer. The pack sounded off in the distance, answering in kind. Cindra looked around the pillar frantically, her eyes open wide to take in all the light she could. The moon had not risen yet and the stars were bright, but not nearly bright enough to benefit human eyes. Her ears pricked at every sound; a breeze rustling a bush, the sea-sounds of the waves below, the far-off evening song of nestling birds. She studied the rocks behind her, looking for a likely approach. *Where would they come from?* There was a steep drop to the city-side and a large craggy rock face behind her, but the area near the head of the trail was a bit more passable and led into the maple trees. *There*, she thought. *They will come through there.*

Surely the guards heard the howling, but they would not help her. The mean guard said the beasts would get her if the sun didn't. Being eaten by creatures was all part of the deal in a trial before the elements. *Think, think, think*, she thought. *How do you scare off wolves? Shepherds did it, surely. That's what shepherds were for. Did they make noise? Wave their arms? What?*

Shadows moved in the undergrowth. The wind from the ocean blew in gusts and made the treetops sway, made a rustling whistle that masked what lurked beneath. They were close, she was sure of it. She felt a chill that had nothing to do with the coming night, felt desperation such as she had never experienced before. *There was nowhere to run, nowhere to hide, nothing with which to defend myself.* She strained her eyes toward the shadows, willing *something* to appear and end the suspense, a husk of hares, a gaggle of geese, a scurry of squirrels, anything but wolves.

Yellow eyes met hers, glowing faintly in the half-light rising from the lighthouse off the edge of the bluff. Another pair appeared, and another, and another. Four wolves loped out of the darkness, pausing to watch her as they spread themselves apart, the largest with his tail upright and his ears pricked forward.

Cindra tried to feel brave but her knees started shaking, already weak as they were, and turned to jelly. Her insides felt watery and loose, as if they might spill out at any moment. Her breathing became quick and shivering, and her heart thumped madly in her chest. *Four! They can surround me!*

The wolves made their way towards her, taking a few steps at a time before stopping and sniffing, making little whines and growls. They were all gray with dark markings, but the low light made them look almost black. She could see the whites of their teeth and their lolling tongues when they paced to encircle her.

Deciding it was better to be bold than dead, Cindra shouted with all her breath, "Get away! Go, GO!" She was pleased that it startled them, watching their stances go wide and ears go flat. But it was only for a moment. She screamed again, a wordless cry of defiance as she rattled her chains through the iron hoop that secured them. They glanced nervously at the lead wolf, which backed away several paces. The others followed suit. Cindra kicked at the air, but the wolves only watched her warily.

Maybe they're as scared of me as I am of them, she thought. Then she thought again. *Who am I kidding?*

The wolves were moving in and this time her shouts and kicks were having less effect. They circled her more quickly, confident that she was all bark and no bite. Cindra was having trouble keeping them all in sight, since the pillar was too wide. She heard a deep growl and a bark, and she tensed. The wolf to her left made a false dash at her, stopping just a few yards away. She wanted to run, but only flinched to the side. Another wolf feigned a lunge at her right and Cindra shrieked. The big wolf before her rushed in, snarling. It got too close and Cindra pressed her back against the stone, lashing out with her foot. She hit the wolf in the nose, making it back away and snort, but the other wolves were moving in around her.

From behind she felt hot breath on her calf, felt a painful pressure. She pulled her leg away just in time, but the wolf caught her skirt in its jaws and began to tug, pinning her against the pillar. To her horror, she found her legs trapped, barely able to kick at the other three now moving in at once. She reached up and grabbed the iron hoop for support and kicked behind her like a mule, her heel impacting the wolf's front teeth. The hem of the dress tore and she was free, but the big wolf before her lunged in and planted its paws on the plinth, going for her belly. She swung her knees up to block it, hanging from the iron hoop for a moment, the pain in her arms overridden by fear. The wolf bit her dress instead, tearing it and pulling her forward. As the others rushed in at her legs, she swung both feet up and kicked the big wolf under the jaw, making it yelp and release its hold.

She was now a flurry of legs swinging this way and that, missing her targets as they stayed just out of range. *They are going to wear me down and kill me once I can't fight back*, she realized. There was a throbbing pain in her calf where the wolf had nearly had her, and it hurt when it supported her weight.

I am going to die.

She began to scream.

The sound was unlike any she had ever heard before, part shriek and part roar, like a savage beast. It frightened her, and frightened the wolves as well, who froze in place before darting away from the pillar. It was getting louder... and closer. There was a rush of air and the beating of leathery wings, and Drahn was there on top of the pillar, screaming that horrid cry at the wolves, making them dart back towards the trees.

Looking up, Cindra could see the dweedragon poised to pounce, his wings fanned out and his horned head shaking with menace. His scales were a deep, angry red, and his chest puffed out as he panted a throaty growl. But the wolves had tasted blood and refused to flee, so he launched himself at them, screaming again and beating the dust before him. The wolves tore off into the trees and the dweedragon followed, his roars echoing into the mountains.

Cindra began to laugh and cry simultaneously; her

body trembled from the after-rush of combat and the strength left her limbs as she slumped against the carved stone. All of her pains came back to the forefront, the wound on her leg screaming the loudest. In the dim light she could make out a dark stain on her dress and feel warm blood trickling down her leg. Her shoulders would no longer support the weight of her arms, and her arms were next to useless anyway.

Her hair had come loose and hung like shabby curtains on either side of her face, blowing into her eyes and mouth in the gentle breeze. Her sobs were reduced to shallow, shuddering gasps, as the black night got blacker. She could not see the stars and the lights of the city were dim and fading. Confusion and exhaustion swallowed her as weak knees buckled and tortured shoulders strained, and with a vague sensation of all-encompassing agony, she hung there from the chains, unconscious and uncaring.

When she next raised her head, the crescent moon was high in the sky and the night was cool and breezy. She could only breathe in painful gasps, and realized that her legs were hanging folded and useless beneath her. When she tried to move, she heard a voice by her feet.

"Don't move pwease," said Drahn from somewhere below her left hip. "I am twying to heal you." She heard the fabric of her dress rip, felt a stab of pain as it was pulled away from her wound, and listened to the strange words the dweedragon spoke in a low, un-Drahn-like voice.

"*Han nith ravesh, nivendiis. Han nith ravesh, nivendiis. Han nith ravesh, nivendiis...*" he repeated over and over. Cindra noticed a golden glow coming from her feet and strained her neck to look down. The dweedragon had his fore paws on her wound and the glow, like the light of a fairy bug, rose around his stubby fingers. She felt tingling and spreading warmth up her leg that soothed her somehow. It was like her calf was out in the sunlight on a cold day, soaking up the heat. Then there was an odd pinching and prickling, like the bites of many tiny ants. Then the glowing stopped and the sensation subsided. Drahn walked around the plinth and looked up at her, his big reptilian eyes reflecting the pale moonlight.

"Can you stand, milady Cindwa?" he asked.

She grunted and strained, pushing her stiff legs to work again. Finally her feet were under her, the muscles of her thighs protesting. She stood with a little help from her arms, and tried shifting her weight from one leg to the other. Everything hurt, but the throbbing pain in her calf was gone, now only a memory. "It... it's fine," she said. "I didn't know you could heal. Thank you, Drahn."

He nodded his head before climbing the carved pillar like a cat, gaining claw-holds on the ancient symbols etched into the stone. When he reached the top, he said, "It is one of the few spells I can do wather well, or so my master says. I noticed your hands are scwatched and have bled."

"A crow," said Cindra. "I was stupid and grabbed it." Her voice was hoarse and it hurt to speak.

"Hmph," Drahn exclaimed, "Cwows are almost as bad as pigeons. At least they don't coat their nests in their own dwoppings. Fiwthy cweatures, pigeons."

He began his chanting again, reaching down and laying his paws on her hands. The mad itching and burning they had suffered subsided and ceased, and she wiggled her fingers experimentally. They were not even as sore as they had been after supporting her weight for so long.

"How long was I unconscious?" she asked him.

"About five hours," answered Drahn. "I didn't want to leave you until I was sure the wolves were gone."

"Leave me?" she asked. "Aren't you going to stay all night?" *Perhaps I smell worse than I thought.*

"Master saw your pwedicament in his cwystal and dispatched me immediately, so I left without your food and water. Once I was sure the wolves had gone, I went back for it." He held up the wineskin with a little smile and began to uncork it. Helping her eat and drink was more difficult than the night before since she was so much weaker, but the provisions were even more desperately needed now.

When she had regained her strength and voice, she thanked him again and asked, "What kind of spells does Master Ildric teach you?"

Drahn corked the wineskin and said, "Anything he can. We have been twying to find something I am good at."

"I thought dragon-kind had magic in their blood?" she said.

"We do, we do," he replied, "But I don't know how to use dwagon magic. Learning to use human magic is like... Wenyssaya says it's like a bird learning to fly by watching men try to build wings. She doesn't say this in fwont of Master Ildwic of course...""

Cindra nodded, "Your egg, I remember now. You were separated from your mother while still in your egg, and you didn't get the proper instruction."

"Yes," Drahn said sadly. "Wenyssaya said-" he gulped, appearing unsettled, "she said there were some evil men who twied to bwing about the end of the world by killing all the dwagon-kin they could find. They... they misinterpreted an ancient pwophecy and..." he sniffed back tears.

"I'm sorry Drahn," Cindra said, chiding herself for bringing up such a tragic subject. She wished she could give him a hug just then. He seemed to need a hug. Unfortunately she was in no position to do so.

He sighed deeply. "She says the Ilvayiin put a stop to them, whoever they were. But the damage had been done to many, many clutches."

"Maybe they were Llomaakittes?" Cindra rasped, wishing for more water.

"Wwomaakittes?" Drahn exclaimed, his eyes growing wide. "That might expwain it. They are cwazy enough to do anything to end the world."

"I still don't understand why anyone would want such a thing," Cindra said.

"They worship Chaos itself," Drahn said. "I am sure their weasons would make wittle sense to you or me."

Cindra really wanted to change the subject. Memories of being surrounded by the vile priests came back clearly now; she feared that in her weakened state of mind the memories would become her reality, and she might forget she was safely tied to a rock on a mountain. "You said Wenyssaya understands your situation?" she asked. "Could she help you learn magic?"

Drahn replied, "She knows little about dweedwagon magic, but she did say that I need to find my element."

Plenty of those up here, she thought grimly, but she asked, "What's that?"

Drahn replied, "The first four dwagons were cweated to be gods of the elements of earth, water, air and fire. Their offspwing were bound to those elements, and took their power fwom them."

"So," she reasoned, "The elements are earth, water, air or fire? That sounds easy enough."

"That's not all," he said, "A dweedwagon must become one with that element somehow. I have twied a few things, but... I am afwaid to do something wrong." He sighed and fiddled with the end of his tail, "Also, there are more than four elements. The dwagon gods made new kinds of dwagons, forming new elements that became part of the world. Fire and water make steam, water and wind make ice, earth and water makes... mud, I suppose? According to Wenyssaya, dweedwagons must undergo some kind of cewemony or witual or something. But I don't know how."

Cindra understood, "And you don't want to try anything reckless because it might not be the right element."

Drahn nodded. "I don't want to dwown or burn or be buried alive. It's a conundwum."

Cindra imagined it would be a terrifying choice, to 'become one' with a roaring fire or a pool of deep water, even if you knew it was what you were meant to do. She thought again of the time she almost drowned at sea. If not for the magic bracelet Ildric had given her, she would have become one with the ocean. She did not envy Drahn his quest to find his element, even if it would make him stronger somehow.

"I'm pwetty sure it's not fire, since I got burned," he said. "And I spend lots of time flying just in case it's air, but..."

"You got burned?" she asked. "Was it on accident or on purpose?"

He answered a bit sheepishly, "I, eh, stuck my tail into a hearth fire and singed it a bit. It didn't hurt at first, but after a few seconds it certainly did."

"Oh Drahn," was all Cindra could think to say. What else was he liable to try? She pitied him as she imagined the little creature testing the limits of his endurance, never sure if it would lead to his goal, endangering his life even, with the hopes that he might pass some unknown test and be rewarded with a new power. She hoped for his sake it was worth it.

Cindra stayed awake to say farewell to Drahn and watch the sunrise. She was so very weary and weak, in spite of the food and drink he had brought. She had gone too long without regular meals and it seemed what little she drank she would sweat away within the first few hours of daylight. She had been exposed to the sun and winds for only two days now, though it seemed like a week. Southern summers could be cruel, and the month of Hwessmoth worst of all. Though named for the goddess of the winds, it applied more to Celvestrian seasons than those of her native Casselvane. Still, there was the sea breeze, so it was not as bad as becalmed weather. *It could always be worse,* she told herself. *Besides, I am a lady of the south.*

The gulls were out in force today, flocking along the

rock faces to the southeast and screaming at each other. She could see all along the eastern coast as the mountains bordered the Crimson Bay with its sandy red shores and little fishing villages. To the west she could see the masts of her father's fleet anchored off the shipyard a few miles from the city. They were no doubt undergoing refits and preparations for winter and the war that would follow.

Beyond the shipyard she saw a cloud of dust rising again, closer this time, following the Red Coast Road. A dust cloud of that size could only be made by the march of a mighty force, probably with wagons and riders on the cobblestones and footmen off to the sides to avoid treading in all the manure. Perhaps it was not beyond the shipyards, but closer? The more she watched, the harder it became to judge the distance. Things were a bit blurry today.

The sun climbed to its zenith and the weather grew hot and muggy. Clouds like a thousand giant sheep moved in from the sea as the day wore on, and she felt her dress clinging to her body as every inch of her skin became warm and moist. The crow had returned and brought friends, but they rarely perched on her stone pillar, choosing instead to walk around its base or circle lazily far above. She wondered what the observers must be thinking, seeing all the crows on the bluff. She hoped her parents were not among them, looking through a spyglass. The brazier on the castle roof was still being tended, though it gave her little cheer.

I might survive this, she thought; *if I stay strong of will.* Being sound of body was of little help now, since it felt like the very life was being sapped out of her by the heat and humidity. She no longer had illusions of snapping in the guards' faces when they came for her, and no pithy remarks or arrogant attitudes were left in her now. She would be grateful if she were conscious to greet her rescuers, whoever they might be. No doubt they would have some water and food for her, and perhaps a litter on which to carry her down the mountain. She was looking forward to it now, and would count the hours till sunset.

Some part of her brain reminded her that her trial would not be over today, but the day after. She begged to differ, but that other part of her brain was insistent. *This is the third day*, it said. *One more night and one more day, and only then will you be freed.*

Nonsense, she thought. *Drahn has come three times... or was it twice in one night? He told me but I can't remember...*

It was so hot, so very hot. The stone burnt her bare feet... when had she lost her shoes? *Probably all that kicking at the wolves*, she thought. *They took my shoes, damn them.* But they hadn't really. Looking around, she saw a shoe lying on the ground nearby, a crow pulling at the laces. It was just out of reach, and even as she stretched out to grab at it with her toes, the crow pulled it farther away.

"Shoo!" she croaked at it. But the crow didn't listen.

Was it the same crow that had scratched her? She couldn't tell. It probably was, since it was stealing her shoe. *It's trying to get back at me for grabbing it*, she figured.

"Shoe," she mumbled. "I'll call you Shoe." She looked around at the other crows perched on the rocks behind her. "And you two are going to be Left Eye and Right Eye." She snorted a laugh and her ribs throbbed for it. "But don't start feasting till I'm dead."

She closed her eyes, leaning her back against the pillar and lowering her head to sleep. She came to as her body began to slump and hang painfully, refusing to let her rest. Had it been minutes? Seconds? It was impossible to tell.

She tried to regain her feet, but her legs trembled at the effort, refusing to support her. Helpless and weak, she just hung there and suffered, letting her legs rest. Breathing was difficult and painful, and her gasps became shallow when she breathed at all. The air was thick and sweltering, and it felt like she was inhaling steam from a cook pot. Only the smell was not that of a cooking meal, but of days of sweat and filth and misery.

A pounding began in her head that got worse as the day wore on, the pain making her nauseous and sick. She heaved several times, but there was nothing in her stomach. The contractions made her ribs throb and she gasped huge gulps of air to appease her burning lungs.

I want to go home, she tried to say, but the words required breath and too much effort. *I don't want to die here. I don't deserve this.*

"No one ever gets what they deserve," said Shoe, looking at her with his black crow eyes. "I wanted your eyeballs, but you went and named me Shoe."

She blinked at the crow near the foot of the plinth, wondering why he hadn't spoken before. "Crows can't talk," she said, or thought she said it. She could no longer be sure.

"And girls can't be knights either," answered Shoe. "What were you thinking?"

"But I did well at the fighting school," she replied. "I did so well, everyone said so..."

"Yes, that's nice." Shoe retorted, "You had everyone fooled, but now the gold cat is out of the bag. Do you think the world will change just for you?"

"I... I..." was all she could say.

"Caw!" said Shoe, and he nipped the flesh of her ankles.

She twitched at the pain but was in no condition to stop him. *I will survive... I am strong of will...*

"I wouldn't count your mind among your assets right now," Shoe said; Left Eye and Right Eye flapped down to join him. "Your body however, that's another matter." They began hopping around her feet, picking at her sunburned skin and squawking noisily.

"Drahn... where is Drahn?" she asked the air. "My friends..."

"Mmm," said Left Eye around a piece of skin, "The dweedragon won't be here till dark, remember? We'll have eaten our fill by then and be in bed."

Black shadows crossed the ground as more winged visitors arrived for the meal. *A whole flock of crows,* she thought. *No, that's not right... what do they call it? Ah yes, it's a murder of crows... a murder.*

They were all around her now, pecking at her feet and legs, pulling at her dress. More were descending, as the cawing grew louder and angrier. Black beaks nipped at one another for the choicest position and black wings stirred the dusty air. She felt pecking at her hands and beaks pulling at her hair. All she could manage was a few desperate kicks to scatter the birds, but they returned soon enough. Blood trickled from the wounds, running down her arms and ankles. *They are murdering me.* She wept silently, helplessly, with not enough moisture for tears.

One black bird landed just beyond the plinth with something in its beak. The dangling object glittered in the sunlight as it hopped forward, sparkling blue like a sapphire. It hung from a finely wrought chain of silver and sent shards of light dancing over her dress. The other crows turned to look with interest as the newcomer dropped the amulet on the plinth.

Then it opened its beak and spoke in a deep, hoarse voice, *"Cimnan-diis!"*

The effect was instant and dramatic. The blue gem flashed and the crows screamed and fled, including the one who delivered the amulet. Suddenly she was alone, her limbs throbbing with dozens of little wounds. She chanced a look around and saw some of the crows perching on the rocks behind her or in the trees above the trail, but none were closer than a stone's throw away.

What was that? Cindra wondered, *more talking birds? No, birds can't really talk... can they?* She remembered Gavagul, the family ember swallow, and how it could deliver messages in anyone's voice. *Oh... perhaps they can. But was Shoe really talking to me, or did I imagine it?*

She decided it did not matter. They were gone and

she was alone again, bleeding, thirsty, delirious and alone.

Cindra had been fading in and out of consciousness for a time, she knew not how long. It seemed to her that the world was growing dark and the harsh shadows were disappearing, but it was not nightfall yet. At some point the clouds must have rolled in and covered the sun, though the heat of the day was not lessened. Looking out across the sea, she saw darker clouds looming over the horizon, smearing the line between water and sky.

She tested her legs and rose with some effort, the exertion making her sick to her stomach. Once she was standing again it became a bit easier to gulp the air, but it hurt sorely. *If I have to hang like this much longer,* she thought, *I shall suffocate.*

Flies buzzed about her body, crawling over her wounds. She felt seasick standing up, but she would not be off her feet again. *Not unless I'm dead,* she promised. Her tongue cleaved to the roof of her mouth and felt unfamiliar as she moved it about; it was so dry, like a piece of soft hide. It took great effort to turn her head around and survey the landscape.

The crows were still at a distance, she was glad to see. The amulet was glowing softly at her feet, and she wondered whom she had to thank for that. The vigil fire was burning atop the roof of the keep, and beyond she could see the gathering of an army across the outer canal way. Tents of many colors were being pitched upon the banks and along the road, and there was a great milling about of men and horses. The top of the western wall was lined with spectators watching the host make camp.

Cindra wanted to be among the city folk and listen to them talk, wondering if they were afraid or anxious or angry. She wanted to hear the soldiers too, as they discussed the coming winter and the battles they would see. She wanted to be anywhere but where she was.

Just one more night, she thought desperately, *and one more gods forsaken day. I don't know if I'll survive this. I am broken and befuddled, and my friends...* Her mind wandered over the past few days, back over all the little favors she was thankful for. *My friends have done all they can.*

Darkness fell with languid ease, the gray of day turning to a charcoal evening, and then eventually to a black, veiled night. A chill came with the darkness, almost unnaturally fast, robbing the air of its hammering heat. A fog rolled in a few hours later, the cool mists caressing her like a lover, soothing her tortured skin and blanketing her in a gentle glow. *It's the glow from the lighthouse,* she thought, and then she noticed the soft blue radiance at her feet as it faded and flickered. *That's the amulet that keeps the birds away. I almost forgot about it.* She reminded herself to thank Ildric Finnael once she was free.

Free...

A flapping of wings disturbed the air and she thought of Drahn, with his nightly food and water. Instead she saw a black bird silhouetted against the glow of the lighthouse, fluttering about as it tried to find her in the gloom. Finally it landed on the plinth, squawked at her once, and took the amulet in its curving beak.

"Thank you," she said as the creature flapped away towards the rosy glow of the city.

She had not noticed it until now, the light about the city; it had become a common sight but for the fog. The mist gave every lamp a faerie glow, a soft luminance that joined with its neighbors, making the whole expanse below her into a warm and magical landscape, painting it in a way it could never be seen from below. The streets became the strands of a spider web, heavy with morning dew that caught the early sunlight. Each wizard lamp shone as a tiny moon, each open flame flickered like a star, and their light was a warm blanket cast over the rooftops.

"I should have come up here sooner," she whispered

to the light. "I should have come here long ago."

Had she done so she knew, the pillar would have been nothing but an ancient curiosity; just another part of the landscape as she viewed the beauty that was Portshia on a foggy night. There had been so many nights like it, and she had always thought them gloomy and something to hide away from. She had been a fool.

Wings stirred the air again, and this time it was Drahn, sweet little Drahn with his cargo of life about his neck and clutched in his fore claws. He landed on top of the pillar.

"Milady Cindwa, are you alwight?" he asked fearfully. She wondered if Master Ildric had told him she was dying. He would know, wouldn't he?

"I'm fine," she croaked. She hadn't used her voice to speak to another being for a while now, and it sounded like the raspy grating of Sir Fedrick Dunlorden, Jaron's aged father.

"You are not 'fine' milady," said the dweedragon as he uncorked the wineskin and climbed down the chains to perch on her arms. The weight of him, little though it was, made her flesh ache. "Dwink this, slowly now..." he held the skin to her lips and watched her, worry showing in his large reptilian eyes. His pupils were dilated in the low light and it made him look rather adorable. She smiled and a bit of water ran down her chin. "Ooops," he said. "Careful, milady."

Her tongue felt like a dried sponge as the water flooded her mouth, expanding and soaking up the moisture, her cheeks tingled and her gums ached as the liquid swirled down her throat. It was as if she was a snail in its shell, waking and revitalizing after the first rain. It would not be enough, she knew. The next day's sun would beat it out of her mercilessly and bake her like the fresh bun she was about to enjoy.

Drahn climbed the chain with the empty wineskin and retrieved her bun, carefully working his way down to feed her.

"I am glad the waven came when he did," he was

saying. "Wenyssaya made the amulet in only a few minutes! It was impwessive."

"Raven?" she said as she chewed. "Wenyssaya's?"

"Yes," Drahn said. "His name is Navithwi, and he is a wascal. Luckily he can follow directions and speak command words, so he is good for something." Drahn climbed back up when she had finished eating. "Wenyssaya created the amulet to ward against animals, so it would even keep wolves and bears away."

"Bears?" Cindra murmured. She hadn't even considered bears.

"Well, mostly crows," he said reassuringly. "I am certain there are no bears about."

She gave him a questioning look, pleading and hopeful.

Drahn said, "I could scare away a bear, if it came to it... but I am not sure I could do it more than once. I am loud but not vewy dangerous."

She tried to smile, but her lips cracked, making her wince.

Drahn changed the subject. "Master Ildwic says the next day will be cloudy with a chance of wain, so there will be water aplenty!"

She nodded at the news. *I might live after all.*

"Also," he said, "it will be dark and foggy, so I can stay with you through the day."

This made her smile for true, making her lips crack painfully, but she didn't care. "I will have a chance after all, with you here," she said faintly. "Yesterday I had only crows to talk to."

"Not vewy good conversation, are they?" he joked.

"They said nothing nice," she whispered, "Shoe told me girls couldn't be knights..."

Drahn gave her a worried look from atop the pillar, wishing his master were here to help. He examined her ravaged hands and arms, clucking his tongue at the damage the crows had done. "I will make sure your wounds do not fester, milady. But my master says I must leave some evidence of the damage so people won't become suspicious. He will heal you pwoperly when you come down." He began to chant and mend the deeper wounds, shielding the glow with his wings.

After he finished with her arms, he moved down to her bloody legs. These wounds were far more numerous and some had become infected from the filthy stone plinth, and Drahn was glad for the coming rain that would wash everything clean. He wrinkled his nose but did not complain about the smell, for he knew she couldn't help her condition. He wondered if there was a spell to remove foul odors, and he resolved to look it up when he got back.

"Talk to me, Drahn," Cindra said. "I need to hear a voice."

"What do you wish me to talk about?" he asked.

"Anything," she replied weakly, "Tell me more about dweedragons."

"Oh," he said, straightening. "I shall tell you what I know fwom experience, but there is much I don't know about our histowy and culture."

"That's fine," she said. "It's all new to me."

"Vewy well." He focused on his pronunciation and began proudly, "Dweedragons are an ancient branch of the line of elder dragons who once ruled the world in a time long before the Ilves. Most of the lesser dwagon-kin died off, never to be seen in the world again. The mightiest dragons succumbed to the Great Sleep, perhaps to awaken one day. No one knows for certain.

"However, there was a line of dragon kind that retained the learning and wisdom of the elder days, though they were much lesser in stature and power. My ancestors were the last generation of eggs before the Great Sleep, learning all their parents taught them in the shell. But they did not hatch, not for many an age. When they did, they were small and weak compared to their mighty sires, but they were the heirs to the elements and scholars of an age long gone."

He cleared his throat, "Ehem. It was around the time of the First Ones when the Dweedragons awoke and hatched," he continued. "The world had changed, the mountains had arisen and rivers had carved out valleys, and all the animals were new to them, but the First Ones were the most like them in thought and wisdom."

"First Ones?" Cindra asked, "Elves?"

"Yes," Drahn answered, "They were called the *Damvayiin*, the First People; later *Ilvayiin*, the People of Light. They became friends of my kin, whom they named *Dwimathii*, New Dragons. The Dweedragons shared the ancient stories and wisdom, and taught them much about the elements and practical magic. At least, this is what I learned from Wenyssaya."

Cindra craned her neck up, "Is she a First One?"

"Oh no," said Drahn. "She was born only a few hundwed years ago, in the Blackwood Forest."

"Few hundred," Cindra remarked, "well-preserved."

Drahn blinked at her. "The Ilvayiin do not age like humans do," he said. "According to her, the eldest of her people are hale and stwong, and when it is their time to die, they simply sleep and do not wake up. Only then do their bodies begin to fail."

"Not immortal?" Cindra asked, using only necessary words.

Drahn shook his head, "Only the First Ones and their next generation, the *Damfayen*, were immortal, if that is the word for it. With each generation, their power diminished and the call of Alhanna came sooner. Now they are but shadows of their fore-bearers... much like me."

All Cindra could manage was a shake of her head. She didn't like it when Drahn was down on himself. She thought he was wonderful.

After a few moments, she gathered the strength to ask, "Are the First Ones all gone?"

Drahn said, "The First Ones all left for Alhanna. Many of the younger generations remained, including the ones who fought with Kraal against Orthicus. To my knowledge there is only one of the *Damfayen* with us, and he is Nixy's father."

It took Cindra's addled mind a few moments to grasp what that revelation entailed. Nixy's mysterious sire was one of the firstborn of the elves? How old did that make him, and what kind of power had he passed to his son? Cindra remembered another story Drahn had told her once of the Sorcerer Kings, born with great magic in their blood, who had ruled vast empires in ancient times. Had their time come again in the form of the street urchin who had stolen her purse?

"Nixy... a Sorcerer King?" she asked it softly, lest the world hear her.

Drahn nodded slowly, "Yes, he could be one day. They were the children of the Damfayen and the newly awakened race of humanity. Wenyssaya says they were born to fight a war against evil."

"What?" Cindra gasped.

Drahn lowered his voice, as if the darkness and the fog were listening, "They were called the *Vylas*, and they were terrible cweatures born of the dark god Llomaak when he defiled the World Mother. Thankfully, the *Vylas* could not breed, but their numbers were vast and they lived as long as the First Ones. The humans had many names for them, but one of the oldest recorded languages of men calls them *Guadim T'drall*."

Cindra recalled Nixy telling her about the troll, the 'Guadim' that nearly killed him, and her blood ran cold. *Gods above and below!*

"They were made to bring chaos to the world, and the Ilves were not numerous enough to fight them," Drahn said. "The Dwivayiin, the humans, were not strong enough, but they had great numbers and bred so much faster."

Cindra's question came between shallow breaths, "Elves... bred with humans... to make soldiers?"

Drahn fiddled with his tail, "Not exactly... They were their children after all. But it is not very diffewent from what people do today. People send their childwen off to fight..."

"But... children aren't bred to fight!" she said with a hoarse voice. "We want peace for them..."

Drahn considered, "But there are so many wars, so very many."

Cindra did not have an answer for that. Now that she thought about it, if she had been born a boy, she would have trained as a page and later a squire, someday to become a knight and a lord. Martial training was given to all noble boys for the sole purpose of fighting and leading others in war. It was something she wanted so badly that she had gotten herself chained to a stone pillar to die for it.

Feeling the fool, she hung her head and sighed. It was true; wars were commonplace in the world, from as far back as history recorded. Her father once said, 'War is how we make peace when all else fails.' She had never asked what he meant by 'all else.' Maybe humans acted the way they did because they had such short lives and so little patience?

Drahn took her silence as anger. "I didn't mean to upset you, milady," he said.

Cindra raised her head, "You didn't. I've been thinking..." she sighed, "First I wanted adventure... to fight our enemies... But now I think... I want to avoid this war."

He folded his wings close and looked down at her. "What do you want to do about the reason you're here, about a knighthood?"

She looked past him at the billowing darkness overhead as distant lightning lit the clouds beyond the mountains. "I am not going to suffer through all this... and not claim myself worthy," she said. "But I won't fight... under the king's banner. I will ask to be made... knight-errant."

Drahn cocked his head, "What is that?"

She answered, feeling stronger, more resolute, "It means I will be without a lord... wandering... finding worthy deeds... like the stories."

Drahn scratched his chin, "I have never heard of a

knight-errant, but then again I don't keep twack of such things. Do you think the king will appwove?"

Cindra smiled, making her face ache, "He can make me a knight... then tell me to get lost."

Drahn nodded, "That makes sense, I suppose. Let us hope the king will keep his word and make you a knight for twue."

Cindra could only agree silently.

The night passed quickly as Drahn told Cindra about the ancient tales of the Dragon Gods, the rise of greater dragon-kind, the lesser dragons and their descendants, and the upheavals and changes wrought upon the world in that longest of ages. By the time the dark shroud of night began to lighten into a gray foggy morning, Cindra figured she knew as much about the Age of Dragons as any scholar outside of the Old Empire.

What she found most interesting was that human tales of 'dragons' in the modern age were only stories of encounters with lesser dragon-kin, little more than savage beasts with animal cunning. She shuddered to think what a real dragon of old would be like, radiating power and possessed of a frightening intellect. Drahn was a 'diminished' dragon and he was as intelligent as anyone she had ever met. She learned he could recall anything he bothered to commit to memory with perfect clarity. He was a born scholar, and could keep track of a treasure hoard to the last copper as well.

The cool evening had been a blessed relief, and helped to ease her suffering greatly. When morning came she was no longer sick and woozy, and Drahn's spells had managed to ease her aching limbs. The water was not enough, for she was still dry and parched, but the promise of rain was keeping her spirits up.

The lights below winked out one by one as the spells on the wizard lamps expired, making the entire city vanish as if swallowed by a cloud. It was wondrous and ominous all at once, and Cindra was unsure how to feel.

There was something very disconcerting about the thick fog, though it kept her comfortable. She wanted to sleep in the cool damp, enjoying the lack of sunlight, but she knew if she sank down and hung by the arms, she would never wake again. Drahn could not lift her if she suffocated, and it took all her strength just to stand leaning against the pillar.

As the day wore on they talked of little matters such as city gossip, the goings-on in the Tower of the Silver Moon, and the habits of Master Ildric. It was impossible to tell the time of day, for the city was still shrouded from view but for the faint light of the vigil fire. Rumbling thunder could be heard getting closer, preceded by the entire world going from gray to pale white. Drahn would flinch with every distant flash.

"It is only thunder and lightning, Drahn." Cindra said to comfort him.

"Lightning and thunder," Drahn corrected her. "And it is not 'only lightning.' I once saw a pigeon get stwuck by lightning; one moment it was sitting on one of the spires of the cathedral, and BOOM! All that was left was a woasted mess and burnt feathers. And the thunder... it was so loud, it shook my insides!"

Cindra imagined a flying creature might fear the lightning more than a groundling, so she conceded his point. "Well, it's not very close, so there is nothing to fear."

"Says you," Drahn replied obstinately.

Later the rains came and Cindra opened her mouth and let the clouds fill her. She hadn't had so much water in days, and the rain was cool and refreshing, washing away her stink and blood, and cleansing the pillar and the plinth as little rivers formed and flowed off the edge of the bluff.

But it was not just a gentle shower; the rain increased in intensity and became cold, pelting her skin with large drops that soaked her to the bone. The dress was plastered against her body and her hair fell heavily in her eyes, doing little to keep the rain from spoiling her vision. It was easier to keep her face low, since trying to drink would only invite water up her nose to choke her.

Drahn was not faring much better as he huddled beneath her legs, taking what shelter he could under the hem of her dress. His little wings were gathered tightly about him and his tail curled close around his feet as he peeked out at the onslaught. His plum-colored scales had shimmered to a deep purple as his mood soured, making him look almost black in the colorless hues of the storm.

"This is not good," he said, trying to be heard over the cacophony.

"Oh, I don't know," she called over the noise. "At least there's no chance I'll fall asleep."

Drahn mumbled something she could not hear, and the rain poured on. Squalls blew about her, making the raindrops fall sideways for a few moments before dying down again. The howling of the wind and the din of the downpour drove all thoughts from her mind as she shivered and shook, her skin growing numb with the constant assault. There was a brief reprieve for at least an hour, during which time it sprinkled lightly, then it started all over again.

Rivulets ran from the mountain behind her, washing sediment and debris past the stone plinth to pour down the trail and over the edge of the bluff. Drahn began to worry as the flow approached the top of the plinth, threatening to wash him away. Finally he climbed up the pillar just as the water reached the girl's feet, and he perched on Cindra's hanging arms, face-to-face with her, using his wings as a shelter.

She managed to talk past her chattering teeth, "You don't have to stay, Drahn. You can go back down." She really didn't want him to leave, but she didn't want him to suffer either.

Drahn shook his horned head as the rain played upon his leathery wings like a drum. "This is not good weather for flying," he squeaked. "I doubt I could find the Tower of Sight unless I cwashed into it."

Lightning flashed and cracked overhead, arcing across the sky in a forked chain of white fire many miles long. Drahn whimpered and huddled close, burying his head in Cindra's neck as one wing folded on her face like a damp washcloth. She felt so very bad for him, but at the moment she couldn't breathe.

"Drrn," she mumbled through his wing, "Merv yer wng, ah cnd brth."

"Sowwy," he said, sniveling. He tried to hold his wings up but he was shivering as badly as she was.

The fog cleared slowly as the rain wore on, but it was not a comforting thing. Now they could see the full fury of the heavens as the storm broke over the Crimson Bay and swirled over the city. *This is not natural,* Cindra thought with growing dread. *This is the work of that mad old wizard, or worse.*

The sky was so dark that there was no sense of the time, but it felt like hours had passed in the cold, drenching torrent. For all she knew, it could be nightfall at last, and someone might already be on their way up the mountain to free her. Drahn was just as uncertain as she, being preoccupied with his misery and terror. His body was warm against her skin, but his shivering and whimpering were heartbreaking.

Braving the rain to look out over the city, Cindra's heart skipped a beat as she took in the sight. A huge dark maelstrom with sides like an inverted funnel was descending slowly, ominously from the turbulent skies, large enough to swallow the city in its black maw. It widened as it sank, the mouth of a horrid colossus of smoke and ash.

She imagined she could hear the screams of the terrified people below, echoing the soundless shriek in her own mind. The vision was so bizarre, mind-boggling, that all she could do was shake her head in disbelief. This was the stuff of nightmares, the wrath of the gods or the end of the world.

No, she mouthed silently. *No, no, no, no...*

She could almost hear the monstrous cloud start to

roar deep in its heart, as bolts of lightning rippled across its mass like the veins of some living creature. Drahn sensed her alarm and peeked out from under his wing, beholding the gathering of the living storm. He screeched in panic and leaped upon the chains binding her wrists, wanting to take flight to somewhere, anywhere, as long as it was away from the dark, twisting throat of the tempest.

Lightning flashed from the clouds to strike the forest, igniting a tree on the far side of the river where the army had camped. Another bolt struck the cathedral spires, its blinding light slashing a blue streak across Cindra's vision. Yet another bolt hit the Tower of the Silver Moon, arcing down the copper-shod edifice with hundreds of greedy fingers as it raced to the ground. The sound was deafening as peals of thunder beat upon her like a drum. She screamed, helpless to do otherwise.

Drahn was clutching the chain and shaking with terror as the thunder rocked the air, each peal louder than the next, each striking like a blow to the heart that threatened to freeze it in mid-beat. Cindra reached up to hold him, her own fears mingling with his as they watched the nightmare unfold upon their home. She was about to cry his name when her world became light and fire, and every nerve screamed in unbelievable agony from her fingertips to her toes, and the poor dweedragon stiffened and grew hot in her grasp as the deafening sound of thunder crushed her consciousness into oblivion.

Then at last there was silence.

Chapter Eleven

Astrellaris

It was a poor joke, but Ildric Finnael recalled it every time he entered the impressive building. *How can you identify a wizard's tower? It gets nothing but stares on the outside, and is nothing but stairs on the inside.* Nowhere was this truer than of the Tower of the Silver Moon, the headquarters of the Order of Astrellaris. Little more than a meeting hall and library, it was nonetheless the most famous site in all of wizardom, if such a word existed.

The exterior was shod with copper plate which had long ago turned to a greenish patina. The wide base tapered elegantly to a narrow middle, before broadening into the upper meeting chamber two-thirds of the way up the tower. It narrowed, rose, and broadened again at the summit, where the library was housed. The edifice was topped with an enormous globe of polished copper that was enchanted to mimic the phases of the moon.

While the exterior was a marvel of architecture and magical engineering, the interior was fairly ordinary. The main lobby at the base of the structure had a high vaulted ceiling and fine accommodations, where wizards could sit in quiet comfort and discuss matters both great and trivial. In its center was a spiral stair that climbed thirteen stories to the circular meeting chamber, which was Ildric's destination tonight.

He greeted some of the familiar faces he met in the lobby, mostly apprentices, servants, and wizards concluding last-minute business before the meeting. He walked to the base of the stairs, spoke the words of command inscribed on the banister, and invoked the spell of ascension. An intangible breeze lifted him and he rose upward, floating inches above the polished wooden steps.

It took little concentration and effort to maintain the spell since the tower was built on a spirit well, where magic flowed in a powerful stream from the earth itself. There was a time when he refused such conveniences, fearing they would make him soft; as it turned out, time itself conspired against him, weakening his knees and making his body miserable if he taxed it too much. So the little indignity became a much-needed luxury, and he ceased to complain.

"Good evening, Ildric," said a reedy voice from above. Grand Master Horamus Orellus was leaning against the railing, resting from his ascent spell; even in this place of power, magic took its toll on the ancient fellow.

"Good evening, Horamus," Ildric said. "Fine weather we're having, is it not?"

"A rare respite from the heat," he agreed, "although it has set my joints to aching. I think rain is coming soon."

"It is," Ildric said as he disappeared around the spiral. "Rain and more, if I am not mistaken." He continued his ascent as the venerable grand master regained his composure, preparing to follow.

Ildric arrived at the top of the spiral stairs in the

middle of the meeting hall. The room was surrounded by tiered seating that allowed everyone a view of the central podium, and half of the benches were already occupied. Wizards of all ages sat within, from fresh-faced initiates in their twenties, to wizened old men with long, white beards. Every member of the order who lived within a few days ride had turned out for this meeting, and more were sure to come in the next weeks. A matter of great import had come to light since Lady Cindra's trial. In truth, Ildric had predicted it long before, but now people were listening.

"Master Finnael," said Ravilus Tage in greeting. The man's long, gray beard and wide-brimmed hat gave him the look most people associated with wizards and scholars, and Ildric wondered if he cultivated that look on purpose.

"Master Tage," Ildric said, taking a seat near him, but not too near. "How are your experiments proceeding?"

"Promising, thank you," Tage said. "The material at hand is not ideal, but it is the most cost-effective. If a crossing is ever to be made, we must acquire maps of spirit wells along the island chains, assuming such wells exist."

"The Minozhians would know, although I doubt they would be inclined to share." Ildric said.

Tage made a grimace of a smile, and turned away.

Grand Master Orellus arrived at the top of the stair, signaling an end to trivial discussion; the wizards all stood as the elder climbed the final steps and crossed to the podium, which was encircled by a brass railing. Once he reached the center, the ancient wizard raised his bony hands, closed his eyes, and chanted the benediction to call the meeting to order. His voice took on the cadence of a priest at mass, "Radiant Lady of Mysteries, shed your light upon secrets unseen, guide our steps on the path to knowledge, and grant us the skill to work wonders in your name. *D'athe Domos.*"

"*D'athe Domos,*" the others intoned.

Upon ending the benediction, the elder wizard's

reedy voice dropped all hint of ceremony and he began speaking as if to a class of errant students. "Now, I think we all know why we are here tonight; recent events have been nothing if not ominous. There are omens for a blind man to see, and most of us have indeed been blind, myself included. The only man who gave us any warning of these impending events was our own Arch Mage Finnael, though we chose not to heed his warnings."

Ildric nodded slightly to the mention, taking no pleasure in the moment. After all, being right about the ending of the world was nothing to celebrate; he would have much preferred to be dead wrong.

"If I may, Grand Master," interjected Tage, standing to speak. He straightened his purple robes and folded his hands before him, "None of us doubt Master Ildric's abilities, or the power of the artifact he carries. What was questioned was his interpretation of non-scriptural prophecy. We cannot doubt that ill times have befallen us and the testimony of the count's late daughter-"

"Begging your pardon, Master Tage," Ildric cut him off, "but the Lady Cindra has not yet completed her trial upon Tirgrim's Bluff, and it is a bit early to declare her dead. That ordeal ends tonight."

"As you say, Master Finnael," Tage conceded. "Her testimony alluded to the Dark Heart's return, despite being based on a dream-memory conjured by an elf witch. Such an occurrence might account for recent events, or they might not. Surely our task is to find the truth of the matter, not simply rush to the most convenient conclusion?"

"What other conclusion did you have in mind, Ravilus?" asked the grand master, looking out from under his raised, bushy brows.

"Surely, I do not know," Tage said, "But the Dark Heart? This... this *testimony* of hers might be nothing more than a story the lady heard, or a fear placed in her mind by any number of people." A general grumbling began among the attendees.

"Any number," Ildric muttered, knowing exactly which singular number Tage meant.

Tage sat down and another wizard stood to speak.

Fildwin Gaddisen was a man of late-middle age with a thin frame, and his robes hung from him as if they were on a coat rack. He said, "I see little evidence of the Dark Heart's involvement in recent events, aside from the suspect testimony." This remark led to caustic burbling. "*Unless... unless* one takes into account the prophecy that Master Finnael has been so roundly chastised for quoting. The non-scriptural nature of this prophecy is not up for debate, but the relevance of it is staggering in light of certain revelations." He gestured in the direction of the castle, "It is reported that a scion of an elf lord is living in Casselvane Keep! A scion of a deathless ruler-"

"That is not the wording of the prophecy," exclaimed another wizard, this one a large, bald fellow with a stylized beard. "It is misquotes and half-understandings that lead to such conclusions."

"Then by all means," said the old grand master, "give us the proper recitation of the text, if you please, Master Mattock."

The large fellow stroked his shaped, trimmed beard, cleared his throat, and recited,

"The Blood Divine returns from distant lands
And deathless ruler once again shall hold
The providence of life in mighty hands
As dark events will thrice again unfold.

The scion then must into danger leap
And take the shard of heaven to contend
With seed of bedlam in creation deep,
Sending one or both to meet its end."

Master Mattock said, "As you can hear, the stanza pertaining to the deathless ruler is separate from that of the scion. However, they have always been assumed to be one and the same; Kraal, in the most common reading." Sensing no interruption, he continued, "The Blood Divine has been alternately taken to mean Kraal, or the Dark Heart itself; Kraal being the son of the King God Arathus, and the Dark Heart being made from the blood of Llomaak, according to the oldest legends. Since Kraal was the last known being to hold the Dark Heart after cutting it from the body of Orthicus, The first stanza pertains to him."

"Allegedly," said Tage.

"Most likely," said Mattock. "The 'scion' and the 'shard of heaven' again refer to Kraal's status as the vessel of holy blood-"

"Possibly," Ildric said.

"*Quite* possibly," Mattock emphasized, "Hence, the prophecy of Kraal's return."

"But you are all missing one tellingly absurd point," Master Tage cried, waving his arms. "Lady Cindra's testimony was that the scion was said to already be in Portshia! Does anyone here think that Kraal the Great, Kraal the Conqueror, *Kraal himself* is in our fine city this very moment? Has anyone noticed him sitting in a tavern or walking through the market? Has he presented himself to the archbishop, the count, or the king?"

Grand Master Orellus, tired of standing, removed himself to one of the benches and said, "Calm yourself, Master Tage. Your point is made without the use of additional theatrics."

"Except," Ildric said, stroking his beard, "my esteemed colleague is assuming that the scion of the prophecy and the scion mentioned by the priests of Llomaak are the same person." All eyes turned to Finnael as Tage cast him a frustrated look. "After all," he continued, "if the Dark Heart has returned, they would not see it go to one who would destroy it, but to one who would use it to bring about the end of all things."

"Then we are back at the start!" Tage exclaimed.

"No," Ildric said, "we simply do not possess all of the necessary information."

"Have you searched for the Dark Heart, Master Finnael?" asked a younger man from the upper tiers.

Ildric turned to the voice, unable to identify the speaker. He replied, "To do so is to court madness. It is a manifestation of chaos, an artifact of greater power than any studied by humans, elves, or their mixed offspring. To attempt to seek it with divination magic is to open a door into your mind through which any manner of insanity might pass."

There was a pause, and the voice said, "So you haven't then?" Laughter passed around the room, thankfully breaking the tension. Ildric could not help but smile. *Rascal*, he thought, *reminds me of me.*

"What do you recommend, Arch Mage?" asked Master Kell, one of the tower's ward masters.

Ildric shrugged, "Supplement the Dead Watch on the cemetery, be ready to aid our professional colleagues in the Casting Guild, listen for rumors, and don't panic. There is little we can do unless we learn more about the Llomaakittes' plans, which is unlikely."

The tower swayed ever-so-slightly, silencing the room. Though its magical construction kept it stable under otherwise impossible conditions, the edifice was not immune to the power of the wind.

"It would seem the storm is picking up," Ildric said. "I have some concern for the lady on the bluff; I wonder if we might adjourn for the night?" he asked.

"There is nothing you can do to aid her, you know." Tage said. "You were forbidden from using magic to protect her, so I do not see what difference your absence will make."

Ildric glared and said, "I do not plan on using magic while she is on the mountain, but her time is up in under an hour, and she will no doubt require magical aid if she has survived."

"I am certain the count and countess have thought of that, Arch Mage. She is their daughter, after all." Tage said. "Is your continual presence there so vital that you cannot see to your duties in the Order?"

Lightning struck outside and thunder rolled across the skin of the tower to punctuate the rebuke.

"Is your lack of interest in her well-being due to your involvement in her trial, or have you always been so callous?" Ildric replied harshly. Another flash of lightning glinted through the small windows and the thunder was almost immediate, causing many to jump in alarm.

"That will do!" called the elderly grand master.

"I will not have my actions questioned in this manner!" Ildric declared. "Had I not become involved in the first place, she would be long dead!"

"Listen to him!" Tage called as the thunder rumbled outside, "Ever chasing his own glory!" He rounded on Finnael, pointing his finger in accusation, "Master Ildric, it is not your place to act as the hand of fate, intervening when and where it suits you! You have duties here, and you shall not ignore them, not unless the gods themselves come down and say otherwise!"

With that, lightning struck the tower, raising hair on heads and chins, and charging the air with the sharp smell of ozone. The lights glowed brightly, and then dimmed, and a flash lit the center of the room, racing about the ceiling and raining onto the podium like white liquid fire. It crashed and dimmed, coalescing into the figure of a man upon the floor. He was naked, pale, and struggling to raise his head from his prone position.

When he finally did, he looked up into the eyes of the stunned men. He brushed his platinum blond hair from his eyes, scratched behind one of his long, pointed ears, and smiled meekly.

"Er... Hello!" Tavenji said, and he began to retch. An acorn bounced onto the podium floor.

Chapter Twelve

Beyond Dissent

Braeden Khrim watched from the shadows as the last of the conspirators filed into the map room. His master, Duke Manon Wolvert, had commanded him to observe the proceedings from a vantage point in the upper gallery where he could see the faces and body language of the seven attendees. Four of them had arrived several minutes apart, flanked by bodyguards and aides who were now standing at a distance, well out of the circle of light that shone upon the large map painted on the floor. Two had arrived in very short succession, and Khrim made note of that. The lords of Deltovane and Alvavane walked with more assurance than the others; they had often been observed talking in private since arriving at the palace, and they had likely just finished another conversation. *They have made exclusive plans as I predicted,* Khrim thought with a touch of satisfaction. *I shall have to learn what those plans are.*

The Aurilonian ambassador was the last to arrive, and Khrim watched the man closely. He was tall and blond like so many of his countrymen, with a neatly trimmed beard and immaculate clothing of lavender velvet and yellow silk. The man wore a long-tailed hood wrapped about his head like a hat, fanning out in a brilliant cockscomb of indigo and gold, which he removed with a flourish upon reaching the gathered guests. The others nodded their heads in response to his bow.

Duke Wolvert gestured to the ambassador, speaking in a rich, clear voice that carried easily to Khrim's ears. "I believe you all know Lord DuDavadorn, ambassador of His Royal Highness King Brahnus of Aurilon."

The ambassador gave a charming smile and said in a thick accent, "It is a pleasure to see you all again my lords, my lady." He took his seat, relaxing easily into the cushions.

Duke Wolvert leaned forward and steepled his fingers. His hair was wavy and black with white at the temples, and receded from his high forehead. Thick, wild eyebrows jutted over stern and creased eyes, which were blue-gray like a storm cloud. A thin beard lined an angular jaw and his cheeks were sharp and sculpted, with pale skin pockmarked from a childhood illness. When he spoke, it was with the authority of regal blood.

"War is upon us," he began, stating the grim news with calm composure. "The king's army has arrived in the north, and is now but a few days' march from the border of my lands. There is also word of a southern force being assembled, which has likely already reached Portshia to harry our flank from the Yanell Foothills." He stood and smoothed his orange doublet embroidered with the red wolf of his house. Taking up a polished cane of black walnut with a wolf's head handle, he drew their attention to the map upon the floor, gesturing to the area between the Calione Mountains and the Cassel Range. "This will be one of many battlegrounds on our path towards independence. It is a natural choke-point, so we must dominate here."

Leeman Jamiston, the Baron DeWensic, spoke first. His long flaxen hair and beard were braided and thick, and his shoulders were broader than the chair in which he sat. He was dressed in a doublet and hose of simple earth tones, with nothing but a gold ring and brooch to adorn his person. "I expect my lands will be hit first to ensure the flow of their southern supply. They will have to take Odex, which is but a garrisoned town and not well defended. From there it is only a three day march to Wensicton or the city of Kenric." He pointed to the painted castles and towns on the map as he spoke, scowling beneath his golden eyebrows. "We will be hard pressed to keep them from crossing in force."

DeWensic was grim and pragmatic, Khrim knew. Leeman had become baron at a young age upon the death of his father and brothers in a campaign into central Aurilon. They had not wished to fight against their cousins, but the king had called them to service and it would have been treasonous to deny him. Their loyalty had cost them their lives, and Leeman took a hard lesson from it.

Wensic was the breadbasket of the eastern kingdom, but harsh tariffs on their exported grains had driven the province into near-poverty. Like much of the east, Wensic had come to depend upon trade and good relations with Aurilon, and marriage alliances had bound them by blood. Leeman's wife and the wives of his sons were from various Aurilonian families. However, those ties were now strained because the king of Aurilon believed *himself* to be the ruler of his own country rather than the Cordobals of Calilon, who had forced the previous kings to pay homage.

Braeden Khrim preferred the Maanok way, where

rule was determined by who was left after all the killing.

The duke nodded saying, "All contingencies must be prepared for, but it is my opinion that the southern provinces are not King Galen's goal. I believe he thinks this insurrection will end quickly if he moves against us here in Ahrnok."

Khrim watched the others, looking for reactions. Baron Kalavek was unsurprised, but Countess Sulund was visibly relieved. Lords DeWensic and DeKenric looked doubtful.

Baron DeKenric cleared his throat to speak. The man was tight-lipped and hard, with steel-blue eyes and sandy hair, thick upon his head and face. A deep scar ran along his jaw, puckered and twisted. He was dressed in a mail shirt and tunic of deep blue, with breeches of black beneath. Leather wrist guards and high boots completed the martial look that so suited Drom Evenast, the contentious Baron of Kenric.

"If they seek to cross Yanelleen province, they will have to fight for every mile," he said. "My forces can be dispatched to burn the sheep lands and flood every town and castle west of the pass with refugees." He leaned forward and boasted, "If an army comes east on the Casselvane Road, they'll be hard pressed to make Kraal-Dromah before next summer! We can slow their advance through the foothills and keep them occupied."

Countess Sulund gave the baron a cold look. "Lord Meldon Hurnwaerd has remained neutral all this time, yet you would sack his lands at the first sign of trouble?" She shook her head saying, "It is possible the king will try to take Kraal-Dromah from the north and *our* lands from the sea. You remember the sea, that large patch of open water on our southern borders?" The baron scowled at her as she went on, "I fear we must see to our own provinces first, lest they decide to take us a piece at a time. We are fighting a defensive battle, despite what Drom Sheep-Slayer believes."

The baron snarled, "If the Great Basin will have any

security at all, it will be with Kenric steel and Kenric men! Kenric and Delving castles are the strongest in the east and have never been taken, and no invader could hold the lands between the Cassel Range and the Spine without vanquishing us first!" He thumped his fist upon the arm of the chair, as if hammering truth into his claim.

Khrim watched the exchange closely, observing the famous enmity between the lord and lady of the Gayles river-lands. Kenric was upon one bank and Sulund was upon the other, the provinces existing in a state of constant antagonism for the last hundred years. Now the two noble houses had produced their most strong-willed personalities at the same time. Drom Evenast was a battle lord, and Anessta Volden was a diplomat, though she rarely practiced her skills with her neighbor. Lord Drom made his home in the iron-rich foothills, while the Lady Anessta lived on the river mouth to the sea. They were earth and water, one immovable and the other constantly mutable, and when they met, they made mud.

"We are fighting a defensive war, to be sure," said Pellas Wenword, the portly Baron of Kalavek, "but we must be sure we are defending the most vital stronghold. If we stay within our own walls, we cannot meet the Loyalists in the field with the proper force." He sat deeply in his chair, stroking his jowls with the pudgy fingers of one hand while the other rested on his ample belly. He was dressed in a fur-lined doublet and thick woolen hose, with a gaudy, floppy hat resting at what he likely thought was a rakish angle, but it only made him look like a cake that was losing its frosting.

"So says the Shield of the North!" scoffed Baron DeKenric. "What do *you* have to fear upon your own borders, save for an invasion of furdeer from the Peningrand, or perhaps a pod of whales beaching themselves on your shores?" Baron Kalavek blanched and pursed his lips, but had the good sense to let the insult slide. "*We* are on the front lines and have much to lose if we try to meet them in the field," added DeKenric. "Better to let them spend their strength on castle walls while we move in and cut off their supplies."

Kalavek snorted, "A moment ago you wanted to march out and stop them! Now you want to wait behind castle walls?"

DeKenric curled his lip in a deadly smile. "You must have a candle's worth of wax in your ears if you heard that. I proposed to slow their advance and cut their supplies while they march to Ahrnok or some other stronghold. Unless they march on Kenric, *I* will be in the field against them."

Khrim watched Baron Kalavek as the fat lord wrapped himself protectively in his cloak. House Wenword had long been vassals of House Wolvert and had always come to their aid in force. Kalavek was a small province and ill-suited for sea trade in the frigid Bay of Kraal, but their lands were among the most peaceful in the realm due to the utter lack of enemies in their little corner of the world. The Maanok were on the other side of the Gartethan Mountains and did not sail the seas, and the Bay of Kraal only saw whaling ships and a few daring traders who braved the dangerous waters. House Wenword's unflagging support of their stronger neighbor made for a mutually beneficial relationship, but to the eyes of other lords, they saw only a master and his dog.

Khrim also made note of who was not speaking. The Count of Deltovane, Lord Kavin Millward, was a cautious man who only spoke in questions, letting others reveal their thoughts while he gave nothing. Deltovane was currently smiling behind his folded hands, enjoying the exchange. The man was of ordinary build for a great lord, having a physique born of years of training to fight on horseback, but had a childlike face and charm. He was shrewd and ambitious as well, though his face hid much of that. His hair was curly and chestnut brown with an untrimmed beard to match, and his eyes were bright and alert. His attire was finely made but modest, with no great adornment save the gold ceremonial badge of rank about his neck and his family crest upon his heart, a red falcon on a field of white.

The Count of Alvavane, Nichol LuVeness, was also silent, though not so amused as his neighbor. Alvavane was of vital importance to the war effort, since he held so much of the wealth in the eastern kingdom. The duke required the count's deep pockets to raise an army of sell-swords and keep the provinces supplied during the upcoming war, lest starvation become a greater threat than enemy swords and arrows.

Alvavane was slight of build and overly soft, being lord of the richest and most beautiful province in the kingdom. His county was known for its precious metals and gemstones from the Spine, fine wines from its vast vineyards, gossamer silks reputed to be of elven make, and great works of craft and art unrivaled in the kingdom and beyond. It had been so for centuries, and it was said that an army from Alvavane consisted of a wagon bearing chests of gold. Duke Wolvert was depending on such an army and requested Khrim to watch the count closely.

But it was Deltovane who spoke next, addressing the duke. "Why does Your Grace believe the king will march past Wensic all the way to this castle? That would leave Kenric and the others behind them to do their mischief, surely?"

Questions, thought Khrim.

The duke walked across the map, pointing with his cane. "The king's army is now at Forgoness, the northernmost part of the Imperial Road." He indicated a painted castle straddling a curving gray line that crossed the north of the continent, "Once they get around the Calione Peaks and reach Castle Velloness, they will be eight day's march from my city walls," he tapped a grand castle on the floor. Its towers, banners and the label 'Ahrnok' were gilded with gold leaf. "They will be supported from Velloness and Castle Vana, guarding their rear. They would be fools to attack before winter, so they will be vulnerable while the army is encamped." He walked to stand on the province of Kenric and gestured to Portshia beyond the mountains. "There is a southern force gathering, though we do not yet know their full strength. However there are plans afoot to stall their advance. When they do come, the forces of Wensic and Kenric must hold fast, or lessen their number if they press south. However, I do not think they will spend much of their strength on the Great Basin."

Count Deltovane smiled and said, "An interesting assessment, Your Grace. But it did not quite answer the question. Why would the king press on to *this* city and focus the greater share of his strength on taking it? Why would he not move more carefully?"

The duke fixed the count with an annoyed glance and returned to his seat, but did not sit. He faced the assembled lords and lady, supporting himself on his wolf's-head cane.

"I have sent an ember swallow messenger to Galen Cordobal III, declaring our respective lands as no longer part of his realm, and declaring myself as the king of the eastern lands from the Cassel Range to the Gartethan Mountains."

Khrim had been waiting for this announcement, just to watch the reactions. The smile melted from Count Deltovane's face, and Count Alvavane sat upright in alarm; the glance they shared said much. *There it is,* Khrim thought. *They wear their alliance like a banner over their heads. But what arrangement had they made, I wonder?*

Barons DeKenric and DeWensic started in disbelief and rising anger, DeKenric going so far as to bark "What?" in his typically outspoken manner. Wensic's gaze turned towards the map, while Kenric's eyes flashed to Kalavek. The fat lord's face was implacable and smug as he returned the stare. Countess Sulund raised her eyebrows at the news, her mouth opening slightly as if to speak, but she kept her peace. She glanced at Deltovane, then the ambassador. *What promises had they made to each other?* Khrim wondered as his eyes narrowed. *I need more ears in the south, more information.*

The ambassador's eyes only flickered at the duke, and then he looked around the circle at the other lords, absorbing their moods, his face unreadable. *He's a dangerous man, this Lord DuDavadorn,* Khrim thought. *He lets nothing show, yet sees everything... like me.*

"When did you do this thing?" demanded Kenric. "It seems you told no one, save your lapdog!" He gestured to Kalavek dismissively. The 'Shield of the North' flinched and sputtered.

The duke said calmly, "I sent the message this very evening." This caused another round of gasps and exclamations. "The bird flew west-by-southwest, a heading that would bring it to Portshia. We believe the king is leading the southern army himself, and will be a guest of Count Casselvane until spring."

Baron DeWensic folded his arms and said, "So you've baited the king. You think he will be so enraged that he will rush past us to strike here? The Black Eagle is no fool, and neither are his advisers or generals."

Baron DeKenric broke in, "My *son* is in that accursed city! I sent him to train at the Freekirk Academy! What of him?"

Duke Wolvert nodded, "As it was said, the Black Eagle is no fool. He will no doubt hold your son for ransom if he is discovered."

Kenric lurched to his feet shouting, "And kill him if I march against the crown! You've just crippled your strongest force, Wolvert!"

"Patience, baron," Wolvert said, putting an edge on his voice, "It is a contingency that has been planned for. We have contacts in Portshia that can aid us in retrieving him safely."

"What contacts?" Kenric demanded. "Who will be entrusted with the life of my son?"

The duke said, "There are sympathetic factions in Portshia that have offered their aid."

"Who?" the baron repeated, "Mercenaries? Nobility? *The Circle of Gold?*"

This last comment was made in jest, but Khrim saw the duke hesitate. Kenric noticed it as well.

"You are joking!" the baron said, "The Circle of Gold? I am to trust the deliverance of my son to a pack of thieves? They will steal him from the king and hold him for an even higher ransom!"

The duke rapped his cane on the floor, chipping the painted map. "Our contacts have a vested interest in aiding our cause. They have declared their wish to see the east become a separate kingdom, and will do everything in their power to aid in our independence."

Kenric sat back down at this, crossing his arms and scowling.

Wensic said, "If the king is with the southern army, then it is sure to be the larger force. This army in the north may be a diversion to draw us out."

Countess Sulund's exasperation was plain, "Does no one think of the sea? Why would he not bring a force around the Cassel Rocks to land on our shores?"

The duke turned to her and said, "We *have* thought of the sea, my lady. In addition to your own ships, we will have the support of Aurilon in the Crimson Bay."

The ambassador gave her a nod and a smile, "Indeed, we have cogs ready to sail from our closest ports, and galleys as well so the wind need not be with us. If the king takes to the sea, we will sink his ships or break them upon the Cassel Rocks."

Lady Anessta raised an eyebrow at this news, "And what will we owe Aurilon for this favor? A fleet to challenge Casselvane's navy will not come cheap."

The ambassador's voice was honey, "We of the Majestic Lands wish only for the best interests of our kin beyond the mountains and sea. To have a friendly realm in place of an antagonistic one... is this not a wise investment of men and ships?"

Lady Anessta was not placated, "A friendly realm? A buffer, you mean. How long may we enjoy the support of Aurilon once we are freed of Cordobal rule?"

"For as long as my lady wishes for good relations with her friends, of course." The ambassador said.

"As for a realm," said Alvavane to the duke, "I do not recall Your Grace asking the rest of us to support you as king over us all. Is this just a ruse to bait the Black Eagle, or do you intend to style yourself our king from now on?"

"A very good question," said Deltovane, "I was wondering, do we address you still as Your Grace, or is it now Your Royal Highness?"

The duke, or king, said to the lord, "Do you dispute my claim to an eastern throne? My house was the house of kings until the Cordobals rose up with their fellow rebels."

"No one disputes your ancient bloodline, Your Grace," said Lady Anessta pointedly, "But we are... *anxious* about replacing one monarch with another, especially if he does not ask for our support before declaring our treason to the king."

"Come now," said Kalavek, "Surely you knew this would come to treason. Do not shy away from it now, my lady."

She rounded on the man, glaring. "I do not shy from the term, My Lord Shield. I know that to lose is to hang, but I do not intend to be dictated to. I rule my own lands, and rule them well. If I am to pay homage to a king, it will be one that I have helped to raise up, not one that simply declared himself with a talking bird."

The duke bristled at this; Khrim could see the man's shoulders tense. Kalavek sputtered and clucked his tongue, his eyes darting between his king and the lady. The other men sat back, nodding in agreement, only Deltovane seemed to be amused at the battle of wills. The ambassador was passive, watching the exchange in silence.

Lady Anessta's dissent had been sparked after the death of her lord husband, when old King Galen II ordered her to wed a lord of Eshlinor in the north and leave her beloved river-lands for the cold rocky plains bordering the Eshlin Bay. A northern lord would have ruled her lands in her husband's stead until she had a male heir to inherit them. Her refusal had been swift and pointed, holding up her Aurilonian family's traditions of female land ownership as precedent. Khrim wished he could have witnessed the ember swallow giving her answer to the old king in the woman's assertive voice. The king's answer had been to enforce crippling taxes on her ports, diverting trade ships to Portshia instead.

The duke-king stood tall, his hands folded on the cane and his chest puffed out proudly. "Am I to surmise that you have plans of your own? Perhaps you all had another king or queen in mind?"

"Why a king or queen at all?" asked Alvavane, "Why perpetuate the old ways?"

Ah, thought Khrim, *the neighboring lords of the Spine must have arranged for an alliance of self-rule. The wealth of House LuVeness and the strength of House Millward, with access to the sea for trade, safely bordered by the southern Blackwood forest and the Gayles River, two little realms tucked away in a corner that no one would bother with. Suspicions confirmed. The tapestry grows. The greater image becomes clearer.*

"Our alliance is of vital importance!" Kalavek declared, "We must be united to defend our lands, and we cannot be united unless we are under one king! Surely you all see this."

Wensic spoke, his eyes roving over his province painted on the floor before him. "I will follow the banner of House Wolvert. I have no desire to carve out a kingdom of my own. The duke has the right of it; his claim to the throne is indisputable."

"A wise choice, to be sure," said Kalavek.

"I'm not finished," Wensic said. "What rankles me is the way of it. We had a shared purpose and a shared dream, to gain our independence from the crown, to recover the honor and prestige we've lost since the Cordobals moved the capitol from Ahrnok and made bitter enemies of our neighbors and kin. We swore to stand together and support each other, to throw off our king, but we never decided what kind of government we would make afterward. I thought that's what this meeting was for, to hammer out our differences and either appoint a king, or many kings, or try something different altogether.

"But now we learn that this very day, you have declared yourself our liege," he folded his arms and glared at Wolvert. "Whatever we might have made of this rebellion has been decided, and our wishes and goals have been discarded before they were even heard."

"Not discarded," said Wolvert, "Only postponed until this conflict is at an end."

Deltovane interjected, "Think, Your Grace, even if you deign to allow us to choose our own paths after the war, how will that look to the other crowned heads of Gartetha? Will they think of you as overly generous to your vassals, or will they see a king unable to hold his new realm together?"

"What has happened once can happen again," said Kenric. "Our combined strength can hold off our enemies, but not if we make enemies of each other."

"That sounded like a threat, my lord," said Kalavek. "A threat directed to our rightful king."

Kenric scoffed, "Hah! No more rightful than you or I, as it happens. We are all traitors to the crown for declaring ourselves, whether as seven kings or one. The claim of Manon Wolvert is two centuries old, and I'll wager most of the common folk have never even heard of the Wolf Kings. Be that as it may, if we find ourselves worse off than we were under the Cordobals, then good

King Manon won't rule for long."

"I take it you will be leading such a rebellion, if it comes to that?" Manon Wolvert asked coldly as he took his seat. Khrim knew his duke had sat just then in case Kenric needed to be subdued. Wolvert was getting out of harm's way.

Kenric asked, "If we have no say as to how we will be ruled, then it falls upon one man, does it not?" His brow creased a twin fissure above his eyes. "However, if we were to write up a charter and sign our names to it, then we'd be bound by honor to make it work, and we'd have no one to blame but ourselves if it goes sour."

Lady Anessta turned to him saying, "I am impressed Lord Drom. You did not think of this yourself, surely."

"I did not," Kenric replied tersely, "but I read books and hear news from other lands. There are merchant lords of Minael that came to such an arrangement with their sovereign half a century ago and the pact still stands. Also the tribes of Raanor have a union that gives them governance of their own territories, but they meet as a council to decide greater matters, each as equals."

Khrim's eyes narrowed, *Unexpected... It seems I underestimated this man.*

"What a specific focus you have in your literary pursuits," Lady Anessta said, "One would think you had ambitions of your own."

"As do we all," said Alvavane. "Let us not pretend. The question before us is how are we to proceed now that His Grace has declared himself king?"

Kenric sat back in his chair and huffed moodily, "I for one will not pledge myself to a king unless we are all agreed to be ruled by one."

"And what manner of governance do you propose, Baron DeKenric?" asked Count Deltovane.

The soldier was not the most eloquent of speakers, but he had apparently given this some thought. "There is a collective of city-states in Abani that rules the whole of their peninsula, a region roughly the size of our eastern kingdom. Each great city controls the region around it and when needed, they can band together and defend their lands from invaders."

"And they fight amongst themselves more often than not," said Countess Sulund. "The Abani do not have the most stable of arrangements. If Celvestria were not so weak, Abani would be easy prey for them once again."

"They rule without a king and defend their lands," declared Kenric with finality.

"As do the Maanok," said Alvavane with distaste, "but I would not wish to emulate *them.*"

Khrim let that comment roll over him. His people were often hated, and with good reason, but taking it personally would interfere with the Way of Wisdom and the Flow of Structured Thinking. *Bias is the bane of understanding, and emotion clouds the mind.*

"If I may," the ambassador said, "It seems that the greatest issue before you is how to best deal with your neighbors. You already have ideas on how to govern yourselves." He stood and gestured to the map at his feet. "United, you are strong; divided, you are weak. This is plain. But whom do you fear? Not Aurilon, surely. The ties that bind us are ironclad, ties of culture and blood. Maanok is across the mountains and you have your Passguard Keep to defend against them.

"Do you fear each other perhaps? Not so much I think, since you have embarked on this course together. Your greatest enemy is therefore the crown of Calilon and its allies. They can surround you and crush you if they bring their full force to bear." He swept his arm about the map as he spoke. "But... if you become part of a greater whole, one that can support you by sea and lend you wealth and numbers in arms..."

"Become a part of Aurilon, under King Brahnus?" Wensic scoffed, "I think you've come to the wrong party, my lord ambassador!" The others agreed, making dismissive sounds.

"Not under the king!" DuDavadorn declared, "Become your own rulers, set up whatever governance you desire, but form a pact with Aurilon to defend against your enemies and share in the bounty of trade that the Cordobals have denied you. Make the crown of Calilon think twice before marching on your lands, knowing that the might of Aurilon is backing you! If you are strong together, think of how powerful we will be combined!"

Khrim observed the thoughts playing across their faces. The ambassador's offer had been brought to the duke earlier and His Grace had consented, but now it fell to the approval of the assembled nobles. An open-ended alliance offered to such a fractured and vulnerable assembly spoke volumes about the mind of King Brahnus. He longed for a foothold in Calilon, and not just for the security of his own lands; his actions spoke of empire building, his aid both weakening Calilon and creating dependence on his support. The rebel houses could be moved to war with grand promises, but the assistance of Aurilon would eventually be withheld until certain conditions were met. One by one the rebel provinces would be absorbed until those remaining could no longer stand without paying homage to the Aurilonian crown.

Khrim had made this assessment in advance, and when Lord DuDavadorn had presented the offer this afternoon, it only confirmed what Khrim had already told the duke. Manon Wolvert had decided to declare himself king for a similar reason; the other provinces would either have to support his claim or fall. It was a great risk, but the Dissenter Houses would be emboldened by the aid of Aurilon given so freely. The truly dangerous game was in letting Aurilon aid them without becoming reliant on it. If the new Wolf King and his lords could not stand without the Majestic Lands to support them, they were doomed to either death or servitude.

Countess Sulund was glaring at the ambassador as she spoke, "The succor of Aurilon is given as freely as candy to children, it seems. It makes one wonder what it is worth?"

There is bitterness in her eyes and voice, Khrim noted. *She likely met with DuDavadorn and Count Deltovane in the south lands, and they were promised Aurilon's support of their sovereignty. What will they do with this reversal now?*

The lord from Aurilon shrugged, "It may be worth more to some than to others."

Deltovane asked, "What plans does His Highness have for the raising of mercenary forces from abroad? Can this new realm afford such expenses?"

Clever question, thought Khrim, *he reminds Wolvert of other alternatives to relying on Aurilon, reminds him of his need for the wealth of House LuVeness of Alvavane, and all in front of the ambassador who shifted his support so easily. This DuDavadorn has been making too many promises.*

Wolvert's jaw muscle twitched as it always did when he was annoyed, "You well know that the success of this venture depends on all of us, and no one house has the gold in its coffers to raise such a mighty force of sell-swords, excepting House LuVeness of course."

"You flatter me, Your Grace," said Alvavane. "I fear the legends of our wealth far outmatch the actual count of our coin."

"Modesty is an ill fit for you, Lord Nichol." Wolvert replied. "I dare say that the realm will be in your debt for rising to the challenge, and repayment of that debt will be of paramount importance once the fighting is over."

"It is easy to speak of repayment, Your Grace," Alvavane said. "But first we must achieve victory in the field. What assurances do we have that you are capable of such a feat?"

Kenric spoke up at this, "My thoughts exactly! I have not heard of your military exploits, Your Grace. I would offer my services in leading your forces," he said as his voice filled with contempt, "but there is the little matter of my son and heir being on the wrong side of the

Cassel Range..."

Sulund broke in, "I share Drom's concerns. Does Your Grace mean to lead our armies, or will you defer to more experienced generals?"

Annoyed, Wolvert said, "It was stated before that this shall be a defensive war. Therefore the strategies we employ must make the most of our smaller forces and make the enemy's greater size into a weakness. There are many tactics we have devised to do this very thing, but we will require not only soldiers, but gold and gemstones to make them work."

Kenric's narrowed his eyes, "I assume you are not using the royal 'we' already. Whom do you speak of when you say 'we' have devised tactics? You and your *financial* advisers?"

Duke Manon Wolvert motioned over his shoulder and a moment later, Braeden Khrim was at his side. Khrim stood at an imposing six and a half feet in height, six inches taller than Wolvert, and was sturdy and muscular beneath his black and gray robes. His face was blocky and chiseled, as if carved from rough stone, and his hair was black with streaks of gray throughout, gathered in many locks of clustered braids bound at the back with a leather cord. His face was weathered and creased, his skin tanned and copper, and a jagged-looking tattoo was etched under his eyes, giving him a frightful countenance. He wore a thick leather belt, leather traveling boots, and a bracelet about his wrist carved of a single piece of blood wood.

Gasps and muffled curses issued from the lords and lady, save for the ambassador, who only raised an eyebrow. Khrim was of Maanok, the land of the savage barbarian tribes beyond the Gartethan Mountains. The tribes of Maanok were the ancient enemies of Calilon and Aurilon, the latter of which was not fortunate enough to have a natural barrier to protect them. The Aurilonian kings had tried both conquest and compromise to deal with the Maanok, with little success either way.

"What madness is this?" exclaimed Wensic, "Are your great war plans the product of a painted barbarian scalper?" He sat upright with feet apart, ready to rise if Khrim rushed him. The other lords were regretting leaving their weapons at the door; their bodyguards, now on high alert, shuffled uneasily in the shadows. Kenric's hand went to his belt and he cursed when he remembered his dagger had been left outside.

Wolvert held up a hand to command their attention, "There is no danger here, save what you will bring upon yourselves. I present Braeden Khrim of the *Baedoch Khoorn*."

"A barbarian warlock," Sulund gaped, "Have you lost your wits?" she amended, "*Your Grace?*"

Manon Wolvert stood and struck the end of his cane on the floor. "Khrim is my trusted council and has been in my employ for several years. The *Baedoch Khoorn* has a fearful reputation in the Majestic Lands, as our dear lord ambassador can attest to."

The blond Aurilonian lord simply nodded his head, not taking his eyes from the warlock. His expression was guarded, vigilant.

Wolvert continued, "My friend Khrim here is a master of unconventional warfare, skills which were developed to fight their neighbors who are better armed and armored, and often more numerous."

"Does he intend to fling balls of flaming dung at King Galen?" asked Kenric. "What good is one hedge wizard against the might of Calilon?"

Khrim answered for himself, his voice deep and even, thickly accented but devoid of a barbarian's expected passion. "Wizards are of little use at the head of an army in the chaos of battle. That is why we work in the shadows and strike where the enemy does not expect us. The tactics used by the *Baedoch Khoorn* are not those of an army, but of a small force, or of one man."

The nobles were clearly shaken by his calm demeanor and mastery of Calilesh. Maanok only spoke their own guttural tongue, or knew just enough to insult or curse a foe; most spoke with their blades or clubs. Khrim was not at all what they had expected upon seeing his face, and he secretly enjoyed that knowledge.

The ambassador spoke in even tones, "*Baedoch Khoorn* means 'Oath Breaker' in the Maanok tongue. They took their knowledge from captured wizards and priests of Aurilon, bending it to their own purposes. They are not bound by the ethics of the Mystic College or the higher orders of wizards. Only the most desperate of great houses employ the warlocks of the Wild Lands."

"I would call our need desperate," Wolvert said, "If we are to survive the coming year, we must strike decisive blows early in this war and break their momentum. We have devised many plans to do just that, and some are already underway."

Kenric scowled at the warlock saying, "This reeks of treachery and dishonorable combat, and I won't have any part of it."

Wolvert rounded on the lord and his voice boomed, "Then you may declare yourself neutral if you wish, or beg the Cordobals to take you back! We must use every advantage at our disposal if we are to win our independence from Calilon, and if that means using underhanded tricks, then so be it!" He pointed at Khrim, "He may well be the only one that can return your son to you." He then turned to the rest of the assembled nobles, "You may either join me in this war and accept me as your king, or cling to your petty ambitions until the Black Eagle marches on your lands and smashes you into pulp!

"Aurilon has offered its hand in friendship, and together we have the strength to gain autonomy for our lands. If you believe you can do better on your own when the fighting is done, so be it. Feel free to build your own little kingdoms and haggle over borders and treaty terms with each other.

"I will let you decide for yourselves after walls have been smashed, crops have been burned and populations have been decimated. But for now, I ask you for your fealty and support. I ask you to stand united with me against a common foe and win our freedom. Calilon has betrayed us; let us not betray each other."

Wolvert took his seat once again with Khrim at his side. The nobles exchanged glances, too cowed to reply. *It was a good speech,* Khrim thought, *but will it be enough?*

He got his answer as one by one the nobles stood and knelt before the new king, some begrudgingly, but they knelt nonetheless.

Braeden Khrim recalled the simple maxim that had guided their strategy for this meeting, *Decisions are clearer when options are fewer.* All had gone as planned, but the real work was ahead of them. *This will be a grand experiment indeed,* he thought. *This conflict might well decide the future of my order, my people, of warfare itself. Let it begin.*

Chapter Thirteen

Marked For Life

Cindra awoke in a comfortable bed with a feather mattress and pillow, covered by linen sheets and shaded from the morning sun by heavy bed curtains. At first she was unsure if she was awake or asleep, alive or dead; her memories were vague and scattered, and there was nothing that made sense. She recalled the stone, the sun, the storm, and pain, but none of that translated into her present condition. She must be dead, surely. This must be Haven, and Lelonetha would soon appear with the Peaches of Bliss.

Moving her limbs confirmed beyond a doubt that she was still alive; her shoulders ached and her joints felt stiff and old, seeming to squeak like rusty hinges. Every muscle had a complaint, as though it were her first week of training at the Freekirk School. She took a deep breath and her ribs throbbed with the effort. As she turned her head, her neck made a ghastly cracking noise.

She looked beneath the sheets and found she was wearing a soft blue nightgown, not the soiled and weather-beaten dress she wore on the bluff. Her hands and wrists were bound with soft linen wrappings, probably to bandage the deep cuts inflicted by the crows. The bandages went all the way down to her forearms though, and she thought that strange.

Straining with the effort, she propped herself up on an elbow and parted the bed curtains. Familiar walls and decorations greeted her in the sunlit room. *I am in the castle,* she thought, *in my own room, my own bed.* The chamber had been recently decorated with new wall hangings and rugs, and fresh herbs were hung about to spread the pleasant scent of lavender and mint. Above the unused hearth was the coat of arms of her family, the rampant gold cat above a half-sun/half-moon, and under three silver crowns, all on a field of blue. The sight made her sigh in relief. She was home, she was alive, and she was safe.

A shadow crossed the curtains, footsteps came around the bed, and a familiar face parted the hangings to look in on her. Cindra almost gasped when she saw Mineth's features; the prominent nose, the large, dark eyes, the pouting lips. But it was not her friend and handmaiden, for she had fallen under a Minozhian knife. *No,* Cindra thought, *it is Lady Vanetha, Mineth's mother.* She had not seen the woman since leaving the castle four years ago.

Lady Vanetha LuKrane had married Baron Malvord DuMaith, but was tragically widowed early on. With a young daughter and few prospects, she was chosen to serve as handmaid to the thirteen-year-old Lady Zara DuMaylione, a distant cousin of her late husband. When Zara was wed to Amon Corrina three years later, Vanetha hoped her daughter Mineth might be a playmate or nanny to Zara's future children. She had been so much more.

"Milady, you are awake!" Vanetha said in her

soothing accent. "You have been insensible for days, and with a fever, poor child! I shall tell your mother immediately." She smiled, placed a warm hand on the girl's bandaged wrist, and left in a hurry. Cindra noticed there were guards outside her door.

My mother's own handmaid is caring for me, she thought. *Of course, she is one of the few that can be trusted.* It comforted her, but troubled her as well. *I am not quite safe, even here.*

Her mother entered moments later, followed by Vanetha, and the bed-curtains were open wide. The eyes of Zara Corrina were moist and sparkled like emeralds in the morning light as they fell upon Cindra's face. She crossed the floor in four long strides and knelt at the bedside before Vanetha could bring her a chair.

"Cindra, kitten!" her mother said, "I am so relieved... when they brought you in, we feared the worst." She stroked the girl's auburn hair, her face, and her bandaged arms.

The sight of her mother was like a soothing balm that took her pains away. Cindra said, "I don't... I'm not sure what happened, mother. How did I get here? I don't recall being brought down the mountain."

Her handmaid brought a chair and Zara took a seat before explaining. Her face was grave, her brow knitted in concern, "There was a storm, a terrible storm. The priests and wizards think it was due to what you said at your trial, about this 'Dark Heart' being in the city, but they will say little else about it. There was lightning and..."

"I remember the storm, and the thunder and lightning," Cindra said.

Zara continued, "A priest was sent to retrieve you, along with a few of our house guards and Sir Jaron Dunlorden."

Cindra was alarmed, "Sir Jaron brought me down?" She had been sunbaked, bloody, and stained by her own filth. The rain storm had been heavy enough to wash most of it away, but still...

The countess nodded, "He would not be kept from the duty," she smiled. "He said that there was a lightning strike on the bluff, just before they made the ascent. A horse was spooked and the priest was thrown from the wagon, the trail had become a treacherous torrent. By the time they reached you, they feared you had been killed."

Cindra remembered the pain, white light and pain. She looked at her arms again, bandaged from hands to forearms. For the first time, she feared what her skin might look like beneath the wrappings.

Zara said, "They found the faintest signs of life in you, and they brought you back down with all haste. Since then we have had healers tending you each day, using all their skills to help you recover."

"Each day?" Cindra asked, "How many days?"

"It has been a week, kitten." Zara said, "Almost twice as many days as you were up on the mountain."

"My arms," Cindra said, holding them up. "What happened to them?"

Zara's face was pained as she said, "The stone to which you were chained was struck by lightning. They say it should have killed you. I think it was a miracle; I do not know which god to thank, so I have thanked them all."

Cindra had figured the gods were all conspiring to kill her on the mountain. She did not relate to her mother the thoughts she had during that time, or the ones she had given voice to. One thought was now in her mind, and it made her chest constrict as it occurred to her.

"What happened to Drahn? Ildric's little dweedragon?" she asked. By the confused look on her mother's face, she feared the worst.

"I... I am not sure what you mean, kitten. Was Ildric's dragon with you on the mountain?" Zara asked.

"He was," Cindra said. "He was keeping me company during the storm." She recalled his terror, his pitiful whimpering as the dreaded lightning flashed and crashed about them. He had been so very brave to be there with her, his bravery all the greater for how much fear he had felt.

She pulled at the wrappings on her hands, uncovering reddish-pink fingers and raw skin. Once her palms were free, she saw the burns in the shape of scales upon them. Her eyes filled with tears as she thought of poor little Drahn, lying dead and forgotten on Tirgrim's Bluff, being pecked by the same crows who had tried to eat her.

The countess moved to the bed to hold Cindra as Vanetha poured a cup of mint water for the girl. She spoke words of comfort to her daughter in her low, soothing accent, "*La shupú, fellí, mesha shupú.*"

When Cindra had recovered a little, she accepted the drink and sat up in bed as Vanetha propped her up with more pillows. The countess stood back and let the woman work, knowing her daughter was in good hands.

Zara said, "Your father has visited your bedside every day as his duties allow; I fear the war effort has taken much of his time. Shall I send for him?"

Cindra smiled and said, "Yes, I think that would be nice. It would be good for him to see I am alive and well. He must have been tormented by his decision the whole time."

"I admit I have tormented him a time or two," said the countess with a touch of guilt. "It is a difficult thing he did, condemning you like that."

"I was condemned from the moment I told the king my identity," Cindra said. "The rest was just politics."

"You are your father's daughter," Zara said with a sigh, "headstrong and canny. You would have made a fine countess." *If only Calilon's traditions allowed,* she thought.

Soon there was a knock at the door and a servant entered, bowing as she said, "Countess, the Arch Mage Ildric Finnael has arrived to... to see Lady Cindra." She had just noticed the girl sitting up in bed and was momentarily stunned. Recovering, she said, "He requests an audience with her ladyship to discuss things of importance."

The countess turned to her daughter with a look of mild surprise and said, "It seems our friend knew the hour of your recovery. He has a most convenient talent, when it pleases him." Turning to the servant, she said, "Give us a moment to make her presentable, and then show him up." The woman curtsied and left.

She went to Cindra's vanity table, took a hairbrush, and began combing out her daughter's neglected hair, "I imagine the two of you have some further conspiring to do. The arch mage has been here often this week, playing the role of advocate in various matters. Your father has allowed this because it pleases him to annoy the king through another's words. I cannot say I disagree, since His Majesty uses that dreadful field marshal to the same end."

"Is the king still here?" Cindra asked.

"No," Zara said. "He and his men have taken up residence in the Winter Palace, as is befitting." She sounded quite pleased and a little bit scornful. "He has taken his prisoners with him, thankfully."

"He has more prisoners?" Cindra was confused, "Other than Maron Theenix?"

Zara said, "Maron was released along with his wife days ago. There were others taken into custody for 'questioning,' as well as the DeKenric boy from the Freekirk School."

"Grigor!" Cindra gaped, "Grigor DeKenric is a prisoner?" She had been afraid of that possibility ever since Jaron mentioned him to the king.

"A hostage. Much has happened, kitten," she said as she examined her handiwork. "There, now you look a proper bedridden lady. I shall leave you to your visitor. If you find yourself growing weak or tired, do not be afraid to tell the arch mage to come back later." She stroked Cindra's cheek and gave her a warm smile before departing with her handmaid.

In the moments she had alone, Cindra found herself

fixated on her bandaged arms. Her morbid curiosity got the better of her and she began unwrapping the linens, quickly at first, then more slowly as she found them pulling at her skin beneath. Whatever wounds she had received were weeping yellowish ichor, but there was thankfully no blood. She undid one arm, then another, staring in disbelief at what she saw; to her horror and fascination, she found that the lightning had left its mark upon her in the most unexpected way.

She had expected to see ghastly burns of red and black, like a piece of fresh mutton left too long on the cook-fire. Instead, she found an almost beautiful pattern of scar tissue that began on her hands and spread to her elbows. It forked and branched like the growth of a mad tree or the tributaries of a river, splitting again and again as it flowed across her ruddy skin. However, the most surprising discovery was the image of Valdak's blind eye burned into her wrists. Apparently, the shackles that bound her had been imprinted on the inner surface with the symbol of the god of Justice and Judgment; whether it was intended to leave a mark or be purely symbolic, she could not tell. What no one expected was that it would leave her permanently branded like livestock.

Her grim inspection was interrupted by a knock on the door. "You may enter," she called, hiding her arms under the covers.

The guard opened the door to admit Ildric Finnael, who smiled as he saw her. He strode across the chamber, his staff clicking on the floor and the thumb of his silver hand hooked over his belt. He wore a robe of blue and gold, as he often did when visiting the castle. His hood was thrown back, revealing short white hair and a trimmed beard that made him look more like a respectable lord than a dabbler in the Art.

Master Ildric took the seat next to Cindra's bed, leaning his staff against the bedpost. He smiled congenially and the lines about his eyes deepened. "Good morning, milady. I trust you are well?"

"Well enough," she said. "I have much to thank you for, but..." her face grew anxious, and she swallowed back tears. "What of Drahn? He was with me on the stone when the lightning struck." She hesitantly showed him her palms with the scale-shaped burns, and the angry traces the lightning had made.

"Alas, poor Drahn," Ildric said. "I am afraid he was properly roasted by the lightning. We found him the next day, all cooked like a holiday goose." As her face grew pale, Ildric's brightened, "But the good news is, he was delicious! Who knew dragon meat was so flavorful!" He picked his teeth with a silver talon of his metal hand.

Cindra stared in absolute shock and horror.

But a voice arose from behind the wizard, "Master Ildwic! You are a tewwible, tewwible man!"

Ildric began to laugh as Drahn's little purple head poked out over the wizard's shoulder, his scales shimmering to crimson. He bit the man on the ear, leaped out of Ildric's hood and into Cindra's outstretched arms.

"Drahn! Oh Drahn, I was so..." Cindra began to cry as she hugged him, careful not to squish his wings.

Ildric rubbed his ear, knowing he deserved it. "Ow. Wretched beast."

"I taste delicious, do I?" Drahn huffed at the wizard. "Well *you* taste like an old shoe!" He explained to Cindra, "Master Ildwic was *supposed* to make it into a happy surpwise, but he has a *vewy* bad sense of humor." The little dweedragon peered sidelong at Ildric as the man rubbed his ear, chuckling.

"But it *is* a happy surprise," Cindra said, taking a good look at him. He seemed unhurt and unburned; in fact he looked better than ever. "How did you survive? What happened up there?"

The corners of the dweedragon's mouth curved up as much as they were able and his voice rose in pitch, "It was my element! The lightning! It was lightning all along!"

Ildric explained, "It is likely the reason you survived the strike, milady. Drahn absorbed the greater share of the power. We still do not know if what happened was proper, that is, we cannot say if others of his kind must experience the same thing in the same way, but..."

"I can bweathe lightning!" Drahn said happily. "I have always wanted to bweathe fire or *something*, but I never could. Watch this!" He hopped to the edge of the bed and looked for something to shoot at, his wings and tail raised in excitement.

Ildric grabbed Drahn by the tail and gave it a tug, "Oh no you *don't*, you silly creature! You are not showing off in here! You still have to repair the wall in my tower."

"But I *told* you master, I saw a wat," Drahn replied sheepishly.

"I don't care if you saw ten rats! I won't have my home smelling of charred rat!" Ildric said. "No, you will kindly practice out-of-doors."

Cindra grinned from ear to ear saying, "Can you do proper dragon-magic now, Drahn?"

Drahn turned and shrugged, wrapping his tail about his feet as Ildric relaxed his guard. "I am not sure," the dweedragon said, "I have no idea how dwagon spells are done, but the few I know fwom Master Ildwic's teachings are stwonger and more potent. Wenyssaya is twying to help me learn, based on things she has heard."

"Well I am very happy for you, Drahn. Maybe you won't be afraid of lightning anymore?" she asked.

Drahn fiddled with his tail, looking uncertain. "Maybe..." he said.

Ildric scooted the chair closer, perhaps intentionally letting it drag with a harsh noise. "There has been much that has happened in the world while you underwent your trial." His face looked serious, and Cindra hoped her joyous reunion would not be too much soured. "For starters, it seems that war is assured. The Dissenter Houses have committed treason in declaring their sovereignty and naming Duke Manon

Wolvert as King Manon I. Those provinces in the east that have remained neutral are likely to fall in with him for their own protection, knowing the Cordobal king or the Wolvert king will make battlefields of their lands either way."

Cindra took this in, not terribly surprised. To her mind, Galen III had made war inevitable when he summoned his banners and marched to the edge of the eastern provinces. Perhaps it was intended only to give him diplomatic leverage, but she had the distinct impression that Galen III was more hawk than dove. *The Black Eagle has much to prove, and little time to do it in,* she thought. *He would not wish to seem weak by staying in the west and sending threats with no force to back them up.*

"I heard that Grigor DeKenric has been taken hostage," Cindra said, remembering the boy as quiet and focused, with few friends. "Is he well?"

"He is," Ildric said, "The lad is being treated with all the courtesies granted one of his station. He has promised not to attempt escape, and so has been given the freedom of the palace. Still, his father is a man of fiery temperament, and no one knows how long this might stay his hand."

"You think he will attack?" she asked.

"Not likely," Ildric said, "but it may not keep him from fighting if the king invades the east. Baron DeKenric might wish to take hostages of his own on the battlefield, hoping to trade. Regardless, tensions are at a great height now."

Cindra thought on that, "Still, it does not make sense that they would declare their sovereignty with Grigor still in Portshia. Jaron always thought that if Grigor left the school, the war would not be far behind. Perhaps they meant to get him a message or call him home, but failed."

Ildric nodded, "That point has been brought up in council. Kenric is a fierce warrior and commands a great host, many of whom are armed with Kenric steel, the finest in the land. He will likely be the first and greatest foe in the coming war. For his son to fall into our hands so easily must either be a great windfall for the king, or a devious trick beyond our reckoning."

"What kind of trick?" she asked.

Drahn answered with a shrug, "One beyond our weckoning."

Ildric smiled, "There is no sense to it, and so we are taking it as a godsend. It is possible that Manon Wolvert simply miscalculated when he sent the ember swallow with his proclamation."

"I imagine the baron must be furious with him then," Cindra remarked.

"Let us hope," said the wizard. "Dissent among the Dissenters can only aid our cause."

Cindra sat there for a moment, moving her toes under the sheets. They hurt. Finally she asked, "What does the king say of my knighthood?" It was what she had suffered for after all. She had little time to think on it since waking, but all the talk of war and intrigue reminded her that she might have a part to play.

Ildric sat up, smoothing his robe. "Ah," he said, "That is, of course, the main reason for my visit; that, and delivering this silly, brave creature to you." He motioned at Drahn, whose wings twitched in response. "The king has little choice but to accept your survival as proof of your worthiness in the eyes of the gods; at least, that is how he phrased it. I happen to think it was a rather shrewd tactic to avoid a lengthy trial and keep the priests of Valdak out of it. The fact is that you were guilty as charged. No amount of counsel could have made your acts sound legal or just; it was only your worthiness that bore any argument, and that was dismissed out of hand because you are of the fairer sex."

"I remember. I was there," Cindra said, looking at her arms. *How fair am I now?* she wondered. "I still don't consider the king my hero for chaining me to a rock."

But Ildric leaned in conspiratorially, "It is now my

belief that His Majesty, while openly turning your fate over to the gods, was secretly hoping we would assist you as we did. Drahn was found with you when they brought you down the mountain; the little fellow was unconscious, so he shared your litter. When you arrived at the castle to be treated, the king was among those in waiting, but no question was raised about Drahn's presence."

Cindra frowned, "Not even from my dearest friend Field Marshal Valthór?"

"He was not present," Ildric said. "His Majesty was only attended by a small personal guard."

"My mother said she knew nothing of Drahn being with me," Cindra said.

"Your mother was waiting at the inner gate, for it was evil weather, and raining heavily. You were met at the outer gate by the king, your father, and Wenyssaya. It was she who took Drahn away before you were brought inside."

"Were you not there as well?" Cindra asked.

Ildric scratched his beard, "Eh, I meant to be, but there was an incident at the Tower of the Silver Moon... I was held up. Wenyssaya met me there with Drahn, and we tended to him while things were sorted out." He quickly changed the subject, taking on a lighter tone. "Incidentally, the king sent his own healer to retrieve you; Reverend Brother Alynar arrived at the head of the army while you were on the bluff."

"I heard he was injured?" Cindra asked.

Ildric nodded, "He was thrown from the wagon when the horse bolted and broke his arm. Still, he made the climb up the mountain just the same; quite a remarkable feat at his age."

Cindra would make a point to thank him when she got the chance, but another thought stuck in her mind. "What about Sir Jaron? May I see him?" Her heart quickened when she spoke his name, although she thought she knew what the answer might be.

Ildric scratched his beard and Drahn's wings drooped

a bit. With more than a bit of discomfort, Ildric said, "It was decided that you should not be allowed to consort with Sir Jaron Dunlorden, since you bore his guilt along with your own on the bluff. Seeing him now might lead one or both of you to, eh... recommence what should be... concluded."

She had expected this, yet she still felt her heart sink at the news. They were going to keep her from her love, even after she had proved herself worthy of donning sword and armor, just as he did. Her face flushed with a rising anger, but at the same time she felt a cold chill in her stomach; a quivering mixture of helplessness, guilt, fear, and finality that made her want to scream at the walls.

Drahn patted her knee, his scales shifting to a deeper shade of purple as he looked up at her sadly. "I am sowwy," he said.

It took her a few moments to recover herself, during which time Ildric pretended to examine the construction of her bed canopy, and Drahn fiddled with his tail. Finally she asked coldly, "Who was it that came to this decision?" She could guess, but would rather not.

Ildric replied, "The king, his advisers, your father and mother, Constable Fingelm and several other advisers, Archbishop Karros..."

She had not expected such a list, and she blushed. "Why were all of these esteemed busybodies making decisions about my love life?" she demanded. "Was there also a special assembly called to discuss who my friends may be, or are they just concerned about whom I choose to sleep with?"

At this, the wizard cleared his throat and studied his boots. He muttered, "Er, the meeting was to discuss how to proceed with your training, milady. Your father will see you provided with arms and armor, as well as any other necessities. But it was agreed that you should not return to the Freekirk school, as it would be too distracting and... ah, inappropriate." He raised his eyes to meet her angry stare. "No mention was made of your future marriage prospects. Only the integrity of the fighting school and your reputation were discussed."

"Hah!" Cindra scoffed, "Marriage prospects indeed! The only man who might wish to marry me is the only man I cannot see! I doubt father could find a house poor enough and desperate enough to marry their son to a lady knight with such... odd beauty marks." She held up her arms.

Ildric had nothing to say to that.

Drahn offered, "Actually, I think they are vewy pwetty."

Cindra asked, "If I cannot attend the fighting school, how will I complete my training?"

Ildric said, "The king has decreed that your ladyship shall live and train at the Winter Palace under the tutelage of Gavadaire LuVestra."

Her eyebrows raised in surprise. "LuVestra? Why him in particular?" She could imagine Jaron's face at hearing *that* news.

"He was one of your instructors, and was recommended by Sir Cord Freekirk as a suitable and quite competent teacher. Really, there was only one choice for Master Freekirk to make."

Cindra supposed that was true. *Damn them all anyway.* It was a wide world out there, and she would be free to find him later. She stifled her defiance and instead asked, "What of Nixy's proposition? Will I be allowed to go with him to find his father?"

Ildric nodded, "You will, but have no illusions milady; this will be no pleasant pilgrimage. There will be scouts from the Dissenter Houses in Casselvane soon, if they are not here already. The road will be dangerous, especially if the purpose of your mission is discovered."

"A secret mission?" she smirked. "What better way to make me disappear? He's a clever one, this king."

"Don't be petulant," the wizard said. "It doesn't suit you."

She shrugged and asked, "How will we find this Shadow Lord?"

Ildric replied, "Wenyssaya believes his home is deep within the woods, past the meeting of the Kelga and Joshian rivers."

"That seems rather vague," she said. "If I recall my maps, that area is as large as half of Casselvane province itself."

"Yes," Ildric said, "It is hoped that her raven might act as a guide, since it was once the Shadow Lord's messenger. However, there is also the chance that the lord of the dark wood might show you the way more plainly."

"Master Ildwic," Drahn said, "You have been in the Shadowood Fowest; could you not act as guide?"

Ildric shook his head, "I delved but a few leagues into the woods, no more. Besides, that was many years ago. Would that I could come with you," he said sullenly. "I would be honored to finally meet the Shadow Lord, but alas I am needed elsewhere. It is not yet decided if I shall travel with the king's army or remain in the city; regardless, I shall be occupied in uncovering the enemy's plans.

"But you will need help on this journey, make no mistake. Wenyssaya and Nixy will be going, of course. Drahn shall accompany you as well; as it turns out, he is not altogether as silly a creature as he seems."

At this, Cindra and the dweedragon shared a smile.

The wizard continued, "You might benefit from a small retinue as well; some trusty men-at-arms to fill out your numbers, so you do not make so tempting a target."

"But not Sir Jaron," she said glumly.

"No... not Sir Jaron," Ildric agreed. "I should remind you that enemy scouts and bandits may not be the only threat on the road; the Guadim creature that Nixyalderthor described is still unaccounted for, and there have been a few more incidents of people leaving the cemetery after being laid to rest."

A chill shot through her as she recalled the vemlok attack that killed Halvoy Quenlorden. "The Dark Heart?" she asked, almost in a whisper.

"The Dark Heart," he said. "I believe it is here, although something has changed. Your last night on the bluff, the night of that freakish storm, was a turning point. Things have calmed down since then, as if we sit in the eye of a tempest. Even the rats are retreating from the streets."

"Well that's good news at least," Cindra said.

"Perhaps, perhaps," the wizard said, obviously not believing it himself.

They sat in silence for a time until Cindra said, "Master Finnael, there is something I have always wanted to ask you." She summoned her courage and said, "You have looked after me for all these years, first with the enchanted bracelet that saved me at sea, then with your spell to protect me from divination magic at the school. You kept my secrets and kept me as safe as you were able, even on Tirgrim's Bluff." Her brow knitted and she asked, "My question is why? Am I destined for some great purpose? Have you seen what will be?"

Ildric gave a wistful smile and said, "A complicated question, to be sure. You are the only surviving child of my lord count, and I owe it to him to do my best; that is one answer. Another is that your fate is tied to that of Nixy DuQuayne, and he is a child the likes of which the world has not seen in many an age. These are both adequate reasons, and there are others...

"But the real reason is my own morbid curiosity." He held up his silver hand to display the dragon-eye stone embedded in the palm. "You have heard me speak of the Eye of Omithys?" She nodded. "It allows me to see more clearly than any other wizard, the future, the past, and the distant present. This you know. But my visions of the future have a limit; I cannot see beyond one *particular* moment in time." His eyes took on a melancholy aspect as he examined the Eye. Drahn's expression was downcast and his wings drooped.

"You mean... you can see your own death?" she asked, dismayed.

"I can see a time when a great conflict rages, when death and danger surround me, and when I see no more," he replied, his voice heavy with dread. "And you are there, Lady Cindra. You are there with me almost every time."

She blinked, dumbstruck.

He stood and took up his staff, turning so the dweedragon might climb into his lowered hood. "But now you must rest. I fear I have caused you too much excitement already. Come Drahn, we have much to do."

The dweedragon waved to the girl and flapped up to the wizard's shoulders, burrowing into the hood.

"Thank you for everything," Cindra said. "I owe you both my life. I don't know how I can ever repay you."

Ildric looked down at her fragile form, haggard and weak from her ordeal; the scarred arms, reddened skin, sunken cheeks, all a testimony to her suffering. He said, "You may repay me by growing strong and fulfilling your destiny, whatever that may be."

And with that, he strode from the room, leaving Cindra to ponder the future.

Chapter Fourteen

Brother's Keeper

The little god was both miserable and ecstatic all at once. He had made it to the mortal world without facing the wrath of his father, and he could begin searching for his lost brother to undo the damage he had done. Of course, first he must get loose from the wizards holding him captive. His powers were practically non-existent, and he had no idea where he was. Mortals built like busy bees, and if you were out of touch for millennium, they could radically change the landscape on you.

"Who *are* you," repeated the wizard for the ninth time this hour. The man had a long gray beard, a wide-brimmed hat, and a staff that he thumped angrily on the floor to punctuate his question. There were a few other wizards in the room with him, several dozen in the chamber below, and a trickle going up the spiral stairs to what appeared to be a library, for they brought down books and scrolls with them.

Tavenji sang, "Chatha Kamrang, Ibli Hilsaam, Grendi ko Tsitse, Lornakra mal Drum..." It was four of his old names in four dead human languages. He had been reciting all of his favorites and was getting to the several thousand he didn't care for, but by the look on the faces of his captors, their patience would expire long before he could run out of names.

"Now look," said Ravilus Tage, "No one knows you are here. You have no advocates coming, not from the civil authorities, and not from the Valdakian priesthood. Your only hope for freedom is to answer our questions."

Tavenji asked, "Do the Valdakians still poke their own eyes out? That is *sooo* stupid. Don't you think that's stupid?"

Tage said, "If you wish to speak of putting out eyes, we may get to that later if you are not inclined to answer."

Tavenji was indignant. "Are you *threatening* me? Do you *know who I am?*"

Tage said, "No, please enlighten us."

"Re-ne-ku-Valam, Dr'aste-Koldu, Ama-B'shelot, Quen-xin-yan-foo..." he sang.

The wizard shook his head in disgust and descended the stairs.

Tavenji was bound in common rope, upon which one of the ward masters has placed a spell of binding. In olden days, when a god could visit the mortal world at will, he could escape from such a trap by wiggling his little toe. Now he struggled in vain against the ropes as his cheeks reddened with the indignity of it all.

After making his sudden appearance, he had been seized by some kind of spell and surrounded by wary wizards, prodding him with staffs and wands. He had been too weak to resist at first, but by the time he was able to get to his feet, someone had gathered a length of rope to bind him with.

The following week had been torture. Not literally, not so far, but having to listen to all of their questions, theories, and propositions had made him want to fling himself out the nearest window; though he was as yet uncertain of this room's height, he was keeping that option open.

At least they had given him a robe, food and water. His prison wasn't bad either; Tavenji guessed that it was meant to be a comfortable sitting room for wizards to chat over a smoke and a glass of spirits. He was tied to a nicely upholstered chair and he spent his time in comfort studying the portraits of self-important human magic-dabblers that graced the curved walls.

Another wizard ascended the stairs, one who had questioned him days before. This fellow had a silver hand, like a fancy taloned gauntlet, but Tavenji got the impression that it was a replacement for a missing limb. He had a dweedragon with him, one of the purple lightning-spitters, if he remembered correctly.

The wizard motioned the others to give them some privacy, and he pulled up a chair. "Good evening," he said, smiling like a host rather than a jailer.

"I'll take your word for it," Tavenji replied. "I haven't seen the outside of this tower. It *is* a tower, I assume? You wizards love to build towers."

"Yes," the wizard said. "I get the impression that you are not native to this plane of existence."

"Whatever makes you say that?" asked the little god with wide, innocent eyes.

The dweedragon said, "Your ears, for one thing. Not even elves have ears so long."

"Well, that's not a crime," Tavenji pouted. "Neither is appearing out of thin air. It's just rather unusual, that's all."

The wizard said, "We have had a rash of unusual events of late, and none of them have led to any good. You must forgive our caution."

Tavenji perked up. "What kind of events? You have all been hinting at things, but no one has told me what's been going on." He found he was straining against his bonds, and forced himself to relax. "Have strange things been happening everywhere, or just here? Where is here anyway?"

The wizard made a thoughtful expression and leaned forward. "Perhaps we can satisfy each other's curiosity. I shall answer your questions if you answer mine."

"A game!" Tavenji cried. "I love games! Very well, ask away."

"I am aware of your fondness for games," said the wizard, sitting back with arms folded. "You have been playing with us all week. I do not intend to waste my time with your cryptic, nonsensical answers."

"Oh, have I exhausted your librarians?" Tavenji asked. "I'm sorry. Perhaps if you had younger ones, they wouldn't be all huffy and puffy from taking the stairs." He nodded towards the upper chamber.

The little dragon spoke, "I have identified a few of the languages you used. One is Bythian, fwom the first dynasty. Another is Kin Dwon, fwom gweater Ayn Gozhi."

Tavenji would have clapped if his hands were free. "Bwavo! Apweva! Congwaduwations! I pwostwate myself to your gweatness."

The dweedragon glared at him, "There is no need to be wude."

The wizard cleared his throat and said, "It is my belief that you are a denizen of the outer realms, possibly of the Abyss itself. During the Time of Chaos, many things escaped into our world, and I believe this is happening again. What realm are you from?"

Tavenji looked hurt. "I am *not* from the Abyss. I am not an agent of Mash, or Llomaak, or whatever you call him in these parts. I am... a denizen of the Void."

The wizard looked to his dragon companion in concern, noticing the little creature had fixed the prisoner with a glassy stare. He said, "What is it, Drahn?"

Drahn blinked himself back to the present and said in a low voice, "Mash... Master Ildwic, I know that word."

"I have never heard Llomaak referred to as Mash

before," said Ildric. "Is it something you read?"

The little dragon shook his head, staring into space. "It was... in the shell, on the day the men came."

Ildric frowned at that. "Are you sure?"

Drahn nodded.

"I have answered your question," Tavenji said. "Now I have one. Where am I, exactly?"

Ildric said, "You are in the Tower of the Silver Moon in the city of Portshia. Does that help?"

"Portshia," Tavenji said. "I know it. There's a tall castle on a bluff facing the sea, and a few hundred brick buildings sit below. Oh! There are also the silver mines where all those little folk toil away. I always liked them."

Ildric considered this, scratching his beard with his silver talon. "My next question: how did you come to be here?"

Tavenji said, "That's a *very* good question. I was in a spot of trouble back home, and the next thing I knew, I was here in this charming tower. I was pushed through the veil, I think. Since your wizard towers are always built on the thin spots, it was a natural place to appear. That's my theory, anyway." He said, "My turn. You said there have been lots of strange things happening. When did they start, and what do you think is the cause?"

Drahn said, "That is two questions."

Ildric waved the remark away and said, "They began over a month ago, when a strange dust storm descended on the city. There has been a plague of rats, camp fever, bizarre weather and strange occurrences; worst of all, vemloks have risen from the cemeteries and attacked people." Tavenji grew very quiet and attentive, and Ildric risked sharing more information. "The rumors are that these events seemed to follow a man from the north, a mad wizard that brings chaos with him. Such a man was sighted in Portshia on the night these events began."

Tavenji sat very still, his eyes wide.

"My question," said Ildric. "In the week we have kept

you here, you have eaten three meals a day, and yet you have not used a chamber pot in all that time. Do you not need to... relieve yourself?" Drahn glanced in surprise, apparently not having heard this news.

Tavenji just looked distracted. "Are you asking if I'm full of crap? I've been told that I am. I'll use the pot if it will make you feel better."

"I imagine it might make *you* feel better, but regardless. Your turn," Ildric said.

Tavenji asked, "Do you know where this mad wizard is now?"

"No," Ildric said, shaking his head. "He exists in a cloud of obscurement, and a great darkness lingers about him, a warning that I dare not ignore. I will not use my powers to seek him out lest I risk madness myself."

"Probably wise," Tavenji said, rather dejected. "Your turn," he muttered.

"Very well, what is this?" Ildric asked, holding up an acorn.

Tavenji's eyes widened and he fidgeted, but all he said was, "It's an acorn?"

"You coughed it up after you arrived. You tried to retrieve it before you were bound, but failed. My powers have only showed me that it is somehow not what it seems."

Tavenji's eyes were fixed upon it as Ildric held it up in his metal talon.

"I take it that it is a thing of importance? Perhaps even an object of power from the outer realms?" Ildric placed it in his left hand and held the silver limb over it. A yellow-green light glowed softly from the dragon-eye stone embedded in the palm, shining on the acorn. He said, "I can take any object and see where it has been, or where it will be in the future. I can see through great distance and time. But I cannot see from what tree this acorn fell, or from whence it came before dropping from your lips that night. Why is that?"

"All I can tell you," Tavenji said miserably, "is that I

am trying to stop this mad wizard from unleashing destruction upon us all. Please, you must release me! I need to find him, and I need the acorn to help me. I'm... I'm on a mission from the gods!"

"Master," Drahn said, "The acorn is one of the older symbols of Eyorona."

"Yes!" Tavenji said. "I was entrusted with it, and it will help me on my quest. Please, you must release me! Don't you see? It was fate that brought me to the same city as the Dark-" He cut himself off abruptly; he would have clapped his hands over his mouth were they not bound.

Ildric closed his hand around the acorn and leaned forward intently. "The Dark Heart; so it is truly here. Would that make you the scion of the prophecy?"

Tavenji frowned saying, "You have asked your question, now it is my turn. This is also for all the other wizards listening in with their magic ears." He raised his voice until it almost squeaked, "What do I have to do before you let me try and save the world?"

The sound of footsteps came up the stairs, and the ancient grand master appeared with several other elders, including Ravilus Tage. Grand Master Orellus spoke in a solemn voice, "You claim to be sent from the gods. Does this mean that they are planning to return? That they have not abandoned us?"

Tavenji sighed and said, "I hate to disappoint you, grandfather, but the gods have even abandoned their own kind. As for their return, that is a tricky question. The gods *might* return, but they won't be the ones you're hoping for."

Drahn stirred at this revelation but said nothing. His wings trembled slightly.

Tavenji shrugged and said, "All you are going to get is me, so take it or leave it. But I warn you, if you choose to leave me tied up in your little club house, you are going to wish you were born in the Time of Chaos instead of the time that's to come."

Tage stepped forward and asked, "I will vote to

release you, if you tell us who you truly are."

Tavenji glared up at the gray bearded wizard and said, "If I thought I could trust you with that, I'd have given you a name you would recognize."

"Ah, but you have," said Tage smugly. "The name '*Quen-xin-yan-foo*' is from the Kin Dwon language. It means 'One Who Makes Life Interesting.'"

Tavenji smirked, "The dweedragon figured that out, not you. Besides, have I not made your life interesting since I arrived?"

"I am afraid," said Orellus, "that without more information, we cannot afford to release you. I am sorry, but those who passed through the veil during the Time of Chaos were mostly a plague upon us; we cannot take the chance that you might do untold mischief were we to set you free."

Tavenji sat and stewed as the wizards descended into their meeting hall. A spell of privacy fell upon the lower chamber, and the little god was infuriated that he didn't even have the power to eavesdrop.

Later that night, after most of the wizards had returned to their beds, a shadow crept down the stairs from the library. Tavenji opened his eyes at the sound of claws clicking on the worn steps, wondering if this was some new scheme to break his will. He was surprised to see the lithe, cat-sized body of the dweedragon making its way down the spiral, his long neck peeking around the corner as he came.

Drahn's eyes reflected the dim luminance as he entered the room, focusing on the wizard sitting at a table, reading by magical light. The council had elected to keep only a single guard, since the prisoner was obviously incapable of escape. This was a mistake, for Drahn's sleep spell could only work on one person at a time. The dweedragon raised his tail over his back and swayed, chanting in a deep, almost inaudible voice. The guard closed his eyes and dropped his head onto the book.

"Well done," Tavenji whispered admiringly. "I take it you intend to free me? Please say you intend to free me."

"I do," Drahn whispered, "Wegardless of what the Order decided; I think you are here to help."

"Wonderful!" he said. "What convinced you?"

Drahn replied, "You said 'Mash' was a name for Llomaak. I wesearched that, and it answered some vewy old questions for me. Also, you mentioned the gods weturning, but not the ones we are hoping for. I think I know what you meant."

"A dragon would," Tavenji said solemnly. "These humans are so devoted to the Divine Court that they forget there are older and more terrible gods."

Drahn's wings quivered as he made his way around the back of the chair to work on the prisoner's bonds. He chanted another spell in that deep, draconic voice, *"Posthe n'thom ves."* He then began to chew on the ropes, loosening them enough for Tavenji to wriggle free.

"Ugh, I can't thank you enough, little friend," he said, rubbing his arms and wrists. "Those fools would have kept me here until the world ended."

"Not all of them," Drahn said. "Master Ildwic bewieved you also, and asked me to give you this." It was then that Tavenji noticed the acorn tied around the creature's neck.

"My acorn!" he cried, hopping about excitedly. "Wonderful!" He held his hands out for it as Drahn removed it from his neck.

"What does it do?" Drahn asked.

"I have no idea," Tavenji said, "It's a gift of Eyorona, so I'm hoping it will give me wisdom and knowledge when I need it."

"Are you weally sent by the gods?" the little creature asked with a touch of awe.

"You deciphered one of my names," Tavenji said. "What do you think?"

"What I think makes no sense," Drahn replied,

fiddling with his tail.

"I know exactly how you feel," said the little god. "Now, how do I get out of here?" He gripped the acorn, wishing for inspiration.

Drahn said, "I came in through the library window. It is how I usually get in to do wesearch."

"Wonderful! Let's go!" Tavenji whispered.

"First," Drahn said, "could you lift the guard's head off the book? I'm afwaid his dwool will wuin the ink."

After tending to the safety of the book, the two headed upstairs to the library. It was a large domed room that held three levels of books, the lowest level being the smaller in diameter. Movable ladders allowed access to the collections, which were kept well-dusted and cared for. The room was lit by a globe suspended from a large central column that hung from the ceiling. On further investigation, Tavenji found that the column was actually a suspended fourth level that kept books and scrolls around its circumference. There was a railing, but no visible way to access it. He had to admire the ingenuity; no doubt those were rare and valuable tomes indeed.

"So where is this window?" Tavenji asked. Drahn led him to an oval-shaped egress set into the curved wall. The angle allowed him to look straight down to the street almost two hundred feet below. "Uh... We're a bit higher than I was expecting. I see humans have improved their tower building skills."

"It is quite a dwop," Drahn agreed.

"What am I supposed to do now?" asked the little god, "Fly?"

"I wasn't sure if you could or not," Drahn said. "Don't you have powers of some kind?"

"If I had powers, I wouldn't have spent a week tied to a chair being pestered by old men with beard fetishes," he said.

"Twue, twue," Drahn said.

"Well, what about you then?" Tavenji asked. "You dweedragons know all kinds of tricks. Can't you get us both out of here?"

"I'm afwaid I don't know how to use dwagon magic," Drahn said, drooping his head. "My egg clutch was attacked before I was taught how. I only escaped by accident."

"Oh, sorry," Tavenji said, more disappointed than sympathetic. "I guess I should have suspected when you cast those spells in Celvestrian mage-cant." He looked at the wealth of information around him. "Aren't there books on dweedragons in here?"

"Only the ones I edited," Drahn said, "They wead more like wildlife catalogs, wather than wecords of a complex culture. There are no spell descwiptions."

"That figures," Tavenji said with a sigh. "But I suppose dweedwagons only twade twicks with twusted twainees."

Drahn gave him a withering look and his scales flushed to deep purple, then to crimson.

"Sorry," the little god grinned. "It's infectious." He tossed the acorn in the air as he scratched his head, pacing about the circular room. Suddenly, he stopped in his tracks with a grin spreading across his face. "That's it. That's it!" he exclaimed, and he picked up the startled dweedragon and rushed to the window. "We can ride the lightning!" Tavenji stepped out onto the ledge, with Drahn under one arm, and the other braced against the window frame to keep them from falling.

Drahn was very upset at this arrangement and let out a whimper as he gripped the man's borrowed robe, "What are you doing? What lightning is there to wide?" If they fell now, he would plunge to his death unless the little man let him go, and with his wings pinned to his body, the drop looked very far indeed. "I told you, I don't know dwagon magic!"

Tavenji felt the acorn shrink in his grip as the knowledge flooded into his brain.

Drahn stiffened as his scales turned blue with fright. "What- what is happening to me?" he squeaked. He experienced a torrent of words rushing into his mind, but they were not the words of the little man holding him; they were words in the language of dragons. The rumbling, sibilant chorus spun inside his skull and coursed down his spine, filling him with a new confidence.

Before he understood why, he was taking a deep breath and reaching for the element that resided within him. His scales turned red with anticipation as he enveloped himself and the prisoner in a charged ball of cracking energy. For the briefest moment, he felt at one with the lightning. Then he exhaled.

Tavenji's whoop of exhilaration was lost in the crack of thunder as they vanished into a white-hot bolt of fire, racing down the length of the tower in an instant. Then it was over, and they found themselves sprawled on the paving stones amid a black burn mark at the base of the structure.

"Whoo-hahaha!" Tavenji cried, spreading his arms and legs on the cold stone and gazing up at the tower looming over them. "That was incredible! I can't believe I've never tried that before!" He scooped Drahn up and held him so that the little dragon was looking down at him. "Brilliant! Thank you, my friend."

Drahn was too amazed to be upset at the unwanted handling. His lips curved into a triumphant smile and he said, "I had no idea that was possible! How did you do that?"

Tavenji set him down and sat up, holding up the acorn, which was decidedly smaller. "Gift of Eyorona, goddess of knowledge and learning!" he said happily, getting to his feet. "Now I need to get out of here and find my- er, that mad wizard," he looked down at himself and sighed, "and perhaps some proper clothes."

Windows were opening and faces were peeking out into the night from the surrounding buildings. The tower's neighbors were a tolerant lot, but the flash and noise of the lightning was more than people were willing to ignore.

"Time to go," Tavenji said. He gave Drahn one last

hug and fled into the night.

The Dweedragon just sat there on the paving stones, contemplating the strange visitor and his own newfound power; it wasn't until the door to the tower opened and wizards came out to investigate that his better sense kicked in, and he scampered into the shadows like a guilty cat.

Tavenji wished he had taken more time to study the vast city from a height before making his escape. Portshia had changed in the last millennium, and aside from the mountains, there were no landmarks he recognized. Even the castle on the seaside bluff was completely different; it sat so low that its ramparts could barely be seen over the wall.

"Where to start, where to start..." he muttered. The streets were deserted but for the occasional city watch patrol, which he avoided. He was conspicuous with his long, pointed ears and over-sized robe, and it wouldn't take a genius of a guard to realize he was out of place.

He wandered the streets at random, peeking in windows and listening at doors. There were dark little shapes moving underfoot in the shadows, squeaking in a pitch that Tavenji's long ears could detect. "Rats," he said. "Rats, rats, rats."

He knelt down near a number of rats who had found a patch of filth to rummage through. "Hello," he said to the rodents. "Would you fellows be local residents, or are you part of the recent plague?"

The rats stopped to consider him, sniffing his robes and looking him up and down with their beady, black eyes. They huddled together, and then squeaked at him at length before returning to their filth pile.

Tavenji stood and folded his arms, "It was *not* a stupid question. You ought to have more respect, you fuzzy little cockroaches." He tromped away, feeling lower than he had all week.

Eventually he came to a bridge crossing the flowing canal that separated the Copper District from the

Temple District. Portshia had no canals the last time he was here, so he stopped on the bridge to admire the view, if not the smell. His attention was drawn to a team of water oxen tied up at a low pier. The beasts made gentle splashes as their heads and horns broke the water.

"Huh, those are new," he said. "At least they made themselves useful." The Time of Chaos produced so many odd things, both from the outer planes and from nature itself. There was no telling what would be popping up soon if he didn't find his lost brother. He shrugged and made his way towards the huge cathedral that glowed ghostly white in the moonlight.

The streets were broad and well-lit, modeled after the avenues of the old imperial capital across the sea. Glass orbs hung from street-poles upon which magic light glowed. The people of the night gathered nearby the pools of light, but not too near, lest they need to slip into the shadows and disappear. At this late hour, few decent folk were lurking outdoors.

Tavenji passed between the temples of Lelonetha and Selvina, pausing to gaze upon the relief carvings of his sisters. The images did them no justice of course, but they did manage to capture Mother Mercy's kindly nature, and Selvina's prowling sensuality. He had the briefest notion to find some charcoal and grace the love goddess with a thick mustache, but he really had more important things to do first. He gave the statues a little wave and skipped on to the base of the giant cathedral, now looming before him.

"How do I find you, brother?" he asked to the air as he climbed the steps of the cathedral and sat cross-legged before the ornate doors, his chin resting in his hands. "Do you even want to be found?" He looked out into the large plaza before the cathedral, seeing the wretched souls who congregated near fiery braziers placed there for the homeless. He might have expected his brother Epoch to be huddled by one, but he had a feeling that the old man was keeping much worse company.

The cathedral was dedicated to the gods of the city, in this case, a mixture of the gods of civilization and the gods of nature. Most had their own separate temples in town besides, but mortals loved to outdo themselves. Each of the twelve towers that anchored the buttresses was dedicated to a god, and it was no surprise that Tavenji was not among them. No one worshiped him anymore, not for a very long time.

Eyorona was represented on the cathedral's carved statues, as was Lelonetha and Obamir. Recalling the other favors he had been given, he felt his stomach. They were in there somewhere, waiting to get out. If he were still a full-fledged god, he could cough them back up at will, but here things were different. How different he was not entirely sure. *I hope I don't have to squat over a bucket and dig them out*, he thought grimly.

He knew the wizard had observed correctly; he didn't have to relieve himself like a mortal would. But could he choose to? Could he be... *selective* about what came out of either end? It was situations like this that no god was ever prepared for, no matter how powerful they had been on the other side.

Taking a chance, he stuck his finger down his throat and wretched. His stomach heaved, disgorging a mixture of oatmeal, bread, and water onto the cathedral steps. Yet, there was no coin and no ring. He tried again.

And again,

And again,

And again,

His ribs ached and his head began to pound with the effort, yet still there were no tokens from his siblings in the growing pool of spew. He noticed a thing or two of interest during the experience, and he ruminated over them as he continued discharging the week's meals. First, there was no sharp smell of bile; in fact, the food came out rather as it had gone in, albeit more soggy and chewed.

Second, the cathedral plaza carried sound quite well, and his retching was echoing across the paving stones, drawing looks from everyone within earshot. Third, the sheer amount of vomit he was producing was now cascading down the cathedral steps like a mighty river, its chunky consistency producing a 'plop, plop' sound as it flowed down the semicircular tiers.

This was all very interesting, and might make for an amusing anecdote one day, but for now it was rather hard work. He put his observations at the back of his mind and focused on the business at hand.

Finally, as he was sure he was about to give himself a hernia, he felt two solid objects pop out of his throat and clink on the stone steps. The lucky coin from Obamir and ring from Lelonetha glittered in the moonlight amid the mess he had made, and he could only gaze down at them on his hands and knees, panting from the effort. Scooping them up and putting them in his pocket with the smallish acorn, he eventually staggered to his feet and shuffled off into the darkness before he could be arrested for desecrating the holiest ground in the city.

Tavenji awoke in the cool dark of an alleyway as the morning sun turned the sky a pale blue. He was wrapped up in his robe, which was liberally stained with crusted puke and rat droppings. The later had been left by the scavengers who were even now leaping off of his back and scampering to a safe distance.

"Ugh," he moaned, rubbing his eyes. "Sleep? I have to *sleep* now? That's all I need." He got to his feet and shook the debris from his robe, looking around to get his bearings.

The alley was one of many that broke up the solid quad-buildings, creating narrow gaps that stood two to three stories high on either side. Behind him was a typical-looking street beginning to fill with morning traffic and before him was a courtyard with a broad, circular building in the middle, adorned with decorative animal-head water spouts. It seemed to have a copper domed-roof, though it did not have the look of a temple.

"Weirder is better," he muttered, and stumbled down the alley to get a closer look.

His curiosity was rewarded by the sight of many poster frames that lined the enclosing walls of what must be a theater. The frames contained delightful posters that had been pasted over layers of older ones, announcing current or upcoming plays. The latest poster advertised something called 'The Fools of Fallow Farm,' and had a picture of a dancing cow and a pair of bewildered farmers, above whom the laughing face of a pointy-eared trickster was looming.

"Well, I'll be a son of a reylok," Tavenji said, his eyes growing wide at the sight. It was not exactly his face of course, but it was a traditional depiction that could be no one else. He giggled despite his miserable condition. All theaters were once dedicated to Tavenji long ago, and he found himself a recurring character in mortal entertainment, as often as any other god. "This is a good sign," he said, "A very good sign."

He found his way in through the stage door, getting only a few odd looks for his ears, hair, and clothing. One of the players, trying to memorize his lines, glanced up and did a double-take.

"Who are you supposed to be?" he asked, looking suspicious.

"Who do I look like?" Tavenji replied, flapping his overlong sleeves, "The dancing cow?"

The player gave him a humorless snort, "We already have a Tavenji," he said. "Those ears are amazing, to be sure, but what are you wearing? Is that vomit on your robe?"

"It's a bit the worse for wear," he admitted, "but it was all I had at the time."

"Wonderful," said the player, noticing the bare skin under the robe. "It looks like you rented yourself out to a wizard with a tender stomach. If you are Tavenji's new understudy, I hope the lead never takes ill."

"How *dare* you!" the little god squeaked, taking offense for the fun of it. "No one plays a better Tavenji than me! I'm no one's understudy!"

"Hah!" scoffed the player. "You better not let our shining star hear you say that if you value your pretty little nose."

Tavenji felt his nose. "It *is* rather pretty, isn't it? Very well then, I'll go and see if that talentless hack has what it takes. I assume they are rehearsing now?"

"We're rehearsing what few scenes we have," he said. "The play opens in a week and we still don't have a complete script."

"Hah!" Tavenji scoffed dramatically. "I need no script! I do my best work when I improvise!" He snapped his fingers and marched into the backstage door, disappearing into the nearest costume rack. He would have spent the whole day playing himself opposite his mortal counterpart, had he the time. Instead, he stole the actor's costume and made off before anyone was the wiser.

Feeling himself again in his traditional jester's motley, green silken coat, and red sash, he skipped into the city streets, which were now abuzz with the life of the morning. He received many odd looks, but also smiles and nods, and it helped alleviate the suspicions of the watch when he called out, "Come one, come all to the theater! See the Fools of Fallow Farm, opening next week!"

He was sure it would be a sold-out performance with advertising like this, and he hoped the mummer company remembered to thank him for the blessing. After all, it was the first he had been able to give in more than a thousand years.

As he wandered the streets, he became aware of the somber faces around him and the overall low mood of the city. There were sick people huddling in doorways, coughing and shivering as they tried to get warm in the summer sun. Others avoided them as best they could, and many doors were marked with charcoal to indicate households taken ill.

There were many priests about, offering soothing brews and poultices, as well as Divine Alchemy for the worst cases. Bodies could be seen lying on the street, covered with linens to await the undertakers. Children armed with sticks guarded the corpses, making a game of keeping the rats at bay.

Tavenji saw that a great many soldiers were in the city, adding to the tension of the populace. They were in the process of quartering in private homes, going door-to-door and requesting permission from the residents to lodge a few soldiers through the winter. Obviously there was a war on the horizon, and the trickster could feel his elder brother's bloody legacy at work. *War is coming,* Tavenji thought, *but it's a war no one will win.*

His wanderings took him closer to the foot of the mountain above the city, towards the place that housed the dwarfs who worked in the city's silver mines. He was happy to see that much of Miner Town still stood, but it had obviously dwindled along with its population. There was no smoke from smelters or smithies, no sign of machinery churning to haul rocks up from the depths of the earth. *The mines must have petered out,* he thought.

He had always had an affinity for the little people, outcasts that they were. He knew what it was like to be seen as an aberration to one's own family, and he felt a kinship to those who were misunderstood and shunned. He loved to play tricks on them of course, but they were tricks of a generous and playful nature, of the kind that friends played upon friends. The dwarfs of Portshia's Miner Town came to know him as 'Uncle Tweak.'

He suddenly felt conspicuous in his garish clothing, and wondered if he should try to blend in better. It was a certainty that the wizards of the big tower were looking for him, possibly with magic. They had kept his arrival a secret, but his escape might be reported to the authorities, and a little man with platinum hair and long pointed ears would not be hard to find, especially if he was dressed like, well, like Tavenji.

He muttered to himself aloud, "I am going to need a disguise, and soon. Come to think of it, I will need other things that I've never needed before." He ticked off the count on his fingers, "I'll need food, clothing, lodging, weapons, and equipment." He switched to his other hand, "a guide, and a horse, someone to care for the horse, a pet monkey, and *money*. Where am I going to get money?" He could steal it of course, but that would create more problems.

He reached into the fold of his sash and retrieved Obamir's luck coin. It was the only coin he possessed, and it was worth more than the whole of the nation's treasury, so he was certain that no one could make change for it. He tossed it in the air as he walked, pondering his new predicament. "If I'm going to get a job, I will have to learn some skills, I expect. I wonder how much money a juggler makes?"

He whistled as he walked, passing out of Miner Town and following a wide road next to a tree-lined wall. It enclosed a large area, like a private park. The tops of white marble buildings could be seen over the wall, as well as a tall tower that overlooked the expanse. It was currently manned with a few soldiers and what appeared to be guild wizards, judging by their robes and twin-tailed caps.

As he approached the iron gates of the enclosure, he saw that it was a cemetery full of mausoleums, monuments, and rows upon rows of simple graves. He wondered at the manned tower, but recalled how the silver-handed wizard had said that vemloks had been stalking the city. *It must be a Dead Watch tower,* Tavenji thought. *Ill times indeed when you need to keep the people* inside *a cemetery.*

Just then he looked up at the temple adjacent to the cemetery gates. The sight made him jump; it was a temple of Valdak, and a very life-like relief carving of the dark, blind god stared down at him, his hooked staff gleaming wickedly in the morning light. Tavenji was so unnerved by the sight that he missed catching his coin, and it hit the ground rolling.

"Agh!" he cried, chasing after the precious metal as it bounced along the worn cobblestones. "No no no no no!" It slowed, wobbled along its path, and headed straight for an iron storm drain. He dove for it, but only managed to scrape his elbows, knees, and knuckles. "NO!" he cried in anguish, listening to the distant 'clink' echoing in the depths of the drain.

He lay there for some time, peering into the darkness as passersby regarded him with curiosity. Finally, he rolled over on his back and looked up at Valdak's blind eyes saying, "It's *your* fault for being so creepy, brother."

It seemed that luck had deserted him, but he was not about to despair. *I'm a god, damn it!* He thought. *I'm not going to give up that easily!* He got to his feet and tried to lift the iron grate. A twinge of pain in his back told him this was not a good idea. "Ow!" he said. "Muscle strain? Really?" This new existence was terrible; no wonder brother Epoch had gone mad.

A horse and wagon loaded with hay came trundling down the road, headed directly for him at a leisurely pace. An idea sprang into his mind, and he hurriedly removed his sash, tucking the acorn and ring down his motley tights. *Pockets,* he thought. *I need an outfit with pockets.* He tied one end of the sash to the grating, and stepped aside to wait for the cart.

As it passed, he tried to look casual, whistling and gazing at the clouds. Just as the horse passed by the grating, Tavenji tumbled under the cart and tied the other end of his sash to the rear axle. The cart gave a shudder and the iron grate groaned out of its fitting, but then the axle broke and dumped the tall stack of hay backwards, nearly burying him in the cascade.

That didn't quite go as planned, he thought as he

kicked aside the hay to find the drain opening. He felt the need to apologize to the driver, but quickly let it pass. The man had tumbled into the back of his cart and into the hay, and seemed in no mood to entertain an explanation. Tavenji quickly found the opening and dropped in. *I'll need a new sash too,* he thought as he fell.

The impact jolted his knees and rattled his teeth, but left him otherwise undamaged. He began feeling about on the damp stone, searching for the missing trinket. The drain passage was sloped, so the coin had likely rolled away again. "I wish I had a light spell or *something*," he said. He tried snapping his fingers, wiggling his nose, and fluttering his hands while imagining a ball of light appearing before him; nothing. He tried chanting in the mage-cant used by human wizards, "*Ildas Oridos!*" nothing again. He uttered an elven spell, "Ilviis galan diis." No result.

"Matches," he said to the darkness. "I'll also need matches."

Finally, after much groping in the dark and damp, he found the coin lying in a puddle of water about thirty feet from the drain opening. He gave a little cheer, squeezed it, and noticed it felt a bit smaller. "Wait a minute," he said with growing suspicion. "There was nothing lucky about that! That was decidedly *unlucky.*" But he was not imagining things; the coin was smaller now, and thinner. Feeling betrayed, he slipped it into his tights with the other two tokens and began to wonder how he was going to get out of the sewer.

He headed in the opposite direction, figuring that up was best. There was no way to reach the drain opening, and there was certainly no one up above who was in the mood to help him, so he trudged up the passage with hopes of finding another shallower grating. What he found instead was a brick wall blocking the passage further up the sewer line. Feeling in the dark, he found what seemed to be a metal handhold set into the stone. There was another above, and another, and soon he was climbing up the wall towards an opening near the top. He straddled the wall for a moment, feeling for a foothold on the other side. To his relief, he found one, then another.

It was quite nerve-racking, climbing about in the dark. He could hear the echoes of deep spaces beneath him, and when he dislodged little pebbles from the wall, he heard them tumble far below. There were small shafts of light that came in through distant drains, but none were near enough to light his path. He only hoped that the hand and footholds would take him somewhere he wanted to go.

It was nearly twenty minutes before he found solid ground under his feet. As best he could tell, he had descended far below the level of the sewer tunnels, and was now someplace cold and very dark. The air barely stirred, and the odors of mold and damp earth could not quite cover the scent of old death.

"Catacombs," he said miserably. "I'm in the necropolis under the city; lucky, lucky, lucky. Yep, lucky me."

Feeling along the walls confirmed his suspicions. His hands slipped into recessed alcoves where he felt the smooth length of bones and the brittle remnants of burial shrouds. Thoughts of vemloks creeping in the dark leaped to his mind, and he wondered for the first time if he could actually die. Death had never been an option before, but now that he was more of a man than a god, who could say? He quivered at the notion and found that his heart was pounding noticeably in his chest.

If I have a heart, can it stop?

He wandered in darkness for what seemed like hours, until to his delight, he saw a flickering orange glow in the distance. At first he thought his eyes were tricking him, but no, it was unsteady torchlight coming from around a bend in the far passage. He began to quicken his pace, still unsure of the level of the floor, but soon found himself running towards the light. He felt like a soul must feel after passing through death to the other side. Then he remembered that a soul's first experience after death was with Valdak the Judge, and he stifled his glee just a bit.

He almost tripped over the bodies. There were two forms on the ground at the bend of the passage, dressed in dark cloaks. He could make out nothing more in the dim torchlight, but he saw its source up ahead. It was flickering because whoever held the torch was wedged into a narrow alcove, and was thrusting it at a figure in the passageway, keeping it at bay.

The figure was thin and pale, wearing a simple white nightshirt; it seemed to be a man, though it snarled and moaned like a beast. Tavenji saw a sleeve of the nightshirt catch fire, but the man did not seem to notice until the fire spread. The pale figure tore at the fabric, ripping the burning section away before slashing into the alcove once again.

"Vemlok!" Tavenji said under his breath, or thought he did. It must have been loud enough to hear, for the pale creature turned its head to look down the corridor at him. Its dark, sunken eyes glowed with points of cold light, and its mouth opened into a cavernous maw, emitting a low moan that turned to a shriek of savage hunger. It lunged at him, covering the distance with inhuman speed.

Before Tavenji could react, the thing was upon him, knocking him back against the wall. He felt strong hands press against his face, felt iron fingers enclose his skull. He saw the chaos-fire in the black eyes as the thirsting spirit drove its host body to feed upon fresh blood, sucking it in through greedy fingers. Tavenji's face turned to pins and needles, going numb as the blood drained from his head.

He didn't even have a chance to scream before the creature's eyes widened in pain and it launched itself back, shaking its hands and arms as if they were on fire. Then they *were* on fire, burning orange and black as the vemlok's body immolated from fingers to toes, leaving a pile of ash and embers to fall at the little god's feet. Tavenji began breathing again, panting in his near-panic.

The torch poked a bit farther out of the alcove, followed by a face peering into the gloom. The little god found he was looking at the face of a dwarf, eyes wide with terror, and hands shaking as he held the flame before him.

"Hello?" said the dwarf, his voice cracking. "Is it gone?"

"Uh, yes," Tavenji said, more than a little shaken himself. "It's dead for good." He rubbed some feeling back into his face.

The dwarf let out a deep sigh, leaving the alcove to step out into the hall. He was about four feet tall, with a thick mop of dark hair and a prominent brow. He wore a dark cloak, like the bodies in the passage, and a dark gray tunic with trousers. "I cannot thank you enough my friend," he said. "But if I may ask, how did you manage to destroy that monster?"

Tavenji had a notion, but he wasn't going to share it with this fellow. Instead he answered, "Oh, it's an old bit of magic that protects me. I give them heartburn."

"Are you... an elf?" asked the dwarf.

"Why yes, yes I am," Tavenji lied. "What are you doing down here in the first place?"

"I might ask the same of you," replied the dwarf. "Some would say that a dwarf is a more common sight underground than an elf."

"True enough," the little god smiled. "But this isn't a mine, and that's a dagger, not a pickax." He pointed to the weapon on the dwarf's belt.

"True enough," said the dwarf. "Alright, I- rather *we*, were on our way to a secret meeting. The vemlok attacked us and my escorts were killed. It was pure luck that you came along when you did, or I would have been his next meal."

Pure luck, Tavenji thought, and his eyes widened as he recalled the shrunken coin in his tights. He said,

"Happy to be at your service. My name is Tweak." They shook hands in greeting as the dwarf recovered some of his color.

"Pleased to make your acquaintance, uh... Tweak. My name is Emen." The dwarf gave him a slight smile, neither unfriendly nor trusting. "I wonder if I might purchase your assistance for the next hour?" he said as he walked over to his two fallen companions. Passing the torch to Tavenji, he began going through their pockets. "It is very important that I get to my meeting, and obviously, my escorts were not up to the task of seeing me there safely. I would gladly pay you for your time if you would act as my bodyguard."

"Oh!" Tavenji said, "Pay, as in a job? Yes, that will be perfect. I only have one coin to my name; that's why I'm here actually. It rolled down a drain and I followed it."

Emen raised his eyebrows and said, "Farther than I'd go for one coin. But here," he tossed Tavenji one of the dead men's purses. "Will that cover your time?"

The little god looked into the purse with glee, fingering through all the shiny silver coins. "Is this a lot?" he asked.

"It's a decent sum," Emen said. "The other purse is yours when I return safely to the surface." He looked at Tavenji's garish clothing, as if noticing them for the first time. "You might want to wear something a bit less flashy," he said. "We don't want to draw undue attention to you; perhaps, a hooded cloak?"

The only clothing in the area that wasn't rotted to dust was currently being worn by the dead men. Tavenji had no problem looting dead bodies; it was considered more distasteful to steal from the souls of the deceased, and he did that all the time. So he shrugged and began undressing the smaller man, donning the drab clothing over his motley colors.

"I hope they don't become vemloks themselves and follow us," Emen said.

"They won't," Tavenji reassured him. "The body

needs to be in contact with loose earth or clay; it's a conduit for the thirsting spirit. The floor and walls here are lined with solid rock. Besides, it takes about three days if it happens at all."

"What about the one that attacked us?" Emen asked. "Where did he come from?"

"He probably rose from a grave up above, and hid from the daylight down here," Tavenji explained, describing the grisly subject with a casual air of one seldom touched by true horror. "Either you made too much noise, or it sniffed you out."

"You seem to know a great deal about these creatures," Emen said.

"Well, we elves know these things," he remarked. "We get around."

"I see..." Emen said.

Tavenji finished adjusting his clothing, admiring his pockets, his belt, and his new dagger. He flipped up the hood to cover his ears, Emen handed him the torch, and they made off into the tunnels.

"So what is this meeting about?" Tavenji asked. "Are we going to a grave-digger's convention?"

"Not exactly," Emen said. "Let us say that our little social club doesn't like others taking notice, and leave it at that."

"Secret meeting is a secret," Tavenji said, nodding. *A thieving guild,* he figured, *or worse, a Llomaakitte cult. This is going to be interesting.*

After many twists and turns, they arrived at a long, torch-lit hall that led to a kind of central junction. There were a few hooded guards bearing crossbows and knives, but Emen spoke the required passwords to permit them to continue. Tavenji noticed that the alcoves here contained not only bones, but subtle spring-traps to impale unwelcomed visitors. The guards disabled them as they approached, and rearmed them after they passed by.

They finally arrived in the central chamber, a deep room that used to be a tomb for a very important family. There were carved sarcophagi around the perimeter depicting men and women in beatific repose; their flowing robes of stone looked so life-like that a breeze might rustle them. In the center of the room was a sarcophagus, now serving as a stone table or alter. The area around the platform was surrounded by seven wooden chairs, each seating a dark-hooded figure. Behind each chair was a passageway leading deeper into the tunnels, and they were guarded by one or two dangerous-looking people standing at a respectful distance.

Emen motioned to Tavenji to place his torch in a wall sconce, and beckoned him closer. He said, "You must stand guard here. Watch my back, and try not to distract anyone." He looked as if he might say more, but thought the better of it and took his seat around the stone platform.

Once all six chairs were filled, a man entered the room with two guards flanking him. He stood before the seventh chair but did not sit. Tavenji peered into the man's hood and saw a cold, stony face staring back at him. The features were craggy and hard, with piercing eyes, a hawkish nose, and a thin line of a mouth. The man's chin was squared and wide, and his cheekbones looked sharp enough to cut through his rough skin.

The man spread his arms over the stone table and spoke in a deep voice that almost croaked, "Place your tokens, so that you may be known."

One by one, the six seated figures arose and placed a small trinket on the stone platform, which the seventh man examined. There was a seashell, a walnut, an iron key, a braided length of sailcloth, and a piece of chalk. Emen placed what looked like a dried chicken's foot on the table before sitting down.

"Very good," said the man before finally taking his seat. "All of the districts are represented. I now call this meeting to order." He cleared his throat with a noise like a barking dog. "You are all aware of the problems our guild will face with the army encamped within and without the city. There will be fewer chances for aggressive activities like pinching, selling protection, and housebreaking, and greater opportunities for pandering and gaming. I expect that your districts will restructure as best as can be for the coming months."

A woman spoke, her rough voice telling of greater age and a lifetime of yelling, but she spoke with low respect, "I've a question, Boss. Will ye be expecting my specialty girls to follow the army north? They're not much for hardship; a powdered tin of pastries, the lot of them!"

"Your girls may go as they choose, Mag," he said, "though I expect you to send handlers along. Their earnings should flow back to you, as I am sure you'll agree."

There were rough chuckles all around. Mag let out a cackle.

Emen spoke, "Boss, forgive my lateness, but we encountered a vemlok in the catacombs under the Silver District." All eyes turned to him and the chuckling stopped.

"Another vemlok?" asked the Boss. "I hope you were not injured."

"I lost two men," Emen said. No one spoke, but many nervous glances were shared. In the silence, Emen cleared his throat and continued, "I have a question about the recent events that have been happening in the city."

"You think I have answers for you?" said the Boss.

Emen said, "There have been many stories from the north about a mad wizard that came south to Portshia, trailing curses and misfortune behind him."

Tavenji's ears perked up at this and he tried not to jump forward.

Emen said, "He was seen in the Outwalls on the night of the freak dust storm over a month ago, and others saw him within the city when the rats began to swarm, and the ill cloud of omens befell the city."

"Is there a question coming soon?" asked the Boss in a flat voice.

"Yes," Emen said meekly. "I was wondering if we of the Circle, with all of our spies and informants, have heard or seen anything of this mad wizard. If he is still in the city, surely we might be the ones to best find him?"

"Why should we wish to?" asked a thin man to Emen's right. His beard poked out under his hood as he spoke. "What is the profit in it?"

"The *profit*," Emen spoke with exasperation, "would be to lift this curse from our city. I know we are not the most civic-minded of persons, but isn't it worth our while to seek out this rogue wizard and put an end to him?"

"You think no one else has tried?" asked an older man sitting nearer the Boss. "Both the Mystic College and the Order of Astrellaris have been searching in vain for him, and no one has gotten any closer. It's said that some have gone mad in trying."

"No doubt they were searching with magic," said a younger man with an erudite manner of speech. "We can search with eyes and ears, and we need not trouble ourselves with disposing of him. I'm sure the Gold Cat or the Black Eagle himself would be quite pleased to do that."

"Exactly," Emen said, glad for the support.

"Master Emen," said the Boss. "I know you have not been a member of this council for very long, but let me assure you that the health and safety of the good people of Portshia are always foremost in our thoughts." There was another round of chuckling as the Boss cracked a rare smile, creasing his face unnaturally. "As for this mad wizard however, he is none of our affair. It stands to reason that if all of the city's authorities are seeking him, then casting our lot with them would expose us."

"I had hoped," Emen said, "that we might mitigate the suffering of our own brotherhood- *and* sisterhood," he added, nodding to Mag, "many of whom struggle already with poverty and ill-fortune. As you know, my pickpockets are mostly orphans and street urchins, and several have died-"

The Boss cut him off saying, "Your predecessor was neither a kind man, Master Emen, nor was he compassionate. Yet Dexer kept his district in line. I expect the same of you. How you wrestle with your conscience is your own affair. As for your losses, I guarantee that there will be many more unwanted orphans to choose from in the near future."

Emen sunk into his chair and did not speak for some time. Yet before the meeting was over, the Boss asked him, "Emen, there is something I hope you can clarify. You said you were attacked by a vemlok on your way here?"

"Yes," Emen said, unhappy at being singled out again. "It killed two of my escort."

"I see," said the Boss. "How did you escape?"

Emen swallowed in a dry throat and replied, "Er, my other man was able to immolate the creature; not a moment too soon, actually."

"Quick thinking," said the Boss. "Is that him back there?" He pointed to Tavenji, and Emen nodded. The Boss beckoned him forward.

Tavenji had been so distracted by the talk of the mad wizard that he almost forgot himself. He snapped back to the present and stepped forward, careful to appear subservient.

The Boss rumbled pleasantly, "What is your name, young man?"

"Tweak," Tavenji said.

"Let me have a look at you, Tweak," said the Boss, and he beckoned Tavenji closer. The little god noticed the man's bodyguards shifting position and fingering their weapons.

Tavenji stepped upon the platform and approached, raising his face to look into the Boss's hood. The craggy face was in stark relief in the firelight, and there were details Tavenji had not noticed before; the man's eyes were subtly shifting color, from hazel to blue-green; his left eyelid drooped slightly due to a scar; the muscles in his jaw flexed and twitched almost imperceptibly, as though they were under strain.

There was much about the face that the little god could see, and what he saw told him that this man's face was not his own. *A duplict?* He thought in amazement, *No... a half-duplict, maybe?*

The Boss also had an eye for Tavenji's strangeness. He took in the fine features, the wide, innocent, almond eyes, and the locks of pale blond hair. Reaching up, he pulled back Tavenji's hood. A gasp of shock went around the room, and Emen groaned.

"What *are* you?" asked the Boss, peering at the little god's ears.

"Um, an elf?" Tavenji offered. By the look on the man's face, that was probably the wrong answer.

"An elf," said the Boss, looking towards Emen Silverthumb, who was hiding his face with his hand.

Emen explained, "I met him in the catacombs. He saved me from the vemlok when my men were killed, and I hired him to escort me here."

"So he's not even a made brother?" asked one of the district bosses in astonishment. "Just someone you *happened* to run into on the way?"

"I was a bit desperate," Emen said. "It had me backed into an alcove with nothing but a torch to protect myself. Then this elf appeared, it attacked him, and the next thing I knew, it had burst into flame and cinders. That's the truth!"

"There will be time for questions and answers later," said the Boss, motioning for his men to take 'Tweak' into custody. "I declare this meeting at an end. Silverthumb, I'll have you escorted back home, where I'm *sure* you'll stay put. You don't mind if I take your elf friend with me, do you?"

Emen shook his head, looking thoroughly wretched. "Do as you will, Boss. Forgive me, I-"

The Boss shook his head and said in a croaking

baritone, "Emen, Emen. There is nothing to forgive. What's important is that we have made a new friend." He turned his unnerving face towards the little god.

Tavenji smiled his most innocent smile at the creature of Chaos, but had a feeling that his new 'friend' had something other in mind than tea and pastries at the end of the tunnel. The point of a dagger pressed in his back confirmed that suspicion.

The district bosses of the Circle of Gold took back their trinkets from the stone altar, and with their bodyguards, swept out of the chamber. Tavenji got a last glimpse of Emen's face before they were taken into opposite passageways. The dwarf gave him a look of regret and sadness, as if he were looking upon him for the last time.

Tavenji had been correct: there was no tea and pastries awaiting him. Instead, he was led through a maze of catacombs and access tunnels, eventually arriving through a secret door into a sub-basement. The chamber seemed to be beneath the level of the sewers and canals, and it stank of mold and mildew. Worst of all, there were cages along the walls and what looked like torture devices in the middle of the room.

The Boss lit the chamber's torches with his own, bathing the sub-basement in warm orange light; it did not improve the mood of the room however. The torchlight struck the cages and wicked iron implements, casting dancing wraith-shadows upon the walls. Dark patches of mold crept across the stone in defiance of the light, creating permanent shadows where there should be none.

"Make our friend comfortable," the Boss said, placing his torch in a wall sconce. The bodyguards nearly lifted the little god off his feet and shoved him into a nasty-looking chair, clasping metal wrist and ankle clamps in place. As they did this, the Boss turned and raised something to his face. When he turned back to his prisoner, he was wearing a bestial mask that hid his features below the eyes.

Tavenji saw that the man's face was already different than before. His eyes had changed to blue and were a different shape, but he still bore the scar over his left eyelid. His eyebrows were darker and thicker, and the bridge of his nose was thinner. The beast mask covered the rest, and it was hideous enough to make one want to divert their eyes.

He's a Llomaakitte, Tavenji realized. *They wear those masks in rituals and secret meetings, where they might be seen by outsiders.* It told him much. It meant that the bodyguards were probably not cult members, and were not meant to see the face the Boss now wore. *He's got Duplict blood, no doubt about it,* Tavenji thought with mounting excitement, *Second or third generation, maybe. He's a child of Chaos and a Llomaakitte, which means he's probably exactly who I'm looking for!*

Unfortunately, Tavenji's captors were preparing to torture him with various, nasty instruments. He was going to have to think fast if he was going to avoid it.

"Now," said the Boss, his voice now an airy tenor. "Perhaps we can discuss what an elf was doing in the catacombs, and what unlikely chain of events led him to my doorstep?"

"First of all," Tavenji said as he watched the Boss select a pair of serrated tongs, "I should tell you that I'm *not* an elf. It just seemed like the best answer at the time."

"Oh?" The Boss opened the tongs, making them squeak at a pitch that made Tavenji's ears ache. "You seem to fit the description."

Tavenji squirmed as the Boss brought the instrument closer. He said, "Considering that most humans wouldn't recognize an elf if one was farting in their ear, that isn't saying much. Many have mixed blood and look human. *You* know about mixed blood, don't you?"

The instrument stopped as the Boss's eyes narrowed over the mask. His muffled voice replied, "Oh, I believe

I do. I know that the blood power diminishes as it mixes with human lines. I know that the best of weapons are the purest of blood, and *you* my friend look like a pure-blood of some kind. Therefore, I believe you are a weapon aimed at my affairs." He quickly grabbed one of Tavenji's fingers, and before the little god could struggle, he had the tongs clamped around it. The serrations bit into the skin, and the Boss increased the grip with practiced slowness.

Tavenji really didn't want to be tortured. He had no idea how much it would hurt, or how long it would take to heal. As a god in all his glory, he could take vast amounts of punishment and laugh about it later. However, he was no longer a god in any way that mattered. He didn't think he would be laughing at all if things didn't change fast.

"So," said the Boss, "what are you, if not an elf?"

The pressure became nauseatingly sharp as the tongs broke his skin and threatened to pop his knuckle. Tavenji blurted, "*Mash bah havaath!*" The pressure ceased as the Boss's grip relaxed as if by reflex.

The masked man's eyes fixed on his captive as he said to his men "Leave us. Your work is done for today." The men exchanged confused glances and departed, looking a bit disappointed.

The Boss leaned in close, "*Gnathii hvevesh ey dwratha-na vizh kwaath?*"

Tavenji translated the phrase. *Tell me why I should not spill your blood?* It was a rhetorical question, really. Tavenji had a great number of good reasons, but he doubted the Boss would accept most of them. He quickly replied, "*Vizha kwaath larwa-thii zhou. Kwaath zhu-Mash larwa-thii zhou.*" *Spilled blood has drawn me here. The blood of Mash has drawn me here.*

The answer seemed to be enough. The Boss withdrew the tongs and stood back, looking thoughtful. Presently he said, "You know the secret tongue, and you know of the Dark Heart, that much is clear. But I cannot think of why you have come, or what part you hope to play. You have not even told me what you are, if not an elf."

Tavenji breathed a sigh of relief and said, "First of all, I am new here, to this world I mean. I came through the Veil a week ago during a terrible storm. I don't know if you people have a word for what I am." This made the Boss's eyes widen with interest. "Second," Tavenji continued, "I have come to find the old man who bears the Dark Heart. He needs me, and I am sworn to help him."

"The Mad One is under my protection," said the Boss. "He is watched constantly, and wants for nothing. Why does he need you?"

Tavenji felt his anger rise at the mortal man's arrogance. "Is he not still mad? Do you think he was always so? I can help him in ways you cannot. It is my reason for being here." As he said the words, he felt an unfamiliar surge of self-righteousness and decency. It was not often that the trickster had reason to experience those feelings, so he took full advantage. "You must take me to him! It is the will of Mash."

It made him feel strange saying those words, 'It is the will of Mash.' It was not as though he was lying in an official capacity as messenger of the gods, but it still disturbed him to his core. *I'm more like a free agent now, or a spy,* he thought. *I'm lying for a good cause, the best of causes. No one can fault me for that, can they?* Well, Uncle Llomaak might fault him, but he never really liked his uncle anyway.

"The will of Mash?" asked the Boss, leaning forward. "What else does Mash say? I have never heard his words before."

"Well, of course not," Tavenji said. "None of the gods have been able to speak beyond the Veil for more than a thousand years. But why should he speak to you anyway?"

The Boss removed his mask, revealing a decidedly more handsome yet sinister face. "I am his High Priest," said Kobus DuChat. "I thought perhaps this might be known to you, if you were sent by Him."

Tavenji regarded him with a mixture of pity and mild amusement. "There was no message for you or anyone else. Choosing a high priest is no longer the affair of the gods, and neither is setting the course of human destiny."

"But he knows we carry out his will, does he not?" DuChat asked. "He knows we work towards the ultimate sacrifice that he made possible with his own blood?"

"I imagine he knows," Tavenji said truthfully, "as all the gods know. Something like that doesn't just slip their attention. But if you're looking for a pat on the head, I'm afraid I don't have an official charge to give you one."

This made the high priest frown and step back a pace. The little god was sure that the man was having an existential crisis right now, but the truth was the truth. Besides, he didn't owe this fellow anything to sooth his ego, even if it might get him out of this chair faster.

"All I can say is that I was charged to see to the 'Mad One' and his well-being. Will you take me to him, or no?" Tavenji was in no mood to sweet-talk this high priest; he was sick of being tied to chairs and threatened.

Kobus DuChat took several moments to consider before leaning back down towards the little god's hand.

He undid the clamps and set him free.

Tavenji was taken upstairs and through another set of basements and secret doors, until finally arriving in the lower rooms of what must have been a large mansion. He was shown into a guarded set of rooms where the Mad One lived with his servant in apparent comfort and luxury, although the untidy odors made his nose wrinkle. The high priest preceded him into the room and spoke briefly with the Mad One's servant, a disheveled man with hard, dark eyes and long, hawkish features. The servant regarded Tavenji with his coal-black eyes, a mix of worry, anger and fear playing across his features.

"This is Omiras Bevek," said the high priest, by way of introduction. "Bevek, this being calls himself Tweak. Please show him to the Mad One, and give him every courtesy."

Bevek did not offer his hand in greeting and Tavenji was glad of it; the man looked like he had the kind of madness upon him that was contagious somehow. "This way," he said, leading the little god towards the darkened bedchamber.

There was a warm fire burning in the hearth, though it was the middle of the day in late summer. The curtains were drawn at the windows, but the poster bed's drapery was opened to admit the heat to the frail, thin figure under the covers. There was a shabby cloak hanging over a chair, and a crooked white staff leaning near-at-hand. The figure under the covers stirred as Bevek leaned over him to speak.

Tavenji waited at the foot of the bed, unable to think of anything to say. In his mind he had pictured this moment over and over again, how he would rush to his brother's side and hug him, chide him, shake him until the Dark Heart fell out of him. He'd ask him why he betrayed his fellow gods, why he would do Llomaak's biding, why he would use his little brother as an unwitting pawn.

But seeing him in this state, like a dying mortal who could not let go of life and slip peacefully away, was too much to process. The little god could only stand there until his elder brother's eyes focused on him.

"You?" The Mad One's voice was weak and dry as the desert sands of his abandoned realm. "You are here. You helped me... in my time of need. You found me, took pity on me and rescued me. You do not deserve this fate, young one. You do not deserve to be here with me."

Bevek raised his head, recognizing the words spoken weeks ago. He thought they had been meant for him.

Tavenji went to his brother's side, sitting in the chair

near the bed. He took his brother's hand and held it as tears began to blur his vision. He had no words, no accusations. All he could manage was, "Brother Epoch? How... how are you?" He felt foolish asking such a question. If Epoch felt half as bad as he looked, he was truly miserable in ways the little god had never imagined.

"I am cold," Epoch said, "Always cold. This world, this body... not meant for us." He squeezed his eyes shut and his grip on Tavenji's hand strengthened with the pain evident on his face. "It was so strong, so much more than I... could control. It twisted... my insides... twisted everything around me."

Tavenji felt his heart breaking for his fallen brother, but was aware that he was talking now about the Dark Heart. He also noticed that he was speaking of it in the past-tense.

"It *twisted* you?" Tavenji asked softly. "Does that mean it is no longer within you?"

"It is gone from me," Epoch nodded, "Gone, yes... but it left me so weak... so weak."

It was the blood of a greater god, Tavenji knew. It would have done horrible things to Epoch, but it would have shared its power with him as well. Now that he was free of it, he would be left diminished and ruined. Tears flowed down Tavenji's cheeks as he cursed himself for his part in it. *This is all my fault,* he thought bitterly. *I thought I was being so clever, so devious and insightful.* He wished desperately that he could hurl himself back in time to undo the damage, but not even a god was capable of such a thing. He could not turn back one minute of time much less four thousand years.

Tavenji leaned close, not wanting the dangerous-looking human to overhear, "Brother, if you do not have it still, where is it?"

Epoch's eyes opened again, though it took a moment to refocus on the little god's face. He croaked, "Gone... given away. It is in their hands now, the mortals... They must choose their own path." He said these last words with bitterness, and turned his head away in anger.

"What will they do with it?" Tavenji asked desperately. "What did you tell them, brother?"

"The prophecy, the scion of ancient blood, he is here," Epoch rasped with growing excitement. "They will give him the heart when the time is right. It is dormant now, waiting... waiting to join with him..."

"Him?" Tavenji asked, now wanting to shake his brother for information; instead, he squeezed his hand tighter. "Who is the scion? What is his name?"

Epoch looked back to his little brother with a weary expression. "You cannot stop this," he said. "It is out of our hands now. We cannot interfere."

"But you *did* interfere," Tavenji said angrily. "You made me a part of it as well! How can you justify this, this... madness?"

He heard Bevek stir in his chair, but did not turn to see the intense frown crease the man's brow.

Epoch's eyes stared past his brother to fixate on the roof of the poster bed. They wandered there as he spoke. "I have been exiled in this world for one thousand and eighteen years," he said. "Ever since the portals were shut, I have walked alone; without peace, without mercy. I have starved to death but not died. I have frozen to death but not died. I have been beaten to death but not died. What I wouldn't give for a moment's peace, or the oblivion of death."

He focused on Tavenji's face again with an expression of despair, "But it never comes. I go on and on and on... without end. If death came for me, would I then be judged by our blind brother? Would he sentence me to more torment for my sins? When will I find peace, little brother? When will I-" His words choked off as his eyes squeezed shut again, drawing his wrinkled features into a web of agony.

Tavenji could not bring himself to wrest any more information from the wretched former god. He knew only a taste of the suffering Epoch had endured, and his deep compassion for him overpowered any other considerations. He wanted desperately to help, and knew of a way to do so, but he would not bargain with his brother for the information he needed. That seemed cruel beyond measure.

Tavenji stood, releasing his brother's hand, and said, "I think I can help you." As Epoch watched, Tavenji patted himself down, pulled at the clothing about his waist and crotch, and started to do a strange little wiggling dance. Epoch looked at him in confusion, but as Tavenji continued his dance, three items dropped out of his pant-leg and clattered to the floor. He bent to retrieve them and took his seat beside his brother again.

He took his brother's hand and said, "This is from our sister. I hope it gives you what you seek." He placed the golden ring upon Epoch's finger and waited.

The effect was immediate. The pain eased from his body, his features relaxed, and the old man breathed a sigh of contentment. He gazed at his young sibling with a look of gratitude beyond words, and a smile spread upon his wizened face, beatific and infectious. Tavenji shared that smile, his heart leaping into his throat as he saw Lelonetha's gift of mercy do its work.

Then his brother's eyes closed and he released his final breath. Tavenji felt the old man's hand go slack in his own, and he became utterly still. The ring upon his finger became thinner and thinner, until it vanished altogether.

"Brother?" Tavenji said. "Brother Epoch?"

He heard movement behind him, and turned to see Bevek, his eyes staring and wild. "What have you done?" croaked the man as he loomed over the little god and the body of the Prophet of Mash.

"I- I have set him free," Tavenji said weakly, defensively. "He suffers no more."

Bevek let out a wild cry of outrage and struck out with a dagger, piercing the little god's heart.

Tavenji felt it stop. *That answers that,* he thought.

Chapter Fifteen

Veins of Iron

Khrim watched the twelve men practice in the yard, noting changes that needed to be made to their techniques before being deployed. According to the scouts, his men had to leave on the morrow to be in striking position on time. It was cutting it closer than he would have liked, but finding men of such skill and bravery was difficult here. He could have picked dozens from any clan back home in Maanok, but the men west of the great mountains were a softer lot. He jumped down from the work table and crossed the muddy ground, examining the men's' positions from a lower angle.

His special soldiers had been training in the way of the *Vortazhi* hunters, Maanok warriors who took their name and tactics from monstrous, color-changing cats that stalked the forests of the Wild Lands since the Time of Chaos. The men wore cloaks of dull earth tones, woven with a pattern of loose, dark twine netting. Beneath the strange mantles, they wore dark traveling clothes and leather armor, but none of that could be seen now; the men were lying on their bellies in shallow depressions in the ground, with their cloaks spread to cover all but their hands and crossbows. The twine netting had leafy branches of foliage, wood bark, and grass trapped in it, creating a little cluster of forest debris on the back of each man. The concealment did not have much effect here in the castle yard, but in the woods to the west near Velloness, they would be nigh invisible.

Even their crossbows were unique; each one was constructed with a lever device for easier cocking, a special bent stock, and a tiller-guard that allowed for more reliable shooting from a prone position. It was an assassin's weapon, and his men were ideally meant to fire only one bolt each. They were all chosen for their marksmanship first and foremost, and second, for their absurd disregard for danger. Their mission would be to assassinate the commanders of the advancing northern army, hitting them all on the road at the same time. If they escaped in the confusion, so much the better, if not... well, they were only needed for this mission after all.

Khrim had scouted the Imperial Road himself over two years ago, disguised as a traveling cobbler. He journeyed first to Velloness Castle, and then north to Landsworth, and west around the Calione Peaks to the city of Forgoness, seeking the best location for a future ambush if the king's forces came along the obvious route. He even made a decent profit from mending the shoes of fellow travelers while he was at it.

As it turned out, the best location was only a few hour's ride from Velloness itself; north of the castle was a narrow stretch of road with a steep rock face on one side, and a gently sloping decline on the other. Trees were sparse near the roadside, having been felled many years before, but the woodlands grew thick a few dozen yards further in. He could place his *Vortazhi* archers on either side, spread over a mile of road; the marksmen farthest south could kill the lead target, causing the entire column to halt, and make easy prey of the others.

A young page, wearing the orange ermine and red wolf's head standard of House Wolvert, approached Khrim nervously, bowing in the mud as he spoke, "Master Braeden? His Royal Highness King Manon the First commands your presence in the great hall."

Braeden waved his hand to dismiss the lad, smirking inwardly at the use of the title so soon after declaring himself, as if it made it so. Not only had he won no crown yet, but it made for cumbersome listening. *'The king,'* he thought, watching the boy depart. *Just say 'the king'.*

Braeden followed many paces behind the page, marking the quickness in the lad's step. They all served a king now, and the distinction made a palpable difference among the castle servants and guardsmen. It was an odd combination of pride and fear that laced their mannerisms lately; as if they owed the new king better service than they had previously given, and hoped no one had noticed any earlier failings.

The warlock took care to kick the mud from his boots before entering the hall, since Manon did not tolerate undue sloppiness. Khrim approached the table where the king was speaking with Lord Drom Evenast of Kenric, and took note of the tension in the air. The king's men were at the arched passageways and none of Drom's men were to be seen, but the angry lord held a certain quantity of menace all by himself. He was not pleased; an ember swallow had arrived days ago to announce to Kenric that his son was a 'guest' of the one true king of the realm, Galen Cordobal III.

It was an unfortunate oversight, to be sure. Braeden Khrim had received an urgent message delivered by pigeon, stating that Master Freekirk had taken most of his students to Cordoshome to bury a fallen companion, leaving Grigor at the school. He had intended for the boy to be on his way home over the mountain pass by the time Wolvert's declaration was sent, but it seemed either Khrim's message, or the man it was intended for, had been intercepted. No one expected the schoolmaster to return so soon, and with the king himself.

We had eyes and ears in the west, he thought. *How did the southern army and the king himself escape our notice?* He sensed the hand of powerful wizards at play.

Manon sat straight in his high-backed chair, his face a mask of regal authority. Drom, on the other hand, was sitting across from the king, leaning forward in his chair and speaking in harsh tones, though not raising his voice enough to be truly impudent.

Drom hissed through gritted teeth, "Submit to the Cordobals? Why in the name of the Eight Storms should I do that?"

Manon steepled his fingers and took on a conciliatory tone, "It is not your submission I want, but the appearance of it. Send your envoy to entreat with Galen Cordobal, offering your pledge not to engage his forces. He will not be so foolish as to accept this, but will likely press for you to submit to his authority and rejoin the realm. If it comes to this, do it. So long as he holds your son, let him think you will even fight on his side."

"Treacherous..." Drom shook his head, "You think your warlock can get my Grigor out of the king's palace?" He turned to glare at Khrim as the Maanok took up his place behind the king. "Your whole plan revolves upon this, does it not? What assurances do I have that no harm will come to him if he attempts escape? And how do you expect to get him out of the city and over the mountains? Fly?"

Manon motioned for Braeden Khrim to answer the question; no doubt the king was weary of his verbal duel with the obstinate warlord.

"I have my contacts in Portshia-" Khrim began.

Drom snorted, "Yes, your Circle of Gold friends. I've hanged more than a few of their brothers in my lands."

Khrim said, "I have taken a more cooperative

approach. Their guild of thieves has 'fingers in many pies,' as you say. I have cultivated a relationship with their spies and have gained the favor of their leadership." Drom's eyes narrowed at this news. Khrim continued, "I shall travel with your envoy to Portshia and seek the aid of the Circle of Gold to assist in the safe retrieval of your son."

"Ha!" Drom laughed, "What makes you think the Circle isn't going to sell him to the highest bidder? Why do you put so much trust in cutthroats and pickpockets?"

Khrim said, "Because I have tasted their heart."

Drom looked uncertain at that.

"An expression," Khrim waved a hand. "I have seen what their leaders hope for, what they are willing to risk much for."

"Which is?" Drom asked.

"Legitimacy," Khrim said. "They wish to play a part in the future, as all powerful men do. They dream of a day when they might act in the open, taking by right what they once took by force and deceit. They wish to be acknowledged."

This made Baron DeKenric sit back and stare. He asked Manon, "And this is the coin you offer for their help? You plan to make them part of your new government with a seat on the council? Or perhaps make them your tax collectors?" He was obviously incredulous, and might have laughed if his son's life hadn't depended on it.

Khrim said, "Of course not. We will be expected to betray each other, but the music is playing and so we must dance.

Manon said, "The footmen do not matter in the end; it is the support of their commanders we want. They can make promises to their cutthroats and pickpockets all they wish, but they know that in the end, only the clever and useful will be rewarded. We may even find some of them worth keeping about."

Drom sat back in his chair, "So you promise them

titles and positions, then whittle them down until all they have to gain is their lives."

Manon said, "It is a nasty business, but there is no place for lawlessness in my future kingdom. I am sure you can agree with that."

"I agree that lawlessness must be rooted out," Drom said, "but I believe in a firm fist, not a knife in the back."

Manon stiffened slightly, "Your honor is affronted, is it? Would you expect such men to deal honestly with you?"

"No," Drom said, "All the more reason to deal honestly with them." Manon scoffed at the notion, but Kenric was in no mood to argue about honor with Manon Wolvert. He asked, "I assume the Circle of Gold will require payment, and I assume this is not coming out of your royal coffers?"

Manon said, "I shall ask our allies to contribute what they may to ease the burden."

Drom asked, "How much of a burden?"

Khrim said, "Fifty thousand crowns."

"Fifty-?" Drom gaped. "I could march on Portshia with five thousand men for that amount!"

"It is a high price for a baron's heir, to be sure," Khrim said dispassionately, "but King Galen would extract a far greater sum, either before or after the war."

Drom scowled at the Maanok, but had to agree.

Manon said, "This is all about the timing. If all goes well, Galen will lead his army into our lands, believing he has rendered you powerless. We will liberate your son, and Galen will be caught between our forces."

"What if the Galen takes Grigor with him on the march?" Drom asked, stabbing the tabletop with his finger, "The boy would be safer in the palace, but easier to execute if he's in the king's camp."

Khrim said, "We will have to be fluid, flexible. The king will not march until spring, so we have time to raise the funds and organize."

"If your 'friends' in the Circle can be trusted," Drom said.

"I am not treating them as friends," Khrim replied. "I am treating them as thieves and liars. Every precaution will be taken to avoid betrayal. But we must leave as soon as we are able."

The twenty-nine day journey from the grand city of Ahrnok to the grim walls of Kenric Castle was not a pleasant one. The warlock got the distinct impression that Drom wanted to kill him and take matters into his own hands. *He is a man of honor and action, and having to rely on my 'underhanded' means is shameful to him,* Braeden knew. He did not hold it against the baron, he simply made note of the reality.

Bias is the bane of understanding, and emotion clouds the mind. It was an axiom of the *Baedoch Khoorn* way of thinking that overcame the Maanok cultural proclivity to fly into a rage and charge into battle. It was Western thinking, more akin to the teachings of the Eyoronian branch of the Grand Magisterium, or the research approach of the Mystic College. It was what made the *Baedoch Khoorn* outcasts in their own tribes, respected, feared, and misunderstood. Guile was the defining trait of the Oath Breakers. This was the truth the first of them realized; this was the reason they took the oaths of ethics and restraint that they had no intention of keeping.

Let the foreign wizards think they are taming the beast, reshaping our minds in their own image. Let them try and make swierdi, *weaklings, out of us. We will learn what we need to defeat the ones who hide in towers and behind walls. We shall be the blade that slips though the gaps in their metal hide. We shall be the thorns under their feet and the mist that veils their eyes...*

As a boy, Braeden had loved the stories of the warlock cult. He had never been eager to rush into the unknown, unlike those brave boys who got hurt about as often as not. He thought about things, analyzed his problems, and pondered his troubles. This earned him the notice of the brotherhood of warlocks, and they took him from his parents on his tenth winter.

A few years later he learned to make his verge, a necessity for any human user of magic. Unlike the wands and staffs of the western wizards, the verges of the warlock brotherhood were fashioned into bracelets of blood wood and hidden silver. His verge was placed upon his wrist after his twelfth winter, and as he grew, it became difficult, then impossible, to remove. Now it seemed no more than a piece of primitive jewelry, not unlike the ones worn by most Maanok warriors. Yet with it, he was armed with the powers of the spirit world; a warrior that could take on an army alone, if he chose. It was all in the strategy and tactics.

Lord Drom and his knights mostly ignored Khrim on the journey, and that was to his liking. He could learn more about the man by watching him with his fellows than he could by trying to play at the niceties of polite conversation, not that Drom observed many niceties. He was more like a warrior of Maanok in that way, feeling and acting before thinking, unless given time to cool his head.

Upon reaching the hilltop city of Wensicton, they were the guests of House Jamiston. Lord Leeman and his wife, Lady Kathia welcomed DeKenric with open arms, but allowed the Maanok within their walls only grudgingly. Still, Khrim was a sort of emissary of House Wolvert, so the strict rules of hospitality took precedence.

Leeman had left Ahrnok before the ember swallow had returned with news of Drom's son, so the tidings brought a somber pall to the feast that evening. Much of the lordly discussion was beyond Khrim's hearing, since he was seated so far to the back of the main hall, but the two barons sent many unfriendly glances his way during their close conversation.

They left Wensicton the next morning, taking a

lesser-used road through the forest and a bridge over the Weness River. The route took three days off their journey, delivering them to the gray city of Kenric and its great stone castle. In the dim, rosy hues of dusk, the stonework of the fortifications were cast in shades of purple, much like the distant peaks of the Cassel Range. The valley scene was dominated by the singular peak of the High Horn, an impressive wedge of craggy stone that tore the clouds, flying them like banners upon its snow-capped summit.

The city of Kenric was both impressive and oppressive, in great contrast to the whitewashed walls and warm, colorful banners of Ahrnok. Kenric was built from the abundant granite that formed the base of the mountain range, granite from quarries that now served as part of the city's borders. There were imposing gray long-houses with slate roofs, drab little stack-stone huts with thatched roofs, and narrow streets hemmed in by tall, gray buildings. All were separated into wards by high walls and gates. The only prominent colors were of the banners of House Evenast, a blue field with white chevron, and a smith's hammer and anvil in gold.

After climbing up the long, curved causeway, and crossing under gate after gate within the concentric curtain walls, they finally arrived at the main keep. Khrim was given a cold, damp room above the main hall, where many of the servants were quartered. It was dark and drafty, like older castles, but there had been little effort to make the spaces more comfortable. Tapestries and glazed windows could combat the drafts, hearths with chimneys could warm the rooms more efficiently than braziers, and some wainscoting and a dash of paint would work wonders. But House Evenast was not known for its patronage of the arts or its love of finery; here, it was considered excessive to cover the floor with sweet-smelling rushes. The warlock did not mind the stark interiors, but it spoke volumes about those who chose to live here.

Lord Drom and his baroness, Lady Heliana, had

eaten a late supper with the lord's escort before the men retired to their barracks. Khrim had not been asked to attend, being served instead in his room. No candles were provided, but that was not a problem for him; a simple 'lamp light' spell cast upon the empty sconces provided all the light he needed. He sat on the firm bed and ate in silence.

Later that evening, Khrim heard the voices of the lord and lady raised in conversation. He knew there were guards upon the balcony overlooking the hall, but they could not hinder him from listening in. He sat cross-legged on the bed and concentrated, building the spell in his mind before drawing upon the power of the spirit world to give it shape. He imagined his eyes and ears floating in the room below, invisible but attentive. The drab little room soon dissolved into the open and airy main hall, with its long table and benches, racks of antlers and trophies, hanging banners of blue and wooden hearth-seats soaking the warmth of a cozy fire. Occupying the seats were the lord and lady, dressed in house robes and soft leather boots.

Lady Heliana had her robe wrapped about her protectively; her heart-shaped face a mask of anger and sorrow. "I cannot believe the gall of that... that *fool!*" she spat. "He has planned this all along, I am sure of it." The lines around her mouth deepened as she scowled; her dark chestnut hair had escaped its braid, giving her a haggard look.

Lord Drom frowned, "How would our son getting captured-"

"Not our son's capture," she interrupted, "his claiming the crown! He waited till all the pieces were in place, and the Cordobals' involvement was inevitable, then he declares himself 'king' and we are in no position to argue." She glared into the fire as if she might fuel it with her rage alone.

"Perhaps," Drom said, "But the duke, or rather, king-"

"Wolvert," she said with a voice full of scorn.

"Wolvert," he repeated, "assured me that our son's return was set in motion *before* he sent the message to King Galen. There was some problem, however…"

"I do not care for his assurances," she said. "He has played us for fools, and now his idiocy has endangered our son. It would serve him right if you chose to fight for the Loyalists when they come marching into our lands."

"I'd not change my colors so easily," he replied. "Given the choice, I'd refuse to fight for either side."

"Well, we may not *have* a choice, not if you want our son to inherit your lands! If this 'Black Eagle' is like his father, he may demand you lead his vanguard. Refuse and the only land our son inherits will be the plot he is buried in." She drew a ragged breath, "Damn the Cordobals *and* the Wolverts."

"My grandmother was a Wolvert," he reminded her.

"And I've never held that against you," she said.

Drom leaned forward towards the flames, sighing and rubbing his hands, "The Black Eagle has not made any demands thus far, but when the money is raised, I'll send an envoy and Wolvert's warlock."

She turned to him, a look of great distaste on her face. "Do you truly believe this Maanok savage can retrieve our Grigor? If the gate guards of Portshia have any sense at all, they'll spear him on sight."

Drom shook his head, "Grigor's last letter claimed there was a Maanok student in the Freekirk School. They are welcomed in small numbers, just not in massive raiding hordes. Still, I imagine the warlock will be in disguise or some such thing."

"Have you asked him how he plans to accomplish this miracle of rescuing Grigor?" she asked.

Drom said, "The plan is to pay the Circle of Gold to aid in stealing him from the palace." His wife's face showed her contempt, but he pressed on, "Wolvert contributed hundreds of crowns, and more is coming from House LuVeness, who are acting as bankers of the war effort. It may take a while"

"Hundreds?" she scoffed, "How generous. That nest of vipers in Portshia will no doubt realize how important Grigor is to Wolvert's war, and price their 'help' accordingly. What is it worth to Manon Wolvert to have House Evenast fight for his new kingdom? Surely it's more than a few hundred gold coins."

"It was what we could easily carry; we had to travel light to make it back so quickly." Drom said, annoyed. Then he muttered, "The sum is closer to fifty thousand crowns."

"Fifty thousand!" she cried, "Gods! I hope that warlock knows what he's doing." Lady Heliana shook her head and stared into the flames for a long while before asking, "If all goes amiss, if our son is beyond rescue or... killed... what do you intend to do?"

Braeden Khrim focused his concentration on the lord.

Drom's eyes went upward to the family crest that hung over the hearth, the underside of the raised relief darkened with years of soot. The motto read: *Veins of Iron*. He took a breath and said, "If we are betrayed and he is killed, I shall slaughter every Loyalist until I reach the Black Eagle, then take his lying head." He ran his fingers through his hair, "If he is beyond rescue... if they hold his life over my head to secure my loyalty..."

Lady Heliana looked at him. "You'll what?" she demanded softly.

"I don't know," he replied. "I don't know."

Khrim ended the spell, allowing his senses to return again to his surroundings, like waking from a dream. He could see the dreary little room again, and hear his own breathing and heartbeat. *He must be rescued,* Khrim thought, *rescued or killed.*

He lay back on the bed and closed his eyes.

Chapter Sixteen

Watchful Eyes

Cindra had only been in the Winter Palace once before, long ago. The old king, Galen II, had invited her family to attend a week of winter feasting when Cindra was seven years old. She remembered the warmth of the great hall, the noise of the banquets, the smells of the kitchens, and the music from the minstrels in the galleries. The palace had been a magical place, so much more elegant and grand than her father's castle, which was first and foremost a defensive stronghold against the sea.

But the king had taken ill in the following years and had not returned. The memories of that magical winter had faded into her own personal mythology until it became a haven for her mind during the cold months in her father's modest halls. The white walls and spires of the palace were a source of longing, drawing her eyes whenever she looked out over the city.

Cindra once again stood in the middle of that great

hall, where those memories had been born. It was a dark and dreary place, with cold light streaming in through high windows and all but one of the four grand fireplaces lit with a meager flame. The banquet tables were absent, as were the rich hangings and drapery she remembered. The floor was a smooth, bare checkerboard of red and white marble, its surface paled with dust that she disturbed with her progress across the hall. Servants busied themselves in the vast chamber, dusting the walls and high places with long poles, and turning the sunlight into white shafts of dancing motes.

"There you are," said an echoing voice from behind her. She turned and saw the king approaching, and she dropped into a curtsy. The servants followed suit, bowing as the monarch passed by.

"Highness," she said, smoothing her dress self-consciously. It was a simple but elegant gown of yellow and black silk, one of several in her new wardrobe. Most of her old dresses were lost at the bottom of the sea; what few remained in her mother's keeping were too snug about the shoulders, back, and arms, and would have to be let out.

The king wore his customary black tunic and hose, embroidered with an eagle in silver and black thread. He wore a dagger at his waist and a silver pin on his cloak, but was otherwise unadorned. He needed no other symbol of office, for his bearing and manner carried all he required. He said, "I feel I am interrupting something. You seem deep in thought."

"No interruption, Highness," she replied. "I was just remembering when last I was here. I believe it was about eleven years ago."

"I recall," he said. "It was the last time I was here myself. I fear the secrecy of my arrival caught the housekeepers off guard. They have since prepared our rooms, but as for the rest of the palace, it will be a while before it matches the memory."

"You were present back then?" she said.

"Yes," he said with a smile, "a week's worth of

feasting and merriment. We met briefly, though as I recall, you mostly looked at my shoes."

She blushed, "I suppose I was a shy child."

"Hah! Not as I could tell. You ran about with the other children, and talked up a storm when given the chance." He glanced about the room, picturing it as it was. "But you were intimidated by me, though I was only a boy of eleven." He offered his arm to lead her as they walked, and she took it awkwardly. "Much has changed, dear cousin. Nothing seems to intimidate you now."

"Oh, I wouldn't say that," she replied. "You still intimidate me."

He smirked, "And all it took was four days tied to a rock." Her steps faltered at that, but he said, "Do not mistake me; I have the greatest respect for your courage and strength of will. It was an unfortunate necessity that required your trial and punishment; I needed to maintain the respect and morale of my barons."

"I know the reasons, Highness," she said quietly. "But they were little comfort on the mountain."

"Of that I am sure," he said with only a twinge of regret. "But I need not justify my decisions to you. As it happens, you survived the ordeal and achieved what you set out to do. Is that not enough?"

She nodded but said nothing. This was the reason he intimidated her still; he was the sovereign ruler of the land, and need not answer to anyone. His word was law, and she was just another subject. She had been raised in a noble house, but being in the presence of the king changed everything for everyone and she had been slow to realize it, to her own peril.

"I trust you are well enough to continue your training?" he asked.

It had been twenty days since her time on Tirgrim's Bluff, and her body had recovered from much of the trauma thanks to the ministrations of the finest healers in the city. The king's personal physician, Reverend

Brother Alynar, had treated her with concoctions of Divine Alchemy that not only eased her pain, but healed many of the cuts and abrasions she had received. Nothing could be done to remove the scars left by the lightning however, and Cindra was grateful for the long sleeves of her dress.

"I am well enough," she replied. "Your priest was able to repair most of the damage to my nerves and sinews, but I can handle a sword." In truth, she still had pain in her arms and shoulders, and numbness in her hands, but she would not list her complaints to the king.

"I am pleased to hear it," he said. "Gavadaire LuVestra will take over your training, and shall arrive within the week."

A thought struck her suddenly, and she asked, "How is Grigor DeKenric? Is he here in the palace?"

"He is here, and he is quite well," said the king. "I have given him the freedom of the tower spires. Unfortunately the palace is going to have too many comings and goings to act as a suitable prison for a noble hostage, so it is unlikely you will see him. Would you care to visit him?"

"I may, if I have the time," she said.

"We have also arranged to have suitable garb made for your exercises," the king said.

"My clothes from the school?" she asked.

"No," he said. "Those were disposed of, I'm afraid. We have inquired with a few local tailors, who are sending their seamstresses to fit you later today."

"What manner of garb does Your Highness deem more suitable for training? Would I not just wear men's clothing?" she asked.

"Unfortunately," he said, "I made an injunction against it, if you recall. We shall have to be creative."

She wanted to ask 'why?' in a loud voice, but she knew she had to remain deferential. She offered, "That seems to be an excessive effort just for my lessons."

He said, "For the next five months, my palace shall be home to my war council, my greater barons, and their knights. They will be training on the grounds, sharing food at table, and many of them sleeping in this very hall," he swept his arm about the grand space. "You shall have your own quarters, of course, but you will be among them for most of the time. You must therefore be a lady first, and a soldier second."

"I'm not sure I understand... will I be training in a dress?" she asked, afraid of the answer.

"Not exactly," he said. "There will have to be allowances made for the needs of movement and comfort, but you must not be seen in men's clothing. It would cause too much dissent."

She could not imagine what more she could do to cause dissent, but she accepted his explanation with mild humor. "Then I shall look forward to seeing what strides in fashion my situation will produce." To her relief, the king smiled.

Cindra had to admit, she liked the new clothes. They were a fusion of southern styles and specialized clothing worn by Galindri women. The dress only looked like a dress at a glance, but had separate legs, so she could run, jump, or ride her horse with total freedom. The *Gatéth-sho'a* women called such a garment *l'lo'pín-ku-doma*, literally a 'skirt with legs,' and she had worn one before when the Galindri taught her to ride in their fashion.

The upper portion was more traditional, with a loose, long-sleeved blouse and a soft leather bodice. She was relieved to find that the bodice was only slightly snug; enough to keep her breasts in place, but not so tight as to push them together and lift them under her chin like a serving wench. The bodice had detached sleeves of matching leather that covered her from upper arms to wrists, leaving her shoulders bare. It was altogether functional and attractive.

Gavadaire liked the new look too, and he made much of it over their first training day together. "Apreva!" he exclaimed, "I cannot decide which is a more beautiful and impressive sight; Milady Cindra Corrina, or this Winter Palace."

"I cannot decide if that is flattery or not, "she replied.

"Ah, but I am not free to flatter as I will," he said. "After all, I am your teacher and you are my student, and His Majesty wishes for us all to avoid further... controversy."

Controversy, she thought. *What an impersonal way to describe a passionate love affair and close friendship.* She could not blame Gavadaire for being blunt, but neither could she maintain her good mood. Her chin dropped and she sighed, not undramatically.

"He thinks of you always," LuVestra said, catching her off guard. "You can see it in his eyes. Even as he throws himself into the training, you are always in his thoughts."

She swallowed back tears and nodded, "Thank you." She had not seen Jaron since they were parted at her trial. He had taken her down from the mountain, but she had been witless at the time. He hadn't even been allowed to visit her during her convalescence.

"Come now," he said, trying to bring her back to the matter at hand. "Have you done your stretching exercises?"

She nodded, following him from the foyer into the training hall. It was a long chamber with white and black checkered tiles and white arched pillars. The king had called it a 'modest' space, but it was more like an elegant dining hall for seventy people. There was a small table in the corner from which she selected a pair of leather gloves and a blunted metal arming sword.

"Good," he said, taking a sword of his own. "Let us practice parry and counters. How is it said? Gher yaas?"

"Gher yaas," she confirmed, raising the sword in a defensive stance. It felt good to hold one again, though her hands and fingers lacked some feeling. They moved within striking distance and exchanged a few light attacks, offering counter-attacks that increased in speed. Within moments, Cindra had been disarmed.

Gavadaire frowned at her, noticing her dismay. She was rubbing her hands as she retrieved her sword. He held out his hand to her and said, "Take it and squeeze." She did so. "Harder," he said, "as hard as you can."

She obeyed, her hand shaking with the effort.

"Shu d'Vaer!" he exclaimed, pulling away. "Is that all? What did they do to you?"

"They put me in manacles for four days," she said. "I was told that my hands were so swollen, they looked like a blacksmith's."

He shook his head in disgust. "Barbaric. Still, we must rebuild your strength; else there is no point to any of your weapon training." He thought for a moment and said, "We will focus on avoidance, in the Su'Kraal way. In the meantime, I will give you exercises for your wrists and hands that can be done throughout the day."

Cindra agreed, and her training commenced. She enjoyed the Su'Kraal method, for it was more like dancing than fighting. She ducked, dodged, side-stepped, and wove herself away from oncoming attacks as Gavadaire advanced with ever-greater speed. She practiced unarmed trapping and striking attacks that slipped in past his guard, aiming false blows at his throat and eyes. He commented on every attack and counter-attack, adding new moves of his own to challenge her. Within hours, she was quite exhausted.

As they recovered on a balcony overlooking the gardens below, she said, "Tell me about this monastery where you grew up. What are the monks like? How was the training?"

He breathed the warm sea air and said, "It was remote, far from the cities and towns. There was only a nearby village, some miles away, that grew vegetables and raised cattle. I was taken from my mother at the age of six and brought to the monastery, but I rarely left."

"Six?" she asked. "Why were you taken from your

mother?"

"She had promised me to them, the Su'Kraal brotherhood. I was not told why; only that it was her wish that I be trained in their ways of combat."

"Did you ever ask her yourself?" she asked.

"I never saw her after," he replied. "I inquired, of course. But the monks told me that she had no home and was a wanderer."

Cindra considered this and asked, "What of your father?"

"I never knew him," Gavadaire replied. "I remember my mother saying he lived far away." He turned to see the troubled look of pity in her eyes. "I cannot remember my mother's face any longer. Sad, is it not?"

She nodded, *Sad*.

"From what I can estimate," he said, "she was made with child by a stranger, and her family sent her away. Then she gave me to the monks when I was old enough to be separated from her, and started a new life elsewhere. It is what makes the most sense, no?"

Cindra shrugged, thinking of other possible stories, none of which would make a difference in the end. He had been abandoned, and that was that. "Were the monks good to you at least?"

"They were strict and difficult masters," he said, "but they were not cruel. I was well-fed and well-trained. I was taught to read and write, and learned strategy, tactics, and history. I was brought up to revere Kraal and his rule, and to respect the gods."

"What of love?" she asked, and blushed at her own intrusiveness.

He laughed, "Your Jaron asked me the same thing not long ago."

My Jaron, she thought with a wistful smile. "What did you tell him?"

"*That* story," he said, "is not for mixed company." Then he gave her a comradely pat on the back. "Come, I will teach you your new regimen for strengthening your hands."

The following days saw an influx of men and equipment as the rest of the palace became 'fit for habitation' according to the royal seneschal. The larders were stocked for the winter; not with the rich foods of peacetime banquets, but with hearty fare that would not soften the men's fighting trim. There was also the danger that the enemy might attempt a siege, and the palace would have to be prepared for that as well.

Barons from many provinces between Regala and Cordo were put up in the palace's many, many rooms. Their knights and retainers set up tents within the palace grounds, or outside the walls around the city Commons. Baggage trains came and went, bringing armor, weapons, food and other supplies that the nobles had to provide for their retinues.

Cindra watched much of this from the balcony near her training hall. Gavadaire's new hand and wrist exercises were helping somewhat, but she was still not strong enough to fight with a weapon, either one-handed or two. She carried the iron weights around with her during all of her training time, and occasionally during her balcony breaks.

Gavadaire had presented her with the weights after their first day together. They were called 'cannonbells,' and were essentially small cannonballs with iron loops for handles. She would hold one in each hand by her fingertips and lift them as she made a fist, continuing to lift as she bent her wrist. Then she would unroll her grip in reverse, as slowly as she had raised it. She would do much the same movement holding them over her head, but had to be careful not to drop them. Her hands protested, but they were growing stronger little by little.

The men moving about the castle showed some interest in her presence, but not much. She looked like just another servant as she walked from here to there, passing their rooms and gatherings out of necessity.

But this changed when a few of them wandered into the wing where she was training one day.

"What's this?" said a voice, booming into the hall.

Cindra was in the middle of dodging Gavadaire's latest flurry of attacks and the voice almost startled her into a painful misstep. They both stopped and turned to see four knights gaping at them. The men wore the colors of different lords, but all had similar expressions.

"This is training," called Gavadaire in his thick Aurilonian accent, "Su'Kraal style."

"You hear that, my lads? We got us an Orry warrior monk!" The speaker was a thick-jawed man with a western accent, and he wore the coat of arms of one of the lesser barons of Cenlind, unless Cindra missed her guess. "Maybe he's on the wrong side of the Cassel Range." He addressed Gavadaire, "Don't you Orrys fight for the Dissenters? Or are you here to teach dance lessons to the ladies of Portshia?"

Cindra started to say something, but the touch of Gavadaire's sword warned her not to. Instead, he stepped forward to say, "I fight for no one at the moment; there is no war here, only a host of men with nothing better to do than wander the halls and intrude. But if it is dancing you wish to learn, I can teach you, Sir...?"

"Sir Kasti Kynmaer of House Dunraey," the man said, taking a few bold steps into the room. Cindra saw the scars on the man's face, including the uneven patch of hair that looked like a piece of his scalp had once been cleaved off. His coat of arms bore what appeared to be a male Kyraine with black wings and eagle's head, carrying a spear. It floated on an emblazoned field of green and white, with seven golden stars surrounding the figure.

Cindra had guessed correctly; House Dunraey held the barony of Emenar in southern Cenlind, covering the lands around Mount Piniwen, from the Vynnar River to the Rokvynnar border. She had passed through those lands during her time with the Galindri caravans.

"You want to teach me to dance, do you?" asked the scarred knight. "Maybe I'll be more entertaining than an unarmed girl?"

Gavadaire just spread his arms wide in welcome, bowing slightly. "I offer you my blade, sir knight." He tossed the blunted weapon to the man, who caught it by the handle.

Cindra knew enough to back against the wall out of the way.

Sir Kasti unhooked his sheathed sword and tossed it to one of the other men to hold. He said, "What is your name, sir?"

"I am not a knight," he replied, "but you may call me Gavadaire LuVestra of the Su'Kraal, if you wish."

"Pick up a sword," Sir Kasti said, motioning to the training table.

"That is not the dance today, sir." Gavadaire replied, and he stepped into the middle of the floor, arms at his side.

The other men made calls and jeers, goading their comrade into action. It worked. Sir Kasti said angrily, "Very well, LuVestra. This is how we dance in the west. Gher yaas!" He advanced with what Cindra knew as the Wind Guard, sword held at eye level for high or low thrusts. The man came on fast with shuffling steps, intending to drive Gavadaire towards the wall. His sword darted out like a striking snake, but the tip never found its mark.

Gavadaire backed away and around, weaving from the advancing blade. But the blade was only the tip of the attack; Sir Kasti waited for his opponent to sidestep into his guard when he turned his shuffling advance into a body-check. Gavadaire's eyes widened slightly, but his footing suddenly changed and he threw the charging man over his hip. The knight hit the floor in a roll, reversing with a sword slash. Gavadaire avoided it, stepped along the blade, and trapped the man's chest under his knee.

"Impressive," muttered Kasti from the floor. "I've heard things about the Su'Kraal fighters that are hard to believe."

Gavadaire helped him to his feet and said, "I would be happy to teach, if you wish. We have all winter."

"Perhaps *we* do," said Sir Kasti as he moved towards his fellows and tossed the blunt blade back to Gavadaire. "However, I've heard that a Su'Kraal can take on several opponents at once." He glared over his shoulder and the other men drew their blades, spreading out into the room. "What say you, Orry? Can you take us all?"

Cindra's eyes grew wide in alarm as she saw what they intended. *Were they insane? They would shed blood in the palace?* Her mind raced for something to say, something that would forestall them, but they looked angry and resolute. Perhaps she was not going to be the only person who might cause dissent among the troops.

Gavadaire motioned to Cindra saying, "Milady, be a dear and fetch the field marshal before someone gets hurt?" He looked wary but unafraid as the men spread to encircle him.

Cindra did not know if he could handle four knights armed with sharpened steel, but she didn't want to find out just now. She headed for the door near the balcony. Ahead was the long passage she would have to run down to get help, but by the balcony doors were the cannonbells she used to strengthen her hands. It was a much shorter trip to the cannonbells.

Gavadaire had maneuvered so that only two of the men could attack at once, and attack they did, slashing to hem him in so they could beat on him with the flats of their blades or the brutish sword pommels. He was able to grab and trap one man's arm while ducking another's blade, but had to disengage behind them to avoid taking a beating. This put him within reach of the other two knights, who rushed in holding swords in a half-hand grip to strike with pommel or cross-guard.

Suddenly one of the men felt a hard blow to both kidneys, like two fists of iron striking from behind. He gasped in pain and fell, giving Gavadaire a chance to throw the second attacker into his friends. The men got to their feet and saw Cindra at Gavadaire's side, her cannonbells in hand.

"I told you to get help," Gavadaire said with an edge in his voice.

"If you like, I can scream," Cindra replied.

"You little bitch!" cried the knight she had struck, and he turned stiffly around to face her. The others scrambled to attack, faces enraged.

Gavadaire intercepted Cindra's insulter, striking him across the jaw with his pommel and knocking him to the floor. Cindra let out a shrill, piercing shriek that hurt the ears and rattled the nerves as it reverberated in the bare training hall. Then she pitched her arms back and rushed at two of the swordsmen, swinging and releasing the cannonbells as she came on. One struck Sir Kasti in the chest, knocking him off his feet, and one caught the other man's upraised elbow. He cried in pain and dropped his sword. Cindra took up the blade and held it in a Water guard position, thankful she could grip the handle with both hands.

"Stand down," Gavadaire warned the men. He stood by Cindra's side, his unsharpened blade in a relaxed grip.

Soon there was the sound of running feet, and three of the king's men came upon the scene, followed by a saucer-eyed servant. Cindra was almost happy to see them, though she had come to associate the king's coat of arms with unwelcome trouble. *I need to get past that notion,* she chided herself.

As she stood before the king and his field marshal, Cindra couldn't help feeling queasy and nervous. Her wrists itched and her knees wobbled, as if her body was anticipating another ordeal on the mountainside. The king's face was unreadable, but the field marshal looked as if he would endorse leaving her up there this time.

Gavadaire stood by her side in the small audience chamber, along with Sir Kasti and his accomplices, Sir Marven of Ashenmon, Sir Jorald of Hyvane, and lastly Sir Dwen of Pinikal, whom Cindra had struck in the kidneys. Aside from the bruising and scrapes, they looked unharmed as they stood at attention to await the king's judgment.

After letting them stand for several moments, Galen finally spoke in a soft voice. "I understand there was a melee in the south wing, involving five knights and one of my guests," he said. "Would anyone care to explain how this began?"

The men shared glances, but it was Sir Kasti that spoke for them, "I-it was my fault, Highness. We... we saw this fellow swinging a sword at the lady, and I thought to teach him manners. His Aurilon accent... well, it gave me cause to act up, as it were."

"Aurilonian accent?" the king said in mild surprise. "Why Gavadaire LuVestra, are you from Aurilon?"

"I am, Highness," he said.

"Did you know this, Valthór?" asked the king.

"I heard rumors, Highness," he deadpanned.

"Amazing," said the king. "One of my own guests is from Aurilon; shocking. How in the world did this happen? You know, now that I think on it, my own dearly departed mother was from Aurilon, as was my dearly departed father's dearly departed second wife. What do you say, Sir Kasti? Is it a plot?"

Sir Kasti's face had reddened with shame, and his eyes wavered about. "No, Highness," he muttered.

"No," said the king. "Then LuVestra must have been invited here for some reason. What reason do you imagine that might have been, Sir Kasti?"

The chastised knight muttered, "He claimed to be training the lady in Su'Kraal style, Highness. But-"

"But what?" the king asked.

"Well, he was playing at swords with this lady,

Highness," he said, nodding to Cindra. "And begging Your Highness's pardon, but he's not a knight. At least he said he wasn't."

"No, he is not," said the king. "What of it?"

Kasti was confused, "Well, it's just that, ah... Your Highness said that *five* knights and a guest were involved, and-"

"Perhaps you believe we cannot count?" asked the king with an edge in his voice.

"No, Highness! I meant only-"

"Lady Cindra of House Corrina is the fifth knight I spoke of," said the king.

The four men looked at each other in total confusion, not daring to question.

"Lady Cindra, step forward," the king commanded. She did so, drawing a shaky breath. The king stood beside her and said, "She saved my life *twice* during the battle at Cordoshome. We fought Minozhians, you understand? She was dressed as a young man, but when I knighted her the next day, she revealed her identity to me as the lost daughter of Count Casselvane. Do you know what I did then?"

The knights, having arrived many days after Cindra's ordeal, only shook their heads.

"I put her on trial for breaking the law. I sentenced her to four days on the nearby bluff, chained to a pillar." He turned to her and said, "Lady, bare your arms, if you please."

Cindra hesitated, and then pulled back her sleeves to reveal the delicate lightning scars radiating from the blind eye of Valdak upon her wrists.

"Do you see these marks?" asked the king. "Take a good look. They are an omen of divine judgment if I have ever seen one. She survived four days, and on the last night, the pillar was struck by lightning. Yet *here she stands*." He emphasized those last words, and it made Cindra's spine tingle despite herself.

"I am no diviner or oracle," the king admitted, "but I take it to mean that she has earned the right to bear the title of knighthood, and all that it entails."

The men could only stare at the marks on her arms. Cindra wished the king would give her leave to cover them up again.

Galen continued. "I had to pull her from the Freekirk School for obvious reasons, but LuVestra had accepted my invitation to continue her lessons here. I had hoped that they might do so in peace, but..."

"We beg forgiveness, Highness! We did not know," Sir Kasti exclaimed as he sank to one knee. The other men followed suit, too cowed to speak.

"Well now you do," said the king. "And I expect that you will let it be known among my host that all is as it should be within these walls, and that none are to cause trouble with the lady or her instructor."

They said in unison, "We swear it, Majesty!"

"Good," said the king. "Also if you wish, you may relate how the four of you were thrashed by one man and his weakened female student who was recovering from hanging by her wrists. That is all." He waved the men away, and they quickly left his presence.

Cindra began to cover her arms again now that her audience was gone, but the king said, "Lady Cindra, you might consider letting those marks show. I do not wish to burden your vanity, but such scars can become a thing of renown, even legend. They might serve you better if they were seen."

Cindra said, "I shall... consider it, Highness."

He smiled and folded his arms, "Now, about the actions of the two of you; I am sure that there was no bravado or provocation involved on your parts?"

Cindra recalled how she almost had sharp words with Sir Kasti before Gavadaire intervened; her instructor's behavior thereafter could easily be seen as provocative.

"There was, Highness," Gavadaire said. "I sought to draw their attention away from my student, so I spoke with... ah, *ma'shuovae?*"

Excessive arrogance, Cindra translated silently.

The king obviously understood. "I see," he said. "It

was a wise course, but only if a fight could not be avoided. If used too soon, it makes one inevitable. Yes?"

"Yes, Highness," Gavadaire said, his voice low in contrition.

"I am glad that I am understood. Remember, Lady Cindra is your charge during our time in the palace, until she is to depart on her quest. I hope you will take more care in future to avoid risking her health and yours before the battle is even joined."

"I shall, I swear it," Gavadaire said.

"Very well," said Galen. He waved his hand to dismiss them.

Cindra and Gavadaire walked from the chamber in silence, not daring to breathe until the doors closed behind them.

Once they were gone, Valthór spoke to the king in a low voice, "I will continue to have their training watched of course, but shaming those knights like that, sire? It seemed a bit harsh."

Galen replied, "Shame is a powerful incitement, Valthór. Besides, I commanded them to tell others only that the lady should not be trifled with; the rest of the story was optional."

The field marshal shook his head. "I fear it will fester in them," he said.

"Perhaps it would against a normal girl," Galen said, "but Lady Cindra is far from normal, wouldn't you agree?"

"To hear it from you, Highness," Valthór said, "one would think she was chosen by the gods themselves! Was it necessary to foster such ideas, even telling her to show her scars to impress others? Begging your pardon Highness, but what is your mind in this matter?"

Galen paced the room and said, "We are facing grim times, Valthór. The pall upon this city will lower morale long before winter sets in, or we catch the first glimpse of the enemy's banners. If the Dark Heart has indeed surfaced again, the priests and scholars fear that the world itself hangs in the balance." He stopped and turned, "But there is hope in new allies and strange omens. If Lady Cindra can gain the aid of this Shadow Lord; if we could have a host of Ilves fighting alongside us, then we might yet secure a victory over our dark future.

"Let the men whisper of omens and gods. Let them wonder at the girl who earned her spurs in combat and earned her scars on the mountain. Let them march to war with the hope that they might have an army of legend at their back." The king smiled even as his eyes expressed doubt, "Who knows? They may even be right."

The month of Frellmoth passed quickly for Cindra, who trained every day in the hall until late afternoon, visiting her horse in the stables, and exploring the palace as much as possible before bedtime. She kept up the hand exercises, carrying the cannonbells with her almost everywhere. Before long her grip was greatly improved, and she could use weapons again without trouble. Her body was becoming stronger, though she still bore the stiffness and pain from her ordeal. It worried her that those pains might never fully disappear, nor would the numbness in her fingertips.

She took her meals in her room for the most part, as any lady might who was not required by marriage or official protocol to attend the king's table. The first exception was the Feast of Frella on the autumnal equinox; Cindra, being a knight in the king's service, was obliged to attend. Because she was also the only lady of station and a royal cousin besides, she would be seated next to King Galen himself. Thankfully, she was shown to her seat ahead of time and was not required to enter on the king's arm.

As she awaited the royal entrance with the rest of the guests, Cindra allowed herself to enjoy the festive setting of the great hall. Now it more closely resembled the palace of her memories; warm hearth fires and low light from the chandeliers gave the space an intimate quality that made her feel like an excited girl again. Colorful banners hung from the walls, representing the lords and knights in attendance, and she was surprised to see her family's own coat-of-arms present. The scents from the kitchen added to the depth of her reverie; her mouth watered at the smells of beef, pork, game hen, venison, and lamb. The aroma of fresh baked bread covered the room like a warm blanket, and she anticipated digging her fingers into a loaf and tearing off a soft, moist chunk with an herb-buttered crust. It was enough to quite mask the smell of so many men-at-arms who had managed what hygiene they could under the circumstances.

"His Royal Highness, Galen III!" called the herald, and everyone stood as the king entered the great hall. Men cheered as their sovereign strode to the head table, and fell quiet as he raised his arms.

"Noble lords, valiant knights, and men of Calilon!" he called, addressing the hall. More cheering ensued. "And of course, my fourth cousin once removed, Lady Cindra of House Corrina, Knight of the Realm."

Awkward murmurings ensued. Cindra could have kicked him for singling her out.

But the king went on, "I welcome you to the Feast of Frella, where we give thanks for a bountiful harvest, and entreat the White Queen to show us mercy. May she grant a gentle winter... on *this* side of the Cassel Range." There was appreciative laughter and cheers, and the king took his seat. The rest of the room followed and the feast commenced.

Cindra said to the king, "I wonder if 'Lords and Lady' might have been more appropriate, Highness?"

Galen replied, "They must come to terms with it, cousin. Besides, I want no mistake in the matter. Rumors must be put to rest."

"As Your Highness wills," she said, sipping her wine. It was good wine, sweet and heady, and she might need a lot more before the night was over.

Seated beside her was an older man with dark, wavy hair and a trimmed beard, both which were sparsely streaked with white. He had a scent of comfrey and peppers about him, probably due to some joint medication he had applied. He turned stiffly in his chair, his deep-set eyes lingering on Cindra's wrists until she noticed his attention. "Milady Cindra," he said, "allow me to introduce myself. I am Duke Vanar Duncora, Lord of Cenlind." They exchanged pleasantries and he said, "I have heard something of your exploits, and I had hoped to meet you myself. Forgive my curiosity, but is it true that you traveled with the caravans of the horse people for over a year?"

"Almost two years, Your Grace," she said.

"Fascinating!" he said. "I imagine it was very trying on you, being away from decent company for so long."

"I have learned," she replied, "that there are many forms of decency, Your Grace." She let that sink in a bit. "While it is true that the *Gatéth-sho'a* people have little use for lavish comforts and high walls, they treated me with kindness and generosity. I was alone and in need, and they took me in."

"Commendable to be sure," he said, sipping at his own wine.

She had a thought and asked, "How are your vassals, Sir Kasti of Emenar and Sir Marven of Ashenmon?"

The duke gave her a look that bordered on a reproach and said, "They are well, lady. Their injuries were minor of course, save that done to their honor. Your teacher is a formidable man, I hear."

"He is indeed," she said, noticing the man had discounted her involvement entirely. "I hope to learn from him all I can. Have you heard of the Su'Kraal monks, Your Grace?"

He sat back and said, "The Sons of Kraal, the warrior monks of Aurleona Province. It is said they practice strange ways of combat in their hidden monastery, somewhere in the Aurleon Mountains, many miles south of the Spine." He smirked as he continued, "It is *also* said that to have them in your ranks will cause the opposing army to flee in terror or surrender." He took a gulp of his wine, "Foolish nonsense used to bolster their reputation, as well as their hiring price. I have no doubt they are skilled fighting men, but there is a difference between a training hall reputation and a battlefield reputation."

"Indeed," she said, and let the matter drop. *I am not going to be making many friends tonight it seems,* she thought. *Perhaps I should play nice.* She waited for the next course before taking up the conversation again. "Your Grace, I wonder if you could answer a question of heraldry for me?"

"If I can, milady," he said.

"I noticed that House Dunraey has a charge that looks like a male Kyraine with an eagle's head?" she said. "I did not think there were supposed to be male Kyraine."

"Ah," he said, "It is actually called a Weynndal, a Rok word meaning 'winged man.' Apparently they were said to inhabit the Highwood Forest, and cliffs along the greater Vynnar River. According to legend, they came about during the Time of Chaos, much as the Minozhian beast men did."

"Have you ever seen one?" she asked, genuinely interested.

"Alas, no," he replied. "They are no more, but of course rumors persist. As for their use as a heraldic charge, they symbolize honor, glory, and martial readiness."

"Weynndal," she said, trying out the word. "I have not studied the Rok language in some time. I suppose in your part of the kingdom there are many more familial ties with them?"

"Not as many as hoped for," the duke said with regret. "There have been... precious few chances to unite our people in an alliance." He returned to his meal.

Cindra felt her face go warm as the man ate, ignoring

her once again. The duke was referring to the wedding her father had arranged, the wedding she had missed by being attacked at sea and traveling with the Galindri nomads.

Of course, she could have asked them to take her directly to her husband-to-be in Rokvynnar, but that would likely have ended in her death at the hands of assassins. It angered her immensely that she still had to defend her decisions on the matter some four years later.

King Galen looked over at her with concern and asked softly, "You do not look well, Lady Cindra. Do you wish to retire early?"

She collected herself, smiled and said, "Actually, Highness, I think I shall remain and make everyone as uncomfortable as possible."

To her surprise, he laughed heartily, lifting his goblet to her before draining it.

In the weeks following the Feast of Frella, Cindra was delighted to find her training shifted towards mounted combat. She had been making daily trips to the royal stables to visit T'ózha, her beautiful Gali bay pony, but she had no cause to ride him. Her mounted training had been cut short by the vemlok attack that killed her schoolmate, and she had precious little experience.

Cindra had no armor yet, but her father had arranged for her to be fitted for a suit. It had been an odd experience, having her measurements taken by a seamstress under the supervision of a coarse and nervous armorer, who was inclined to look away as often as not. In the meantime, she would have to make due with whatever she and Gavadaire could scrounge from the palace armory. Most of it was too large, but she didn't need much to learn the basic skills.

Gavadaire accompanied her to the Commons for her mounted training, but while he was formidable on foot, he was not a knight. Instead, he attended as her temporary squire, helping with her horse and gear.

Her mounted training was placed in the hands of Sir Gerard Valdoy, one of her father's own knights. Sir Gerard lived in the northern Outwalls and was tasked with patrolling the Casselvane Road, which he often did just for the chance to ride about and glower at people. Cindra wondered who had assigned this man to instruct her and why. She was beginning to think his main qualification was his even temper; that was to say, he was evenly dreadful with everyone.

"I'll put you through your paces with that skinny dog," Sir Gerard called, indicating T'ózha, "but you'll do better to use him for a pack horse, not a war horse!"

Cindra grimaced as she rode T'ózha around the Commons, turning at the flags planted in the trampled earth. She said, "Don't listen to the bad man, T'ózha. He doesn't know you like I do." The horse tossed his head in response, dashing towards the next flag.

"Never saw a Gali breed in a heavy charge," he called. "Never saw a little girl in one either! You're going to get mashed into paste before you even reach the enemy line!"

Sir Gerard was standing on the edge of the course, where dozens of other knights and their squires were camped, watching outside of their pavilion tents. On the occasion a spectator called out their own insults however, Gerard would round on the offender and shout him down. "See to your own poor excuse for a horse and rider, you lice-infested son of a Minozhian cow! If I want your opinion, I'll yank it out past your teeth!" Such tirades kept the jeers to a minimum, or at least not loud enough to be heard by Cindra.

Sir Gerard was an unkempt and wild-eyed man, with dark blond hair that he never brushed after waking up. He had a long face with wide-set, intense blue eyes that bulged when he stared. It was perhaps these 'crazy eyes' that kept the other knights in line, rather than the man's colorful swearing.

Cindra brought T'ózha to a halt as Gavadaire took the reins. She dismounted and patted her steed on the neck with approval, but her trainer had more to say.

"What's your intent? Hm? What's your plan when the trumpets sound the charge?" Sir Gerard looked down at her from his impressive height, his unsettling eyes boring through her.

She frowned, but was too intimidated to take it personally. She said, "I don't understand."

"No, no you don't, do you?" he nodded to himself, confirming some internal dialog he had been engaged in. "You think you can just slip into a suit of armor and ride into battle, sword swinging for king and country? Cavalry is a unit, girlie. A unit! It has to work together as one. You bring that little rouncey-"

"He's not a rouncey," she exclaimed, defending her horse. "He's a courser. He hasn't got his full growth is all."

"That," Gerard stabbed a finger at T'ózha, "is a rouncey. A pure breed Gali doesn't get more than fourteen hands high. Look around you at the real war horses! Sixteen to eighteen hands if they're an inch!" He loomed over her with hands on hips saying, "Heavy cavalry needs heavy horses, and men that can fight from the saddle. You come up against a big man on a charger, little girl on a little horse, and your head will be at the perfect smashing height."

"What about light cavalry then?" she asked.

"Hah!" he barked, "Light cavalry is for harassment! Battles aren't won by light cavalry; they just pester people until someone makes them go away!"

Sounds like me, Cindra thought. She put her hands on her hips and said, "Can you teach me to fight in a light cavalry?"

He threw his hands in the air, "Oh, for the love of-" he couldn't decide which god to invoke, so he bellowed at her, "I was ordered to train a *woman* how to fight on horseback like a *knight*. Right after I laughed my *ass off*-" he leaned close to her face, eyes bulging, "-I find out she's got no sword, she's got no lance, she's got no shield or armor, and she rides a horse not much larger than my average morning *shit!*" He straightened, folding his arms. "*Now,* you want to learn how to fight in a light cavalry. Do you even have a *bow?*"

Despite his awful manners, Cindra broke into a wide grin.

Her light cavalry training was more challenging than she thought it would be, and difficult to do in the small space of the Commons. The jousting field was big enough for a high speed charge, followed by an impact in the middle, and slowing towards the ends. Cindra's mounted archery practice required her to get up to speed and fire arrows down range; preferably at the targets, and not at the surrounding pavilion tents, or into the street beyond.

"If you can't nock an arrow at a gallop, you can't be in a light cavalry!" her trainer was yelling. "Learn it, or take your Gali horse and your Gali bow and join a Gali circus for all I care!"

It went on much like that until sundown.

The next weeks were better, for she practiced in her room at nocking arrows while bouncing on the balls of her feet, mimicking the rhythm of a trotting horse. Her trainer showed her how to use the half-seat position while shooting, placing her weight on the stirrups and not the saddle, to give her more stability. She had to relearn how to ride without reins, like the Galindri did. T'ózha had been trained for both methods, but Cindra had not practiced it with him for almost a year. She shortened T'ózha's reins with a knot so they would not fall to his legs, and worked on guiding him with the pressure of her legs. By the end of the month, she was shooting at low targets on the ground, and could release three arrows with some accuracy before running out of field.

"I wonder," she asked Sir Gerard, "If we might try using the wider fields beyond the walls instead of the Commons. It's getting so crowded here."

"Oh, aye, that's a *fine* idea," Gerard said.

Cindra got the impression that he didn't really think

it was.

He helpfully elaborated, "There's not a patch of open ground within miles that doesn't have a soldier's ass planted on it. They've been trying to quarter men in the city where there's room, but come winter, most will be camping along the roads. Add to that the baggage trains, pack animals, privy trenches, space for the camp mothers..."

"Camp mothers?" she asked, annoyed. "Is that some colorful term for whores?"

"That," he said, "is the term for the women who keep the camp clean and free of disease. They pick out lice and fleas, clean wounds and change bandages, boil water for drinking, do the washing," he scratched his matted hair thoughtfully, "sure, there might be some of them that are whores, but..."

"So the answer is 'no' then," she said impatiently.

"Unless you want to play on their sympathies," Gerard said. "Tell them how it's so crowded up at the palace that you can't ride about like a free little bird-"

She gave him one of the rude hand gestures she had learned at the Freekirk School, turned her back on him and walked away.

So she didn't get to see Gerard's good-humored smile.

As Frellmoth passed into Tavenmoth, Cindra became more proficient at her horsemanship and archery, much to her relief. Shooting arrows from horseback while wearing a dress was enough to make even the most jaded passer-by stop and gawk, and it helped that she could hit her targets and stay in the saddle. Even Sir Gerard's insults were fewer and farther between, though no less creative.

"Guide him with your legs, just like any other man!" was his favorite comment.

The month grew colder a bit early, which most took as a bad sign. Cindra almost felt guilty not having to worry about shelter during the coming winter, but she could not trade places with the entire army beyond the walls. Besides, southern winters were mild and seldom offered snow. Her concern was for the northern army that was supposedly gathering at the base of the Calione Peaks at the city of Velloness. A brutal northern winter could ruin the entire campaign, leaving only the southern army to fight its way to the pretender-king in Ahrnok.

Her training became split between mounted combat in the morning, and foot combat in the afternoon. While she got to spend her afternoons with a much more genial teacher, she dearly loved her time with T'ózha on the Commons. He was growing steadier and at ease around the other, larger horses, and his introduction to close mounted combat went better for him than Cindra.

Sir Gerard had been right about fighting alongside larger horses; the men she sparred with on the Commons were seated upon full-grown coursers and chargers, and their height advantage was plain when they met side-by-side. She spent most of the time under her borrowed shield, fending off mighty blows from on high. Rarely did she get to strike at anything but an armored leg.

She did better with a spear than a sword and shield. The long reach and the agility of her mount put her opponent on the defensive, and she could score unbalancing blows when she got lucky. It still took a great deal of strength to unseat an armored knight, and she had to retreat more often than not.

Pestering them until they make me go away, she thought.

Gavadaire's role in her morning training was mostly to stand by and hand her things. She felt badly for him, for he seemed bored most of the time, studying the fighting techniques and gear of the knights; watching the city folk pass by the Commons; flirting with the occasional maid; or just watching dutifully as she attacked targets with spear, arrow, or sword.

A thought struck her one day, and she shared it with him on their way to the field. They were walking down the path from the palace gate, which was crowded on either side by the encampments of still more knights and fighting men.

"Gavadaire," she said with a conspiratorial tone, "would you mind running errands for me during the mornings, instead of tending to me?"

He glanced sidelong at her, "That depends on the manner of errands... Do I make my boredom so plain?"

"You do," she laughed, "I've never seen you look so listless."

He shrugged, "Duty is not always exciting. What did you have in mind?"

"Well," she said, "I will first need supplies to write with..."

"Aaah," he smiled and she blushed, "You want me to be Selvina's messenger, delivering your love notes. I am not sure the king would approve."

"The king doesn't have to know," she said in a sly voice.

"You think he will not find out if we do not tell him? What of his spies?" Gavadaire asked.

"Spies? You think he is spying on us?" she said, sounding scandalized.

"Of a certainty," Gavadaire replied, "Perhaps not at all times, but we are watched; you may rely upon it."

"Then," she said with a grin, "We shall have to be extra sneaky."

He shook his head and laughed, understanding Sir Jaron Dunlorden's feelings for the lady somewhat better than before.

Chapter Seventeen

The Bird Man

The trek up the Iron Pass was strenuous and exhausting. Although the summer had supposedly ended more than a month ago, it was still warm and humid, and storm clouds threatened from the horizon on a daily basis. Khrim was dressed in light, earth-toned peasant clothing, with a leather vest over a long tunic of linen, and breeches tucked into his thick boots. The envoy was dressed in the official garb of a herald, all blue silk and velvet with gold and white trim, and the hammer and anvil badge of House Evenast upon his breast. The man was sweating profusely and drinking often from his wineskin, and Khrim wondered if the man had been wise enough to fill it with water. Wine or ale was a more common drink when one did not trust the water, but wizards could purify water for drinking if asked. No one had asked him anything.

The envoy was traveling with a six-man escort, and behind the envoy was a short train of goods and merchants bound for Portshia. They had been encouraged to join partly to take advantage of the armed escort, but mostly to cover Khrim's presence among them. The Maanok was leading a donkey, laden with pewter goblets and tableware that he had purchased from a tradesman in Kenric, intending to pass them off as wares he was going to sell in Portshia. This made it less suspicious for him to carry large sums of money for bribes and information; it would only appear to be part of his purse, as Maanok merchants were known to not trust bills of exchange.

The four-day journey up the Iron Pass led to a high, barren valley in the midst of the Cassel Mountains, where runoff from the winter snows gathered to feed the countless small tributaries in the Gayles Basin. Both sides of the valley were fortified; the Iron Pass ended at the Iron Gate, and across the gray expanse stood the Silver Gate, which lead to the Silver Pass into Casselvane. Khrim had seen maps of the area, but first-hand scouting was invaluable. He might have to return here later to cause trouble, and it was always good to know the lay of the land.

The distance between the two gates was long enough that an army would have to commit to the field, exposing themselves to attack before setting up siege weapons to break the opposite gate. Even cannon fire could not hope to reach from one gate to the other, and each gate was armed with cannons, arrow slits, and ballistae. The real tactical question was the manpower at the gate. Braeden had counted five men visible on the Iron Gate; hopefully the Silver Gate would keep the number low until the end of winter.

The caravan reached the Silver Gates by midday, pausing under the symbol of Casselvane province: a triple-peaked mountain and a wild boar rendered in worn colors and trimmed with silver paint. Two guards exited a sally-gate and approached the caravan, their halberds at the ready; they wore the gold cat of House Corrina upon their blue surcoats. The crossbowmen stood upon the battlements above, eyeing the armed escort. *Five so far,* Khrim thought.

A soldier spoke to the envoy, noting his colors and badge. "Evenast men," he remarked. "What is your business in Casselvane?"

The envoy spoke proudly, "I am Sir Rynard DeVine, envoy of Lord Drom Evenast, DeKenric. I am on a mission of mercy to secure the release of his son and heir, Grigor Evenast."

The guards exchanged a look and grinned at the man saying, "Your purse seems a bit light for that, sir herald. Do these men carry the ransom for you?" He indicated the merchant train.

Sir Rynard's eyes narrowed, "These men are free merchants with business in the west. They are taking advantage of the protection of my men-at-arms."

The guard walked down the line of mules, wagons and men, looking for anything suspicious. He asked each man where he was bound and what he was carrying, inspecting the goods carefully for smuggled contraband. The wagons were searched thoroughly.

It would be difficult to smuggle a man out through the gate, Khrim thought. *If the alarm is raised in Portshia, none will be allowed to pass this way.*

When the man reached Khrim, he stopped and peered at his tattooed face. "Maanok," he said with more than a hint of disdain. "Speak Calilesh?"

Khrim answered with his thickest accent, "Yus, maah." *Maah* was a Maanok word that meant both 'warrior' and 'brave', though he would wager this man was neither, without his fellows and their crossbows above.

"What's your business, savage?" asked the guard.

Oh yes, brave indeed. Khrim smiled stupidly, "Selln me wahres, tablefare uf pyuter." He removed a flap on one of the donkey's saddlebags, revealing pewter cups of decent quality.

The guard poked about in each bag with a dagger, looking for who-knows-what. When he reached the coin stash, he peered suspiciously at Khrim, who stiffened. "There's a good sum of coin here, and a few jewels as well! The pewter trade must be better than I imagined."

Braeden let himself seem anxious and tense, as any Maanok would when a stranger was diddling his loot. "They's me wulth, maah. Is paymen fur long myles uf walkin." He became indignant, "Not be taking writ fur coin. Not a fool!"

The guard stepped back a bit, giving his archers a better shot. The look on his face said he figured Braeden indeed to be a fool, or at least not wise enough to be a spy or threat to the province beyond the gate. He was about to turn away when Braeden sneezed loudly, making a sound like a bark. The result was amusing but dangerous; the guard jumped at the sound and the archers raised their crossbows to take aim. Braeden just wiped his nose on his sleeve, looking innocent. A few of the other merchants chuckled nervously.

"Get on!" said the guard, waving the caravan through. "Open the gates!" he called to the men above. The archers did not move, but the portcullis gates opened, one at a time. *There is at least one more within,* Khrim noted. *Six men might be dealt with at once, if I am careful.*

The last obstacle was an official collecting a toll to use the road beyond. Once the travelers were relieved of a few coins, they crossed through the gate and onto the Silver Pass, heading for Portshia.

The village below the pass was called Silverbottom, a once-thriving mining town that produced lead, zinc, and most importantly, silver. Now, it mostly served as a way station for travelers going up and down the mountain, but traffic had lessened in recent years due to the poor relations with Kenric. The lone business, known simply as the Inn at Silverbottom, provided a large common room for travelers to eat and sleep in;

there was also stabling service, a kitchen, and traveling supplies of smoked and salted beef, horse biscuits, and dried fruit, when in season. The envoy was not greatly pleased to share a room with the rest of the caravan, but his host could do no better.

Khrim waited until the innkeeper had finished seeing to everyone's needs before approaching him in private. He used better speech than he had for the gatekeeper, and tried his best to look nonthreatening.

"Pardon, master inn-keep," he said in a soft voice. The bent little man jumped regardless.

"Ah!" he exclaimed, clearly unnerved by the foreigner's facial tattoos and wild hair. "What is it? What do you want of me?" His balding head was damp with sweat and his face was pockmarked and ruddy. He wiped his hands on his apron as he peered up at the Maanok.

"I hear there are rumors of war," Khrim said, "and we passed mighty gates on the mountain. Tell me, what will they do if an army comes from Kenric over the pass? Can they truly hold them?" He did his best to sound worried.

The innkeeper looked Khrim up and down before replying, "Hmph, the Silver Gate's not as big and strong as the fortress at Passguard, the one that keeps your lot on the other side of the mountains." He thought a moment and added, "Though it didn't stop you, obviously."

"So the Kenric will break the gate above?" Khrim asked.

"If they've a mind," said the innkeeper. "No one's tried in living memory, mind you, but with cannon nowadays... who knows? It might come down faster than anyone's guess."

Khrim shook his head, "But they will call for help, surely? We saw but a few men on the gate."

The innkeeper glanced into the common room to see if anyone might have lost their Maanok, but no one was paying the big savage any mind. "They've got their ways," he said. "There's but six men there now; we send them regular supplies, don't you know. But they'll be reinforced before spring, now that the king's army is in the province."

"But what if the Kenric come before spring?" Khrim pressed.

The innkeeper became suspicious, "Why? Know something, do you?"

He replied gruffly, reminding the man who he was talking to, "I know my own people would rather brave the cold and fight six men, than wait until the weather is nice and fight a hundred."

The innkeeper seemed to take the hint, becoming a little meeker, though it was not in his feisty nature. "Well er... well, if there's a sneak attack, they'll send a hawk with a call for aid. Better than a pigeon, since a pigeon can be ate by a hawk!"

"Ah," Khrim said, "this sets me at ease. I thank you." He bowed to the little man and joined the others in the common room, releasing the innkeeper from the unwanted conversation. The man gave his apron a flap and went about his business.

Khrim stroked his chin as he leaned against a wall, keeping to himself. *Interesting,* he thought, *they do not have an ember swallow, so the news must be written and sent to Portshia. If the bird is not trained to return to the gate, they will have no means of sending more.* He had forgotten to ask if the innkeeper knew how many hawks they had. It was too late now, for the man would become suspicious. *It can be dealt with,* he figured. He drew his limbs in close and slept.

It was another three days before the party reached the outskirts of Portshia. The last plowing of the year was underway as the temperatures began to drop, obstinately settling the warm southland into autumn, more than a month and a half past the official equinox. Sheaves of wheat were drying in the fields, ox-teams were churning up furrows of earth, and seeds were being sown while children followed behind, scaring off the birds with drums and songs.

The envoy, being in no great need to wait for Khrim or the others, proceeded with his escort at a better pace and left the slower merchants behind by several hours. The roads were well-patrolled, so their absence made little difference. The merchants' goods would be safer here than among the dense humanity of the market square, where thieves abounded. The road to the city was crowded with encamped soldiers, most of who seemed to be conscripted footmen by their simple armor and weapons. They paid him little mind, more concerned with preparing for the long cold months ahead.

It was a gamble for this King Galen to march his army so far before winter, Khrim thought. *The weather might defeat his forces before they even reach the Dissenter lands.* He wondered if Portshia and Velloness had put on extra supplies for the effort, or if the king had kept his movements so secret as to give them no warning. He put the thought aside for future inquiry.

The warlock arrived at the gates of Portshia on the 10th day of Eyoromoth, over three and a half months since leaving the grand city of Ahrnok. Khrim felt elated, or would have, had the gate guards let him pass unmolested. Yet he expected no different.

"What's your business in Portshia, Maanok?" one of them asked. The other walked around the donkey, flipping open the leather saddlebags and peering at the tableware.

Khrim grumbled in a moderate accent, "Got Kenric pyuter fer de markit squaar. Gud qualy, see de mark?" He pointed to the pewterers' trademark on the underside of a goblet. "Is late enuf today to sell me in de squaar. Dey makin outsiders wait tul afternoon, ya know. Sa guild rule, tis. Den fees and tax, maah, fees and tax," Khrim shook his head ruefully.

The guards gave the saddlebags a quick check and let

him pass, losing interest in his broken shop-talk.

It was his first time in the port city, but he had familiarized himself with its ways back in Ahrnok, studying street maps and striking up conversations with merchants who knew it well. He wanted nothing more than to spend a day sleeping at a cheap inn, or soak his feet in hot water, but he had urgent business first; he had to find his contact in the Circle of Gold.

The man lived in Miner Town in the Trade District, just down the North Wall Walk from the gate through which Khrim entered. It was an older community, built centuries ago to house workers of the nearby silver mines, long before the city walls extended so far. Now it was a ramshackle collection of ill-kept buildings in the farthest corner of the city-proper.

The first thing one noticed about Miner Town was the odd proportions; for it was a community built for dwarfs. They had been drawn together by their limited employment options and outcast status, giving up their old family names and choosing new ones, and raising their children on the outskirts of society. Now, over a century after the mines closed, they still lived and worked together.

Khrim found the house easily enough; it was the only one that kept a large pigeon coop and a long hen house. He knocked on the door, noting the house's lower-than-average latch and windows. While he waited, he tried to ignore the frightened looks he was getting as parents urgently led their children inside.

Emen Silverthumb opened the door and found he was looking at Khrim's knees. His eyes grew wide in alarm as he gazed up at the giant barbarian before him, but to his credit, he composed himself and managed a nervous, "Yes?"

"I am Braeden Khrim," he said, holding his right hand over his left, palms both facing his chest in the traditional Maanok greeting. "You are the Bird Man?"

"Ah... I *raise* birds, but..." Emen said, looking about the yard as if expecting an invading horde to come pouring down the street. But it seemed Khrim was a horde of one.

"Chickens and pigeons," Khrim nodded, *"Homing* pigeons."

Emen cleared his throat and his shoulders tensed. "Uh, do come in," he said, stepping aside and sweeping his arm in welcome.

Khrim had to stoop to enter the low-ceilinged building, tilting his head to one side until Emen found him a sturdy chair. Sitting, he looked about the room. It was tidy but for the ubiquitous bits of feathers that hid in the corners and drifted across the floor at the slightest breeze. The rack of pots and pans hanging from the wall, the cupboard with the kiln-fired crockery, the shelves with trinkets and tools, the table and kitchen counter, all were of smaller size to accommodate the small man before him. It made Khrim feel like a giant indeed, and could well imagine how the rest of the world might seem to his host.

Emen was a little over four feet tall, with a mop of dark hair, a prominent brow, and wary eyes. He wore a simple tan tunic over his green trousers, and his boots were stained with bird droppings. His hands were covered with scars; whether from handling chickens or some more violent occupation, Khrim could not tell.

"May I offer you some wine?" Emen asked, eyeing his guest as if he were a bear who had wandered into his camp.

"Please," Khrim said, surprising the dwarf with his manners.

Emen poured a cup for him and leaned to pass it across the table, not wanting to get too close. "So, what brings you to Miner Town?"

"I have sent messages to your associates over the last few years," Khrim replied, downing the wine in a gulp.

"My associates?" Emen asked. "I am not-"

"You are Emen Silverthumb, Portshia Bird Man of the Circle of Gold," Khrim said.

The dwarf jumped at the words, waving his hands for

silence. "Yes!" he hissed, "yes, alright. I am their Bird Man. It's not something I advertise; else I would hang a sign on the door." He checked the window before saying, "How did you learn of this, and who do you work for... if I may ask?" he added, keeping his tone polite.

Khrim sat back, grateful to be off his feet. "I represent a power among the Dissenter Houses, and we have had dealings with the Circle. As for how I learned of you, well... each chapter has their own Bird Men, as I am sure you know."

"Of course," Emen sighed. The birds could only fly messages one-way; pigeons from other cities had to be sent to him directly to await messages, just as the birds he raised had to be delivered to those cities. All of the Circle's Bird Men knew each other by name and address at least, though they were not inclined to say for whom they were mainly employed. Emen wondered if his counterpart had given up his name willingly. "So what can I, a simple bird handler, do for the Dissenter Houses?"

"You are aware that the guild leaders have made overtures to us in the past?" Khrim asked.

"I know of no such thing," Emen said, holding up a hand. "I simply handle the birds. I don't read the messages."

"Ah, I see," he said, rotating the clay cup on the table. "We share rumors and the like. But of late, there have been more pressing matters."

"The king's army," Emen said grimly.

"Indeed," Khrim said. "I must speak with someone in authority. I have no direct contacts here, but I do have you," he said, making Emen freeze in place, his own cup trembling in his hand. "Do not fear, I mean no harm. But I need you to make introductions for me."

"Ah," Emen said, reanimating enough to take a chair opposite the table and sip his wine. "That will not be easy. They don't like new faces, and yours is the... ah, *newest* I have seen in quite some time."

"I am sure," Khrim said. "I passed an inn near the prison tower, the Crow's Bill. I shall be staying there."

Emen said spuriously, "That's a rough place."

"It appeared so," Khrim nodded. "Make the arrangements, but not until morning. It has been a long journey." He stood to leave, keeping his head low. "Oh, and one more thing," Khrim said, looming over him now.

Emen gulped, "Yes?" The sound of cooing and clucking from outside filled the space for a breathless moment.

"I will give you a pewter goblet for two of your chickens," Khrim said.

Emen breathed a sigh of relief and led his guest outside. The donkey and its cargo had been untouched, but there was a group of men milling about, brandishing farming tools like weapons. Some of them were of normal size; Khrim thought it likely they were children of dwarfs who did not inherit their parents' condition.

One of the older, if smaller, neighbors called in a high voice, "Everything in order, Master Silverthumb?"

"Yes, yes, everything is fine, Master Leadbottom." Emen waved. "Just selling some chickens." He made the transaction with the big barbarian, and then spoke to Khrim in a softer voice as the makeshift militia dispersed. "I will contact them tomorrow, and I shall tell them what I will tell you. Be careful."

Khrim nodded, cracking a rare half-smile, and led his donkey out of Miner Town.

The Maanok barbarian awoke the next morning and feasted on his second chicken, then prepared his bathing ritual with a pitcher of cold water and a clean linen rag. It had been a good sleep; as good as he had gotten since leaving the palace of Duke- rather *King* Manon Wolvert. He had cast spells of alarm and warding on the room, and the security they provided had allowed him to relax his guard and get some true rest. This was good, for the coming day would be less than restful. He dressed and moved the bag of pewter goods away from the door, which were his second layer of alarms in case his spell had failed for some reason, and headed down to the common room.

His presence made the room go quiet for a moment, just as it had when he came in last night. *If there were a minstrel playing in the corner, he would have stopped,* Khrim mused. He had that effect on the soft folk of the 'civilized' lands; one man even got up nervously and left. Khrim walked to a table near a window, and with his back to the wall, ordered ale.

He had truly expected the Circle of Gold to collect him last night, and was almost disappointed they did not. Now he had an entire day to waste in waiting. *If they come for me now,* he reasoned, *it will likely be in the evening when dark deeds are done.* Therefore it was a complete surprise to him when a young boy entered the inn, searched the room until his eyes fell on Khrim, and approached in minor terror. The boy held an object in his hand, which he tossed at Khrim before scampering to the door. Khrim caught it in mid-air; it was a circular wooden chip bearing the mark of a gaming house.

The Maanok got to his feet, finished his ale, and walked to the door. The boy dashed out into the street, weaving between the morning's striders until he reached an alley entrance, and looked back. *So I am to be lead at a distance until I reach the gaming house,* he thought. *Then the boy will disappear down a bolt hole and I will be met by larger, more dangerous guides.*

This indeed happened, and a bit sooner than he expected. The boy turned a few more corners and entered the side door of a gaming house called the Rolling Fates, where he disappeared within. Khrim found himself in a narrow alley with few other doors and windows. The view from the street was blocked off by a horse-drawn cart, no doubt placed there on purpose. Three men came out of the gaming house door, and three entered the alley behind Khrim. Of curious onlookers or city watchmen, there was no sign.

"Word is," said one of the men, "you wanted to meet the Circle of Gold."

Khrim nodded, his hands empty at his sides.

"I hope you got a good night's sleep friend, because you came a long way for nothing." The speaker was a man in his late twenties with trimmed hair, a clean tunic and hose, and quality boots. His companions were more of the lean and hungry types, not as well-dressed or groomed as their leader, but they all knew each other and worked together. Khrim could tell by the way they spoke with their eyes.

He said to the leader, "I hope you speak for your guild masters, because if you have decided this course for yourself, you take orders from a fool."

The leader took a moment to work this out, deciding it was indeed an insult. He nodded to his men and they moved fast, surrounding Khrim with dagger blades. One put an edge to his throat and pressed, drawing a hairline of blood. Khrim felt hands searching his person, looking for anything like a weapon. The Maanok had none but his wooden bracelet that was too small to be removed. It contained a core of silver that allowed him to pull upon the forces of magic, but he would not use it yet.

The search concluded and they stepped back a few paces, ready to close in and strike if ordered to. Khrim had worn a small purse with a few coins inside, just to make a searcher think he had found something worthwhile. It had the effect of distracting the man, whose mind would now be partly on how to divide the spoils or keep it from his companions.

The leader stepped back towards the door, motioning Khrim with his blade, "We'll see who's got a fool for a boss." He entered the gaming house and the Maanok followed under heavy guard.

The Rolling Fates was a loud and boisterous two-level

hall with men and women alike cheering and jeering at each other as they played games of chance or skill. There were dice tables, spinning wheels, card games, and many that involved rolling balls of various sizes through gates and holes. All was watched over by large men in black jackets, and no one wanted to attract their attention. Khrim was being led down a back hallway however, and did not attract any attention himself.

The men took him down through a cellar door, where the leader withdrew a glowstone from his pocket and said, "*Ilda*," igniting the crystal's cold glow. They walked through a long storage room lined with barrels, bags and wooden crates. Scouts of a hidden rodent army peered out at them from the shadows, their red eyes disappearing as the glowstone passed by. Reaching a far wall, the leader reached for a shelf containing clay jugs. Tipping one of the jugs forward caused the wall to swing away, revealing another room beyond. They passed through and the wall closed behind them with no visible means of opening it again.

In case I try to escape the way I came, Khrim observed with admiration. *No mere thugs, these men.*

The new room was another storage cellar containing large barrels of pickled food and salted meats. A stairway led upward, but they took a different path deeper into the bowels of the city. The light of the glowstone was enough to guide someone who knew their way, but Khrim found precious few sights to mark in the gloom. Before long he admitted he was lost; even if he could overcome his guards and light his way with a spell, he doubted he could make it to the surface streets without hours of searching.

Finally they came to a passage with a stone door. The leader took a rock from the ground and rapped on the door six times, ignoring the obvious pull-cord that would have been Khrim's choice. *Misdirection even down here,* he thought, once again impressed with their precautions.

The door opened and the face of a small child peered

out, blinking at them with wide eyes. The room beyond was lit with lanterns and magical trinkets, some held by young hands as they practiced assembling small devices or cleaning small metal tools. They all stopped to gape at the Maanok, but returned to work as the leader shot them warning looks.

"Welcome to the Warren," said the leader.

"These children are part of your guild?" Khrim asked.

"When they earn their keep, they will be," the leader said. "We don't run a charity down here."

Khrim approved of the practice, for it was similar to how Maanok raised their own children, teaching them survival skills as early as possible. His own childhood ended when he could declare "No!" and withstand the beating that followed without tears. Still, he knew that this society would frown upon keeping children in the dark and training them to be thieves and killers. It was what they feared, and was therefore something that could be used against them if it came to that.

Eventually they arrived in a vaulted chamber that smelled of wine and candle wax. Iron candelabras stood along the walls, with puddles of solid white beneath them like melted ghosts. The floor was covered with rugs that tried to brighten the room with vivid colors, but only served to contrast the cold arched ceiling overhead. An iron fireplace warmed the far side of the room, where there sat a wooden desk and a few upholstered chairs. Behind the desk was a small figure clad in a dark tunic and undershirt. His feet dangled several inches above the floor.

Khrim smiled. "The Bird Man," he rumbled.

Emen Silverthumb nodded in return as his men waited with tensed muscles, ready to strike on command. "Welcome to my parlor," Emen said. "I trust you got the tour?"

"It was illuminating," Khrim said. "Shall we talk, or do you intend to kill me?"

"Are the two mutually exclusive?" Emen asked.

"Hopefully," Khrim shrugged.

Emen motioned for the Maanok to take a chair, then said to the man who led Khrim's escort, "Garreth, I wonder if you would please get us some wine?" Garreth bowed his head and withdrew. Emen turned to Khrim, "You said you wanted to meet with the Circle's leadership. As it happens, I am the Silver District boss. Bird Man is only my day job. How can we be of assistance to the Dissenter Houses, Braeden Khrim?"

The Maanok said, "Have I been corresponding with you, then? Or have my messages been passed on to a higher authority?"

Emen said, "I spoke the truth about the messages. I keep my nose out of them, lest it be cut off. We outlaws are a very private people, you see."

Garreth returned with a wine bottle and two glasses. He poured and offered one to Khrim, who waved it away.

"So you do not know about the prisoner?" Khrim asked, purposely being vague.

Emen frowned and thought a moment. "You mean the DeKenric boy," he said.

Khrim nodded, "He is the guest of the king. I was told that the Circle could help free him for a price."

Emen gulped his wine in surprise. "Were you indeed?" he said. "Why would we do such a thing?"

"You might ask the one who read my letters," Khrim said.

Emen said, "Are you aware that the boy is being kept in the Winter Palace?"

Khrim's expression was unchanged.

"The Winter Palace is currently the heart of the entire southern army," Emen said. "The king and all of his ministers are there, along with his barons and their knights. The place is a fully-manned fortress." The dwarf sat back, as if the matter was settled.

Khrim shrugged.

"Don't shrug!" Emen said. "It's nothing to shrug about. I assume that your messages were sent before the army arrived, when the palace was only staffed by servants and rats. This is totally different!"

"In my experience," Khrim said, "anything that looks familiar will be ignored, even in a busy castle."

"Then it is plain that neither you nor I will be involved in his rescue," Emen said, sipping his wine. "Tell me, how did you begin this correspondence anyway?"

Khrim said, "I got to know local Circle men in the city of Ahrnok in Kraal-Dromah province. They were smugglers and merchant-spies who traveled to Portshia when the need arose. Through them, I gained the ear of your council. I assumed you would have heard of this?"

Emen said, "I have been on the council for less than a year. My predecessor might have heard of such things..."

"Ah," Khrim said, filling in the gaps. "Then I shall inform you. I received a letter from your smugglers; it instructed me how to address future letters. I was to mark the outer edge of the message with an arrow and a backwards bow," he drew the sign in the air. "I was to address my messages with an inverted crown of Arathus."

"A foreign spy wishing to contact the council," Emen interpreted. "I remember receiving several of those in recent years."

"As you say," Khrim said. "I was told to sign the messages with a cross mark, followed by two dashes."

"The cross mark is a compass," Emen explained. "The first dash indicates it came from the east, the second that it came from... farther east."

"Interesting," Khrim said. He had not considered that the symbols might reveal his land of origin. No doubt the smugglers had mentioned his heritage to their masters.

Emen said, "Messages addressed to the council do not reach the district bosses, but are routed to the Boss himself. I don't know the specifics; the courier network is as convoluted as it is effective. If the Boss deems it worthy of the council's consideration, he will present it to us when we meet."

"Have you informed this Boss that I am here?" Khrim asked.

"I have," Emen said. "He had me arrange this little meeting, you see." He waved his hand about the room, indicating his men. "If you were unable to confirm that you were the man who sent him those messages, then I was to have you killed." He made a shooing gesture to the men, who withdrew into the shadows. "I for one am glad you don't have to die; I rather enjoy your company."

"Do you?" Khrim asked, surprised. "You are a rare man indeed, Emen Silverthumb."

"Well, like you," Emen said, "I am a man out-of-place." He waved a hand in the air dismissively, "I have no idea why the Boss elevated me to this post. I'm not a thief or murderer, I can't pick a lock to save my life, and I don't intimidate anyone. I don't even impress the orphans who work for me; I leave discipline to a few of the older boys. So why am I here? What could a dwarf bird handler possibly bring to the council?"

"You seem to be much more than a mere bird handler," Khrim said.

"As you are no ordinary barbarian, begging your pardon," Emen said. "Most dwarfs from Portshia can read and write, did you know? Many of our fellow citizens cannot. Miner Town ceased to be a labor pit long ago; now we teach our children letters, numbers, and anything that will give them an advantage. All that holds us back is our height, and that is quite enough of a challenge to overcome."

"Perhaps the Boss wished for such a different perspective?" Khrim offered, speaking from his own experience.

"Ha!" Emen laughed. "From down here, everything looks big. How's that for perspective?"

Khrim smiled saying, "There must be a reason for everything, whether we see it or not."

"You know," Emen said, "there are rumors that we

are living in the last days of the world. I find myself wondering if the Boss believes it."

"Why?" Khrim asked.

"I fear *that* might be enough to explain his reasons," Emen said, draining his cup. "What will it matter?"

Khrim and Emen made their way through the chill catacombs with Garreth and two other men as escort. They were all carrying torches at Emen's insistence, just in case they met any of the restless dead.

"What are we supposed to do if we see a vemlok anyway?" Garreth asked.

"Try not to die," was Emen's reply.

They had discussed blindfolding Khrim, but it was decided that if they were attacked by some undead monster, it would be best for the big Maanok to be able to see.

"Such a maze of tombs," Khrim said with awe. "Who would think there was such a vast city of death beneath the living one?"

"It is a surety that most people who have lived here are dead," Emen said. "I just hope they stay that way." They turned yet another corner, keeping eyes and ears alert for any sound beyond the lick of the flames and their dusty footsteps. Part way up the corridor, Emen came to a stop. His eyes had fallen upon a figure in a low alcove. He held his torch before him and bent to get a better look.

The figure was not tall, though not as short as Emen. It was wrapped in white linens, and there was a dark stain like old blood near the chest. Dust had only just begun to gather on it.

"What is it?" asked Garreth in a nervous whisper.

"A corpse," Emen said, "Recent by the look of it. The linens are new, not the rotted rags full of bones like the rest."

"This is unusual?" Khrim asked.

"No one comes down here to bury their dead," Emen replied. "The gravediggers take our coin to keep certain passages free of living eyes."

"Some poor bastard that ran afoul of the Circle?" said one of the other men.

"Likely," Garreth said. "Come on, nothing to be done. That is unless you think there might be loot?"

The men shook their heads, continuing up the passage. Emen gave the corpse a last look, wondering if it was someone he knew.

The council convened as the district bosses placed their tokens on the stone altar and the Boss called the meeting to order. Khrim stood behind Emen's chair, looking at the faces of the secret council. They were dressed in similar dark robes or tunics, almost like members of the priesthood. Khrim wondered if it was intended to create a mystique of unity, discouraging the individualist manner common to thieves. All gave him curious and worried looks, as he had come to expect, but their expressions told him much. Obviously, the Boss had not yet informed the council of his plans with the Dissenters.

"Friends," said the Boss in his deep baritone, "We have a guest, as I am sure you have noticed. This is Braeden Khrim, a representative of the Dissenter House of Wolvert. He has come to seek our aid in a matter of great importance."

"He's a Maanok!" cried a younger man with the sound of wealth in his voice.

"Sharp as ever, Taymen," the Boss said. "He is one of their warlocks, a man of cunning and hidden power."

Emen looked up at Khrim in surprise. Khrim shrugged.

"What does House Wolvert want with us?" asked an older man near the Boss. His face was set in a creased mask of hostility and mistrust.

The Boss said, "They have asked for our assistance in freeing the son of Baron DeKenric, who is being held in the Winter Palace."

No one made a sound. They shared incredulous looks all around, except Emen and the Boss, who watched the others.

"If I may," the older man asked, "what would motivate us to commit treason against our king and threaten the success of his campaign?"

"Treason, my dear Kaplin?" said the Boss. "We have done worse in the name of profit before, if you recall."

A thin man with a stiff beard spoke, "But this is a civil war! If we help the Dissenters, it could mean the fate of the kingdom! Why would we risk the stability we now enjoy?"

"A good question, Elmir," the Boss said. "What have we to gain if the king loses the lands east of the Cassel Range?"

Khrim knew the question was not for him. If he read the Boss correctly, the man was setting the council up for his Grand Plan.

The Boss walked around the stone table, his hard, craggy face meeting each of his underlings. "We are people of the shadows, hiding our true selves in the light of day. We hold power over others, but that power is weak and based on fear. The law of the crown governs all, whether they be high or low, worthy or no. Arathus himself gave us this rule, and we are still expected to follow it, even now that the gods are silent and pay us no mind.

"But I tell you, there is another way," he continued. "Without the crown, without the tyranny of a monarch, there is a chance for each land to govern as it will. Imagine if Portshia and its surrounding lands were a nation unto itself? Imagine sitting on a council, not in a darkened tomb, but in a palace of state with the blessings of the people? What wealth we acquire could be worn openly and honestly, not squirreled away out of sight of the *authorities*." He sneered the last word.

"You mean to go on the straight and narrow," said an older woman with a hoarse voice. She sounded shocked and appalled.

"I mean to rule!" the Boss exclaimed. "There is nothing new to us on the other side of the law. Power begets power, and wealth begets wealth. If we make sure that the kingdom fractures into pieces, we can take those pieces and make kingdoms of our own!"

"This is madness," said the younger man. "You cannot rule without the nobility!"

"Nobility is an outdated notion," the Boss said. "They ruled us because they had the ownership of the lands, the wealth, and the weapons. Now the merchants and men of business hold a greater share, and armies are bought with coin, not with loyalty to a lord."

Emen spoke up, "Even if you could convince this council to support such a notion, how would you change the minds of the people? Don't they have to agree to make you their ruler in place of the king?"

"Look at what their king is doing," said the Boss. "He has gathered a great host on their doorsteps, and is demanding more troop levies before winter. He is draining the winter stores of the city, lodging his soldiers in peoples' homes, and demanding purveyance from merchants and farmers alike for his campaign.

"And consider how the north will suffer this winter! His army at Velloness is at least as large, and they have been harvesting the cities and villages for men and food as they march. How difficult would it be to create an uprising in the absence of most of the city's fighting men?"

A man with a laborer's accent spoke from under his hood, "We don't have an army, only a mob. Do you expect to storm Casselvane Keep and toss the Gold Cat off the cliff? I'd like to see that, mind you, but the people are a different matter."

"All we need to do is sow dissent among them," said the Boss. "We spread the word like a fire. When the time comes, they will be ready to be led. We will insist the count step down from power, and if he resists, we will compel him. Other cities will take our example to heart, and a new revolution will be born."

Taymen spoke again, a defiant edge in his voice. "But who are *you* to lead them? You may be the Boss of the

Circle of Gold, but you can't exactly say that to an angry mob, can you? They'd hang you from the nearest lamppost."

"My friends," said the Boss, "I am not intending to announce myself as the Boss. I have another face, a more public face, and it is one that the people will rally behind."

"Do you?" Emen asked. "I must admit, I've never seen your face outside this chamber."

The Boss smiled with his thin lips, making his hard face crack with lines. He lowered his head for a moment and raised it again, drawing back his hood. The other district bosses gasped, some leaping from their chairs. Bodyguards were on alert, and weapons were held at the ready as the tension in the chamber soared. The other bosses knew *this* face well.

Kobus DuChat cast his gaze around the silent room, placid and full of assurance. When he spoke, it was with the mellow tenor of a scholar and diplomat. "We can do this, my friends. This is our time, our age. We will make the broken land into our own private paradise, feeding on the corpse of the dead kingdom as we tend our gardens with the compost. I shall lead the way, and the people will follow me."

And another great enemy of my people shall fall, Khrim thought with satisfaction. *Calilon will fall.*

Chapter Eighteen

Bitter Cold

Jaron flexed his arms and chest as Sir Cord adjusted the armor's fittings for the last time. The sound of twisting leather straps and metal rings sliding together was comforting, and when the tempered steel plates collided, it was almost musical. After many years of saving, he had finally acquired a full plate armor suit.

Now I am a knight, he thought with satisfaction. *Too bad there is no mirror.*

"Would you like me to fetch you a mirror?" Cord asked, stepping back to admire his former squire. Laughter came from the gathered students who were peeking in on the fitting.

Jaron smirked at Cord, who grinned and passed him his helmet. He slid the metal enclosure over his mailed and padded head, locked it closed, and flipped the visor down over his face.

"Can you see?" asked Cord.

"Well enough," Jaron said. "It's better visibility than

a jousting helm, though not by much."

"Head outside into the yard," Cord said. "Let's put a few scuffs on that polished metal."

Jaron clinked and clanked out of the room and into the training yard of the Freekirk School, marveling at how light and flexible the armor was. The weight was distributed over his shoulders and limbs, making the 45 lbs. feel almost natural. The only hindrance came from the helmet, which impeded his vision and hearing. Still, it was a small price to pay to avoid getting his head smashed in or being stabbed in the face.

The remaining students gathered in the yard to watch the action. A few more had departed in the last month, bringing the total down to thirteen. Maadi Gaavi had taken ship for home, having no interest in fighting a civil war, and Minas Koorla had to return to his house in the city to tend to sick family members.

Jaron drew his sword *Valdiroth*, igniting its blue flame, and tested his range of motion. Swinging the blade left trails of whooshing fire as Jaron performed the practice movements of the *Daerbrik* and *Haevrbrik* styles, his armor rattling with each graceful step.

"Take a tumble or two," Cord said. "Learn to recover your feet."

Jaron complied, rolling back over his shoulder and gaining his feet with little difficulty. He rolled in the opposite direction, mirroring the movement. His forward roll was a little less graceful, and he found the knee joint and chest piece hindering his follow-through. Faking defeat, he collapsed onto his back, arms spread at his sides.

"Arrrrgh," he cried into the muffling helmet.

"Get up," Cord said. "You're no turtle, though I have seen more agile turtles."

"They have a lifetime of practice," Jaron said, regaining his feet. The students made good humored applause. Mat Belvine even came over with a handkerchief and made to dust off the armor, adding a polish with his elbow. Jaron himself had to laugh at that.

"Alright ladies, the fashion show is over," Cord said, "Back to your training." The students fell in line and began their morning exercises.

Jaron sheathed his flaming sword and opened the helm, taking in the crisp morning air. "Ah, it's stuffy in here," he said. "I'd hate to think what it's like fighting in full plate during the summer months."

"It's a special kind of torture," Cord said. "But moist air makes it worse; you'll sweat away several pounds just sitting in the saddle. That's why you don't wear it until the morning of battle. Which reminds me," he lowered his voice, "You might want to take on a new squire before we march off to war in spring."

Jaron's spirits fell instantly. He did not want to be reminded that Cindra was, for all practical purposes, out of his life. "I'll consider it," was all he said.

"Good," Cord said. "You know, you could do a lot worse than some of our students here."

"Hm," Jaron said.

"Granted, it's a short list," Cord said. "DeGhat and LiKeska will probably be knighted before spring, as will Gaius..." He avoided saying 'Corrina,' but Jaron sighed all the same. "Victhor and Korbison are spoken for, so that leaves-"

Jaron said, "The beanpole, the nightmare brothers, two mercenaries I couldn't afford to pay, and Cindra's three best friends."

"That's about the size of it," Cord agreed. "Let's assume you don't want Belvine, Stansig Gebthor, or the er... nightmare brothers. Four young men to choose from are better than none."

"Who would you pick," Jaron asked.

Cord considered, "For sheer usefulness, I'd choose Bradric Hyne. He's a big, strong lad who knows horses better than most. He can care for tack and harness, and he's a fair cook."

Jaron nodded, but said nothing.

Cord put his hands on his hips, getting annoyed. "Do you want to offer him the post?"

Jaron only shrugged, making his armor clink.

"Fine," Cord said. "Then I'll take him. That leaves you three to choose from."

"Hey!" Jaron exclaimed, shaken out of his mood. "That's not fair!"

"Love and war, boy, love and war; all is fair, remember?" Cord poked Jaron's metal chest. "I need a squire too, and I'm not eating the kind of slop my last one prepared."

"Liar! You said you *liked* my vegetable stew," Jaron said.

"I didn't want to hurt your maiden-like feelings," Cord said. "Besides, Champ is a great charger, and he needs a strong handler. There's little other choice for me."

"Then why did you bother to recommend him to me?" Jaron asked.

"It's called 'being nice,' you cretin," Cord said. "I can handle a green squire who doesn't know a horse from an ass; I've done it before. Now figure out a choice and do it before winter sets in. You'll need to train him up before the good food runs out, or you'll be eating grass stew on the march." He slapped Jaron on the back with a loud 'bang' and walked away to oversee the morning exercise.

Jaron realized that there was no one left to help him out of his armor, so he wandered around a bit, his shining suit casting shards of sunlight on the courtyard walls.

Later in the morning, Gavadaire LuVestra paid them a visit. He arrived through the main gate with his hat in hand and his cloak swaying in the breeze. Most of the students paused in their training to wave or shout a greeting, and he waved in return. He stepped up to the covered porch and nodded to Master Cord, then occupied himself with examining the coats-of-arms of the school's former students.

When the activity ended, Cord spared his former instructor a moment. "Welcome, Gavadaire. What brings you back? Has our Lady Knight mastered your teaching already?"

Gavadaire chuckled, "No, she has mounted training in the mornings with a scoundrel named Sir Gerard Valdoy. I am not needed until afternoon."

"Gerard Valdoy?" Cord said. "How in the Abyss did he get the post? I recommended Sir Darcy Rendoc." Cord motioned Gavadaire to follow him into the hall. "Jaron!" he called. "Jaron, where are you?"

"Here," Jaron called from the top of the stairs to the private quarters.

As they came up, they found him in his room with old Elmore, who was trying to get the armor straps loosened with his old fingers.

"Let that be, Elmore. We can get him sorted," Cord said, dismissing the old caretaker. Once he had departed, Cord turned to Jaron and asked, "Just who did you instruct the quartermaster to see to Lady Cindra's mounted training?"

Jaron looked up in surprise, seeing Gavadaire for the first time. He said, "Uh, Sir Gerard?"

"Sir Gerard," Cord nodded. "Is there a reason you changed my recommendation?"

"She was my squire," he said. "Besides, Sir Gerard is very competent and knows how to train a rider."

"Sir Gerard is an ass," Cord said, "Not a fit teacher for a- wait a minute..." He folded his arms and glared at Jaron, who seemed to shrink into his armor like a turtle. "Sir Darcy is younger and handsome, that's it isn't it? You thought he'd be a rival!"

"Hardly!" Jaron said. "He's a cad and a lecher. I was protecting her from his advances!"

Cord threw up his hands, "It takes one to know one. I have half a mind to tell the Avenoth brothers that you need a new squire and they have to fight each other for the honor."

"You wouldn't dare," Jaron said.

Cord just sighed and shook his head. "I'm sorry you had to see this shameful display of pettiness, LuVestra. It's most unbecoming of a knight."

"Think nothing of it, master." Gavadaire said. "I have come to see Sir Jaron after all."

"Have you then?" Cord said. "Then I leave him to you. I've had enough of his antics for today." He left the room and stomped downstairs.

Gavadaire began to help Jaron out of his armor, and Jaron asked, "Why have you come to see me? Is Cindra well?"

"She is," he said, "She has made me her personal courier, actually."

"Her courier?" Jaron asked. "Delivering what?"

"Can you read?" Gavadaire asked.

"Well enough," Jaron said. "She sent a letter?"

"The first of many I fear," he said. "I will help you out of this fine suit first, and you can read it in private." When he was finished, he tipped his hat and left.

Jaron was grateful beyond words, regretting all of the unworthy thoughts he had harbored against Gavadaire since he first came to the school. He was especially upset upon hearing that the dashing foreigner would be instructing Cindra in the palace, but it seemed that his fears were for naught. He read the letter to himself by the open window, hearing her voice and seeing her face.

Dearest Jaron,

I want you to know that I think of you every day. I regret the events that lead to our separation, and if I could live the last few years over again, I think now I would rather have vanished into the wilderlands with you to start a new life together. But fate has a way of twisting our wishes and dreams into paths we would not have chosen with foresight.

It is likely that our paths will not meet again for some time. When they do, it will be in some other land on a distant battlefield, or in the ruins of our former lives. Regardless, I look forward to that day, and hope that you will feel the same.

I do not know how many more letters I can send, so I felt it important to set these words down first. My future letters will be about lesser matters, like the time Gavadaire and I got into a fight with four knights who interrupted my training, or about the lout of a man who is teaching me to fight in light cavalry. I leave you with those stories to look forward to.

Please try to find happiness outside of my company. I know you are prone to melancholy, but while I miss you desperately, I will not mourn you. I have hope that we shall meet again, and you must share in that hope. Take comfort in your friends and family, and try not to upset Master Cord overmuch.

With   love,
Cindra

It took Jaron several days to compose a reply. He was not a writer, and had only ever written lists and orders. Yet he found the words to respond in kind, telling her of his love and hopes, his wish that they might meet again someday when all of their struggles were behind them. It was difficult to maintain his tone however, and he found his thoughts slipping towards that melancholy that she warned him against.

Gavadaire returned the next week with a new letter, and Jaron gave his own to deliver, thanking the man with heartfelt sincerity. As he read Cindra's stories, he tried to picture the grand surroundings she only alluded to. He had never been in the Winter Palace, but assumed it was far more impressive than Casselvane Keep. He pictured her sparring in halls of silver and gold, with diamonds on the ceiling to mimic the stars. He imagined her dining in a vast space filled with knights and barons, with a warm, soft light that shone down upon her from above. He winced as he read of her first encounter with Sir Gerard, and felt more than a touch of guilt at having been responsible. Still, he did not feel guilty enough to reveal his part in it. Not yet.

For all he knew, Gavadaire had told her already.

Every Massday, he went to Casselvane Keep to visit his ailing father. Sir Fedrick had wasted away in the last few months; his once sturdy frame was now frail and thin, his skin had become pale, his limbs shook as he sat at rest, and were nearly useless for normal activity. A servant had been assigned to care for him, and the old man was no longer of a mind to complain about it.

"Father," Jaron said as Sir Fedrick opened his eyes. The old knight had been describing his latest aches and pains, and had drifted off to sleep.

"Jaron?" he said, confused. "When did you get here, lad?"

"Less than an hour ago; you fell asleep." He squeezed the old man's hand.

"Ah," Fedrick said. "I thought maybe I died. I always think I'm closing my eyes for the last time now. I try not to do it, but I can't help it."

"You shouldn't avoid getting rest," Jaron said. "If you are tired, you should sleep." He did not want to address his father's fears. It was increasingly difficult for Jaron to cope with how much fear he saw in his father's eyes lately.

"I sleep too much," Fedrick said. "I never see the sun anymore; just this dark room with its tiny window."

"I can arrange for a litter to take you outside," Jaron said. "It's chilly, so you will need blankets, but the sky is clear."

"I'd like that," Fedrick said. "So much you take for granted, like the sun, the wind." He closed his eyes for a few moments, and Jaron feared he would drift off again. But Fedrick opened his eyes and said, "There are things we wait too long to say, things we should say every day." The old man's eyes began to fill with tears, and he raised a shaking hand to wipe them away.

It was more than Jaron could bear. He rose and said, "I will get you a litter and some help to bear it, and we will take you into the sun." He kissed his father on the forehead and said, "I will be right back."

Fedrick watched his son leave, his mouth trying to form words that would not come.

Jaron stepped out into the hall and put his hand to his eyes, squeezing them shut lest he begin to cry as well. It was so very painful to see the man brought low by age and illness. He had always been such a strong and brave example, a knight of quality and renown, noble in all but birth. Now he was a frightened old man who did not know if each day would be his last. It was not that his father had feared death in the past, but he had always faced it on his own terms, with a sword in hand.

He called for servants to bring a litter and more blankets, and he returned to his father's room to prepare him for the excursion.

Sir Fedrick was slumped in his chair once again, his chin on his chest. Jaron did not want to wake him, but he had to dress him in warmer clothing, so he leaned over and gave his father's shoulder a gentle squeeze. "Father?" he said.

Fedrick did not stir.

"Father?" Jaron said a bit louder.

The personal servant arrived with blankets, placing them near at hand. He came to Jaron's side, concerned.

"Father, can you hear me?" Jaron asked, his voice tinged with panic. Fedrick did not stir.

The servant placed his finger under the old man's nose, feeling for breath. He felt for a pulse in his neck. He looked up at Jaron, his eyes telling the young man everything; nothing.

Jaron stepped back, a cold finger tracing down his spine. "Father," he breathed. When he breathed again, it came in a sharp gulp of air. "No..." he said, and sank to his knees beside the chair. He held the old man's limp hand, feeling its warmth and knowing it would not last.

The funeral was held three days later in the private chapel of Casselvane Keep, with all of the knights of House Corrina in attendance. Jaron had never seen such an assembly before, and it reminded him of the great debt of honor the Corrinas owed to his father, their once champion and protector. It had been Fedrick, a lowly conscript and farmer, who had saved the life of the former count when his bodyguard had fled in the face of the enemy. Sir Fedrick had carried *Valdiroth,* one of the three Corrina Honor Swords, and had passed it to his son. Jaron wore it even now, and silently renewed his oath to remain worthy of it.

Rows of knights stood in their blue and gold tabards and blue berets, solemnly intoning the responses to the priest. High Commander Fenwald himself led the service, his armor shined to a high polish and his hair dyed a deep, rich red. His voice boomed through the small chapel and out beyond the doors where the remainder of the congregation stood. The sound was ominous in the darkened halls; heavy curtains of mourning were draped over the windows, making a symbolic tomb of the castle itself.

Cindra and her family were present, standing beside Jaron and Sir Cord. Their reunion had come much sooner than either expected, but it was not what either would have wished. The count and countess were dressed in somber colors of deep burgundy and blue, and Cindra wore one of her mother's dresses of green velvet and gold, having no formal clothing of her own. Though they were together, they were apart, separated by grief and the presence of others.

Sir Fedrick Dunlorden laid in repose before the small altar, his pained face finally peaceful. He wore his suit of polished plate armor, and a blue and gold tabard of House Corrina. His hands gripped a sword at his chest, and his shield lay over his legs with his coat of arms displaying a brown cow on a field of green. The scars on his face were a pale white against the yellowing skin, and his white beard seemed stiff and unreal.

Jaron wondered what his father had meant to say in those last moments. The old man had never been one for kind words, but he said things that were important. What had Jaron missed when he left his side to hide his own weakness? He stared at the face, as unmoving as a sculpture of clay, and wondered if he would ever get the chance to ask in the next life. Would they even meet in the next life?

The High Commander was finishing his eulogy, "Sir Fedrick had seen many battles in his long life, and been victorious in most. His courage and sacrifice were an inspiration to all, and his time upon Balkon's Field of Strife shall surely be brief. May he find the rest he deserves in Haven, under the care of Mother Mercy, before his spirit moves on to its final peace."

"*D'athe Domos,*" the gathered mourners recited.

Jaron and his fellow pallbearers lifted his father's body on its litter and made the slow procession to the catacombs beneath Casselvane Keep. It was a great honor for a knight to be buried in the family tombs of his lord, and if any deserved it, Sir Fedrick did. The mourners followed behind as the pipers played the dirge "First on the Field," the traditional hymn for fallen warriors. Jaron mouthed the words silently, unable to raise his voice.

They heard the battle trumpets call,
They saw the wind in banners swell,
And taking weapons from the wall,
They bid their wives and kin farewell.

March for lord and countrymen,
March for fame and fealty,
The commoner and noblemen,
March to meet their destiny.

The ordered ranks with bow and spear,
The cavalry with lances high,
Proceed to give mighty cheer,

And loose the arrows to the sky.

And who will be first on the field?
And who will be the first to fall?
Who will be borne upon their shield?
Their name engraved on Balkon's Wall?

They reached the entrance of the catacombs and descended into the greater darkness.

It was late in the day before the mourners walked out of the shadowed castle halls and into the light. The sun was partially covered with a veil of clouds, but the change was still painful to bear. Yet it was not as painful as other changes.

"I'm so sorry, Jaron," Cindra said. She touched his arm; it was their first touch in ages.

"Thank you for coming," Jaron said with a weak, shaking voice. It was all he could think to say, foolish though it was. It was her home after all; he was the guest in this place, the outsider.

She took him in her arms, not caring what anyone would say.

Jaron knew she would hold him for as long as he needed. He could feel it in the steady pressure of her embrace. Days ago, he would have wished for nothing more, but now he felt he had to break their intimacy. He pulled away, eyes awash with pain, and he kissed her on the brow. He could not look at her overlong, lest the grief became compounded, became too much to bear. He gave her hand a final squeeze as he turned to walk down the Highcourt road.

The grand mansions of the Highcourt were bedecked with black banners of mourning, but Jaron had declined to have the rest of the city follow suit. There were far too many black flags and black strips of cloth tied on door latches already, and there would be many more to come in the following year. He knew his father would not have wanted to further burden the populace with his own passing. He had been a peasant knight, an oddity in the social order. When he had chanced to talk of his death, it was of simple burial with little circumstance. Yet the count had offered a greater honor. A decade from now, Jaron would be tasked to carry his father's bones to lie beside his mother's on the ancestral farm. He hoped he would be alive to do this, but he knew his own bones might be buried in some distant land by then.

He was distantly aware of the other knights of House Corrina who were drifting away nearby. They had come to honor the father, not comfort the son. Jaron knew most of them, and knew that most of them had no great love for him. Whether they were jealous of his position as Knight Champion, or of his relationship with Lady Cindra, or of the scandal he had brought by making her his squire... it did not matter. He had nothing to say to anyone, and no one offered to speak to him outside of the funeral service.

Each week brought more messages from Cindra, delivered by a dutiful Gavadaire LuVestra. Each week he had nothing to send in return. Her notes came more frequently and were full of concern and fear for him, but all he could bring himself to do was thank Gavadaire and bid him tell Cindra he loved her. Like the waning daylight, Cindra's notes became shorter, but no less heartfelt. Yet his quill and parchment sat unused and the ink congealed in the fountain, a dead man's wound, black and crumbling.

It was on her birthday, more than a month after his father's death that he finally brought himself to write. He composed it in the frost-blue light of morning, which came imperceptibly earlier than before with slender, grasping fingers over the mountain.

Dearest Cindra,

I am not one for long letters when I write at all. Forgive me for my silence, but my heart has been a tempest. There was a time, not many years ago, when I was brought low with the news of your 'death' at sea.

But now it is my own mortality that haunts me. I have looked upon the coming war with fear, not that I might die, but that I might not die well. It is not that I wish for it. But if it comes, as it must, I would have it be in combat on the field of honor. Old warriors face a long, weary battle and a slow, inevitable defeat. Young warriors gain glory in death, but lose the battle much too soon. Which is better? I do not know. I fear I will not know until I look death in the face once again.

Since you may again face that same question, I will not burden you with my struggles. All I have left to offer you is the love I will carry for you, and the oath I shall take for you. May I see you when battle is joined, in this life or the next.

Eternal Love and Honor,
Jaron

He sealed the letter, and placing it on the dresser to await delivery, went down to the cold ground below to ready himself for the coming march of spring.

And who will be first on the field?
And who will be the first to fall?

Chapter Nineteen

Pestilent Waters

Braeden Khrim studied the drawing on the table, watching as Emen Silverthumb moved little dice around to represent guards and obstacles. Joining them at the table was a peculiar-looking man by the name of 'Twist,' whom the Boss had insisted they use for the rescue mission. Apparently this Twist had abilities similar to the Boss himself, able to change his appearance to look like other men. For now, his face was a jumble of mismatched features that made Khrim very uncomfortable.

The candelabras in the parlor had been brought close to illuminate the table and the conspiracy forming there. The parlor in the Warrens was the only place that three such unusual people could meet without drawing attention. *A foreign barbarian, a dwarf, and a twisted man; it was like the beginning of a joke,* Khrim thought.

Emen was shaking his head, saying, "I don't see it. I

don't think it can be done." He poked at the map of the Winter Palace, disturbing several dice. "There are at least a few hundred men inside. Most of them are fighting men with nothing to do. The ones on watch are vigilant, looking out for spies and assassins." He sipped his wine, shaking his head some more.

"The challenge," Khrim said, "is not getting in; it is getting out with Grigor DeKenric. Getting in unnoticed is the easy part."

"Oh?" Emen said. "Easy, just like that?" He snapped his fingers.

Khrim said, "Agents could be sent inside to do common work. After a time, they would become part of the landscape."

Twist spoke in his reedy, lilting tenor, "Time is not something we have in abundance, but we are in luck. The Boss already has a few spies in the palace."

Emen looked up, "Does he now? Good of him to tell us."

"Spies don't work if everyone knows they are there," Twist said, sideways.

"Who are they?" Khrim asked.

"Servants," Twist said. "We've had years to sink our hooks into the palace staff. Most times they work in the city, living their lives, accumulating debts and needing favors. All we ask is for them to keep an ear to the door when the king is home."

"How can that help?" Emen said. "Forgive me, but I am new to this spy business."

"They have already helped enormously," Twist said. "Because of them, we know DeKenric is being kept in the tower wings at the rear of the palace." He indicated the three tower spires on the map, and the raised walkways that connected them. "We know he has the freedom of all three towers, and that he cannot leave the wing without a two-man guard. Each tower has its own parapet into the main palace, and each is guarded by two men at the outer doors, and two at each stairway."

"In other words," Emen said, "we know how insane this whole idea is."

"What about scaling the rear walls?" Khrim asked. "This area next to the mountain is unlikely to be heavily fortified."

"Why is that?" Emen asked.

"The slopes are very steep," he said. "Between the wall and the mountain, there is rubble and bad footing. Anyone trying to assault the wall from here will be killed from above; there is no place to hide or run. Also, I have noticed avalanche traps on the upper slope."

"Charming," Emen said.

"So it is unlikely they will watch the foothills. Even during a siege, only a desperate man would attempt the climb," Khrim said.

"It would be trickier than it looks," Twist said. "The rear wall does not give access to the tower walkways. You would need to enter the palace itself; either that, or climb down into the courtyard and up again to the tower parapets. Doing so unseen would be..."

"Impossible?" Emen offered. "Yes, I believe I'd made noises to that effect."

"I could do it," Twist said. "But again, getting in is the easy part. Once inside, we need to get DeKenric out. He cannot change his face."

Emen said to Khrim, "You're a warlock, can't you... I don't know... cast a 'disguise spell' on DeKenric or something?"

"I would have to be there next to him to cast a spell," Khrim reminded him. "Even if I managed to be in his presence, there is no magic I can summon to change a man's face." He looked at Twist again, his discomfort palpable. Maanok were a superstitious people, and it was difficult to overcome the fear bred of old childhood stories.

"I suppose if it was common magic, DuChat's revelation wouldn't have been such a shock to us all," Emen murmured. "Still, there must be some spell-" He looked at Twist and asked, "How did DuChat do that?

How do you do it? It's a spell, surely?"

Twist only gave him a half-smile, further distorting his features.

"I know of a spell that can make a man see what he expects to see, ignoring what is out of place," Khrim said. "But it is cast on the beholder, not the beheld."

"And that is not useful in a castle full of watchful eyes," Twist said.

The men sat in silence for a few moments, mulling things over. Emen pushed the dice around, each one representing a seemingly insurmountable problem.

Emen said, "What kind of large, heavy package could be removed from the palace without being searched?" The other men looked at him. He said, "If something is delivered to DeKenric, a footlocker for example, he might be smuggled out inside, but only if it is something that will not be searched."

"Perhaps," Khrim said, "he need not be smuggled out in a container, but in different clothing?"

"I think they would recognize his face," Emen said.

"What if his head is covered?" Khrim said. "What if he has bandages disguising his features?"

Twist's face twisted in thought as he sat back, his fingers tapping un-rhythmically on the arm of his chair. His knee began to jump in anticipation.

Emen leaned over the map, "The disguise must be something they don't want uncovered, or that will only be uncovered once. Plague victim or leper? No, they'd be turned away... some kind of bleeding wound? No, that would draw attention of the wrong kind; a servant with a bleeding head wound shouldn't be wandering about." He tapped his temple with his fingertips. "What, what, what..."

Khrim said, "The bandaged man should not be alone, but should have one with him that will draw more attention."

"Sounds like you are volunteering?" Twist said with that disturbing half-smile.

"It is my mission after all," Khrim shrugged.

"But why would they let a Maanok wander into the palace?" Emen asked.

"To carry something heavy," Khrim said. "Some package the prisoner has requested."

"Like?" Emen asked.

"Books perhaps," Khrim suggested.

Emen nodded, "But first we need the DeKenric boy to request them."

"Easily done," Khrim said. "The envoy, Sir Rynard DeVine, visits the baron's son once a week. He could suggest such a thing in private."

"The boy must be let in on the plan, of course," Emen said. "After all, much will be expected of him. Can we send him a note?"

Twist replied, "All messages are inspected by the king's spy-masters. A secret message could be passed, but the risk of discovery..."

"The less we write down, the better," Khrim agreed.

"What if..." Emen snapped his fingers, urging the thought to take shape, "What if Twist took DeVine's place? He could fill Grigor in on everything he needs to know, and get some first-hand intelligence on the route?"

Twist stood up suddenly, his back arching as he stretched, cracking and popping his neck and spine. The noise echoed off of the ceiling and set Khrim's teeth on edge. The face-changer grinned down at Emen, his hands fluttering with nervous energy. He said, "I love it. When do we start?"

It was late in the month of Kraamoth, in the depths of winter, when they were finally able to attempt the escape. Sir Rynard had taken much convincing, mostly by Khrim himself, to consent to let the twisted man borrow his clothing and visit the heir of Kenric in his place. The mission was accomplished, the agreement was secured, and Twist returned with an order to deliver goods to Grigor DeKenric.

The day of the rescue was set for Midwinter, and was

overcast and bitter cold. There was a mixture of snow and horse manure on the road, which had been stamped and tramped into a murky slush. Patches of ice had not yet thawed from the evening's freeze, making the way more treacherous still. Yet it was the best street in the city; a straight, even path connecting the Grand Portshia Cathedral and the Winter Palace.

"I hope they are not too heavy?" Twist said as he walked behind the big Maanok. "We don't want you to fall and break anything."

"They are very heavy," Khrim panted. "That was the point." The plan had required Grigor DeKenric to ask for law books, so that he might search for a legal means of freedom. His father and the king were not at war when he was taken prisoner, and the act might be seen as a kidnapping. It was a good plan, Khrim had to admit. A prisoner occupying himself with law books was unlikely to be planning an escape. They had Emen Silverthumb to thank for that insight. Emen also knew from personal experience that books of law were damnably heavy. Khrim carried several over his shoulders in the saddlebags he had used on his trip to Portshia. The donkey and pewter wares had been sold.

Twist was following behind, bearing a leather case containing a writing set and parchment. If Grigor was going to be studying law, he would have to take notes after all. The face-changer was dressed in a thick wool tunic and breeches, with fingerless gloves and leather boots. The cloak he wore was hooded and dark, concealing his frame. Under the hood he wore a wrapping of black cloth that left only his eyes exposed. Khrim had noticed that the man's mismatched eyes had changed to dark brown; hard chips of obsidian under a set of thick eyebrows. *DeKenric's eyes,* Khrim thought. *Twist will look very much like Grigor on the way in, so Grigor will resemble him on the way out.*

The road ahead was crowded with the pavilion tents and campfires of the king's favored host, and Khrim attracted many odd looks and hostile stares. This was also according to plan. Almost no one was paying Twist any mind.

They reached the main gatehouse of the palace, where gate guards were just a formality; there were more than enough men-at-arms within a stone's toss to discourage anyone who had no right to be there. But duty was duty, and the guards stepped forward to challenge the big Maanok and his hooded friend, confident that they had an army at their backs.

"Halt," one of them called. "What business do you have here, barbarian?"

Twist stepped out from behind Khrim's bulk and passed the guard a folded document. "We are delivering goods to the prisoner, Grigor DeKenric. It was all arranged by the baron's envoy and approved by the king."

Even his voice has changed, Khrim noticed.

The guard looked the document over and passed it to his companion. The other guard nodded and said, "It's got the seal on it. These are in order." He gave the document back to Twist and said, "You may pass."

Twist nodded and muttered, "Go, go," prodding Khrim's foot with a boot tip.

Khrim obeyed with an appropriate scowl and grunt.

The inner courtyard was now an army encampment with an elegant, paved road down the middle. Men and horses stamped about, keeping warm and conversing with steamy breath. The pair walked with eyes straight ahead, although Khrim let his gaze wander up to the high tower spires and impressive facade of the palace.

The white walls had been enhanced with white and dark bricks set in diamond patterns, and beautiful arched embellishments decorated the foundations and the high windows. There were ground level entrances for the kitchens and storerooms, which were abuzz with activity as servants prepared food for the king and his barons. The knights in the courtyard got to share in the hot meals as cauldrons of stew and porridge were brought out.

The duo climbed the stairs to the palace doors, and after a short talk with the guards, was escorted inside. Khrim let his eyes grow wide at the sight of the grand chamber and the many-colored banners, the light of morning beginning to shine in over the mountains. It was what was expected of any visitor, although he had to admit that the hall was more impressive than he had imagined. It had been constructed many centuries after the old royal seat of Ahrnok, which itself had been refurbished dozens of times. If Manon Wolvert hoped to reclaim the glory of his ancestors' line, he would have to start by transforming his own somber palace to match this one.

Khrim and Twist stopped in surprise, making their escort turn and scowl. They had caught sight of the king at table, and farther down sat Grigor DeKenric, looking anxious. *This was not the plan,* Khrim thought.

"Move along, you," said the escort, his hand on his sword hilt.

Twist muttered words to that effect, urging Khrim to move. They made their way along the perimeter of the hall towards one of the staircases. The Maanok's presence caused the barons and their men to shift in their seats, watching them with open curiosity. Twist bowed to the king and waved to Grigor, hoping the boy could accompany them to his chambers. If not, this whole affair would be for nothing.

Field Marshal Valthór rose and strode forward, intercepting them at the stairs. Two men-at-arms appeared at his side, anticipating trouble. "Hold," he said. "What is your business here?"

Twist stepped forward and offered the parchment bearing the seal, grinning under his cloth mask. "Delivery of books and writing implements for Grigor DeKenric, Your Grace," he said.

Valthór gave the parchment a cursory glance and looked at the Maanok. "Who is this barbarian?" he asked with open loathing.

"Local hired muscle, Your Grace," Twist answered.

"He's better than a mule for carrying books. He can't spook and bolt, you see?"

Khrim sneered at the remark, mindless of the armed men.

"Who are you, and why is your face covered?" Valthór demanded, looming over Twist. "Unmask yourself."

Twist hesitated enough to make the guards draw their swords an inch or two from their scabbards. 'I-uh, I've a disfigurement, you see Your Grace," he said as he set down his pack, pulled off the hood, and began to unwind the mask. "It's a growth, actually. Nothing to do with plague, mind you, but not pretty to look at." He undid the wrap over his face, turning away from Khrim and toward the men in the room. There was a general look of disgust on their faces, and Khrim imagined their appetites were diminished.

Twist appeared now as a young man with a series of angry red boils on his forehead and cheeks, and a large, drooping mass of tissue sagging down the left side of his face. The tumor was purple and pockmarked, with thick hairs growing out of it in patches. "I wrap my face so as not to put anyone off, you see? I mostly work indoors with my books, not bothering anyone. When I go out, I wrap myself up so I don't frighten the children, Your Grace."

Valthór gave the man's face a good look, clearly unfazed. Then he nodded and said, "Wrap it up then. You'll be escorted to the prisoner's quarters. Leave the goods there and begone."

Khrim looked unhappily at the stairs, hiding his fear. *This is not how it was to be. Why is Grigor down here?*

Twist looked confused and said, "Begging your pardon, Your Grace, but I was told to instruct the young master on the care of the books and the use of the writing kit. Might we wait in his rooms until his breakfast is finished?"

Khrim noted the request. *Ask for more than they are willing to give. Good. They will not want us to stay overlong in the palace.*

"You may not," Valthór said. He looked to the king, who motioned for Grigor to join them. The young man looked very relieved.

Do not look too pleased, Khrim thought. *They must not suspect that this is your last hour in these walls.*

Grigor approached, greeting Twist with a smile and a nod. He asked, "Are these the law books I requested?" indicating the Maanok, but not getting too close.

"They are, young master," Twist said. "I was told to instruct you in their care, since they might be in your keeping for... er, for a while."

Valthór motioned for the escort to take them upstairs saying, "If these two stray from your orders, kill them." The escort nodded.

They proceeded to the upper levels and took the passageway to the central tower access. *Too many cursed steps,* Khrim thought. Numerous times he had to lean on the wall to keep his balance. They passed a guarded door leading to the high parapet between the main palace and the center spire. *Higher than I anticipated,* Khrim thought, happy they had not chosen to scale the walls and infiltrate that way.

They finally reached the door of the tower spire, and Grigor led them inside as though he were entertaining guests. "Thank you for coming so soon," he said. "I'm sorry I don't have many refreshments. Would your friend like some wine?"

Khrim gratefully took a cup and downed it in a gulp. He then left to sit outside in the warm sunlight. His part was done for now; it was up to Twist to make this work. As he sat rubbing his legs, he smiled at how the guards kept their distance at the other end of the parapet. This allowed Khrim to insure privacy for their plan and act as a door sentry. *That could have gone much worse,* he thought.

After about fifteen minutes, the door opened and Grigor emerged with Twist following behind; only Twist was now Grigor and Grigor was now Twist. The prisoner would be smuggled out in the dark mask and hooded cloak, while the face-changer would rejoin the king at breakfast. Rejoining the escort, they returned to the great hall.

"It is a rare opportunity, dining with the king," the man wearing Grigor's face remarked to no one in particular. "If my friends knew, they would be so very jealous."

Khrim realized this was a request. Twist wanted him to inform the Circle of Gold about his new access to the king. *Would they order an assassination? Would they be so foolish or bold?*

As they descended the stairs, Grigor joined the king at table. Khrim marveled at how perfect the disguise was. Not only did Twist look like Grigor DeKenric, but he sounded like him, moved like him, and even wore the same uncomfortable manner that the young man had displayed when they first saw him. Gone was Twist's fidgeting, nervous energy. It was a total transformation, a truly terrifying display of unnatural power. *He could replace the king if he wished,* Khrim realized. *What if that was his plan? Assassination would be child's play by comparison.*

Before they could leave the palace, they were intercepted by the field marshal once again. An older man stood next to him, his kindly eyes smiling as they approached. He wore the orange robes of a Lelonethan priest, and carried a staff topped with the symbol of the golden winged hands. Over his shoulder was a finely crafted leather bag for his medicines.

"This is Reverend Brother Alynar, the king's own physician." Valthór said. "His majesty has asked him to see to your ailment." He was addressing Grigor, who flinched under the face wrappings. Khrim stiffened.

When Grigor spoke, it was in a voice just like Twist had used. Khrim realized that Twist's disguise had been tailored to what Grigor himself could manage, if the need arose.

"M-most kind, Your Grace," the young man husked, "but I have had treatments before. Not much to be done for it."

Alynar stepped forward, unconcerned with the large barbarian who was now free of his burden. He said, "Come friend, what harm is there in an examination? His Majesty has authorized the use of Divine Alchemy, if it be needed."

Grigor's eyes darted between Khrim and Valthór; his shoulders tensed and he began to tremble. Khrim thought the young man might bolt for the doors and take his chances in a mad dash. *Keep your head, boy! Keep your head or you will lose it!*

Valthór noticed the behavior and narrowed his eyes, but Alynar interpreted it differently. The priest said, "Do not be afraid or ashamed, child. I have seen many ailments and have treated many unwholesome growths in my time. Come, we will withdraw to a private place away from judgmental eyes."

Grigor nodded mutely, following the priest to a secluded alcove. Khrim followed at a distance, trying to look confused. It was an effort, for what he felt now was the cold hand of fear tracing a path down his spine and into the pit of his stomach.

As the priest began unwrapping the mask, Grigor's breathing became rapid and shallow. Khrim's mind raced as he considered his options. *I could cause a distraction and risk getting myself killed, but that would not insure that Grigor would escape. Many eyes are upon us even now, and the king's man is suspicious.* The mask was almost undone. He had to act now.

It was a risk, casting a spell upon the priest. Wizards and priests who trained in magic were more sensitive to its effects on their perceptions, and were difficult to beguile. This man was a priest of great rank, and certainly had training in the Arts. Regardless, there was no time and no choice.

Khrim focused his thoughts on the wooden bracelet on his wrist, tapping the magical energies through the silver hidden within. He let the power flow into his mind, filling the thought-shape he had constructed there. It lit up his awareness and grew in intensity until it was ready to be unleashed, twisting inside his brain and down his spine, washing away all fear. He spoke the words softly, barely a whisper, *"Thavath thiwe thi."* The spell flowed out of him and gently wrapped around the mind of the priest. The old man cocked his head slightly, as if remembering or forgetting something.

Khrim moved forward, placing himself between Grigor and Valthór's prying eyes. The spell would work on the priest alone, and he could not risk anyone else seeing Grigor unmasked.

The young man wore an expression of defeat and surrender, but the priest did not seem to notice anything amiss. He examined the lad's features with an appraising eye, turning his head this way and that, and finally stepped back.

"I think I can offer you some relief," Alynar said. "I have a poultice that will reduce the swelling and sooth the skin, though it will take many applications over many weeks. I cannot say that the effects will be permanent, but it should improve your condition greatly." He reached into his leather bag and withdrew a ceramic jar with a hinged lid. "This is called essence of Limlindal. It is infused with the gifts of the Goddess, and can cure minor wounds and many ailments of the skin. I think it will help you."

Grigor blinked in confusion, but accepted the jar. "Th-thank you, reverend brother," he said. He placed the jar into his tunic and hurriedly wrapped his face. He bowed to the king's table on the way out. Khrim and a visibly shaken Grigor DeKenric walked out moments later at a pace that bordered on frantic.

"How did he not recognize me?" Grigor asked once they were safely in the crowd of the market square. "That priest knew my face!"

Khrim said, "I used a spell on him. He saw what he expected to see. He saw a face covered in growths and corruption."

Grigor let out a sigh. "You might have warned me," he said.

Khrim shrugged.

"So the uh, face-changer, whatever he is, he said my father sent you?" Grigor asked.

"I was sent by Manon Wolvert, on behalf of your father," Khrim said. "My mission is to see you safely to your father's castle before spring."

"How are we going to do that?" he asked.

"First, we rescue you from the palace," Khrim replied. "After that, we think of a plan."

"I see..." Grigor said. They hurried further into the press of the crowd.

Twist decided to spend the rest of his first day in the Winter Palace just wandering around as much as he was able. He took a walk through the halls, examining the portraits and expensive wall hangings, admiring the gorgeous furnishings and decor, and generally drinking in his surroundings. It was a rare thing to have access to a royal palace, especially in the guise of someone who had so little to do. *I had better enjoy it,* he thought. *The road will get rougher come springtime.*

He strolled through the upper galleries, looking down on the great hall below. He walked through rooms that were appointed for dignitaries and courtiers, but were now the winter barracks of His Majesty's favored barons and men-at-arms. He climbed to the roof and looked down over the assembled army filling the courtyard below. The smells of cooked food, campfires, and horses wafted up to him. The sun had fallen well past its zenith, making the shadows of the tall trees in the courtyard lean towards the mountain. A cold breeze blew in from the sea, infiltrating the seams and openings of his fine leather coat and tunic, and he shivered with pleasure.

Then he descended the stairs into the southern wing of the palace, where he heard an old schoolmate of Grigor's was to be found.

Cindra and Gavadaire were dressed in full protective gear, circling each other with blunted blades of tarnished metal. They would step carefully yet swiftly, darting in and out as they tested each other's guard. Then swords would clash and slide together as the combatants fought to gain an attack that could not be countered, seeking advantage in leverage, footing, and grip. If none could be had, they would withdraw and start again.

Gavadaire noticed their visitor first and stopped the match. "Lady Cindra, we have a visitor!" he said, pointing.

Cindra was reluctant to look, fearing a trick, but she turned and pulled off her helmet upon seeing him. "Grigor!" she said with a smile, "Grigor, it's good to see you!"

The pair came over and Twist smiled at them with a hint of embarrassment. Hands were shaken and shoulders were slapped in greeting.

"We heard the king was giving you more freedom of the castle," Cindra said. "We didn't think you would visit us so soon."

Twist shrugged Grigor's shoulders saying, "I was tired of the same old faces. I thought I would seek out some familiar ones from better days."

"I am glad you think of the school as better days," Gavadaire said. "I know there are few who were friendly with you because of... politics."

"At least none of you arrested me," Grigor/Twist said without irony. Cindra cringed a little, remembering Jaron's warning to the king.

"So," Cindra began, "I guess we should be reintroduced? I'm not the man I used to be."

Grigor smiled slyly as Gavadaire laughed and said, "Grigor DeKenric, may I introduce Lady Cindra Corrina, knight of the realm."

She curtsied and Grigor bowed. Cindra said, "Pleased to meet you, Grigor. I hope we can still be friends?"

He shrugged and said, "I suppose that depends on

whether or not you will ride into my father's lands and engage him in battle."

Cindra said, "Actually, I have my own mission that will take me in another direction. I am supposed to escort a young prince to meet his father."

"Oh?" Grigor/Twist said, interested. "A prince? You mean the rumored elven prince living in your father's castle?"

"It's true," Cindra said, shaking her head. "As much as I find it hard to believe, the young boy I rescued from the streets is actually a half-elf prince."

"Then I wish you luck on your mission," he said. "May your road be swift and safe." He turned to Gavadaire and asked, "What of you, Master Gavadaire? Do you plan to march over the mountains into Kenric lands and beyond?"

Gavadaire shook his head and said, "I did not come to fight in a war, but to train myself in a renowned fighting school. I might set sail for home come springtime."

"Does His Majesty know this?" Grigor asked. "I am sure he would hate to lose you."

"We have discussed it," Gavadaire said. "I am not one for politics, but the ties are strong between the south and east of Calilon and Aurilon. I would hate to take sides."

"I see," Grigor said. "Then we can remain friends as well." He shook Gavadaire's hand. "Incidentally, if you are indeed returning home by spring, I have a favor to ask of you. Could you see me in my tower later tonight during the Vigil?"

Gavadaire cocked his head curiously, but said, "Of course."

The Long Night was a time of quiet contemplation and moderate drinking. It was spent awaiting the return of the gods by holding a vigil until two hours past midnight, when most agreed that they would either announce themselves or wait another year for their triumphant return. In truth, after twelve centuries, few cared anymore.

LuVestra arrived at Grigor's residence in the central spire of the palace at the appointed time. The night was cruel and cold, and a haze of smoke hung over the city as peasant and noble alike stoked their hearth fires for warmth. It was the winter solstice, the longest and darkest night of the year, and the moon was new and veiled in shadow. The usual eerie luminance of the white spires was subdued, lending themselves instead to the yellow-gray light of torches and wizard lamps that peeked from their windows.

Grigor DeKenric greeted LuVestra at the door, his smile as welcoming as the glow of the fire behind him. He swung it wide and gestured for his guest to enter. Gavadaire stepped into the balmy chamber, noting the large books opened on table, chair, and couch; there were additional candles for reading; parchments with scrawled notes scattered about; a half-empty wine bottle on the mantle, and a few wine glasses posted like sentries at each pile of books.

"You are very busy, are you not?" Gavadaire asked. "I can return later..."

"No, no, do come in," Twist said, clearing a spot for him to sit. "I know it is the Long Night, and I am sorry if you had to interrupt your vigil. I get few visitors, and I fear that my time will be occupied for much of the remainder of winter. Care for some wine?" he offered a fresh glass.

"Yes please," Gavadaire said. "The guards asked my business, but all I could say was that you requested a visit."

Twist heard the implied question and replied, "It is unusual, I know, but necessary." He poured a glass and offered it to Gavadaire as he spoke, "You see, I have a favor to ask of you, a rather large favor. I believe you are a man of your word, a man of honor, and most importantly, a man who is not beholden to obey King Galen III."

LuVestra listened warily. He said, "I hope you are not going to ask me to do something-"

"Treasonous?" Twist cut in. "No, gods no," he laughed. "It is more of a family matter. Tell me; are you familiar with your family line? When I first heard your name, I figured we might have something in common."

Gavadaire said, "I know that my mother was supposedly from the lands of Vestra in Aurleona province. That alone is the source of my name. I never knew my father, or anything of him."

Twist nodded, making a smile of confirmation creep across Grigor's face. It perhaps held more than that, but he turned toward the fire before Gavadaire could notice. Twist said, "My paternal grandmother was from Vestra, one of the Houses Minor actually. She bore the LuVestra name as well, though she retained it through her mother's land holdings, and her grandmother's before her." He spun on his heel and lifted his own glass in a salute. "We are both men of Vestra, it seems."

"Interesting," Gavadaire said. "I had no idea." His face betrayed a bit of his confusion. "Why did you not mention this during our years at the school?"

Grigor shrugged. "I did not wish to appear that I was seeking your favor. Besides, better late than never."

Gavadaire smiled and lifted his own glass. "To the lands of Vestra, mother to us both," he said, and they both drank. "So, what is this 'rather large favor' you would ask of me?"

Grigor/Twist set his glass down and looked serious. He sat by Gavadaire and said, "When I was taken, I had a family heirloom on my person, something I could not allow to fall into the king's hands. It is something that has been in the Kenric family for many generations, and it is passed from each baron to his heir."

"Go on," Gavadaire said, interested.

"I am afraid that the king will take me on the march with him, holding me hostage. If this is his plan, then my accommodations will not be as large and luxurious as this," he gestured around him, "and the heirloom will be far more difficult to keep hidden."

Gavadaire nodded, finally understanding. "So you wish me to take this heirloom and keep it safe?"

"If you could," Grigor said, looking relieved. "It would mean a great deal to my family. My father, Drom Evenast, may fall in battle, or I may die myself, but the heirloom should go to the next Baron DeKenric. It is a tradition that goes back farther than the Evenast line."

Gavadaire considered for a moment and said, "I do not see the harm. I will do this thing for you."

Grigor shook his hands and said, "Excellent! I cannot thank you enough, Master Gavadaire." He then arose and went to his bedchamber. When he returned, he bore a small object wrapped in scarlet cloth. He sat next to LuVestra and passed it to him. "I must ask that you do not leave it unattended. I rarely do so myself. It would be best to wear it on your person. I always keep it close to my heart."

Gavadaire accepted the bundle and slowly opened it. Lifting the last bit of cloth away, he beheld a strange and beautiful jewel about the size of a man's fist, bound with a leather cord. It was the color of a dark amethyst and blood, and seemed to absorb the light of the hearth, keeping it greedily to itself and spreading it within to its innumerable facets. He felt his pulse beat in his open palm; no, it was almost as if the stone had a pulse, a steady *thrum, thrum, thrum,* which reverberated through his body. Something within him was both drawn and repulsed by it, a warring desire that told him to fling it away and hold it close. It was the essence of human nature, with its beauty and ugliness, distilled and refined into one crystalline form.

"You have my family's eternal gratitude, Gavadaire LuVestra," Twist said, "We shall remember you until the ending of the world."

Gavadaire stood with a look of grave concentration on his handsome features. He wrapped the bundle and placed it into his tunic, donned his cloak, and said, "I shall do my best to keep it safe." With that, he turned and left the tower, an inner turmoil beginning to swell within him.

As Twist watched the man depart into the night, he recited the ancient prophecy in his mind. *And he shall willingly take the blood of Chaos unto him, as a man that drinks from pestilent waters, and it shall mix with the blood of the Eternal Rival, and he shall be overcome.*

"*Mash bah havaath,*" he whispered, closing the door.

Chapter Twenty

Lady Knight

Casselvane Keep was decorated with festive sky blue banners to celebrate Cindra's birthday. The chill breeze brought the tangy scent of ocean life and salt spray, refreshing the air within the walls of the bailey. The banners snapped and flowed in its currents, waving lazily from the alabaster walls.

A dusting of snow had fallen on the city the previous evening, turning to mush by mid-morning. The castle grounds were crunchy with frosted grass and tiny patches of stubborn ice. A wagon rolled up through the gates, bearing several bulky objects wrapped in linen. The man driving the cart would have been familiar to Lady Cindra, for he had supervised the measuring for her armor with partially averted eyes. He brought his mule to a stop before the gate guards, and the men exchanged words with frosted breath.

Within the castle walls, the fires were lit and stoked high, and the aromas of the upcoming feast wafted through the drafty halls. Minerva the kitchen mistress was bustling about, supervising the beehive of activity by the dim light of the ovens. Her eyesight had become a fog of light and shadow, but her nose had lost none of its prowess, and she knew her way around the kitchens and larders like a mole in its tunnels.

Cindra was oddly reflective this day, sitting in the family chapel by herself. The altar was adorned with symbols of the household gods, which tradition and marriage had passed down: the gold, three-pointed crown of Arathus, god of law; the entwined roses of Selvina, patron of Cindra's mother; the mace of Balkon, handed down from warrior ancestors; the oak leaf of Eyorona, goddess of wisdom and learning. Cindra pondered how these gods had shaped her life, if not by their actions, then by their examples.

She had been raised with her mother's hopes and devotions, for there had been little else for her to look forward to as a noble girl. Selvina had given her hope of finding love, if not with her future husband, then with the more perfect love of a devoted admirer. Things had gone rather differently, but she had no regrets.

Balkon had been the source of her childish fantasies of battle and brave deeds, and she had gotten into trouble for it more than once. But she now found herself on the war god's path, against all odds. Whether it was a path she could stay on without losing herself, she would find out in time. Playing at war was far different than fighting for one's life, or taking the life of another.

Arathus was as distant from her thoughts as he had ever been. He was a god of kings, rulers, and all ordered society. It was on his authority that laws and traditions were made, regardless of how unfair or absurd. Cindra harbored a belief that had the gods not gone silent, they might have a thing or two to say about the things done in their names.

Eyorona was her father's patron. He was never much for fighting, and had only been in one battle in his life;

it had left him with a wound that had nearly killed him before he was Cindra's age. Since that time, he had left the fighting to others and cultivated wisdom and learning, making himself into a formidable ruler. He had guided his daughter's education, hoping to make her a great asset to whichever great house she would marry into. Cindra wondered how much wisdom she had actually used in her life.

"This is the last place I would have thought to find you," said her father. He had entered the chapel without her notice, and it startled her.

"Oh! Good morning, father," she said. "I did not hear you come in."

"I always measure my steps here," he said. "One should enter a holy place with reverence and humility."

"I think you like sneaking up on people," she said with a smile as he sat beside her. "I was just wondering about my past and future, wondering if there is a purpose to it all."

"That is something every man and woman wonders," he said, "but if there is a purpose, it is not known to mere mortals. Only the gods know our fates."

"Do they?" she asked. "I wonder if they do. What if they are as surprised by us as we are of them? What if they have plans for us, but we can change those plans?"

"Like parents and their children, hmm?" he asked, making her blush. "I suppose it's possible. They left us to our own ways when they fell silent. We could easily have gone astray."

"But is it going astray if it's your own choice?" she asked. "Maybe they wanted to be surprised. Maybe they grew tired of knowing how everything would turn out."

"That hardly seems like the will of the god of Order," he said. "That sounds more like Chaos to me."

"I think we need a little of both," she said. "It's no good if either side has their way completely."

"Like parents and their children," he said, and he stroked her hair.

"Just so," she said, leaning into him.

The feast was splendid, as Cindra had come to expect from the excellent castle kitchens. Many of her friends were present, including Nixy DuQuayne, Wenyssaya, and Ildric Finnael. Even Drahn the Dweedragon attended, which was a first for castle hospitality. He sat upon a stool and a pillow, raising him up to easily reach the table top. Wenyssaya cut his food for him into bite-sized pieces when needed, like a mother with her child.

However there were those who were conspicuously absent for one reason or another. The king had been invited of course, but he had declined, wisely keeping the celebration centered on Cindra. Jaron and Cord had been invited, but had declined, wisely avoiding the disapproval of the count. They sent their best wishes and regards in writing, and Jaron sent Cindra her wooden training sword that she had named the *Maiden Blade*. Seeing it again made her smile and think of better times.

Other seats at table were occupied by Reverend Sister Lyneth Pelmont, high priestess of Selvina and a good friend of the countess; Constable Fingelm, the family's closest adviser; Elrude Mamfett, Duke of Kelgar and old friend of the count, and his son Elburd, the Baron of Waynwell.

Minstrels were playing a soft melody from the gallery, and a harpist was hired for the occasion. The serving boys brought out each course with the pride and pomp of a military honor guard. There was roast boar and venison from the forests near the south Shadowood, duck and pheasant from local farms, and an assortment of stewed vegetables, tubers. Fish and crab filled out the feast, and a nice selection of wines put down eighteen years ago for the celebration were opened. Cindra's personal birthday wines had been either plundered by Minozhian pirates or sunken beneath the waves along the Red Coast.

"This is the best birthday party I have ever been to!" Nixy exclaimed. He looked very fetching in his tailored coat and embroidered vest, though his hair still defied gravity in places. "I've never heard music like this either." When the harp had started, he was transfixed by the sound.

Cindra agreed, "I love the harp. I never learned to play, though I wanted to."

Countess Zara added, "She took lessons for a week when she was eight, but she was too impatient. She only wanted to strum all the strings, all the time. The harper was so patient with her, poor thing."

"A week?" Cindra asked. "I don't remember it lasting so long. Anyway, I think I was soon out leading my army after that."

"Your army?" asked Lord Mamfett, "Milady led an army as a child?"

"My Army of Mischief, that's what my mother and father called it. It was made up of all of the castle's children who wanted to get out of work."

"She recruited so heavily," said the count, "that the parents brought an official complaint before me." He laughed, "I decided that Trelladay would be a day of rest for the castle children, and they could have their play when their weekly work was done. That was, until *the incident.*"

"Oh-ho! I remember 'the incident' quite well!" said Lord Mamfett, explaining to his son. "I had been visiting Casselvane Keep when the cannon went off, shaking the windows and rattling nerves! We thought we were under attack!" His broad shoulders shook with laughter as he thumped the table. Mamfett was loud and boisterous, but prone to laughter and good humor. Cindra had always liked him from their brief meetings. His son Elburd was large and broad, but less so than his father. He was also far more reserved in manner, though this did not include the admiring glances he cast in the elf woman's direction.

I might as well get used to that, Cindra thought glumly. *She is going to be turning heads until we enter the Shadowood.*

"Oh, let us not mention the incident with the cannon any further," the countess said. "It was used against Cindra by that horrid priest Fenwald..." she trailed off, not wanting to bring up the trial at the dinner table.

"The High Commander is a temperamental sort," said Reverend Sister Lyneth, diplomatically. "But that is encouraged in his order. Passion of that manner plays well on the battlefield. I prefer passion of another kind."

"As do we all, sister, as do we all," Mamfett said. "Damn this war and damn the Dissenters. That Wolvert fellow has gone and done it, he has. Hopefully our preparations will be more than he bargained for, and this will all be over by late summer, if not sooner."

"A worthy toast," Count Amon said, raising his glass. "To a quick resolution, and a hasty return to those we love!" All followed suit, except Drahn, who could not hold a glass. Wenyssaya held one up for him, and he placed his fore-claw upon it.

The countess gave her husband a side glance and asked, "I hope you are not entertaining the idea of riding off to war yourself?"

The count looked uncomfortable, the way he did before dropping heavy news. "I plan to ride with my banners until we reach my brother's keep at Syngmore, *no further*," he stressed as his wife began to protest. "The men need to see that I am with them. I will give leadership of our forces over to my brother, and he shall take them into battle."

"And you are then coming right back home?" the countess asked.

Amon Corrina looked uncomfortable again.

Cindra knew what he was going to say before he said it. "You are going to take command of the castle at Syngmore, aren't you?" she declared. Her father nodded.

Zara Corrina frowned in dismay, but would not rage in front of her guests. "But why?" she asked. "You are not a soldier anymore. Let one of his commanders do this. We need you here at home."

"I am not needed as much as that," he said. "Our generals believe an attack to be unlikely, but if it comes, it will be at our supply lines along the Casselvane Road. Portshia is well defended by sea, and if they capture the mountain pass, their forces will be caught between Syngmore in the north and Portshia in the south. They have to come down the mountain to fight."

"But why is it so critical for you to hold Syngmore Keep instead of another man?" the countess asked. "Does your brother not trust his captains?"

"I have offered to do this," the count asserted, "so that I may take an active role in the war effort. My injuries have kept me from vigorous fighting for so very long, but this is something I *can* do." He then softened his voice and said, "Whether here or there, my role will be the same. Yet the need is greater at Syngmore. Speak on it no more, my love."

Her mother relented, but Cindra could see in her face that she would indeed speak on it again in private.

Ildric spoke up, "If I may be so bold, my lord count, I would advise that you not take matters at home lightly. While the city may not fear an attack from without, I fear there may be trouble brewing within its walls."

"Indeed?" asked the count. "Sedition? Rebellion? What manner of trouble will my populace stir in my absence, arch mage?"

"Really, everyone..." Cindra began.

"These are ill times," Ildric said. "The war effort has come at a time of sickness and cold, when food stores are needed by peasant and king alike. Yet I fear what little people have is being appropriated for the army as we speak."

Lord Mamfett said, "It was damned unconventional, the king marching his army all this way. Gods, the logistics! And camping them all at the start of winter... I hear the northern forces have it bad, worse than usual, what with that cursed sneak attack."

"My lords," Cindra said more firmly.

"A devious, cowardly attack," the count agreed. "Eleven barons killed or injured before reaching Velloness! It was lucky that Hathroy travels in disguise, else he'd have taken an arrow in his coat of arms as well."

"My lords!" Cindra slapped the table, getting everyone's attention. The eating, the conversation, even the music stopped. "May we please keep matters light and pleasant? This is supposed to be a birthday party." She motioned for the minstrels to continue, and the music began again.

Properly chided, the men arose and bowed to her, muttering apologies. The women smiled to themselves, and Drahn lapped at his wine, observing with interest. Nixy hardly seemed to notice as he attacked his roast duck with gusto.

"I think perhaps it is time for presents?" the countess said. There was a muttered agreement, and at the ringing of a silver bell, the servants entered with packages great and small.

Cindra stood and walked around the curved table, standing in the central area where she might receive and then show off her new treasures. In younger days, she had slipped under the table, but was more dignified now, much to her mother's relief.

The first package was from her mother, containing a new dress in the style of her training clothes. "There are several more up in your room," the countess said with a smile. "At least you will not want for something to wear on your travels."

The next was from Reverend Sister Lyneth; a small pot of Essence of Elder, a product of Divine Alchemy. "It can treat minor blemishes with very small doses," she explained, "and damage from burns and abrasions in larger doses. Also, dabbing some under the nostrils can keep the smell of corruption at bay and improve breathing."

Cindra thanked Lyneth for the gift, and wondered if this magical concoction was the secret to the priestess's flawless skin. *Perhaps it will work on my scars,* she thought.

Wenyssaya's gift was a beautiful weapon belt made of black leather. It had silver buckles and clasps, and a special sheath for Cindra's Minozhian *Kos* knife. It was embossed with delicate tracery of ivy vines.

"It's beautiful!" Cindra exclaimed, fawning over it as she tried it on. It must have been expensive, but the elf woman could have purchased it with a smile, for all Cindra knew.

Nixy had purchased a gold medal embossed with her family crest, and a ribbon that read 'For Valor.' "Because you saved me, and you're my hero." He said with a sheepish grin.

She pinned it on her dress with a blush. She would have hugged him were he not on the other side of the table. "Thank you, Nixy," was all she could manage, wondering at the feelings this little token evoked within her.

Lord Mamfett said, "Forgive us, milady, but we were unprepared for your celebration. Let us then take up the modern practice of offering gold in place of our foresight." His present was a small coffer of gold and silver coin, enough to easily outfit her adventure into the Shadowood.

"My thanks, Your Grace," Cindra said, curtsying. "I will spend it well."

Drahn's gift was perhaps the most unusual, and it needed some explaining. He stepped between the plates of food and sat on the edge of the table as Cindra opened his small token. "It is one of my tail scales," he said. "It was knocked loose by the lightning stwike. Wenyssaya wemoved it when she was tweating me." He showed her the bare patch on his tail. "Anyway, I had a hole dwilled in it, and had a jeweler melt a coin or two fwom my hoard..." The polished, shimmering purple scale hung from a delicate golden chain, with a small clasp at the back.

"Oh Drahn, it's beautiful!" Cindra said. She placed it

around her neck, and managed the clasp herself, since Drahn could not do it for her. The little dweedragon looked very pleased as she presented the necklace to her audience, and the scale turned from purple to magenta, much as Drahn himself did at that moment.

"It changes color!" Nixy said, "Just like Drahn!"

"It matches her moods," Drahn said. "That color means she is happy, as am I."

Cindra gave him a little hug, and he returned the gesture, folding his wings about her shoulders.

The last of the presents were the large packages from her father. Cindra knew what they were of course, for she had been measured for it, but seeing the new armor for the first time was a great thrill. It was a plate mail suit crafted in the newer style known as 'white armor,' made to be displayed in all its polished steel glory, rather than covered by a surcoat. It had better coverage at the joints, utilizing solid plates instead of chain mail. There was a close helmet with a pivoting visor, pauldrons with raised neck guards, and 'demi-gauntlets' that left her fingers free to shoot a bow.

"Oh father, I love it!" she said, tilting the pieces this way and that, letting the light play off the shiny surfaces. "It's perfect!"

"It may need some additional adjustments," Amon Corrina said, "but that can wait. I dare say that you will need assistance in putting it on..." He trailed off, and Cindra heard his unspoken thought. It was a strange thing to consider, and perhaps her father had not even considered it until this moment.

"I will need a squire, I suppose," she said. "I can't imagine there are many young men willing to serve a lady knight."

"Or perhaps more than would be fitting," Lyneth said slyly. Knowing laughter carried across the table.

"I would recommend choosing from those you already know," Ildric said. "There are, no doubt, young men at the fighting school with whom you are friends?"

"There are a few," she agreed, "though I have hardly

spoken to any since my secret was revealed. For all I know, they all shun me now."

"I'll be your squire if no one else wants to," Nixy offered.

Wenyssaya said, "That hardly seems fitting, little prince."

"It's not like I have prince things to do," he said with a shrug. "Besides, if she needs the help..."

"Being squire to a knight who serves a king is no small matter," said Lord Mamfett, then added, "er, your Highness. There is much more involved than helping hi- um, *her* with *her* armor." His mouth twisted in an uncomfortable smile. "It's just so damnably odd to say!" he laughed, slapping the count on the arm.

"Try being her father," said the count, chuckling.

It took Cindra a while to come down from the joy of her new armor. When she did, she noticed that one guest had conspicuously not given a present, and it was his present that she had been almost dreading.

"Master Finnael?" she said, "I have been anticipating your gift almost to the point of distraction, once I learned you had accepted my invitation. Your last one was so very... appropriate."

The wizard cleared his throat and arose, his cheeks flushing almost imperceptibly. The magic bracelet he had given her four years ago before her fateful ocean voyage had saved her life, as he knew it might. It had made its way by strange hands back into his keeping, but she would have no use for it now.

He said, "Forgive me, milady knight, but I had hoped to offer it in a more private manner."

She placed her hands on her hips and said, "Not this time, arch mage. Your last gift anticipated an unlikely attack at sea and my near drowning. If you are giving another such present, I would have everyone know what we may expect." It had been bold and brash, but she had said it. She would not be saved by a magic ring, bracelet, or bauble, only to lose another friend.

Ildric looked shocked, then angered, then troubled,

all in the course of a moment. Finally he said, "That gift was in response to a limited vision of what might have been, milady. But now my visions of the future are failing me. To that end, I have chosen a gift that is more... unspecific." He withdrew a small, hinged box from his pocket and handed it to her.

She accepted it with a little trepidation. *Unspecific?* She wondered at that. Had he looked into her future and found nothing specific? Was it truly unpredictable and beyond his guidance? That was almost as scary as *knowing* what was in store for her.

She opened the box and found it contained a stud earring, a small green gemstone in golden filigree. She withdrew it from its velvet confines, holding it up to the light. "It's beautiful," she said, admiring the glow of the strange inner light. "Is it... magic?"

"It is," he said. "It acts as a focus for a spell I have concocted."

"Oh!" Drahn exclaimed, "I think I know which one!"

"Contain yourself, Drahn," Ildric chided. "You sound like an eager school boy." He explained to Cindra, "When I have need to contact you, when my need to reach you is most dire, I shall use the spell. The earring will give you the summons, like the call of a distant, high trumpet. You will feel it as well as hear it; the call will be difficult to ignore."

"But why?" she asked. "Why would the need to contact me be so dire?"

"I cannot say," he replied in all honesty. "The future is moving like never before, a flood rushing towards a cliff. I do not have an ember swallow at my disposal, and I may not be near those who do. In the event, the *unlikely* event, that I need to contact you, the message will be brief and to the point, for I can send it only once. If you hear the call, brace yourself for important news."

"Good news I hope?" she asked, watching his eyes.

"None can say," he replied. "But I cannot imagine what good news I would relay in this manner, only urgent and important news.”

“I see,” she said, lowering her eyes. “Thank you, arch mage. I am sorry if I embarrassed you.”

“Unlikely,” he scoffed. “I think you rather enjoyed it, and I dare say that I had it coming.” She looked up in surprise, but he continued, “I have been called a meddler on more than one occasion, and by more qualified minds than your own. It is true, I have stuck my nose into people’s business more than could be justified, and into yours even more so.”

“But you did save my life,” Cindra offered. She was not ungrateful for that.

“I did not save everyone,” he said. “I might have, had I greater wisdom and less power. I might have saved you all a great deal of trouble.”

“Master?” Drahn asked, his scales turning a deeper shade of purple.

“No, it is time I admitted it.” He raised his silver hand to stop the dweedragon’s protest. “I do not have all the answers, correct or otherwise. My power is best for mundane matters of little consequence. My attempts to see a greater whole have failed utterly, and I am sorry.”

“Come, my friend,” said the count, rising and walking about the table. “You have greater insight than any of us, but none of us are gods. No man could be expected to see all ends, or know all there is to know.” He put a hand on the wizard’s shoulder, saying, “You have done great service to my family, and we shall always be grateful for that.”

“Agreed,” Cindra said.

“Perhaps,” Ildric sighed, lowering his eyes. “But I am fearful now, times being what they are...”

“And what are they?” Cindra asked.

“Dwindling,” he answered, looking up at her through his white brows.

Cindra returned to the Winter Palace the day before the New Year, hoping to spend the Long Night away from the somber observances of her family. She had never enjoyed the vigil until she spent it with people who cared little for the return of the gods, and preferred wine and song and laughter.

But while the vigil had been enjoyable in the company of the king and his men, Cindra could tell that her friend Gavadaire was troubled. Something had changed his mood, something after the start of the New Year. Had Grigor given him some bad news? He would not discuss it, and their training became sullen and cheerless. Grigor himself was not to be disturbed; he was apparently studying books of law, looking for a way out of his predicament. She wished him luck, for he would need all the luck he could summon.

Regardless of the pall that had fallen over her instructor, she would not let it dampen her spirits. During her own Long Night's vigil, she had reflected on what her life might have been had Arch Mage Finnael not 'interfered' as he did. Here she was, eighteen years old and a knight of the realm. Had she made it to her betrothed in Rokvynnar, she would have been wed at fourteen, although cohabitation and children would not have been expected until she turned at least sixteen. Physicians agreed it was safer this way, and her mother had told her that with a little coaxing, a physician might give her a few extra months of clemency. Such a life was unthinkable now.

The afternoon session later that week was almost useless; Gavadaire was so distracted by his troubles that his head and heart were not in it. He broke into a sweat and did not look well at all, and Cindra called a halt to their sparring.

"Are you alright?" she asked, really concerned now. "And don't tell me you are, because I won't believe you."

Gavadaire looked wearily as he lowered his weapon and scratched his chest. "I-I do not know. Nothing seems right, somehow. I do not feel like I should be here."

She came forward and placed a hand on his arm.

"Everyone is worried about the upcoming conflict," she said. "I'm not even going to war in the east, and I'm worried sick about it."

"It is not that," he said a little sharply, shrinking from her touch. "I am not afraid of a battle, though I have not yet decided if I should fight. It is... complicated."

She softened her tone, not wanting to offend. "I know the Dissenters have many ties to Aurilon. So does my family; my own mother is from there. It will not be easy for any of us to fight our cousins."

"It is not that either," he said. "I cannot explain it. I have been given a charge, and I do not know if I can carry it out."

Her interest piqued, though she tried to hide it. "What kind of charge? Was it something Grigor asked of you?"

He shied away from her, walking towards the balcony and into the pale sunset. She followed, her split skirt making whispers about her feet. They stood together in silence for a time, watching the men drilling on the cobblestones below.

She said, "I can keep a secret, as I'm sure you know."

He did not see her sly smile, but perhaps he heard it in her voice. He said, "It is a charge to... uphold the safety of an old family tradition."

She could not imagine what that might encompass, or how such a thing could affect him so. "It doesn't involve, um, doing something that goes against your honor, does it?" she asked.

"No," he said, huffing a heavy sigh. "No, but it weighs on me for some reason. I can't explain it, but it feels wrong somehow."

"What is this family tradition?" she asked, truly interested now.

"I cannot say, or it might endanger my efforts," he replied. "I am sorry. It is not that I do not trust you, but the less I speak of it, the better."

The walls have ears, she thought. It was no leap of imagination to assume that the king was having them spied on. During her time here, other knights had approached her during training, and the king's men appeared most conveniently to make sure nothing went amiss. *What else are they listening for?* she wondered.

"Well if it's anything I can help you with, please let me know," she said.

"Thank you," he replied, scratching his chest under his shirt. His fingers moved something dark beneath, something tied to a leather cord around his neck. She had not noticed it before, but it seemed a bit cumbersome to wear during training, whatever it was.

"We should postpone for the time being," he said. "I need to rest and think."

"Fair enough," she said. They left the training hall and went their separate ways, but she could not help casting a concerned glance at his back.

King Galen summoned Lady Cindra to breakfast the next morning, asking her to sit by him at table. It was an informal occasion, or as informal as breakfast with the king could be. The knights and barons made bows to her as she entered, uncertain of her. She was not a married lady of station, or titled in the traditional way, but she was a knight and might have been called 'sir' if such a thing were appropriate. *What did one call a Lady Knight?* she wondered. Perhaps the king has an answer for that as well.

The king entered shortly after her arrival, and all stood. "Good morning my lords," he called. "Lady Cindra," he smiled and nodded. She curtsied in return. All took their seats after the king. No one offered to hold Cindra's chair for her, and she had to seat herself. It was an unusual but strangely welcome change given her circumstances.

"How did milady sleep last night?" the king asked.

"On my side, Majesty," she replied.

The king laughed, lightening the mood in the hall. "Indeed, indeed," he said. "I trust your time with your family was pleasant?"

"It was, Majesty," she said.

"And your birthday celebration?" he asked, as a pageboy poured his ale.

"It was quite a haul, Majesty," she said. "My father presented me with a suit of plate armor, and my mother with many new dresses in the manner you arranged for me."

"Excellent, excellent," he said. "I see you have a new necklace? It is an interesting token." His eyes lingered on her neckline, examining the shimmering purple diamond shape on its gold chain.

"It is a dweedragon scale from my friend Drahn," she explained, holding it up for him to see. The scale turned slightly red as she did so. "It came loose when the lightning struck us."

"Ah, the creature that shared your litter when you were brought down from the mountain," he said in understanding. "The elf woman bore him away before you were brought inside."

"Yes," she said, and the scale turned crimson as her cheeks flushed. "Drahn bore most of the lightning strike, but as it turned out, he is better for it. His kind of dweedragon needs lightning to awaken their powers, though he did not know it at the time."

"How could he not know?" asked the king with a curiosity that bordered on suspicion.

"He was an orphan, majesty," she explained. "He never knew his own kind. He was even deathly afraid of lightning, but he stayed with me in the storm."

"A noble creature, to be sure," the king said.

"He is," she agreed. "I shall be taking him with me on my mission into the Shadowood."

"Have you chosen any other companions?" he asked. "You may need servants at least."

"I intend to return to the school and recruit some of my old classmates, if Your Highness approves," she said.

"That sounds like a wise notion," he said. "If any would accept you as master, it might be those with whom you have trained and proved yourself.”

They ate in silence for a time, and Cindra listened to the conversations of the barons and fighting men. No one was talking about her, so far as she could tell.

“I was wondering,” said the king, “if milady would be interested in having an official knighting ceremony?”

Cindra was taken aback. *He is asking my opinion? Is this another test?* She thought for a moment and said, “I can see the good and bad sides of the idea, but I am not sure which is greater.”

The king smiled at her appraisingly. “Let’s start with the good. What benefits do you see?”

A test then, she thought. “Well, I will get to show off my new armor!” The king smiled at that. “Also,” she continued, “it will settle the notion in the minds of doubters.” Her glance flickered to the barons and knights eating their breakfast. “There might be some benefit for the people of the city, and the army as well, to see House Corrina make such a commitment.”

“A good answer,” said the king. “What benefit do you see for the populace and the army?”

She considered carefully before saying, “Your Highness once hinted that my story might become one of legend, and that it may help me to encourage that. While I do not see myself as legendary at all, I can see how it might inspire an army, or the people of the province itself.”

The king nodded and said, “And the bad side?”

Well that’s easy, she thought. “The bad side, Majesty, is that I might be completely wrong about the good side.”

He laughed again, though not so heartily as before. “Indeed,” he said. “I have shared the same doubts. It is much to ask that my knights accept you among their ranks, but they do so out of obedience, not approval. An official ceremony might be a bit much for them to swallow.”

A loud belch, followed by cheers, rang out from one side of the hall. Cindra made a face and said, “It’s hard to believe that there is something these men cannot swallow."

"Just so," said the king. "I considered arranging an official ceremony, but I wanted your thoughts first. Do you wish for a ceremony?"

As much as she relished the thought of making everyone deathly uncomfortable, she said, "I think not, Highness. After all, legends are made by deeds, not ceremonies. If I fail in my quest, then it doesn't matter what my knighting ceremony was like."

"Well spoken," said the king. "I shall let my barons know of your decision, and let them chew on *that* for a while."

The rest of the meal was quite enjoyable, and Cindra was glad that the conversation had not killed her appetite.

Cindra rode from the Winter Palace to the Red Eagle Inn, which shared the courtyard with the Freekirk Daerbrik School. She stabled T'ózha and purchased a room, then walked around to the front gates of her old school. The remaining students were in the yard, finishing their exercises before the midday meal. She watched them for a time, wistfully remembering the camaraderie and friendship they had given her when they thought she was one of them, when they thought she was a young man.

There were only thirteen of the original twenty students left, and she watched each of them in turn, thinking of the past two years they had shared. Some were friends, some not so much, but all were dear to her in a way. Mat and Stansig, the two mercenaries, had finally been warming up to her after she had taken some lumps. Demel and Lukas, once team mates of her nemesis Rejick Ratham, had treated her with more respect after she beat him in a match. The Avenoth boys... they were familiar faces at least.

But the faces that gave her joy were her circle of friends, a circle which looked much larger now that the school had lost over a quarter of its students. She saw Adric and Padison, two unrelated boys called 'the twins.' One was tall, the other short; one was handsome, the other homely; one soft-spoken and mild, the other with a tongue of sharpened steel.

There were her peers and teammates Morrin and Inis, two who would either return to serve their knights in the war, or be knighted themselves. Big Bradric and skinny Filbert were there also, and Cindra worried for them in the upcoming conflict. Neither were great fighters, though their hearts were in it. Then there was her cousin Gaius, whom she had not spoken to since her secret was revealed.

Master Cord and Sir Jaron were the first to notice her enter the courtyard. Their eyes were wide in surprise, but their faces were uncertain, and Cindra immediately felt she had made a mistake. Her heart sank a little until Cord called out, "Lads, we have a visitor!" Then her heart leapt into her throat.

All eyes turned to see her walking across the yellowed grass, her split skirts churning up little clouds of dust. There was no great cry, but no muttered curses either. Everyone just looked her up and down, some smiling, some not. She felt painfully awkward and her cheeks flushed. A meek little smile crept over her face, and for the first time she felt truly out of place in a dress, as if she had been born a boy and decided to change one day on a whim. The eyes upon her were not unfriendly, but there was that uncertainty that opened a gulf between them that yawned wider with each pounding heartbeat.

Padison broke the tension when he cried "Dillon!" and rushed forward. He put his hands on her shoulders as if to hug her, but his better sense stopped him at the last moment. Cindra didn't mind, for the bubble had been burst and the others were coming towards her now with glad faces. She hugged the boy close, making him blush in turn as he pulled away. It was terribly improper, but she couldn't have cared less.

"Lady Cindra," said Adric, as he elbowed Padison and

took her hand, bowing. She laughed despite herself. Others came forward with clumsy bows, nods, and awkward handshakes, but all faces wore smiles. Inis and Morrin both made flourishing, low bows with impish eyes, which Cindra returned with a curtsy and a rude noise with her tongue. Laughter rang out in the courtyard, until Sir Jaron came forward.

She and Jaron held each other's gaze for a moment, and the unspoken words and worries passed between them with the speed of a hummingbird's wings. At last they embraced, holding one another with ferocity that neither had planned for.

"Jaron, Jaron!" she gasped, as his arms crushed her against him.

"My lady," he said with a shaking voice.

There was a noise of sentimental approval coming from her classmates, a collective "Awwww," that brought chuckles and fake tears.

"Oh, Bradric!" Padison cried as he hugged the big lad, who shoved him away.

"Alright, you mugs," Cord said, "Get to your lunch, or I'll have Elmore and Celia feed it to the soldiers camped along the wall. Most of them have marched through the autumn to be here, and they don't get to eat as well as you clowns do."

The students turned away to enter the hall, looking back at Cindra with smiles. Gaius caught her eye, and his smile and salute meant much to her. *So he doesn't reject me,* she thought, *none of them do, really. But that may change when I ask for a squire.*

She and Jaron broke their embrace, and Cord came up, boldly clapping a hand on her shoulder. He said, "You might have given a little warning, lady."

"I am sorry, Master Cord," she said. "But I only decided to come when I left the palace this morning. I have been putting in orders for supplies for my quest, and I... well, I will need a squire."

"So," Jaron asked, "the king intends to send you into the Shadowood to find this elf lord?"

"*The* elf lord," Cindra said. "He is believed to be one of the eldest left in the world, and he might be the key to victory in the upcoming war. At least, the king hopes so."

"Of course he does," Jaron said. "But what if he has no interest in our battles?"

She shrugged, "Then at least we will reunite him with his son, Nixyalderthor. That's got to be worth something."

Jaron was about to retort, but Cord interrupted, "Come in and join us for lunch. I'm sure Celia can make up another plate." He put his arms around their shoulders and led them inside.

Lunch was typically when the instructors ate with the students in the hall, but Cindra immediately noted that Cord and Jaron were having their meals served to them by none other than Bradric and Filbert, respectively. Jaron looked a little uncomfortable as Cindra watched the lanky young man perform her former duties.

"You have taken Filbert Gaddisen as a squire?" she asked after the lad had returned to his table. Jaron only nodded. She said, "An interesting choice."

Jaron said, "The Gaddisens gave me food and shelter during my second winter in exile. I owe it to his family to look out for him."

"Fair enough," she said, digging into the bowl of rabbit and potato stew, "I assume that the list of candidates is small?"

Cord said, "There are the Avenoth brothers, Padison Pemwreth, Adric Hywahl, Mat Belvine and Stansig Gebthor. All the rest are spoken for as squires."

"I see," she said, dipping some bread into the stew, "Perhaps I could see them all together after the meal?"

Cord nodded, "I'll arrange it."

The tables and benches had been cleared away and the students were given an hour's liberty, all but the six candidates who stood within the master's quarters. Cord and Cindra sat in the upholstered chairs by the fire as the six men stood at ease before them. There was curiosity in their faces, and nervous energy in their limbs. Cindra's sudden return had left little time for rumors to fly, but the six gathered in the room knew full well what they all had in common.

Cord confirmed it when he said, "You six are here because you are the only remaining students who are not squires to a knight. Come springtime, the others will join the ranks of their lords and masters, while you few will have to enlist as mercenaries in the king's forces. This is your chance to rise in station and responsibility before then, so consider well."

Cindra noticed Adric and Paddy share a look, and the Avenoth brothers smirk and whisper. Mat and Stansig only nodded.

She stood and said, "I am not going to choose from among you, because of my... special status." She tried to focus her gaze on each of them in turn, not wanting to let her hopes show through. "Our king has given me a quest before his armies march, and it requires a small retinue. We will be traveling north along the Joshian Road through the Shadowood."

Mat Belvine asked, "What kind of a mission is it?"

Cindra said, "An escort mission."

"I hate escort missions," Mat grumbled.

Stansig nodded in agreement, "Tiz troth. Dey al-wys be fyndyn troubil."

"Who are we escorting?" Paddy asked.

Cindra noted his wording and repressed a smile. '*We.*'

She said, "The mission is to take a boy to meet his father. That's all I can say for now."

"Sounds exciting," Finnas said. His brother Ferrol smirked and snorted a laugh.

Cindra had rehearsed her speech in her mind for weeks, but found it hard to say now that her friends and classmates were standing before her. The moment had seemed so much more dignified in her imagination. She drew herself up and said, "I now ask which of you would serve a knight of the realm as a faithful squire, forsaking all other ambitions until your duties are at an end." She took another breath, "I ask which of you would serve a woman as one would serve a man, granting all the respect due my station."

Her heart beat in her ears as she waited. Her knees felt weak. This was one of those moments, one of those tests that she dreaded. If none of these men would follow her, who would?

Mat spoke first, "I fight for gold, not honor and glory. I appreciate the offer, lady, but I'll be selling my sword, not swearing it."

Stansig nodded, "Saym."

The Avenoth boys just shuffled their feet, which was fine with Cindra. Her real hopes were laid upon Adric and Padison, her closest friends in the school. But they were looking uncertainly at the wall behind her. Padison looked up at Adric. Adric looked at the floor.

"No one then?" she asked, her heart sinking. Her next breath was trembling and uneven. She was afraid for a moment that she would cry, and cursed herself for it. *I will not start bawling like a child!* she thought. *Not here, not now!* But the thought made it harder to resist.

Adric spoke in the silence. "I will be your squire, lady."

Padison let out a loud sigh. "Gods, I was waiting for you to say that! What took you so long?"

Adric turned to his short friend, "No one was keeping you from backing out!"

"I want to go *with*, but not as a *squire*," Padison replied. "You'd make a better squire, we both know it."

Cindra wanted to laugh and hug them both, but she choked back her emotions and placed her hands on their shoulders. "I accept you both, Adric Hywahl as squire, and Padison Pemwreth as a member of my retinue!" Smiling, she added, "And if neither of you had volunteered, I would have smacked you both over the head!"

"Aw, we wouldn't let you go off alone," Padison said. "We've been through a lot together."

Adric chuckled and said, "Much of it due to Chatty Paddy's mouth! I hope you know not to let him talk to people on the road, milady."

Cord waved his hand to the others and said, "Alright, the rest of you are dismissed. Let's give these intrepid adventurers some time to make plans." The four students left the room, and Cord followed, shutting the door behind him.

Cindra left some written instructions with Jaron before departing the school. She said her goodbyes and returned to her room at the tavern, where she ordered a bath and relaxed in the warm water for as long as she dared. It wouldn't do to make herself all pruney. She brushed out her hair, which had been allowed to grow longer these four months, and slipped into a simple bed shirt. All that was left to do was apply the Oil of Nim she had obtained from the Selvinian temple; it was a bit of Divine Alchemy from the reverend sister that would have been inappropriate to receive in front of her parents and guests.

Less than a half hour later, there was a soft knock on her door. She cracked it open to peek out. It was Jaron, looking groomed and clean, and wearing fresh clothing. *Good,* she thought. *He can follow instructions.*

"Come in, sir knight," she said softly, and opened the door, hiding behind it until he stepped inside.

Her skin was still slightly moist, and the nightshirt clung to her taut form. She was a vision and she knew it, even without the assistance of a mirror; the look on Jaron's face was all she needed. They drew together with a crash of passion, kissing with a desperate need, as if each other's lips were life itself. His hands roamed over her body beneath the flimsy nightshirt, and a moan of longing passed from his mouth into hers. She began to pull at his clothes, simple and uncomplicated garments with few laces and buttons, just as she had specified. He helped as best he could, kicking off his boots and flinging his shirt over his head. It fell into the bathtub, but neither of them cared.

Cindra's pulse filled her ears and tingles shot throughout her body like lightning; not the kind of lightning that would leave scars, but the kind that set her soul aflame and made her feel truly alive. Her body trembled and shivered, and all of her plans and fantasies fell away. Their bodies moved of their own volition, entwining and grasping, giving and receiving, with no thought for the world beyond and no care for the morrow.

Winter in the south could be soft and kind, or harsh and cruel, but it was usually short. The snows were infrequent so close to the sea, but the uplands along the Cassel Range could be bitterly cold and icy. The king's army would need at least a month more to wait before marching into Dissenter lands.

But in Selvimoth, the second month of the New Year, Cindra's party was ready to depart on their quest. A wagon sat in the courtyard of Casselvane Keep, attended by Padison Pemwreth and a newly squired Adric Hywahl. Both wore warm traveling clothes and cloaks, and both wore swords at their hips. Adric stood straighter now than he had before, making Padison seem a little shorter in comparison.

Drahn sat upon a folded bundle on the wagon seat, exchanging a few final words with Ildric Finnael. The dweedragon had little in the way of luggage, though he had entrusted Cindra with a small purse of gold and gems from his personal horde. He had insisted on purchasing his own supplies, scrutinizing everything before spending even a copper.

Nixy and Wenyssaya sat upon their mounts, awaiting the leader of their expedition. The elf maid sat upon Thasimé, her white mare, which wore no saddle of harness. Wenyssaya wore a dress of leather and fine linen, and a thick cloak of wool against the cold. The raven Navithwi sat upon her shoulder.

Nixy was dressed warmly in wool and leather, and sat

upon his new horse which he had named 'Nibbler' for obvious reasons. He wore his mother's magic knife under his tunic and his favorite glowstone around his neck. He looked nothing at all like a prince.

Cindra stood upon the top of the steps before the castle doors, looking down upon her companions. *My very own quest and my very own retinue,* she thought with more than a touch of pride. *It will be a grand adventure, no matter what happens. I had never imagined I would come so far.*

Before her satisfaction got the better of her, she was joined on the steps by her father, her mother, and the king. Galen III had presented her with a tabard of royal service, which she now wore. It was dark gray with silver trim, and a black eagle embroidered upon the breast. She wore her embossed weapon belt with her *Kos* knife, and a serviceable arming sword hung at her hip. Her armor was packed away in the wagon, awaiting employment.

But her father had one final surprise for her. He took a sheathed sword from his own hip and presented it to her. "This," he said, "is *Vyzeroth,* the Bright Blade. It is one of the three Corrina Honor Swords forged in the time of your thrice-great-grandfather Amos. It has not the burning power of *Valdiroth,* nor the icy bite of *Noviroth,* but it will guide your way as you travel into the wood of shadows."

Cindra unclipped her own sword and scabbard, attaching the magic sword to her belt with trembling fingers. "Th-thank you, father," she said around a lump in her throat. "I did not think I would ever carry one of the three." She smiled up at him with tears in her eyes.

"Who better than my own blood?" he said, beaming down upon her. "Bear it with honor, and it will not fail you."

Her mother came forward and embraced her, not wanting to let her go. "Be safe, my child, my kitten. I cannot lose you."

Cindra made herself be brave for her mother,

knowing she had already mourned her daughter once already. "I shall do my very best, and then some," she replied, hugging her mother with strong arms, "No matter what may come, I shall return home again."

Finally, the Black Eagle himself stepped forward and placed his hands upon her shoulders saying, "I bid you to go with my blessing and gratitude, Lady Cindra, Knight of the Realm. May your quest be a boon to us all, and may you return triumphant."

It was a traditional benediction, Cindra knew, but she couldn't help feeling the weight of her king's greatest hopes resting on her shoulders. He greatly desired the aid of the elves, like in the legends of old. Well, all she could do was try.

She bowed low before him, and again to her parents, and stepping lightly down the stairs, she swung up onto T'ózha's back. Taking one last look at her family, she guided her Gali steed through the gates of her ancestral home, her friends in tow. The sun was bright and the air was crisp and cold, and there was not a cloud in the sky. It was the first leg of a brand new journey, one she was beginning on her own terms, and would see through to whatever end.

If they want to make this moment part of a legend, she thought, *so be it. It's as good a place as any.*

The Author

Mark Rude, also known as Markalf the Going-Gray, is a wizard from Phoenix, Arizona, deep in the land of Mordor. He studied the Arts at Northern Arizona University, in the age when painting was done with paint, not pixels, and a photo shop was a place where you worked with something called 'film.'

It was in this age that he forged the story of Cindra Corrina, intending to make the story into a graphic novel, though it was not overly graphic, and not entirely novel. The comic book he called *Passage* kindled the spirit of the story. Three issues were forged in the land of Mordor, in the fires of Phoenix, before the effort was abandoned; yet the spirit of the story endured.

Cindra's tale was of epic proportions, untellable in quarterly comics that came out only once a year. Yet there was hope. Using fewer graphics, and with more emphasis on words, Cindra's story grew like the light of dawn over a darkened land. Markalf was able to spin his yarn as never before, making a nice sweater, some hand warmers, and a scarf.

Markalf the Going-Gray lives alone in a high tower, where he plots the doom of characters great and small.

www.markrude.net
www.facebook.com/markrude.net

www.ingramcontent.com/pod-product-compliance
Lightning Source LLC
Chambersburg PA
CBHW050611110726
47899CB00001B/65